Virginia Tech:

MAKE SURE
IT DOESN'T GET OUT

DAVID CARIENS

High Tide Publications, Inc
Deltaville, Virginia

High Tide Publications, Inc.
1000 Bland Point
Deltaville, Virginia 23043
Www.HighTidePublications.com

Quantity sales. Special discounts are available on quantity purchases by corporations, associations, and others. For details, contact the "special sales department" at the address above.

Virginia Tech: Make Sure It Doesn't Get Out, 3rd ed.

Printed in the United States Of America
Cariens, David: Virginia Tech: Make Sure It Doesn't Get

ISBN   978-1-945990-04-5

Dedicated to the Victims and the
Families of April 16, 2007.

CONTENTS

Acknowledgments   i

Introduction   1

1   I Write   5

2   Crime Scene Analysis #101   21

3   Seung Hui Cho   46

4   Norris Hall   72

5   The Defining Moment   92

6   The Governor's Review Panel Report   112
  (And TriData the Hired Gun)

7   Did Virginia Tech Break the Law?   137

8   Politics Is The Art Of Keeping From   161
  People The Things They Most Need To Know

9   Denial And Deception   184

10   The Hokie Spirit Memorial Fund (HSMF)   217
  (The Unsavory Side)

11   The Lawsuit And Trial   228

12   The Families Need To Move On   253

13   What Parents And Families Can Do   275

14   Doing Nothing Is Not The Answer   288

Epilogue: Where Are We Now?   305

Appendix A: VT Emergency Preparedness, Key Committees,   313
and Witnesses not Interviewed by the Review Panel

Appendix B: Composite Virginia Tech   321
And Gun Violence Timeline

Index   346

About the Author

ACKNOWLEDGMENTS

The research and writing of this book has taken nearly four years. It began when I received an email from Michael Pohle asking me if I would write a book about the Virginia Tech massacre from the perspective of the victims and their families. I owe Mike and his family my heartfelt thanks for putting their confidence and trust in me. Indeed, Mike was the prime mover behind the book, and it would not have been possible without his help, encouragement, and friendship.

Mike was aware that I am a victims rights advocate and that I have written extensively on school shootings, including the tragedy at Blacksburg. After some initial discussions with him, I agreed to write this book, but asked him if he would check with the families to see if anyone objected to the project. The result of his query found no objections. The answers ranged from, "We wish you the best, but please do not use our child's name in the book," to those who wished to contribute their own recollections and perspectives. In all cases, I can only be grateful for the support I received.

More than once I found the subject matter was so overpowering and the stories were so gut-wrenching, that a suffocating black cloud engulfed me and I wanted to throw in the towel. But with the encouragement of Mike and the other Virginia Tech families I continued. I drew on the strength of those Virginia Tech families.

The more I learned about the tragedy, the victims, and the families that were so deeply scarred by the events of April 16, 2007, the more my admiration grew. For nearly fifty years I have made my living writing, but I struggle to find the right words to describe the Virginia Tech massacre and the impact it has had.

At every step, at every turn, I have tried to respect the victims' families and the survivors" wishes. Everyone who agreed to talk with me has approved his or her contribution to the book. I will forever be indebted to them because without their courage and conviction, this book would not exist. I hope that in some small way my words will help give them solace.

Out of respect for the families, there are no pictures of the victims, dead or wounded, in this book and only the names of those interviewed appear in the text.

To Tricia and Mike White, and their son Evan, I can only say thank you so much for sharing your story and for sharing Nicole. She was a remarkable young woman and anyone who reads the words about her cannot help but feel the pain of losing her. And to Tricia's sister Kathy Field, my deep gratitude for your help in pulling parts of this book together in support for Tricia, Mike, and Evan.

To Dr. Diane Strollo, whose daughter was wounded, I can only tell you how much I appreciate your repeated expressions of support for my writings and for this book, as well as your willingness to share the story of your family.

To Suzanne Grimes, whose son was wounded, your words and encouragement helped me press ahead when my own words would not come. Your fight to return to some semblance of a normal life helped me persevere.

To William O'Neil and his wife Jeanne Dube, I hope you will find some solace in knowing this book has helped expose the truth. Nothing will ever replace Daniel. Nothing can ever replace a child. But perhaps the truth will, in some small way, help your family. Thank you.

To Colin Goddard, my deepest admiration to you for trying to turn April 16, 2007 into something positive. The courage and determination you show in your work with the Brady Campaign are inspirational. Your devotion to doing something, anything, to help stop gun violence speaks to an inner strength and the finest of human qualities. And to your father, Andy Goddard, my sincere gratitude for the time you spent with me and for sharing your thoughts and notes.

I greatly appreciate the support Lori Haas has given this book and all my writings. Lori, whose daughter was wounded at Tech, continues to work tirelessly to stop gun violence. From all of us who want to see something done to stop the killings, thank you; thank you so very much.

To Karen and Harry Pryde, your determination to hold accountable those who failed in their duties on April 16, 2007, gives everyone hope. We admire your courage and determination. Thank you so much for taking the time to be interviewed in this book and to tell us about your wonderful daughter.

To Priscilla La Porte and her mother Barbara, thank you for sharing your remembrances of Matthew, an unsung hero who tried to stop Cho's murderous rampage. How proud you must be of him. How fortunate we all are to get to know him through your words.

To Beth Hilscher and her family, just as with the others who lost children on April 16, 2007, I know that it was not easy to tell me your story, but I thank you and hope you, and the other families, will find the words in this book helpful in coming to terms with the loss you have suffered.

To Lynnette Alameddine—thank you so much for sharing Ross with us. You, as all the parents, have shown great courage in confronting this tragedy, a tragedy of unspeakable proportions. I greatly appreciate your repeated efforts to support this book.

My admiration for Professor Jerzy Nowak, who lost his wife Professor Madame Jocelyne Couture-Nowak, knows no bounds. Professor Nowak turned a personal tragedy into a cause for hope by establishing the "Virginia Tech Center for Peace Studies and Violence Prevention." Thank you, Jerzy, for contributing to this book.

No acknowledgment would be complete without a word of thanks to the members of the police response teams whose prompt actions at Norris Hall saved many lives. They performed in an exemplary fashion. I specifically want to thank Virginia State Police Trooper Gary Chafin, whom I interviewed. He was not only a hero that day, but he has continued to support the La Porte family, with whom he established a bond.

To Bryan Griffith, a close friend of Ross Alameddine, I appreciate your support and enthusiasm for this book. You helped me gain insights into your friend and into Cho. I would also like to thank Ross's friend Valerie Weeks for her contribution to the book and her support.

To Bill Jenkins and his wife Jennifer, thank you for your work in helping to stop the gun violence. And, thank you for taking the time to talk to me. Bill lost his son Will who was killed in a separate shooting incident here in Virginia.

I would be remiss if I did not thank, lawyer Robert Hall for his work on behalf of the Pryde and Peterson families and for his support of this book. He and the members of his law firm are truly outstanding representatives of the legal profession.

Many others played a role in this book and I have to begin by thanking my editors, Carolyn Miller, Peg Monahan-Pashall, and Janice Cariens who proofed the completed manuscript. The insightful suggestions and contributions of these three women were invaluable and added depth and context to my writing. I would be remiss without thanking John Wilson, a good friend and former newspaper editor, who read the finished text and offered his words of support. And, to the numerous people (there are too many to mention by name) who were aware of the project and who kept encouraging me to continue my research and writing, I can only say,

"Thank you so very much, you helped give me the will to keep moving forward with my writing."

My journey in dealing with the horrific subject of school shootings began on January 16, 2002, when Angela Dales, the mother of my oldest grandchild, was gunned down at the Appalachian School of Law, in Grundy, Virginia. In the ensuing months and years, as I tried to come to terms with that tragedy; help Angie's parents and brother deal with their profound grief; support my granddaughter as she struggled with the murder of her mother; and help my wife and son as they fought to heal, I gained an agonizing insight into these tragedies. I also came to realize that most of these shootings could be avoided if the warning signs were heeded.

My writing has been cathartic. I hope the publication of this book will help the victims, their families, and me find peace and resolution.

David Cariens
Kilmarnock, Virginia
June 2015

Americans detest all lies except lies spoken in public or printed lies.

Edgar Watson Howe (1853 - 1937)

INTRODUCTION

There are certain tragedies that are burned into our consciousness. No matter how hard we try to forget the memory we cannot. We know where we were when we heard the news; we can see everything just as it was at that moment. The murders on April 16, 2007 at Virginia Tech fall into that category. The events that day in Blacksburg, Virginia were so horrific that we all knew in some way, not fully explainable, that from the moment we heard about the shootings, our lives would never be the same.

If you have the misfortune to not only hear about such a tragedy, but find out that your own family has been directly touched by it through the loss of a loved one, then that moment stretches out over days, months and even years, as one by one the agonizing details come out. If you are lucky, there is justice and a moment when you are able to move on. If you are unlucky, there are justifications, excuses, and lies that tie you tighter to the tragedy every day. But no matter what happens, there is that overwhelming and inescapable loss.

For those of us whose family members were victims of school shootings, there are no words that can capture the impact of that loss. For me it was the mother of our oldest grandchild killed at the Appalachian School of Law shooting on January 16, 2002.

What is my goal in writing this book? There are three main goals: first, to expose the abdication of leadership and authority by politicians, school officials, and law enforcement personnel in connection with all aspects of the Virginia Tech tragedy; second, to raise public awareness about what happened at Virginia Tech before, during, and after the shooting, and in so doing give support to the Virginia Tech families' efforts to bring about changes in state and federal laws to tighten school security; and third, to help all families understand what they can do in insisting that universities and colleges have in place effective security measures and that those measures are understood by faculty, staff, and students.

My purpose is not to be vindictive, but to hold people accountable for their actions or inactions in an effort to lessen the chances of future school shootings. My purpose is to expose the shortcomings and inadequacies of our society that have made too many of our schools shooting galleries for the mentally ill and emotionally disturbed. My purpose is also to expose the lengths that those in leadership will go to in order to hide the truth, including their failure to abide by their own written policies, so as to maintain a steady stream of financial gifts. The simple fact is that until there is accountability, our schools will not be safe.

I do not pretend to have all the answers, and I recognize that violence in America today is part of a broader problem in society, including a crisis in masculinity—men and boys have carried out all the school shootings in the U.S. to date. Males do around 97 percent of the mass killings and serial shootings in this country.[*] I also recognize that many of our core values and beliefs need to be re-examined. For example, we need to re-examine individual rights. A potentially dangerous student does have rights, but not at the cost of other lives. We seem to have lost sight of that fact. To quote Kellner, "Ultimately addressing the problem of societal violence requires a democratic reconstruction of education and society, new pedagogical practices, new social relations, values and forms of learning" (Kellner, page 159).

It is not enough to tell the families of the shooting victims that no one could have prevented the Virginia Tech tragedy. For one thing, that simply is not true. The only way you can say it could not have been stopped is to gloss over the fact that people ignored the warning signs. If people ignore multiple warning signs then of course these shootings cannot be prevented. In my opinion, to ignore warning signs is tantamount to being an accessory to murder before the fact.

As long as people maintain that no one could have stopped Seung Hui Cho, the families of his victims will be prisoners to the agony of their loss. The road to recovery starts with the recognition that Cho's rampage could have been prevented. Indeed, the first step in moving on from the loss of life on April 16, 2007 is to understand that we will never fully recover because the Virginia Tech massacre was preventable.

In Virginia, politicians fell prey to political agendas and opted to cover up and obfuscate. Fear of the impact of those agendas blocked a thorough

---

[*] *Guys and Guns: Domestic Terrorism and School Shootings from Oklahoma City Bombing to the Virginia Tech Massacre*, Douglas Kellner, Paradigm Publishers, Boulder and London, 2008, page 25

examination of events of April 16, 2007, turning the Governor's Review Panel Report of the tragedy into a glossy canard. Indeed, the failure to include a representative from the families on the Governor's Review Panel Report proves French writer Paul Valery's assertion that "politics is the art of preventing people from taking part in affairs which properly concern them."

Second Amendment advocates and the National Rifle Association have so manipulated and defined the problem of school shootings that no one is willing to rise to discuss campus shootings without first saying, "I support the Second Amendment." This statement is usually followed by a tirade about the individual's rights to own guns. The politicians' anticipation of right-wing opposition to any dialog on gun violence has meant that issues such as mental health and keeping weapons out of the hands of the mentally ill never get fully explored. No one seems willing to hear about problems in society or pathologies that might be feeding into the minds of the unstable and contributing to their violent reactions to real or imagined threats. The Second Amendment advocates have paralyzed discussions about the prevention of school shootings. The radical gun-rights advocates have done our society a terrible disservice.

It is because of the inadequacies of the response by Virginia Tech and the fact that not nearly enough has been done to alert the public to the continuing danger of school shootings, that I feel obliged to write this book. Just because *some things* were done in response to the Tech shooting, does not mean that *the correct things* or *enough things* were done. Indeed, the voices of those who wanted to look at all the factors surrounding the school massacre appear to have been drowned out by a chorus of some conservative activists who poisoned the attempts at a thoughtful, sober, and thorough investigation of the tragedy. How else can you explain the omissions and errors that still exist in the Governor's Review Panel Report of the Virginia Tech shooting? I examine the flaws in that report in detail in Chapter VI.

A variety of causes—including broken communications, misunderstandings of our laws on privacy, failure to follow emergency procedures as written, and the incompetence of some people in positions of power—played into the terrible events before, on, and after April 16, 2007. There were a variety of interacting causes that aided and abetted Cho's shooting rampage. There are a multiplicity of causes that led to this nation's worst school shooting and for intelligent people to brush the tragedy aside saying "no one can be responsible for when or how others will act" is nothing less than cowardice to face the truth and a shameful willingness to exploit and manipulate a tragedy for personal or ideological reasons.

The Virginia Tech families cannot move on or begin to heal as long as the lies and the half-truths persist. If one parent reads this book and then takes action to protect the life of his or her child, then I will consider myself to have been successful. If one politician, after reading the book, has the will to push through legislation to keep guns out of the hands of unstable people, and if he or she finds the determination to address the societal problems that make the U.S. so violent, then I have been a success. If my words can help prevent just one campus shooting, then I have met and exceeded my expectations for this book. So I write.

CHAPTER I

I WRITE

*"The world is a dangerous place, not because of those
who would do evil, but because of those who look the other way."*
~Albert Einstein, German-born theoretical physicist

You get over tragedies by addressing them, and that is what I am doing.

Almost 100,000 people in America are shot or killed with a gun every year. Nearly 13,000 people are murdered every year in this country by guns and another 45,000 are shot in a wide variety of criminal attacks; over 17,000 people commit suicide with guns and some 3,000 survive suicide attempts with guns. According to the Brady Campaign, over a million people have been killed with guns in the United States since 1968 when Dr. Martin Luther King and Senator Robert Kennedy were murdered. Since the killing of John Kennedy in 1963, more Americans have died by American gunfire than perished on foreign battlefields in the whole of the 20th century.

Norwegian white supremacist, Anders Behring Freivik, murdered 77 people, over 60 of them by gunfire (the rest by bombing), in mid-July, 2011, and the world was shocked. According to the Brady Campaign, an average of 80 people are killed by guns everyday in the U.S., and it often goes unnoticed.

The statistics are staggering. The United States is saturated with guns of all kinds, and gun-related violence has reached pandemic proportions.

We work, we sacrifice, we nurture, and we send our children to college and university, and all too often they become targets for unstable and disturbed individuals who seek revenge for real or imaged insults; individuals who should never be allowed to own a gun.

Partial List of School Shootings 1969-2007

1969 (October 27) **University of California Berkeley**—Student Prosenjit Podder stabbed and killed fellow student Tanya Tarasoff. Podder had confided to a psychologist his plan to stab and kill Tarasoff. No one warned Tanya or her family about the threat.

1974 *In a landmark decision, the California Supreme Court ruled that mental health professionals have a duty to warn individuals who are being threatened.*

1996 (February 2) **Moses Lake, Washington**—Two students and one teacher were killed and one person wounded when a14-year-old boy opened fire in his Algebra class.

1997 (February 19) **Bethel, Alaska**—A principal and one student are killed, two others wounded, by a student in Bethel, Alaska.

1997 (October 1) **Pearl, Mississippi**—Two students were killed and seven wounded by a 16-year-old student.

1997 (December 1) **West Paducah, Kentucky**—Three students were killed and five were wounded by a 14-year-old who was also accused of killing his mother.

1998 (March 24) **Jonesboro, Arkansas**—Four students and one teacher were killed, ten others were wounded outside Westside Middle School as it emptied during a false fire alarm. A 13-year-old and an 11-year-old shot at their classmates and teachers from the woods.

1998 (April 24) **Edinboro, Pennsylvania**—One teacher was killed and two students wounded at a dance at James W. Parker Middle School. A 14-year-old was charged.

1998 (May 19) **Fayetteville, Tennessee**—One student was killed in a parking lot at Lincoln High School.

1998 (May 21)	**Springfield, Oregon**—Two students were shot and killed and 25 others were wounded at Thurston High School. The shooter's parents were later found dead at home.
1998 (June 15)	**Richmond, Virginia**—One teacher and one counselor were wounded in a hallway at Armstrong High School.
1999 (April 20)	**Littleton, Colorado**—Twelve students and one teacher were killed at Columbine High School. Twenty-three other students were wounded.
1999 (November 19)	**Deming, New Mexico**—A 13-year-old boy was shot and killed by a 12-year-old in the lobby of Deming Middle School.
1999 (December 6)	**Fort Gibson, Oklahoma**—Four students were wounded when a 13-year-old opened fire with a 9mm semiautomatic handgun at Fort Gibson Middle School.
2000 (February 29)	**Mount Morris Township, Michigan**—A 6-year-old was shot dead at Buell Elementary School near Flint, Michigan. The killer was a 6-year-old boy with a .32 caliber handgun.
2000 (March 10)	**Savannah, Georgia**—Two students were shot and killed by a 19-year-old while leaving a dance sponsored by Beach High School.
2000 (May 26)	**Lake Worth, Florida**—A teacher was shot and killed at Lake Worth Middle School by a 13-year-old with a .25 caliber semiautomatic pistol.
2000 (September 26)	**New Orleans, Louisiana**—Two students were shot and wounded during a fight at Woodson Middle School.
2001 (January 17)	**Baltimore, Maryland**—A student was killed in front of Lake Clifton Eastern High School.
2001 (March 5)	**Santee, California**—Two people were shot and killed and 15 were wounded by a 15-year-old.
2001 (March 30)	**Gary, Indiana**—A student was killed by a 17-year-old who had been expelled from school.

2002 (January 16)	**Grundy, Virginia**—A former student killed the dean, a professor, and a female student at the Appalachian School of Law. He also wounded three other female students.
2002 (October 28)	**Tucson, Arizona**—A 41-year-old student at the nursing school of the University of Arizona killed three female professors and then himself.
2003 (April 24)	**Red Lion, Pennsylvania**—A 14-year-old killed the principal of Red Lion Junior High before killing himself.
2003 (September 24)	**Cold Spring, Minnesota**—Two students were killed at Rocori High School by a 15-year-old.
2003 (October 30)	**Washington, DC**—A 16-year-old was shot to death in front of Anacostia Senior High School. He was killed by a 15-year-old "who was aiming at someone else."
2004 (February 2)	**Washington, DC**—A 17-year-old student was shot to death by another student.
2005 (March 21)	**Red Lake, Minnesota**—A 16-year-old killed his grandfather and companion, then went to school here he killed a teacher, a security guard, five students and then himself.
2005 (November 8)	**Jacksboro, Tennessee**—A 15-year-old killed an assistant principal at Campbell County High School and seriously wounded two administrators.
2006 (August 24)	**Essex, Vermont**—A 27-year-old, looking for his ex-girlfriend, shot two teachers, killing one and wounding the other. Before going to the school, he killed his ex-girlfriend's mother.
2006 (September 26)	**Bailey, Colorado**—An adult male held six students hostage at Platte Canyon High School and then shot and killed a 16-year-old girl.
2006 (September 29)	**Cazenovia, Wisconsin**—A 15-year-old shot and killed the Weston School principal.
2006 (October 3)	**Nickel Mines, Pennsylvania**—A 32-year-old male entered a one-room school house and shot 10

	schoolgirls, ranging in age from 6 to 13 years old. Five of the girls died as well as the shooter.
2007 (January 3)	**Tacoma, Washington**—A 17-year-old was shot by a fellow student at Henry Foss High School.
2007 (April 16)	**Virginia Tech University**—A 23-year-old student, Seung Hui Cho, killed two students in a dorm. Over two hours later he killed 30 students and faculty in Norris Hall, and then killed himself. Some 17 others were wounded. **This shooting is the most deadly rampage in U.S. history to date.**

So many people are gunned down in this country that what would have been a shocking crime 50 or 60 years ago barely makes the news crawl on CNN. Few in positions of authority appear willing to spend the time or money to stem this epidemic of gun violence. Most politicians are counting on the fact that violence is so much a part of our society that it has desensitized people to suffering, pain, and death. They appear to be right. Elected officials do not pay a price at the polls for failing to tackle this problem. When school shootings happen, politicians and luminaries from all segments of society say all the right things: they meet with the victims' families, they cry, they appear to exude sympathy and compassion, they wring their hands, and they promise to do something to help prevent future shootings. In fact, however, when push comes to shove and they are given the opportunity to support tightened campus security they do not. For example, in early 2010, then-Virginia State Delegate David Nutter voted against a bill to amend and reenact the Code of Virginia related to crisis and emergency management for institutions of higher learning. At the time Nutter was both an employee of Virginia Tech and a member of the legislature.

Despite the statistics, despite the anguish, despite the suffering, there has been no real public outcry—until Sandy Hook. It has taken the slaughter of 20 elementary school children and six adults to galvanize the public into demanding that something be done to stop the shootings on school grounds and campuses. But even this public outrage appears to be producing only modest results such as calls for universal background checks, proposed laws to make it a crime to buy a gun for someone who may not legally own one, and, possibly, a ban on high capacity ammunition clips. But even with all the public outcry, when push came to shove, the Senate could not muster enough votes to pass a bill for universal background checks. The chances of banning the purchase of semi-automatic and automatic military-style weapons appear slim, at best.

Security Plans

If you read, as I have done, the official reports of both the shootings at Columbine and Virginia Tech, there is repeated emphasis on the importance of the schools' security plans and the role of those plans in preventing campus shootings. Yet time after time, the schools' security plans were not given teeth to make them effective.

Those of us who do try to look at the root causes of America's gun crisis are rarely given a chance to speak out in the national media. What we have to say is not shocking; it is not earth shaking, but it is critical to identifying potential killers who stalk our schools. We want the violence examined in terms of mental illness and other factors in society that make us ripe for these crimes. The rightwing of the American body politic, however, has foisted off on the public the fallacy that a liberal media and liberal politicians want to take away citizens' Second Amendment rights to own guns. The clamor of these extremists is so loud that Republicans, Democrats, Independents—almost all of them—are frightened of doing anything about stemming this tide of gun-related violence because eventually the subject of keeping guns out of the hands of the mentally ill and those prone to violence will have to be addressed. Any talk of restricting gun ownership brings down the wrath of the National Rifle Association (NRA)—one of the most influential organizations in America today and one of the most powerful lobbies on Capitol Hill.

How can we remain silent when politicians in Arizona, and elsewhere, fire guns at their campaign rallies or worse yet, run for office and openly advocate the use of firearms if they do not get their way? These people seem oblivious to the impact their words have on the emotionally disturbed. Most of them claim to be devout Christians and rant and rail against public expressions of nudity, such as bare-breasted statues of lady justice. Somehow they see the sight of a naked human body as having the potential to influence people into doing all sorts of "unseemly" sexual activities. They want to regulate artistic expression because in their suppressed lives they see words and statues as undermining this nation's moral values. However, they don't see their words and their outspoken advocacy of the use of guns as having any influence on people who are mentally ill or emotionally disturbed.

In the 99th District of the Virginia House of Delegates, a candidate, Catherine Crabill, running for office addressed a political rally in Heathsville, Virginia on July 15, 2009. During the rally Crabill asserted that if she and her followers could not get what *they want* at the ballot box or the jury box, they would get it at the "bullet box." Her words were repeated throughout the country on the evening news. Her utterances were so disturbing that they even made the international news.

Ms. Crabill's words so deeply upset several of the families of the victims of the Virginia school shootings that they drafted an open letter calling on the voters of the 99th District to reject her. When the ballots were counted, Crabill received an alarming 48 percent of the vote, narrowly losing to the Democrat incumbent. Apparently a large number of the electorate in the 99th District did not care if a candidate advocated gun violence. And yet some ask me why am I upset and why do I write.

The simple truth is that politicians such as Catherine Crabill make headline news. They call themselves "patriots" and they apparently feel that the use of that word gives them the right to advocate gun violence. Crabill is not alone. Look at Jesse Kelley, the candidate who opposed the reelection bid of Representative Gabrielle Giffords (D-Arizona). In June, 2010, Kelley urged his supporters to "target" Gifford in the November elections and help remove her. One of his campaign slogans was, "Shoot a fully loaded automatic M-16 with Jesse Kelley." His words were grotesque; his candidacy represents what appears to be a failure of ethics among people seeking public office throughout this country. Kelley clearly showed himself and his campaign to be based on superficial emotionalism, rather than substance and issues.

Even on the national level, politicians cannot resist using the image of guns to rally support. Politicians from both sides of the aisle often tell their supporters to "lock and load." Former Vice Presidential candidate Sarah Palin "targeted" Giffords for removal on her now infamous map of politicians in the crosshairs.

On January 8, 2011, Jared Laughner, a demented and seriously ill young man, took Kelley and Palin up on their words. He shot Giffords in the head, seriously wounding her. He killed six people including a nine-year-old girl who had just been elected president of her student council. Laughner wounded 12 others. To say that words such as those used by Crabill, Kelley, and Palin don't influence the Jared Laughners of this world is sheer nonsense. However, to say the three advocated killing is also nonsense. The crime is that Crabill, Kelley, and Palin do not recognize the power of their words to influence the emotionally disturbed.

Guns, as a symbol for redressing real or imagined wrongs, permeate our political life. We now have a governor of Texas who brags about shooting coyotes while he is jogging and poses for pictures holding a pistol in the air. In the 2008 primary season, minister and former governor of Arkansas, Michael Huckabee, and his wife frequently posed in hunting outfits, holding guns as part of his efforts to get the Republican nomination for president. Not one of these politicians—not even the minister—will engage in a serious conversation about the root causes of school shootings. That is a crime.

Those of us who would like to talk calmly and soberly about all aspects of the gun-violence problem are not given a chance to be heard. UCLA Professor Douglas Kellner has done some excellent research on the media's biased handling of the Virginia Tech shootings. In his book, *"Guys and Guns Amock: Domestic Terrorism and School Shootings from the Oklahoma City Bombing to the Virginia Tech Massacre,"* (Paradigm Publishers, 2008), Kellner argues that school shootings and other acts of mass violence are indicative of an of out-of-control gun culture and male rage, both of which are heightened and glorified by the media.

As part of his research, Kellner monitored talk shows on the major networks for several hours on Sunday, April 22, 2007 (six days after the Tech shootings) revealing "the almost unopposed supremacy of the right-wing slogans of the day, with only one gun control advocate portrayed, in a brief segment on ABC's *Good Morning America*." When it comes to gun violence and school shootings, Kellner's findings do not support the right-wingers' assertion of a liberal bias in the media. What his research exposes is a horrific right-wing feeding frenzy in the media (Kellner, page 55) "...None of the guests mentioned gun control or had anything constructive to say about the serious problems of school safety evoked by the tragedy, suggesting that it is highly unlikely that establishment politicians will contribute anything to making the schools and country more secure."

Kellner's research also exposes the duplicity of one of this nation's leading conservative columnists—Charles Krauthammer. Krauthammer did not hesitate to turn his serpentine tongue to exploiting the Virginia Tech tragedy for his own agenda. Kellner writes, "But the most extreme example of rank hypocrisy and political manipulation of the Virginia Tech tragedy was a dual intervention by *Washington Post* columnist Charles Krauthammer. Krauthammer, one of the most enthusiastic advocates of the Iraq war ... reasonably wrote in his April 19, 2007 *Washington Post* column that it is terribly inappropriate to exploit tragedies like the Virginia Tech shootings to make ideological arguments. But later in the day and less than 48 hours after the shooting, Krauthammer was on *Fox News* explaining the shootings to promote one of his personal hobbyhorses. ... Krauthammer just couldn't help running to *Fox News* to explain why the Virginia Tech shooting and the killer's 'manifesto' are connected to Al Jazeera, the Palestinians and other Muslim Enemies who dominate Krauthammer's political agenda. ... " (Kellner pages 46-47)

"... Krauthammer's blaming the massacre on Al Jazeera, the Palestinians and other Muslim Enemies" gives us insight into Krauthammer's mind that sees his Muslim enemies at work everywhere from Iraq to Blacksburg, Virginia." (Kellner, pages 46-47) Not only do

Krauthammer's words give us a glimpse of his true thinking, but he also exposes his willingness to stop at nothing to get his agenda across, even if it means stepping over the bodies of 32 dead students and faculty at Virginia Tech.

"Already by the end of the first week (following the Virginia Tech shooting) ... it was clear that conservatives and hard-core gun advocates would make the Virginia Tech massacre an issue of mental health and 'privacy' laws which they were completely willing to exploit to deflect focus from the gun culture." (Kellner, page 58) Indeed, President George W. Bush made mental health and the need for more government spending on mental health, the centerpiece of his response to the tragedy. The facts behind the mental-health problems of the shooter, Seung Hui Cho, were so glaring that at last there seemed to be, at all levels of federal and state governments, a recognition of the seriousness of mental illness and the need for something to be done. And indeed, following the Tech tragedy, Richmond promised more money for mental-health care and services. The state allocated additional funds for mental health and indicated that it would be a high priority. Within a year, however, Virginia cut the state's mental health budget by 15 percent, and the following year by another 15 percent. Virginia now spends less on mental health than it did before the Tech shootings. Yet Virginia is one of a few states to consistently run a budget surplus.

Both shooters at The Appalachian School of Law and Virginia Tech suffered from mental illness. Both slipped through the cracks. The system failed. Now, Virginia intends to make the situation worse. The state plans to privatize Virginia's mental-health care will make the system even worse, raising the specter that more potential shooters will not get the care and attention they need. I look at Virginia's decline in mental health care allocations in greater detail in Chapter XIV.

We Don't Seem To Learn

On March 11, 2009, a disturbed 17-year-old named Tim Kretschmer killed 16 people at a secondary school in Winnenden, Germany wounded another 11 people, and then committed suicide. On March 13th *Denver Post* columnist Mike Littwin wrote a poignant article capturing the frustrations most of us feel over these school shootings. His words are worth repeating:

"We are coming up on the 10th anniversary of Columbine, and you can expect new pages filled with tear-stained memories of that horrible day. After 10 years, the old questions will inevitably be asked anew. And we'll struggle again to discover some kind of meaning from that day.

"But it turns out the story won't hold, not after a week of fresh horror. Instead, the old unanswerable questions are being asked in other places. ...

"And if there is one lesson to take from Columbine, it is that whatever happens, we never seem to learn anything. That's how we come to meet again at the intersection where disturbed young men turn into psychopaths with access to guns."

"Years later, after too many massacres, the killings are treated more like natural phenomena—they come, like tsunamis, and then drift from our consciousness, leaving death and sorrow in their wake.

"In each new town, the story line emerges—the flowers, the poems, the candles, the turn to religion, the questions about a just God, the young people learning far too young the meaning of tragedy, the photographs of the faces twisted in disbelief, the lives of the victims burned into memory.

"And I go to Virginia Tech, where the warning signs we had supposedly learned were ignored so completely that looking for answers seemed beyond hope.

"At Virginia Tech, we saw a student with serious and documented mental-health issues, who thought that Klebold and Harris were martyrs. Still, he was able to get guns and, as they say, do a Columbine. And those of us who covered Virginia Tech wondered again, if we were contributing to the next one—and what we could possibly do about that.

"In this story (Virginia Tech) if you remember, the killer had sent a video manifesto to NBC-TV, which had to decide whether to run it. The video gave voice to a killer who barely spoke at all. It was chilling, and it was disturbing and it gave voice, too, to the problems of the modern media.

"By now, we know too much and too little. Do video games make killers? Not likely. Do would-be killers find a home there? Of course. Do we know enough about guns and disturbed young men and tragedy? Sure. Did we decide in the ongoing culture wars, not to fight about guns anymore? You know the answer."

Lost Our Way

At least with regard to higher education in the United States we have lost our way and we are paying a terrible price—in lack of security for faculty, staff, and students. If faculty members are concerned about their safety and the safety of their students and if school administrators ignore signs of abnormal violent behavior on the part of students or staff, then the atmosphere is counter productive and certainly not conducive to learning. One college professor told me that every day she wonders, "Will this be the day a student brings a gun to class and kills us all?"

There is no simple answer to why security has deteriorated on so many of the nation's campuses—but one of the greatest contributors to this deterioration has been the tendency to see state-funded colleges and universities as businesses rather than institutions of learning. Learning in a safe atmosphere conducive to intellectual pursuits appears to be totally absent from the thinking of this new breed of university and college presidents.

Robert Bickel and Peter Lake, in their exhaustive and thorough look at risk and responsibility on college campuses, *THE RIGHTS AND RESPONSIBILITIES OF THE MODERN UNIVERSITY,* (Carolina Academic Press, 1999) point out that "by far, this (the business model) is the dominant current conception of modern relations, if one aggregates the cases." The net result is that most college presidents today are "glad-handers" and fund raisers—not educators.

Even worse, some—such as Charles Steger the President of Virginia Tech—are woefully lacking in crisis management skills. Indeed, Virginia Tech's President is a prime example of the problem we face. Read his biography or listen to his defenders—the repeated emphasis on how much money he has raised for the school drowns out all else. His leadership was absent on April 16, 2007; this lack of leadership may have cost 30 lives. But, he is an outstanding fund-raiser—unfortunately that seems to be what counts in Blacksburg and elsewhere.

The fact of the matter is that in order to make our colleges and universities safer, we will have to spend hundreds of millions (if not billions) of dollars on such things as security training and equipment, and mental health programs. These expenditures cannot be tallied on a profit sheet—they are expenses on behalf of the safety of our children and on behalf of this nation's future; they are long-term investments we must make to preserve this nation's greatness.

To run state colleges and universities on a "for profit basis" is not only counter-productive in the long run, but it has cheapened the quality of education and undercut campus security. For example—if you pay for your daughter or son to go to college, under the business model some lawyers argue that you have paid money and established a contract—your child is owed a degree. The result has been a lowering of standards. A friend of mine was an English professor at a major university in the Washington, DC area. She developed an English test that all seniors had to pass to show that they had a certain degree of facility and understanding of English. So many seniors were flunking that the alumni association was up in arms and the school was forced to do away with the test.

In blindly following the business model we are paying a price in so many ways, and not just campus security and the quality of education, but in our nation's security. I witnessed the latter a short time ago. I was working with non-native English speaking Americans who were doing translations for our fighting men and women in Iraq and Afghanistan. In my classes I give these students a laminated translation aid on rules dealing with some of the problem areas of English—areas critical to their work. The laminated study aid costs $4.95. The CEO of the multi-billion dollar consulting company I was working for wanted to cut non-essential costs to help raise the stock price, so he cut the study aid. I guarantee you that wrong decisions will be made based on poor translations—decisions that may cost lives. But, the company's stock price went up.

To say that this country is in a sorry state of affairs doesn't begin to describe the magnitude of the problem. Our values seemed turned upside down; we measure everything including human life, only in terms of dollars and cents. Few recognize that making a profit in higher education is not synonymous with our national interests; making a profit is not synonymous with securing the safety of our children. On the other hand, increasing the size of an institution's donor base and value of its endowments are high on the priority list. I once read, "to be ruled by ideas for which there is not evidence … is generally a sign that something is seriously wrong." There is no evidence that turning our colleges and universities into businesses improves the quality of academic training. If fact, the opposite appears to be true. One consequence of turning schools into businesses is that when it comes to making our schools safe it appears that many in positions of responsibility and authority are intent on limiting information in an effort to manipulate public opinion and prevent people from being held accountable for their actions or inactions. That was certainly the case in the shootings at Virginia Tech, which I will detail in later chapters.

Perhaps the most frightening and discouraging part of the problem of school safety can be found in the excellent research and writing of Professor Helen de Haven. Professor de Haven was a member of the founding faculty of the Appalachian School of Law in 1997, was the first Dean of Students at the school 1999-2000, and was at the school on January 16, 2002—the day Peter Odighizuwa shot and killed Dean Anthony Sutin, Professor Thomas Blackwell, and student Angela Dales—the mother of my oldest grandchild. De Haven is currently an Associate Professor of Law, John Marshall Law School in Atlanta, Georgia.

Professor de Haven's article, "The Elephant in the Ivory Tower: Rampages in Higher Education and the Case for Institutional Liability," raises disturbing questions about safety on this nation's institutions of higher learning. Her article appears in *The Journal of College and University Law*, a peer-reviewed journal published by the Notre Dame Law School—the citation for the article is 35 JC&UL 503 (2009). Her words leave the reader with the impression that many of this nation's schools approach the threat of gun violence on campus with apathy, confusion, and a denial of responsibility.

When de Haven wrote her article it was 10 years after the shooting at Columbine; seven years after the killings at the Appalachian School of Law; and two years after the Virginia Tech massacre. There have been numerous school shootings since then, most notably the horrific rampage at Sandy

Hook. Her words were prophetic because far too many in positions of authority remain mystified and perplexed over how to deal with the threat of school violence.

She further asserts that, "Though they are still relatively uncommon, school shootings in higher education are happening more frequently, and they are likely to increase unless we in the academy learn from our collective history. We need a new consensus about how best to keep ourselves safe without destroying academic freedoms and pedagogical values that best define us." De Haven's words were prophetic, Sandy Hook and Chardon, Ohio attest to that fact.

Professor de Haven's words imply that many who run our academic institutions harbor one or both of the following: an inexplicable naiveté or a disregard for human life. I would also not rule out an element of bureaucratic incompetence and mediocrity. In fact, reading some of the explanations and statements put out by individuals defending the actions leading up to, during, and following the shootings at Virginia Tech University, I could not help but wonder, "Are these schools run by carnival shills?" For example, faculty members expressed fear for their personal safety to senior management—yet Virginia Tech denies prior knowledge that Cho was a threat.

Having read Professor de Haven's words and examined the events surrounding school shootings here in Virginia, I can only say that unfortunately the academic community is far from reaching a consensus on how best to tackle the problem of keeping our schools safe. Here in Virginia, for example, school officials at Virginia Tech did not sufficiently heed the concerns and warning of faculty members. When schools ignore faculty expressions of fear for their personal safety, as well as for the safety of their students, something is terribly wrong!

Indeed, Professor de Haven asserts: "… universities have a legal duty as well as a professional obligation to make academic spaces as safe as they reasonably can for students. … We have not yet owned up to the ways in which academic cultures ignore the legitimate safety concerns of their faculty and students, disable appropriate support services, and enable dangerous and violent student behaviors."

Professor de Haven is not the only academic to identify a problem with institutional responses to faculty complaints about threatening students. Professor Carol Parker at the University of Tennessee and her colleagues tell the following story:

"A law professor was being stalked and threatened with death by a student who was failing his class. He and his colleague went to the administration. Sadly, he later reported, 'They simply stuck their heads in the sand and said nothing was happening. For the administration, this do-nothing strategy was a win-win situation. If they took action, they might get sued. However, in the small chance that the student actually carried out his threat and killed the professor, we figured that they would hire a cheaper faculty member."' (Smith, Thomas & Parker: *Violence on Campus Practical Recommendations for Legal Education*) Carol Parker's article is accessible free on the Social Science Research Network (SSRN).

Reflecting on this disgraceful attitude of a school administration, I could not help but think that this was the exact same way of thinking that typified the shootings at Virginia Tech and in many respects made the tragedy inevitable.

Good people make terrible decisions with horrific results. The more I delve into the school shootings in this country, the more apparent that fact becomes. It also becomes crystal clear that our society needs to hold "good people" accountable for their actions and inactions—particularly when they result in death. I am not talking about revenge; I am talking about removing people who clearly do not understand the law, override experts in mental health, or do not do their jobs.

Many of the poor decisions I am talking about are made for fear of lawsuits or to protect careers. In doing my research I came across a similar example of poor decisions made in connection with the murder of a freshman student at the University of California, Berkeley.

On October 26, 1969, Prosenjit Poddar murdered Tanya Tarasoff, a University of California Berkeley student. Poddar had met Tarasoff at a social event, fell in love with her and proposed marriage. When Tarasoff rejected the proposal, Poddar began stalking her.

Poddar voluntarily sought psychiatric help, saying he had thoughts of violence and getting even with Tarasoff. He had around eight sessions of outpatient therapy with Dr. Warren Moore over a period of two and a half months. When Dr. Moore challenged him about his violent tendencies, Poddar became angry and broke off therapy.

On August 20, 1969, Dr. Moore called the campus police and reported that Poddar was dangerous to himself and others. He provided the police with a letter from the acting head of the psychiatric department concurring with his diagnosis of paranoid schizophrenic reaction, acute and severe. Dr. Moore proposed a 72-hour emergency detention order if the police would pick Poddar up and take him to the hospital.

Three police officers interviewed Poddar, and based on their interview, decided Poddar was not dangerous and did not detain him. To my knowledge, none of those officers had any experience or training in mental health, but they overrode the recommendations of two highly trained mental health experts.

No one warned Tanya Tarasoff or her family of the threat Poddar posed.

On October 27, 1969, Poddar found Tarasoff alone at home shot her with a pellet gun and then chased her into the back yard where he stabbed her to death with a kitchen knife.

In 2002, people in positions of authority ignored the warning signs at the Appalachian School of Law—requests for campus security from the faculty, the soon-to-be murderer taking over classrooms and ranting and raving, a doctor calling the killer a time-bomb waiting to go off, police ignoring the very basic rules of triage and allowing a critically wounded student to bleed to death when the hospital was 10 minutes away—I could go on and on. A few weeks before Peter Odighizuwa killed three people and wounded three others, then-law-school President Lucius Ellsworth responded to requests from female faculty for campus security (the school had no security) by saying, "Oh you women, and your hormones, nothing will happen, it will be all right." Ellsworth was never held accountable, or even asked to explain his words.

As for April 16, 2007, at Virginia Tech, volumes could be written about the warning signs centering on Seung Hui Cho. He was deemed a threat to himself and others, but no one put his name on the list making him ineligible to buy guns in the state of Virginia; a faculty member threatened to resign because Cho frightened students and faculty alike, but he was not barred from campus. On top of this, on April 16, 2007, the school administration failed to follow its own security procedures and standards and as a result 30 people were slaughtered at Norris Hall.

On August 21, 2006, eight months before the Tech massacre, William Morva escaped from custody in Blacksburg, killing two people. There was no evidence or indication that Morva was on the Tech campus, yet the school closed down. On the morning of April 16, 2007, two students were found shot to death in a school dormitory, there were bloody footprints leading from the crime scene, and the school hesitated and vacillated over whether or not to even warn the campus. While administrators dithered, Cho made his way unhindered to Norris Hall, finding 30 more victims. And, no one has been held accountable.

To make matters worse, the state of Virginia paid a small fortune to a contracting firm to write a report that covers up, glosses over, or does not address many of the actions that would make people culpable and accountable. I will examine *The Governor's Review Panel Report*, and TriData, the firm that wrote the report, in great detail in Chapter VI.

Some argue that there is no way to prevent tragedies like the shootings at Berkeley, the Appalachian School of Law, and Virginia Tech, saying that history does not repeat itself. They are right, history does not repeat itself, but we can learn from history. The future cannot be predicted with exact certainty, but based on warning signs you can predict that the conditions exist and the stage is set for violence. We should and can learn from the past. We can learn from 1969, 2002, and 2007. If we will finally face the hard facts and realities of what led to these shootings, if we can make people in positions of authority accountable for their actions or inactions, we can prevent some of these kinds of shootings from happening again. We can make it a crime for a university president and school officials to ignore warning signs; we can adopt laws that keep guns out of the hands of those who have been deemed a threat to themselves and others. We can and should learn from history.

Just because something has been done in the wake of the Virginia Tech shootings, does not mean the right things were done, and it is certain that not enough has been done. So I persist, I write in hopes that my words will sensitize the public—particularly parents—to the seriousness of the problem of school tragedies and the fact that much more must be done to prevent future shootings.

CHAPTER II

CRIME SCENE ANALYSIS #101

"Failures are divided into two classes—those who thought
and never did, and those who did and never thought."
~John Clark Salak, author

Here is the "Law Enforcement Oath" of Honor ascribed to by the Virginia Association of Chiefs of Police:

"On my <u>honor</u>,
I will never <u>betray</u> my <u>badge</u>,
my <u>integrity</u>, my <u>character</u>,
or the <u>public trust.</u>
I will always have the <u>courage</u>,
to hold myself and others
<u>accountable</u> for our actions.
I will always uphold the Constitution,
the <u>community</u>,
and the agency I serve,
so help me God."

Before Police Officers take upon themselves the "Law Enforcement Oath of Honor," it is vital that they understand what it truly means. An oath is a solemn pledge someone voluntarily makes when they sincerely intend to do what they say. The key words in the "Law Enforcement Oath of Honor" are defined thusly:

<u>Honor</u> *means giving one's word as a bond and guarantee.*
<u>Betray</u> *is defined as breaking faith and proving false.*

The <u>Badge</u> is a visible symbol of the power of your office.
<u>Integrity</u> is firm adherence to principles, both in our private and public life.
<u>Character</u> means the qualities and standards of behavior that distinguish an
   individual.
The <u>Public Trust</u> is a duty imposed in faith to those we are sworn to serve.
<u>Courage</u> is having the "heart," the mental, and moral strength to venture,
   persevere, withstand, and overcome danger, difficulty, and fear.
<u>Accountability</u> means that we are answerable and responsible for our
   actions.
<u>Community</u> is the municipalities, neighborhoods, and citizens we serve.

There is no reason to belabor that those investigating the murder of Ryan Clark and Emily Hilscher violated several basic rules of crime scene investigation—such as using common sense, asking the right questions, and avoiding knee-jerk judgments. As a result of these errors in judgment and procedure, the actions of the police on the morning of April 16, 2007 played a role in the deaths of 30 people and the wounding of at least 17 others. The stunning lack of professionalism on the part of some members of the police force needs no hyperbole; the facts speak for themselves.

During my research for this book, I found that the guidelines and standard operating procedures for investigating a crime scene—specifically murder—are broad and general. I thought there would be a manual of standard and specific procedures, but as far as I can find out there is not. This lack of specificity is probably because there is no typical crime or crime scene and therefore there is no typical approach to investigating a crime. But the lack of detailed guidelines is no excuse for what happened on the morning of April 16, 2007. A crime scene is where logic meets harsh reality, requiring a careful, well-executed and methodical examination of the evidence; something that was lacking on the part of certain members of the police that terrible April morning.

The decisions that are made and the questions that are asked in the first few minutes of arriving at a crime scene can be, and usually are, critical to preventing future violence and/or solving the crime. Interviewing witnesses to the crime or other individuals who may have pertinent information is of paramount importance. In other words, asking the right, poignant questions, even when unpleasant or difficult, is critical. Equally important is listening to the answers.

In the case of the police personnel called in on the morning of April 16, 2007, there were serious blunders in both the questions that they asked and in the analysis of the answers they received, and these had catastrophic consequences. Mistakes in judgment were made in the first hour after Hilscher's and Clark's bodies were found, not just once, but over and over again. No matter what label Flinchum and others put on the West Ambler

Johnston murders—"targeted," "domestic," or "love triangle," they cannot hide the fact that they ignored the best practices of their own profession and were tragically wrong.

2007 (February 2)	Cho ordered a .22 caliber Walther P22 handgun online from TGSCOM, Inc.
2007 (February 9)	Cho picked up a handgun from J-N-D Pawnbrokers in Blacksburg, across the street from Virginia Tech.
2007 (March12)	Cho rented a van from Enterprise Rent-A-Car at the Roanoke Regional Airport, which he kept for almost a month. (Cho videotaped some of his subsequently released diatribe in the van.)
2007 (March 13)	Cho bought a 9mm Glock 19 handgun and a box of 50 9mm full metal jacket practice rounds at Roanoke Firearms. Cho waited the 30 days between gun purchases as required by Virginia law. The store conducted the required background check by police, and found no record of Cho's mental health issues. (This was clearly a breakdown in the system designed to keep people such as Cho from being able to buy guns. The Governor's Review Panel Report does not adequately address this flaw and does not say which organization dropped the ball or who was at fault.)
2007 (March 22)	Cho went to PSS Range and Training, an indoor pistol range, and spent an hour practicing.
2007 (March 22)	Cho bought two 10-round magazines for the Walther P22 on eBay.
2007 (March 23)	Cho bought three additional 10-round magazines from another eBay seller.
2007 (March 31)	Cho bought additional ammunition magazines ammunition and a hunting knife

	from Wal-Mart and Dick's Sporting Goods. He bought chains from Home Depot.
2007 (April 7)	**Cho bought more ammunition.**
2007 (April 8)	Cho spent the night at the Hampton Inn in Christiansburg, Virginia (a town adjacent to Blacksburg) videotaping segments of his manifesto-like diatribe. **Cho bought more ammunition.**
2007 (April 14)	An Asian male wearing a hooded garment was seen by a faculty member in Norris Hall. The faculty member later told police that one of her students had told her the **doors were chained. This may have been Cho practicing. Cho bought more ammunition.**
2007 (April 15)	Cho placed his weekly Sunday night call to his family in Fairfax County. They reported the conversation was normal and Cho said nothing that caused them concern.
2007 (April 16)	(5:00 a.m.) One of Cho's suitemates noticed he was awake and on his computer.
2007 (April 16)	(around 5:30 a.m.) One of Cho's suitemates noticed Cho was clad in boxer shorts and a shirt brushing his teeth and putting on acne medicine. Cho returned from the bathroom, got dressed and left.
2007 (April 16)	(around 6:45 a.m.) A student spotted Cho loitering in the foyer area of West Ambler Johnston Hall, between the exterior door and the locked door. He had access to the mailbox foyer, but not to the interior of the building.
2007 (April 16)	(around 7:02 a.m.) Emily Hilscher entered West Ambler Johnston Hall, after being dropped off

	by her boyfriend, Karl Thornhill. (The time is based on her swipe card record.)
2007 **(April 16)**	(around 7:15 a.m.) **Cho shot Ryan Christopher Clark (an RA whose room is next to Emily's). Clark apparently came to investigate noises in Emily's room. Cho then shot Emily Hilscher, who had sought refuge under her bed.** Both of the victims' wounds prove fatal. (Ryan died almost instantly, Emily died after being evacuated to a Roanoke trauma care hospital.) Cho exited the crime scene leaving bloody footprints and shell casings.
2007 **(April 16)**	(7:17 am) **Cho's access card was swiped at Harper Hall which is near West Ambler Johnston and was Cho's dormitory. He went to his room to change out of his bloody clothing,** canceled his computer account, and made preparations for his rampage.
2007 **(April 16)**	(7:20 a.m.) **The Virginia Tech Police Department received a call on their administrative line reporting that a woman in room 4040 of West Ambler Johnston Hall may have fallen from her bed.** The caller was given the information from another student whose room is near room 4040.
2007 **(April 16)**	(7:21 a.m.) **A Virginia Tech Police dispatcher notified the Virginia Tech Rescue Squad that a female student may have fallen from her bed in room 4040 of West Ambler Johnston Hall.**
2007 **(April 16)**	(7:22 a.m.) **A Virginia Tech Police officer**

	was dispatched to room 4040 West Ambler Johnston Hall to accompany the Virginia Tech Rescue Squad—this is standard operating procedure.
2007 (April 16)	(7:24 a.m.) The Virginia Tech Police officer arrived at West Ambler Johnston Hall and found two people shot in the room, and immediately requested additional police resources.
2007 (April 16)	(7:25 a.m.) Cho accessed his university e-mail accounts and erased all his files.
2007 (April 16)	(7:26 a.m.) The police dispatcher was advised that there were two gun shot victims. The officer requested his supervisor.
2007 (April 16)	(7:29 a.m.) Virginia Tech Rescue Squad 3 arrived at room 4040 West Ambler Johnston Hall.
2007 (April 16)	(7:30 a.m.) Additional Virginia Tech Police officers began arriving at the crime scene in West Ambler Johnston Hall. They secured the crime scene in an effort to lock down the dormitory, with police inside and outside. The police started their preliminary investigation. Interviews with residents failed to produce a description of the suspect. No one on Hilscher's floor in the dormitory saw anyone leave room 4040 after the initial noise was heard. A housekeeper in Burruss Hall told Dr. Ed Spencer, Associate Vice President for Student Affairs and member of the Policy Group, that an RA in West Ambler Johnston Hall had been murdered. (The housekeeper received a call from a housekeeper in the dormitory.)

2007 **(April 16)**	(7:35 a.m.) Police on the scene said they need a detective.
2007 **(April 16)**	(7:40 a.m.) **Virginia Tech Police Chief Flinchum was notified by phone of the shootings in the dormitory.** Chief Flinchum tried repeatedly to reach the Office of the Executive Vice President.
2007 **(April 16)**	(7:51 a.m.) Chief Flinchum contacted the Blacksburg Police Department and requested one of their evidence technicians as well as a detective to assist with the investigation.
2007 **(April 16)**	(7:55 a.m.) **Dr. Ed Spencer, Associate Vice President for Student Affairs arrived at West Ambler Johnston Hall** after walking from Burruss Hall. He called Zenobia Hikes, Vice President of Student Affairs.
2007 **(April 16)**	(7:57 a.m.) Chief Flinchum got through to the Virginia Tech Office of the Executive Vice President and notified them of the shootings.
2007 **(April 16)**	(8:00 a.m.) **Classes begin. Chief Flinchum arrives at West Ambler Johnston Hall** and found Virginia Tech Police Department and Blacksburg Police Department detectives on the scene. A local special agent of the Virginia State Police had been contacted and responded to the scene. The Tech and Blacksburg police began to "process" the crime scene. They canvassed the dorm for possible witnesses, and searched interior and exterior waste containers and surrounding areas near the dormitory for evidence. They also canvassed the rescue squad for additional evidence or information.
2007 **(April 16)**	(around 8:00 a.m.) **The Virginia Tech Center**

	for Professional and Continuing Education locked down on its own.
2007 **(April 16)**	(8:10 a.m.) **President Charles Steger was notified by a secretary that there had been a shooting. He told her to get Chief Flinchum on the phone.**
2007 **(April 16)**	(8:11 a.m.) **Chief Flinchum talked to President Steger on the phone and reported one student was critical, one was fatally wounded, and the incident seemed to be domestic in_ nature. (Nowhere in the Governor's Review Panel Report is this assumption adequately explained.) Flinchum reported no weapon was found and there are bloody footprints (leading away from the crime scene—this point is not made in the timeline of the Governor's Review Panel Report until the first addendum was issued over 2 years after the original edition was published. The motivation for not correcting the timeline may have been a recognition that the correct timeline would have undercut and had a negative impact on the tremendous pressure being placed on the families of the victims to settle with the Commonwealth of Virginia.). President Steger told Chief Flinchum to keep him informed. President Steger decided to convene the Policy Group no later than 8:30 am.**
2007 **(April 16)**	(8:11 a.m.) Blacksburg Police Chief Kim Crannis arrived at the crime scene.
2007 **(April 16)**	(8:13 a.m.) Chief Flinchum requested additional Virginia Tech Police Department and Blacksburg Police Department officers to assist

in securing West Ambler Johnston Hall entrances and with the investigation. He also ordered the recall of all off-shift personnel.

2007 **(April 16)** (8:14 a.m.) **Emily Hilscher's roommate, Heather Haugh, arrived at West Ambler Johnston Hall.**

2007 **(April 16)** (8:15 a.m.) Chief Flinchum requested the Virginia Tech Police Department Emergency Team respond to the scene and then to be ready n Blacksburg in the event an arrest or search warrant was to be executed.

2007 **(April 16)** (about 8:15 a.m.) **Two senior officials of Virginia Tech had conversations with family members in which the shootings were discussed**. In one conversation, the official advised her son, a student at Tech, to go to class. In the other, the official arranged for extended babysitting.

2007 **(April 16)** (8:16 a.m.-8:40 a.m.) **Hilscher's roommate, Heather Haugh, was interviewed by detectives.** She told them that on Monday mornings Emily's boyfriend, Karl Thornhill, usually dropped Emily off and then went on to Radford University. She told the detectives that Thornhill owns a gun and practices shooting. Police then seek Thornhill as a person of interest. **(Note: University President Charles Steger would tell a press conference a press conference at 7:40 p.m.—some 12 hours after the double homicide—that he was that told at there was a "person of interest" at 7:30 a.m. In fact, *no "person of interest" was identified until sometime between 8:30 a.m. and 8:40a.m.*)** Thornhill's vehicle was not found on the campus and officers assumed he had left the school. Virginia Tech and Blacksburg police were sent to Thornhill's home; he was not there. The Thornhill home was put under surveillance.

2007 **(April 16)** (8:16 a.m.-9:24 a.m.) The police continued canvassing West Ambler Johnston for possible witnesses. The Virginia Tech Police, the Blacksburg Police Department, and the Virginia State Police continued processing Hilscher's room gathering evidence. Investigators identified the two victims. Police allowed students to leave to 9:00 a.m. classes in Norris Hall. **(This last sentence is misleading. The lockdown was apparently in place at West Ambler Johnston Hall** *after* **9:00 a.m. Two students pleaded with the police** *after 9:00 a.m.* **to be allowed to leave the dormitory. Those two, Henry Lee and Rachael Hill, were killed in the French class in Norris Hall. The police agreed to break the lockdown and allow them to go to class. Lee and Hill arrived just moments before Cho entered Madame Couture-Nowak's classroom.)** The Policy Group convened to plan how to notify students of the double homicide.

2007 **(April 16)** (8:19 a.m.) Chief Crannis requested the Blacksburg Emergency Response Team assistance.

2007 **(April 16)** (8:25 a.m.) The Policy Group convened to plan how to notify students of the double homicide. **Police cancelled bank deposits and pickups.**

2007 **(April 16)** (8:40 a.m.) Chief Flinchum told President Steger in a phone update that Hilscher's boyfriend was a person of interest and probably off campus. **(Note: President Steger will state at a press conference some 10 hours later that he was told of the "person of interest" over an hour earlier and that is part of the excuse for not warning the campus. Steger has never explained the press**

conference error. Even more puzzling is the fact that Chief Flinchum was at the press conference and never corrected Steger.) A Policy Group member notified the Governor's office of the double homicide.

2007 **(April 16)** (8:40 a.m.-8:45 a.m.) Phone calls were made from the Blacksburg Police Department to its units and to the Montgomery County Sheriff's Office and Radford University police to be on the lookout for Thornhill's vehicle.

2007 **(April 16)** (8:45 a.m.) A Policy Group member e-mailed a Richmond colleague saying one student was dead and another critically wounded. "Gunman is on the loose," he says, adding, "This is not releasable yet."

2007 **(April 16)** (8:49 a.m.) The same Policy Group member reminded his Richmond colleague **"just try to make sure it doesn't get out."**

2007 **(April 16)** (8:50 a.m.) **First period classes end.** The Policy Group member began composing a notice to the university about the shootings in West Ambler Johnston Hall. The Associate Vice President for University Relations, Larry Hincker, was unable to send the message at first due to technical difficulties with the alert system.

2007 **(April 16)** (8:52 a.m.) **Blacksburg Public Schools locked down until further information is available about the incident at Virginia Tech. The school superintendent notified the school board of this action by e-mail. The Executive Director of Government Relations, Ralph Byers, directed that the doors to his office be locked.** His office is adjacent to the school

President's suite, but the four doors to the President's suite remain open.

2007 **(April 16)** (9:00 a.m.-9:15 a.m.) **Virginia Tech Veterinary College locked down.**

2007 **(April 16)** (9:01 a.m.) Cho mailed a package from Blacksburg post office to NBC news in New York that contained pictures of Cho holding weapons, an 1,800-word rambling diatribe, and video clips in which he expressed rage, resentment, and a desire to get even with his oppressors. He alluded to a coming massacre. Cho prepared this material during the previous weeks. In the videos Cho acted out the enclosed writings. Cho also mailed a letter to the English Department attacking Professor Carl Bean, with whom he had previously argued.

2007 **(April 16)** (9:05 a.m.) **Second period classes began in Norris Hall. Virginia Tech trash pick-up was cancelled.**

2007 **(April 16)** (9:15 a.m.) Both police Emergency Response Teams were staged at the Blacksburg Police Department in anticipation of executing search warrants or making arrests.

2007 **(April 16)** (9:15 a.m.-9:30 a.m.) Cho was seen outside and then inside Norris Hall (an engineering building) by several students. He was familiar with the building because one of his classes was there. **Cho chained the doors shut on three public entrances from the inside. No one reported seeing him chain the doors. A faculty member found a bomb threat note attached to an inner door near one of the chained exterior doors. She gave the note to a janitor who hand carried it to the Engineering School dean's office on the third**

floor. A Virginia Tech police captain joined the Policy Group as a police liaison and provided updates as information became available. He reported one gunman at large, possibly on foot.

2007 **(April 16)** (9:26 a.m.) **Virginia Tech administration sent an e-mail to campus staff, faculty, and students informing them of a dormitory shooting "incident." The message contained no specifics, no one was made aware that one student had been killed and another seriously wounded, and there was no hint that a killer might have been roaming the campus.** (*The gravity of the situation and seriousness of the threat was played down.*)

2007 **(April 16)** (about 9:30 a.m.) Radford University Police received a request from the Blacksburg Police Department to look up Thornhill's class schedule and find him in class. Before they could do this, they got a second call that he had been stopped on the road.

2007 **(April 16)** (9:30 a.m.) The police passed information to the Policy Group that it was unlikely that Hilscher's boyfriend, Karl Thornhill, was the shooter (though he remained a person of interest).

2007 **(April 16)** (9:31 a.m.-9:48 a.m.) A Virginia State Police trooper arrived at the traffic stop of Thornhill and helped question him. A gunpowder residue test was performed and packaged for lab analysis. (There is no immediate result from this type of test in the field.)

2007 **(April 16)** (9:40 a.m.) **Cho began shooting in room 206 in Norris Hall.**

*   *   *

The immediate goal of the investigating officer when he or she arrives on the scene is to gain, as much as possible, a clear understanding of what has happened. Common sense mingles with keen observational skills. Theories about what happened are fine—that is part of the initial investigative process. But investigating officers should never zero in on a theory or theoretical suspect to the exclusion of all else, particularly when there is little evidence to go on.

If the crime is violent, one of the critical questions is, "Is there a blood trail leading away from the victim(s)?" If there is, that trail tells an investigator that the perpetrator is on the loose. The blood trail also dictates that the investigating officer(s) do everything possible to warn and alert that a murderer is at large. This is simply common sense meeting harsh reality. Indeed, notifying the campus community when a dangerous criminal is loose is part of most universities' emergency plans, including Virginia Tech's.

I have to reluctantly conclude that the failure of the Virginia Tech police and other law enforcement officials to follow this elementary first step in crime scene analysis doomed thirty people at Norris Hall. Indeed, in reviewing media accounts of the morning of April 16th and the court room testimony concerning that same time frame, it is clear that law enforcement personnel involved in investigating the crime scene violated a basic principle in crime scene analysis, which is that investigating officers need to make decisions that will help prevent follow-on violence and crimes related to the one being investigated. But you, the readers, can judge for yourselves.

Let's look at the events of the morning of April 16, 2007 and what the police found and did.

Somewhere between 7:05 a.m. and 7:12 a.m. a then unknown gunman shot a black male and a white female in room 4040 of West Ambler Johnston Hall on the Virginia Tech campus. A call was made to the campus police saying someone had heard a noise and that a female may have fallen out of bed. The rescue squad was sent to the dormitory, arriving sometime between 7:21 a.m. and 7:24 a.m.

When the Virginia Tech police arrived at room 4040 on the fourth floor of West Ambler Johnston Hall, there were two bodies on the floor—one dead and one severely wounded. A black male was lying up against the room door. He had been shot in the face and bled profusely before dying. The other was a young white female barely alive with a wound to the top and back of her head. She had been shot at a downward angle and the bullet had exited her jaw. The police found two spent 9 mm shell casing indicating the weapon was a semi-automatic pistol, but there was no pistol.

The absence of the murder weapon eliminated the possibility of a murder suicide.

There were thirteen bloody footprints leading away from the murder scene, apparently made from a size 10 sneaker. The footprints headed down the hall and stopped at the door of a stairwell—one of 12 entry/exit points in the building. There was a bloody thumbprint on the stairwell door handle. The stairwell leads to the ground floor and to a door exiting the building. All indications were that the killer was on the loose, was possibly still on the campus, and that the killer was almost certainly armed and dangerous. At that moment (sometime around 7:30 a.m.), a warning was justified and called for.

No warning went out.

Virginia Tech Police Chief Wendell Flinchum was notified of the murder and wounding around 7:40 a.m. and immediately tried to reach the office of the school's Executive Vice President. Court records indicate that at 7:51 a.m. he contacted the Blacksburg Police Department and requested "technical assistance." A few minutes later, at 7:57 a.m., he got through to the Executive Vice President's office and notified them of the shooting. At approximately 8:00 a.m. Chief Flinchum arrived on the scene.

At this point, the investigation of the crime was fully and squarely in the hands of Virginia Tech Chief of Police Wendell Flinchum. He was running the show and making all the decisions. Flinchum had an excellent reputation and was well thought of in the law enforcement community in southwestern Virginia. His background included ten weeks of training at the Basic Police Academy and in 2005, and he had been nominated for and was sent to the FBI for training that included 44 hours of homicide instruction. His nomination for this training at Quantico was, to use his own words, a special "honor."

By this point it was nearly an hour since the shootings occurred and according to court documents, no one was looking for a shooter on campus. No one had issued a be-on-the-lookout for the killer, especially one with bloody clothes and shoes.

One of Flinchum's first actions was to assign the homicide to a young detective with no prior homicide training and no homicide schooling of any kind. The detective however, did follow good police procedure and began to interview people on the fourth floor. She learned that a number of them had heard screams and loud bangs, but there were no eyewitnesses.

Chief Flinchum later testified on the witness stand that he never raised the subject of a campus lockdown with school president Charles Steger. In fact, he even went so far as to say that *if* he considered issuing a warning that morning, he doesn't recall it. The chief also testified that he had the authority to issue a warning per published university procedure, but did not because the police did not have the technical means to do so and the evidence suggested the shooter posed no threat to the wider campus.

What evidence gave that suggestion? The two bodies—one dead and one dying? The gunshot wounds? Or perhaps it was the bloody footprints leading out of the building? In the first hour or two following the double homicide there was a dearth of evidence. About the only intelligent thing you could say was the killer was out there somewhere, might be on campus, and was armed and dangerous.

We know at this point that President Steger and Chief Flinchum were in contact though we have no way of knowing what was said. However, notes taken by Kim O'Rourke and Lisa Wilkes at the Policy Group meeting convened to discuss the shootings, state the police (read Flinchum) indicated there was no need to rush to warn or to lockdown the campus. (Two families whose daughters were killed at Tech, the Petersons and the Prydes, refused to settle with the state and sued Virginia Tech. In Chapter XI, "The Lawsuit and Trial," I discuss the discrepancies between Chief Flinchum's statements on the stand, and the notes taken by O'Rourke and Wilkes. Chief Flinchum claims that the idea of warning was not considered in his communications with the Policy Group, but President Steger testified at the Pryde and Peterson trial that Flinchum indicated there was no need to rush to warn the campus. No one has explained this inconsistency and no one has ever adequately explained why or how Flinchum felt there was no need to rush to warn or lockdown.)

While all of this was going on, the young man and the young woman in room 4040 were yet to be identified by the police. There were pictures of Emily Hilscher and Heather Haugh, with their names, on the door of dormitory room 4040. The wounded female student was almost certainly one of those young women. It is not unreasonable to think that the medics who worked on Emily would have been able to quickly recognize her features from the photo on the door. For that matter, the university had records of who lived in that dorm room and neighbors could also have provided names. Emily remained, for the moment, unnamed.

Ryan Clark, who was a Resident Advisor (RA) for the dorm, lived in room 4042, next to the crime scene. His name was on the door. The door to that room was open and pair of trousers had been thrown on the bed. The young man in 4040 was found in his undershorts. The police had still not made an official identification at the one-hour mark.

Unofficially, however, the cleaning staff had already identified the male victim. We know that because Ed Spencer, the Associate Vice President for Student Affairs, knew Clark and knew that he was gay. Soon after the shootings Spencer had been informed by a member of the cleaning staff that the "RA had been murdered" in West Ambler Johnston Hall. To quote from the *Petition for Rehearing*, Record No. 121717, "Ed Spencer, Associate

Vice President for Student Affairs, arrived on the scene [Norris Hall] shortly before 8:00 a.m. He informed police that the RA 'was active in the gay community,' thus negating the sexual-liaison theory."

Even if no one had told Spencer, it would have taken him a very short time to realize that the murdered male was Ryan Clark. Because Spencer knew Clark, he should have reported instantly who the murdered black male was. It seems logical that Spencer could have provided assistance in identifying the female victim as well, or at least with contact information for the two females listed as living in that room. As far as the records show, none of that happened.

It is odd that the cleaning staff identified Ryan Clark within 30 minutes of the shooting, but the police did not. The failure of the police to at least give a tentative identification of the victims is puzzling. It is also puzzling that police decided the double homicide was a domestic incident—a love triangle. As already noted, Ryan Clark was gay. Spencer knew that and even if he had not, one question by the investigating officers to any student on the fourth floor of West Ambler Johnston Hall would have put the domestic incident theory to rest.

As far as I have been able to ascertain, it took a little over an hour after the shootings took place to identify Clark, but the timeline in the Governor's Review Panel Report does not pin down the precise time of the identification.

You may be saying that this delay is not too bad. And, in and of itself, you are probably right. But coupled with the rest of what was going on at the crime scene, it is another indication of the lack of coordination and communication among those who were at West Ambler Johnston Hall. It would seem that despite the presence of an experienced police chief, Wendell Flinchum, there was little or no organization or systematic approach to investigating the crime scene.

A good crime scene investigator considers all possibilities and rules nothing out. Who might have committed the murder, was it a random act of violence, was it a robbery or drug deal gone bad? Nothing should be excluded and while a suspect may be identified in the interview process, no one suspect or person of interest should be singled out to the exclusion of others—particularly in the absence of strong evidence. So how did it happen that Chief Flinchum focused the investigation on Karl Thornhill, Emily Hilscher's boyfriend, as the only person of interest?

Let's take a closer look at this "person of interest." Who decided that the West Ambler Johnston crime scene was a "domestic incident?" When was that decision made? How was the conclusion reached that murderers in a domestic crime should not be considered a threat to others? The only evidence that Flinchum had to support his belief that this was a domestic incident appears to be that one of the victims was male and the other female—and, that they were clad only in their pajamas and underwear respectively. It does not appear that the trousers flung on the bed of the next-door room, left unoccupied and with the door hanging open, were taken into account.

A far more likely explanation of the crime scene was that what Ryan Clark had heard concerned him so much that he didn't take time to put his pants on before going to investigate. He was probably the only person, and certainly the last, to hear Emily's cry for help. He did the heroic thing—he went to her aid. But, the police, because the two were not fully dressed, put the tawdriest explanation on what they found—the two must have been having sex; the shootings must have been part of a love triangle. It apparently was beyond the investigating officers' thinking that what they found could be anything else but some spin on a sex crime. The exact opposite appears to be the truth—Ryan Clark died a hero's death.

Let's look more closely at the question of issuing a warning and instituting a lockdown. Only the Virginia Tech police and the school's Policy Group know what took place in the deliberations and conversations following the double homicide at West Ambler Johnston Hall. Only they know if a lockdown was suggested; only they know if and how vigorously a campus-wide warning was recommended—and by whom. And they are not talking.

A key concept in crime scene analysis is the "person of interest;" the identification and apprehension of such a person is key to any investigation, and especially important in a violent crime. First, a reasonable suspicion of who may have committed the crime—based on facts—must be determined. Then, if that person is still at large, investigators must determine whether that person is planning to engage in further criminal activity. Only once investigators have the evidence to substantiate their suspicion, should they identify that individual as a "person of interest."

These principles were violated at Virginia Tech. The Virginia Tech police identified Karl Thornhill, Emily Hilscher's boyfriend, as a "person of interest" and concentrated on him to the exclusion of all else. The "evidence" pointing to the boyfriend was a photo of Thornhill holding a rifle, not a pistol, at a firing range.

In fact, a large number of college-age males in southwestern Virginia own guns and many go to firing ranges or engage in target practice. On this basis alone, any number of young men in West Ambler Johnston Hall could have been designated a "person of interest." There was no evidence in the room or from witnesses that Karl Thornhill had been there that morning, and no hints that the couple had been unhappy.

Compounding the error was the fact that the police and school proceeded as if they had found their killer. By zeroing in on Karl Thornhill, Chief Flinchum and all the police investigators violated one of the very basic tenants of crime analysis: they believed what they wanted to believe, they assumed someone was guilty with the flimsiest of evidence and apparently excluded other possible culprits in their investigation.

Flinchum and others may try to argue that it was reasonable to focus on Karl Thornhill. Reasonable suspicion, however, is determined from the totality of the circumstances and information known to the investigating officers. There was no totality of evidence pointing toward Thornhill. Reasonable suspicion is subject to neither wishful thinking nor is it subject to formulaic analysis in the absence of evidence. Crime scene investigators should never zero in on one suspect to the exclusion of others. This basic mistake by Flinchum, and others, would become a mutating monster at Norris Hall in less than two hours.

In examining the missteps of the investigating officers in the early hours of April 16, 2007, you have to look at the questioning of Emily Hilscher's roommate Heather Haugh. If the police suspected that the murders were the result of a domestic dispute such as a love triangle, what better person to ask that than Haugh? Yet, there is no evidence such a question was asked.

Had anyone thought to follow up on the possibility of a love triangle with any of the dorm residents, rather than assuming it was true based on the location and genders of the bodies, investigators could have quickly found out that Ryan Clark had no interest in Emily Hirscher beyond her being a student he was assigned to help and watch over in his role as a RA. Hilscher had none in him, other than as a neighbor, RA, and possibly the person who answered what may have been her last cry for help.

As far as I can tell, no one asked Heather Haugh about the relationship between her roommate and her RA. Haugh returned to the dorm room at 8:14 a.m., an hour after the shooting, 45 minutes after Spencer had arrived, and only 14 minutes after Chief Flinchum. Shortly after that point in time the police had to know that Emily Hirscher was the wounded student (although the timeline of the Review Panel Report does not specifically state the time of Hilscher's identification). It is not until the questioning of Haugh begins that the police identify Hilscher's boyfriend, Karl Thornhill, as the person of interest and that takes place sometime around 8:30 a.m. A lookout for Karl Thornhill was issued between 8:30 a.m. and 8:40 a.m. However, although he was a "person of interest" and a student at Radford University, apparently Virginia Tech police did not notify the Radford University police of that fact for some time. This delay in asking for help to find Thornhill, "a person of interest" in a double homicide, is puzzling.

Strangely, President Steger would claim at a press conference on the evening of April 16th that Thornhill was a "person of interest" at 7:30 a.m.

Only years later, and following a painful jury trial, did families find out for certain that such timing was impossible.

Still, it is clear that by 8:40 a.m. the university police had decided on a suspect and issued a be-on-the-look-out for him. It is also clear that the young man was not in custody, and the police did not know where he was. They had delayed in contacting Thornhill's school, and so they could not confirm whether he was in class or at his dorm. What they did have was thirteen bloody footsteps leading away from a double murder scene, and someone with a gun, whether it was Thornhill or not, potentially loose on their campus.

Still no warning was issued. It was not until 9:26 a.m. that the school issued a notification reading: "A shooting incident occurred at West Ambler Johnston Hall earlier this morning. Police are on the scene and are investigating."

All references to a homicide and a possible active shooter were absent from the notice; there was no mention of the fact that the killer was armed, dangerous, and still at large.

The police said they locked down one building on the morning of April 16, 2007, and that was West Ambler Johnston Hall. But even then, they got it wrong. Despite statements that the dormitory was "locked down" while the building was being searched, in fact it was not. Students still had access into and out of the building. Students such as Henry Lee and Rachael Hill were allowed to leave the building during that time period to go to their French class—where both would later be killed. The two arrived at class sometime between 9:15 a.m. and 9:30 a.m., just minutes before Cho. A particularly heart-wrenching aspect to this story is that Hill, while walking across campus, called her parents to tell them there had been a shooting in her dormitory, but she was OK.

Cho's rampage began at 9:40 a.m.

The bottom line is that at the one place where the police instituted a lockdown, they didn't get it right. If a true lockdown had been in place, Hill and Lee would be alive today.

As the dust settled and the horror of the Tech massacre began to sink in, there was widespread suspicion that the school leadership was trying to figure out how to handle the negative publicity of a double homicide less than two weeks before the largest on-campus fundraiser in the school's history—was that why there was no warning; was that why there was no lockdown? Surely the upcoming gala was known by these senior administrators who had most likely been involved in discussions during the planning for such an important event. This evidence is circumstantial, but is at least as good as the evidence that allowed police to target Karl Thornhill as the killer in a domestic dispute.

Some argue that it is unfair to criticize Flinchum, Steger, and others because hindsight is 20-20. But I believe it is fair to criticize them for lack of professionalism, poor leadership, and unsound judgments. Consider this, Chief Flinchum prior to April 16, 2007, was extolled by many as "one of the best" in his profession. If this is true, his poor decisions and lack of action when confronted with a murder scene are open to question and are valid areas of criticism.

Flinchum's actions and inactions on that fateful morning are not only mystifying, but are certainly not commensurate with "one of the best" in his profession. Indeed, his actions on April 16, 2007 are something more akin to an amateurish response than the actions of a senior, professional police officer.

We need to skip forward for a moment until sometime around 6:00 p.m. on April 16, 2007. That is when school President Steger and Larry Hincker, Associate Vice President for University Relations, and possibly the school's legal counsel, apparently mapped out a strategy for handling the press and fielding questions about the delay in issuing a campus-wide warning.

A press conference was scheduled for 7:40 p.m. that night so they needed a plan and they needed it quickly. The two apparently decided that Steger would read a prepared statement and then the floor would be turned over to Police Chief Flinchum. Flinchum had not been at the Policy Group meetings, the deliberative body that debated when and how to alert the campus, so he wasn't privy to what the group had discussed that morning. Nevertheless, the chief would field the questions.

Prior to the press conference, at 7:05 p.m., an email detailing specific wording that President Steger would ultimately present at the press conference was prepared on the laptop of Virginia Tech's head of University Relations, Larry Hincker. The email could then be forwarded to his computer for printing for release to the media. At a trial five years later, Hincker—under oath—denied that he had written the email on his laptop and had no idea who had composed it, yet it was sent from that laptop to himself, and was read almost verbatim by Steger 30 minutes later on television in front of reporters.

The prepared statement read by Steger included an erroneous timeline of events, along with other untruths. The incorrect timeline identified 7:30 a.m. as when a "person of interest" was identified, and police were already searching for him. But, as we have already shown, "the person of interest," Karl Thornhill was not identified until the questioning of Heather Haugh over an hour later—sometime between 8:15 and 8:30 a.m. The school needed a 7:30 a.m. time in order to give them some degree of cover for the delay in notifying the campus.

I have serious doubts about the statements made by Hincker relative to his being so clueless about the source and author of what was about to be released to the national media by the school president. It is odd that apparently a phantom got access to Hincker's laptop at 7:05 p.m., typed a timeline that lied about key aspects of the crime, sent it to Hincker, and then left before the real Hincker returned to his keyboard. Following that, the document mysteriously was printed for the president of the school to hand out to the press corps, presenting false information as fact, and getting these inaccuracies into the public record—yet still its origin is unknown. Granted, there was a great deal of confusion and angst that day, but by anybody's standards the strange comings and goings regarding Hincker's laptop stretch the limits of credibility.

Even if you accept the phantom timeline writer, it is hard to explain why Chief Flinchum, who knew there was no person of interest until after 8:30 a.m., remained silent at the time of the press conference and for a very prolonged period of time thereafter. In fact, he did more than just remain silent; at one point he apparently contradicted himself and verified the lie.

In March of 2012, during the trial where Virginia Tech, as agent of the state, was found guilty of negligence, the *Roanoke Times* reported that retired Virginia State Police Superintendent Gerald Massengill, chairman of the Virginia Tech Review Panel appointed by Governor Kaine, testified under oath that Flinchum and Blacksburg Police Chief Kim Crannis had both verified the erroneous timeline in a private meeting with Massengill held in June of 2007. The meeting attendees were purposely limited because had their numbers exceeded a certain level, then, by law, the meeting would have to have been open to the public.

What is even more egregious is that in May of 2007, just one month earlier, Flinchum had presented the timeline of events to the Virginia Tech Review Panel in a PowerPoint presentation which was published almost verbatim in the official report released by then-Governor Tim Kaine in August of 2007, which actually showed the correct start time of the interview. I say "almost verbatim" because even though Flinchum's PowerPoint presentation of May, 2007 showed the critical interview of Heather Haugh actually began at 8:16 a.m., and led to the identification and search for a person of interest almost thirty minutes later, the false timeline entry surrounding that event remained in the official record.

True, over one year later Flinchum would finally lay out the correct timeline. However, that correction was only made after approval of a legal settlement offer was accepted by all but two of the families. Prior to the settlement, there was no mention of the false timeline, or other errors, by anyone from the school, former panel members, or the state. His silence on this critical point, particularly early on, is troubling because the incorrect timeline made it into the first official version of the Governor's Review

Panel's report. The motivation for not correcting the timeline may have been a recognition that the correct timeline could have undercut and negatively impacted the tremendous pressure being placed on the families to settle with the state of Virginia.

Another complete falsehood contained in Steger's comments dealt with whether the campus had been notified and warned of the homicide at West Ambler Johnston Hall. According to the school president, the answer was—of course. At the press conference, and in the press release, Steger stated that the school had been notified of a "homicide." That simply is not true. "A shooting incident," the exact words found in the first email sent to the campus at 9:26 a.m., is not a double homicide; "police are on the scene and are investigating," in no way indicates that the murderer is unidentified and is still at large.

It is impossible to disguise or gloss over these errors in information and evidence gathering. The "love triangle" was allowed to stand, and then for reasons no one has explained, the police built on that theory, calling the double homicide "targeted" killings, making the murders and murderer seem less a threat to the campus at large. Where did Flinchum and the Virginia Police come up with that? The term "targeted" was apparently an afterthought as police kept looking for excuses. "Targeted" is not used in the timeline of events in the Governor's Review Panel report and only gains prominence in testimony given at the trial in connection with lawsuits the Peterson and Pryde families filed against Virginia Tech. (See Chapter XI, "The Lawsuit and Trial.") A murderer is a murderer. There is absolutely no way to measure the threat posed until the killer is in custody. There is no reason to ever say that a murderer is not a threat. But the school and law enforcement argued that because this was "domestic" or "targeted" there was no urgency to warn.

Let's take a closer look at the words "targeted killings." According to the American Civil Liberties Union (ACLU), "targeted killings" refers to the killing of individuals whom the U.S. government deems to be an enemy. The ACLU says this about "targeted killings:" *"The CIA and the military are carrying out an 'illegal killing' program in which people far from any battlefield are determined to be enemies of the state and are killed without charge or trial. The executive branch has, in fact, claimed the unchecked authority to put the names of citizens and others on 'kill lists' on the basis of secret determination, based on secret evidence that a person meets a secret definition of the enemy."* Indeed, most authorities who have looked at "targeted killings" refer to it as an intentional killing, by a government or its agents of persons who are allegedly taking part in an armed conflict or terrorism, whether by bearing arms or otherwise, and who have allegedly lost the immunity from being targeted that they would otherwise have under the Third Geneva Convention.

I think that what the Virginia Tech Police really meant when they used the term "targeted killings" was a completely different term and concept: "targeted violence." "Targeted violence" is used by specialists who study violent crimes and is a completely different concept from "targeted killings." "Targeted violence" has been used in discussing school safety, but from what I can determine, it does not apply to a love triangle on a campus, anywhere. Did Flinchum really mean "targeted violence?" The mixing of the terms "domestic incident," "targeted violence," and "targeted killings" gives credence to the fact that the label "targeted killings" was applied in a rush, without thought, and as part of an afterthought to provide an excuse for both the police's and school's inaction.

Another nagging question is why there was no campus lockdown.

One of the excuses repeated by school officials is that they did not call for a campus lockdown because they wanted to avoid a panic similar to the one that occurred in the late summer of 2006 when William Morva escaped from custody in Blacksburg and killed two people.

On August 20, 2006, Morva, while awaiting trial for armed robbery, was taken from the Blacksburg jail to the Montgomery Regional Hospital for treatment of a sprained ankle and wrist. After using the bathroom, Morva assaulted and knocked out deputy Russell Queensberry with a metal toilet-paper holder. He then took the officer's gun and killed Derrick McFarland, a hospital security guard.

The next morning, on August 21, 2006, Morva shot and killed Montgomery County sheriff's deputy Eric Sutpin. In response, Virginia Tech canceled classes and closed the campus—a lockdown. In other words, the school locked down even though the victims were not students and there was no evidence the killer was on the campus. Later on the 21st, Morva was captured hiding in a briar patch 150 yards from where he killed Sutpin.

When asked why Virginia Tech did not follow its own example of eight months earlier, President Steger and others in the school administration said they did not want a repeat of the panic that occurred at that time. The only problem with that is in talking to people who were there at the time and reading the newspaper accounts, there was no panic anywhere on the Tech campus.

*   *   *

If you look back to the Law Enforcement Oath of Honor ascribed to by the Virginia Association of Chiefs of Police, you have to ask where was Flinchum's integrity and character when a flawed timeline was knowingly allowed to stand for nearly two years and make it into the initial draft of the official report on the Tech tragedy. Where was his courage to look at all the possibilities in a crime investigation instead of choosing an easy answer that fit the needs of a fund raising schedule? Looking at the actions of some members of the police on April 16, 2007, and in the months and years that followed, you search in vain for courage, accountability, character, and integrity. The duty to serve the community and uphold the public trust, and in so doing honor the badge is, if not betrayed, wanting.

CHAPTER III

SEUNG HUI CHO

"Our lives begin to end the day we become silent
about things that matter.

~Dr. Martin Luther King, Jr.,
Baptist minister and civil rights leader

1984	Seung Hui Cho was born in Seoul, South Korea. He had serious health problems from the time he was 9 months old until he was 3 years old.
1992	The Cho family emigrated from South Korea to Maryland.
1993	The Cho family moved to Fairfax County, Virginia.
1997	Seung Hui Cho was in the 6th grade. Teachers meet with his parents about his **very withdrawn behavior.**
1999 **(April 20)**	Columbine shootings—12 students, one teacher killed and 21 students wounded.
1999	One of Seung Hui Cho's papers depicted suicidal and homicidal ideations. **The paper referenced and celebrated the Columbine shootings.** The school requested that his parents ask a counselor to intervene, which led to a psychiatric evaluation at the Multicultural Center for Human Services. **Cho was prescribed anti-depressant**

medication. He responded well and was taken off the medication approximately one year later.

2000   Seung Hui Cho began his sophomore year at Westfield High School. After a review by a local screening committee, **he was diagnosed as having an emotional disability and was enrolled in an Individual Education Plan (IEP) to deal with shyness and lack of responsiveness in a classroom setting.**

2002 **(January 16)** Appalachian School of Law shootings—one student, one professor, and the dean were killed and three students were wounded.

2003 **(Spring)** Seung Hui Cho graduated from Westfield High School with a 3.5 GPA in the Honors Program. **He decided to attend Virginia Tech against the advice of his parents and counselors who thought the school was too big and he would not get adequate individualized attention.**

2003 **(Fall)** Seung Hui Cho entered Virginia Tech as a business information systems major. He had a difficult time with his roommate over neatness issues and changed rooms.

2004 **(Fall)** **Seung Hui Cho began his sophomore year and moved off campus.** He complained of mites in his apartment, but doctors told him it was acne and prescribed minocycline. He became interested in writing. His sister noted his growing passion for writing, though he was secretive about content.

2005 **(Spring)** Seung Hui Cho requested to change his major to English. He submitted an idea for a book to a publishing house; it was rejected.

2005 **(Fall)** **Seung Hui Cho started his junior year and moved back into a dormitory on campus.** Cho was taken to some parties by his suitemates. **On one occasion he stabbed at the carpet in Margaret Bowman's room with a knife in the presence of others.**

2005 **(October 15) Professor Nikki Giovanni wrote a letter to Cho expressing concern about his behavior in her class and about the violence in his writing. Professor Giovanni asked the head of English Department, Professor Lucinda Roy, to remove Cho from her class.**

2005 **(October 18) Professor Roy informed Mary Ann Lewis, Associate Dean of Liberal Arts and Human Sciences, and others that Cho read a violent and upsetting poem in class that** day, and that her students told her Cho had been surreptitiously taking photos of them. Dr. Roy also said she had contacted Tom Brown, the Dean of Student Affairs; Zenobia Hikes, Vice President of Student Affairs; Detective George Jackson at the Virginia Tech Police Department; and Dr. Robert Miller at the Cook Counseling Center to report the incident and seek advice. Roy said she could remove Cho as long as there was a viable alternative to Giovanni's class. The Cook Counseling Center advised that though the poem was disturbing, there was no specific threat. They suggested that Cho be referred to the counseling center. Frances Keene, Director of Judicial Affairs, and Tom Brown both wrote to Professor Roy to advise Cho that any future similar behavior would be referred to Judicial Affairs.

2005 (October 19) Professor Roy and Cheryl Ruggiero met with Cho regarding his situation in Professor Giovanni's class. They discussed the impact of his writing on the class, and warned him that unauthorized picture-taking is inappropriate and is taken seriously by the school. Cho said his writing was intended as satire and agreed not to take any more photos of classmates and professors. Cho was advised of the study alternative that was available. He was advised to seek counseling. This advice was reiterated in an email to Cho following the meeting. Cho was removed from Dr. Giovanni's class and Professor Roy tutored him one-on-one with the assistance of Professor Frederick D'Aguiar. Cho refused to go to counseling. Professor Roy informed the Division of Student Affairs, the Cook Counseling Center, the Schiffert Health Center, the Virginia Tech Police, Department (VTPD) and the College of Liberal Arts and Human Sciences of the arrangements made for Cho. Cho's problems and his removal from Professor Giovanni's class were discussed at a meeting of Virginia Tech's Care Team. (The Care Team is a student assistance team convened by the Dean of Students' Office that coordinates timely responses to student emergencies.) The Care Team considered the problem solved.

2005 (November 2) Cho's roommates and dorm residents thought Cho set fires in the dorm lounge and said in emails that they reported it to the police. No written police report exists.

2005 (November 27) Jennifer Nelson, a resident of West Ambler Johnston (WAJ) residence hall, filed a report with the campus police indicating that Cho had made "annoying" contacts with her via the Internet, by phone, and in person. The police interviewed Cho; Nelson declined to press charges, but said she would testify at a disciplinary hearing. The investigating officer referred the incident to the school's disciplinary system, the Office of Judicial Affairs. The Office of Judicial Affairs later contacted Nelson, telling her they could only proceed if she filed a written complaint. She declined and no hearing was held.

2005 (November 30) Cho called the Cook Counseling Center following his interaction with the police and was triaged on the phone.

2005 (December 6) Emails among Resident Advisors (RAs) reflected complaints by another female student, Christina Lillizu, who lived on the 3rd floor of Cochrane resident hall, regarding derogatory Instant Messages (IM) with foul language sent by Cho under various strange aliases. The RAs also reported the incidence of IMs Cho sent to Jennifer Nelson, and his visit in disguise to her dorm room. Lisa Virga, a resident advisor, sent an email to Rohsaan Settle, a member of the Residence Life staff, detailing a list of complaints about Cho, including reports that he had knives in his room.

2005 (December 9) Cho sent unwanted Instant Messages to a third female student, Margaret Bowman. Later he left her messages on the marker board outside her room.

2005 (December 11) Cho left a new message, a quote from Shakespeare, on Bowman's marker board.

2005 (December 12) Bowman returned from an exam and found more text added to the message from the day before. She then filed a report with the Virginia Tech police complaining of multiple "disturbing" contacts from Cho. She requested that Cho have no further contacts with her. When questioned by students (apparently his dorm mates) about the notes to Bowman, Cho said "Shakespeare did it." Cho called and canceled a 2:00 p.m. appointment at the Cook Counseling Center, but then called back and was triaged on the telephone a second time.

2005 (December 13) The VTPD notified Cho that he was to have no further contact with Bowman. Cho's suitemate received a message from **Cho saying, "I might as well kill myself now."** The suitemate notified the campus police. The police took Cho to the Virginia Tech Police Department where a pre-screener from the New River Valley Community Services Board **evaluated him "an imminent danger to self and others."** A magistrate issued a temporary detaining order, and Cho was taken to Carilion St. Albans Psychiatric Hospital for overnight stay and mental evaluation. **No one contacted Cho's parents.**

2005 **(December 14)** (7:00 a.m.)The person assigned as an independent evaluator, psychologist Roy Crouse, evaluated Cho and concluded that **he did not present an imminent danger to himself.**

2005 **(December 14)** (prior to 11:00 a.m.) A staff psychiatrist at St. Alban's evaluated Cho, concluded he was not a danger to himself or others and recommended outpatient counseling. **The staff psychiatrist gathered no collateral information.**

2005 **(December 14)** (11:00-11:30 a.m.) **Special Justice Paul M. Barnett conducted Cho's commitment hearing and rules in accordance with the independent evaluator, but ordered follow-up treatment as an outpatient. Cho made an appointment with the Cook Counseling Center and was released.**

2005 **(December 14)** (Noon) The St. Alban's staff psychiatrist dictated in his evaluation summary that "there is no indication of psychosis, delusions, suicidal or homicidal ideation." The psychiatrist found that "his insight and judgment are normal ... Follow-up and aftercare to be arranged at Virginia Tech; medications, none."

2005 **(December 14)** (2:35 p.m.) **Cook Counseling Center received a fax from Carilion Health System with copies of St. Alban's discharge summary and the Pre-admission Screening Form completed by the Community Services Board evaluator the previous day at police headquarters.**

2005 **(December 14)** (3:00 p.m.) Cho appeared for his appointment at the Cook Counseling Center. Dr. Miller, the Cook Counseling Center director, received an email notifying him that Cho had been taken to St. Alban's the previous night. Dr. Miller emailed the Cook Counseling Center staff to alert them "in case this student is seen" at the Center. A Cook Counseling Center staff member emailed back that Cho already had been seen in the afternoon.

2006 (January) The Cook Counseling Center received a psychiatric summary from St. Albans. **Neither the Cook Counseling Center nor the Care Team took any action to follow up on Cho.**

2006 (February) Dr. Miller was removed from his position following a management study of the Cook Counseling Center. **In his hurry to vacate the office, Miller packed Cho's file and the files of several other students in a box and took them home. (The file was only discovered in July 2009 after 30 families had reached a settlement with the state.)**

2006 (April) **Cho's technical writing professor, Carl Bean, suggested that Cho drop his class after repeated efforts to address shortcomings in class and inappropriate choice of writing assignments. Cho followed the professor to his office, raised his voice angrily, and was asked to leave. Professor Bean did not report the incident to Virginia Tech officials.**

2006 (Spring) Cho took Professor Bob Hicok's creative writing class. Professor Hicok later characterized Cho's writing as not particularly unique as far as subject matter was concerned, **but remarkable for violence.**

2006 (Fall) Cho enrolled in a playwriting workshop taught by Professor Ed Falco. **Cho wrote a play about a young man who hates the students at his school and plans to kill them and himself. The writing contained parallels to the subsequent events of April 16, 2007, as well as the recorded message to NBC that same day.** Professor Falco conferred with Professors Roy and Norris, who told him that in the fall of 2005 and in 2006, Professor Roy and Professor Norris, respectively, had alerted Associate Dean Mary Ann Lewis about Cho and his behavior.

2006 (September 6-12) Professor Lisa Norris, another of Cho's writing professors, alerted Associate Dean Mary Ann Lewis but, according to the Governor's Review Panel Report, the dean "finds no mention of mental health issues or police reports" on Cho. **Professor Norris encouraged Cho to go to counseling with her but he declined.**

2006 (September 26-November 4) Cho writes three more violent stories for an English class.

2007 (February 2) Cho ordered a .22 caliber Walther P22 handgun online from TGSCOM, Inc.

2007 **(February 9) Cho picked up a handgun from J-N-D Pawnbrokers in Blacksburg, across the street from Virginia Tech. The timeline in the Governor's Review Panel Report does not indicate whether or not the pawnbroker did a background check.**

2007 **(March12)** Cho rented a van from Enterprise Rent-A-Car at the Roanoke Regional Airport, which he kept for almost a month. (Cho videotaped some of his subsequently released diatribe in the van.)

2007 **(March 13) Cho bought a 9mm Glock 19 handgun and a box of 50 9mm full metal jacket practice rounds at Roanoke Firearms.** Cho waited the 30 days between gun purchases as required by Virginia law. The store conducted the required background check by police and found no record of Cho's mental health issues.

2007 **(March 22)** Cho went to PSS Range and Training, an indoor pistol range, and spent an hour practicing.

2007 **(March 22) Cho bought two 10-round magazines for the Walther P22 on eBay.**

2007 **(March 23) Cho bought three additional 10-round magazines from another eBay seller.**

2007 **(March 31) Cho bought additional ammunition magazines, ammunition and a hunting knife from Wal-Mart and Dick's Sporting Goods. He bought chains from Home Depot.**

2007 **(April 7) Cho bought more ammunition.**

2007 **(April 8)** Cho spent the night at the Hampton Inn in Christiansburg, Virginia (a town adjacent to Blacksburg) videotaping segments of his manifesto-like diatribe. **Cho bought more ammunition.**

2007 **(April 13)** Anonymous bomb threats were made to Torgersen, Durham, and Whittemore halls. The threats were assessed by the Virginia Tech police and the buildings were evacuated. There was no lockdown or cancellation of classes elsewhere on campus. (Later, during the investigation of the April 16, massacre, no evidence was found linking these threats to Cho's bomb threat note in Norris Hall—based, in part, on handwriting samples.)

2007 **(April 14)** An Asian male wearing a hooded garment was seen by a faculty member in Norris Hall. The faculty member later told

> police that one of her students had told her the **doors were chained. This may have been Cho practicing. Cho bought more ammunition.**
>
> 2007 **(April 15)** Cho placed his weekly Sunday night call to his family in Fairfax County. They reported the conversation was normal and Cho said nothing that caused them concern.
>
> 2007 **(April 16) Cho committed his murderous rampage, killing 32 students and faculty at Virginia Tech—the worst mass**

*   *   *

Cho's Early Years

It is true that it is not always easy to predict when a person is going to become violent, but it is also true that in some cases there are clear warnings. In the case of the Virginia Tech massacre, the warnings were there, yet Virginia Tech's response and treatment were not. Seung Hui Cho's medical history at the university was largely one of institutional inaction, pervasive ignorance of the law, individual incompetence, and bureaucratic indifference.

Cho was born in Korea on January 18, 1984. He was the second child of Sung-Tae Cho and Hyang Im Cho. Their daughter, Sun Kyung, was born three years earlier. As a child, Cho was frail. He developed whooping cough and then pneumonia when he was nine months old. When he was three, doctors diagnosed him with a hole in his heart; some medical records refer to it as a heart murmur. At age five doctors conducted cardiac tests to examine the heart. Those tests may have included an echocardiograph or cardiac catheterization and apparently had a traumatic effect on the child*. From that point on he did not like to be touched. His parents describe him as being sick a great deal of the time while growing up.

In 1992 when the Cho family emigrated from South Korea to the United States none of the family spoke English and the transition to their new life was not easy. It took the Cho children approximately two years to learn to speak, read, and write English. During that time both were teased,

---

* Note: The rendering of Cho's medical history in this chapter is, in large part, taken verbatim from the *Governor's Review Panel Report—The Addendum.* For a more complete examination of Cho's background see Chapter IV of that report, *Mental History of Seung Hui Cho.*

but Cho's sister said she took it in stride. There apparently is no record as to Cho's reaction to this teasing.

Cho's parents indicate that he was quiet and gentle; they do not recall tantrums or angry outbursts. As a youngster he took Tae Kwon Do, watched TV, and played video games. He reportedly liked basketball and collected both figurines and remote controlled cars. Cho was a very shy child and did not communicate much with his parents but when he did talk he avoided discussing his feelings. Cho remained introspective and the fact that he talked little with family members became an increasing concern to his parents. His mother and sister worried that he was being bullied at school, but he never mentioned it. According to the Review Panel Report, when interviewed, Cho's sister did know that when he walked down the hall a few students would sometimes taunt him.

Throughout Cho's elementary school years, his lack of communication became more and more of a concern for the family. Mrs. Cho, in particular, tried to socialize him by encouraging him to go to church, but to no avail. In the end they decided to "let him be the way he is."

In mid-1997, the Chos sought therapy for their son at the Center for Multicultural Human Services (CMHS), a mental health facility offering treatment and psychological evaluations to low-income, immigrant families. His first counselor was not a good fit (the Review Panel Report does not explain this point), so Cho began working with a specialist trained in art therapy. Art therapy is used with young people who do not have sufficient language or cognitive skills to utilize traditional spoken therapy.

Cho also saw a psychiatrist who diagnosed him with social anxiety disorder. He continued to work with the mental health specialists, but made next to no improvement.

Then came the Columbine shootings in April 1999. After that tragedy, Cho wrote a disturbing paper for his English class in which he expressed thoughts of suicide and homicide and indicated he wanted to repeat Columbine. The school contacted Cho's parents and urged psychiatric care.

Again, Cho was evaluated by the CMHS. The psychiatric intern who evaluated him was an experienced child psychiatrist and family counselor. (As good as the intern may have been, he or she—the Review Panel Report does not specify whether the intern was a male or female—was not an expert. An intern, by definition, works under someone's supervision.) The Cho family explained that they were facing something of a crisis, as their daughter, the one person with whom Cho would communicate, was getting ready to go away to college.

The doctor diagnosed Cho with selective mutism* and major depression: single episode. He prescribed the antidepressant Paroxetine 20 mg, which Cho took from June 1999 to July 2000. He did so well that the doctor stopped the medication, feeling he was so improved that he no longer needed the antidepressant.

Cho entered high school in the Fall of 1999. The teachers noted that he was shy, not verbally active, and that there was practically no communication between Cho and his peers or teachers. The Review Panel Report does not indicate how much, if any, communication there was about Cho between his elementary school, middle school, and high school. When Cho talked, he could barely be heard.

Furthermore, he did not speak in complete sentences, but his grades were high and he was always punctual. The school apparently noted no other unusual traits or behaviors. When a teacher asked him if he would like help in communicating he reportedly nodded his head yes.

In high school Cho met with a guidance counselor who asked him if he had ever received mental health care or special education assistance at his previous schools. He reportedly indicated he had not.

Cho was brought to the attention of the high school's Screening Committee in October of 2000. Federal law requires that children with learning disabilities be given the opportunity to learn in the least restrictive environment and to be mainstreamed in classrooms. Cho was then given a series of tests to diagnose his problems and to guide the school in preparing an Individual Education Plan (IEP).

School representatives met with Cho's parents to learn more about their son. Mrs. Cho, in what was an ominous glimpse of what was to come, expressed concern about her son's future and how he would fare in college given his poor social skills.

The Screening Committee decided that Cho was eligible for the Special Education Program for Emotional Disabilities and Speech and Language. The school developed an IEP for Cho that included curriculum and classroom modifications: First, a modification for oral presentations, and second, a modification for grading based on oral and group participation. It was recommended that Cho receive language therapy, and he did. Other modifications included allowing Cho to eat lunch alone and to provide

---

* *The Addendum* defines selective mutism as an anxiety disorder characterized by a constant failure to speak. The unwillingness to speak is based on painful shyness. Children with selective mutism are usually inhibited, withdrawn, and have an obsessive fear of hearing their own voices. They may show passive-aggressive, stubborn, and controlling traits. Doctors are not clear about the relationship between autism and this disorder. Major treatment for depression and selective mutism include psychotherapy and anti-anxiety agents such as Selective Reuptake Inhibitors.

verbal responses in private rather than in front of the class where his manner of speech and accent drew derogatory comments from his fellow students. Cho's grades were excellent.

In the eleventh grade, Cho's weekly counseling sessions at the mental health care center ended. He resisted further sessions. Despite evidence of slight improvement and while his parents were not happy over the termination, Cho was turning 18 and legally they could not make him continue.

Cho's high school grades were very high, he finished school with a 3.52 in an honors program and his SAT scores were very good. On that basis, he was accepted to Virginia Tech. His guidance counselor, however, in talks with Cho and his family, strongly recommended that he go to a smaller school where the transition to college life would be easier. But Cho's goal was Tech.

The counselor was apparently so concerned about Cho that she made sure he had the name and contact information of a school district resource that he could call if he encountered problems in Blacksburg. There is no record that Cho ever sought this help while at Virginia Tech.

The Student Scholastic Board

There is a standard cover page that accompanied Cho's transcripts to Tech. On the lower right corner of that page there is a section marked "The Student Scholastic Record" under which there are boxes to be checked. There is a subheading labeled "Special Services Files." There are six boxes: Contract Services, ESL, 504 Plan, Gifted and Talented, Homebound, and Special Education. Only the ESL box was checked for Cho. There was no indication that he had Special Education treatment for psychological problems. The university, then, had no inkling of Cho's past problems or treatment. Thus, the first warning sign was absent.

The excuse for not checking this box was "personal privacy." One common fear is that an individual will be stigmatized or denied opportunities because of a mental or physical disability. The fact is that the Family Rights and Privacy Act of 1974 (FERPA) *does* allow secondary schools to disclose educational records (including special education records) to a university. The law simply prohibits a school from making a "preadmission inquiry" about the specifics of the applicant's disability. After admission, the school can make a confidential inquiry about the disability. Therefore, the failure to check the box demonstrated a misunderstanding of the law—not to mention lack of common sense. Furthermore, a nonspecific reference to a special need can help, not hinder or prejudice, a school in meeting students' needs once accepted.

Warning Signs

In August 2003, Cho entered Virginia Tech as a business information technology major. His parents were so concerned about him and his adjustment to college life that they visited him once a week, every week, during his first semester. Cho was not happy with his roommate and requested a change, but other than that, his freshman year appears to have gone fairly well. His grades were good, and he ended his first year with a 3.0 GPA.

On November 6, 2004, Cho sent an email to the English Department head, Lucinda Roy. *The Addendum* notes that this appears to be the first concrete evidence of what sparked Cho's interest in writing. He told Professor Roy that he had attended her poetry writing class the previous semester and asked for advice in finding a publisher for a short novel he had written. She responded by recommending two books with tips on finding literary agents.

In Cho's sophomore year he moved off campus, sharing a condominium with a senior who was rarely home. He took more math and science classes and his grades began to slip. During his second year, Cho decided to switch his major to English beginning in the Fall of 2005—a move that has puzzled many because of his dislike of words, but also because English was his second language and it had not been one of his stronger classes.

Cho's sister began to notice he was bringing home books on literature and poetry. He seemed to be developing a passion for writing. In the Spring of 2005, Cho took three English courses. He did not do particularly well, earning a D+, C+, and a B+ respectively in the three classes. About that time, his sister found a rejection letter from a publisher. She encouraged him to keep writing and explained that many successful writers go through numerous rejections before finding a publisher.

In the Fall of 2005, however, foreboding signs began to emerge. From that time on, Cho would become known to students and faculty as withdrawn and hostile. His family noticed he was not writing as much and that he seemed more withdrawn. When he did write, his writings took on violent overtones and his behavior became threatening. He registered for French and four English classes. One of the English classes was Professor Nikki Giovanni's Creative Writing Poetry.

Cho's odd behavior soon began to alarm Professor Giovanni.

What was Cho's disturbing behavior? First, he wore reflector glasses to class and pulled his hat down to obscure his face. Professor Giovanni took class time to ask him to remove his hat and glasses and stood next to his desk until he complied. He next began wearing a Bedouin-style scarf wrapped around his head—an action that Giovanni believed was intended to intimidate her.

Second, Cho was uncooperative in both presenting his papers and changing their content. When asked to revise his drafts he would turn in exactly the same thing the following week. He read from his desk in a barely audible voice. The situation went from bad to worse.

Third, one of Cho's papers was especially disturbing. Entitled, "So-Called Advanced Creative Writing—Poetry," Cho accused his fellow students of eating animals. The Governor's Review Panel Report quotes Cho as writing, "I don't know which uncouth, low-life planet you come from but you disgust me. In fact, you all disgust me. ... You low-life barbarians make me sick to the stomach that I wanna barf over my new shoes. If you despicable human beings who are all disgraces to [the] human race keep this up, before you know it you will turn into cannibals—eating little babies, your friends. I hope y'all burn in hell for ass murdering and eating all those little animals."

Fourth, Cho began taking pictures of his fellow students without their permission, an action that caused alarm and concern and prompted a number of students to stay away from class. Giovanni asked one of the students what was going on and he responded, "It's the boy ... everyone is afraid of him."

Giovanni took her concerns to the head of the English Department, Professor Lucinda Roy. In fact, Giovanni was so concerned for her wellbeing and the safety of her students that she threatened to quit unless Cho was removed from her class. That should have been warning enough for the school to take immediate action for psychological counseling and care—but it was not. Giovanni was offered security, but declined and said Cho was not welcome back in the class. In the final analysis, Cho was offered, and accepted, private tutoring from the head of the English Department, Professor Lucinda Roy.

Roy contacted Tom Brown, the Dean of Student Affairs, the Cook Counseling Center, and the College of Liberal Arts. Roy asked Cho be given a psychological evaluation and wanted to know if the picture-taking violated the code of student conduct. At this point, with this warning, the school should have taken swift and prompt action to deal with Cho's menacing behavior. But nothing was done.

Dean Brown emailed Roy saying, "There is no specific policy related to cell phones in class. But, in Section 2 of the University Policy for Student Life, item #6 speaks to disruption. This is the 'disorderly conduct' section that reads: 'Behavior that disrupts or interferes with the orderly function of the university, disturbs the peace, or interferes with the performance of the duties of university personnel.' Clearly the disruption he (Cho) caused falls under this policy if adjudicated.'"

In addition, Dean Brown added, "I talked with a counselor … and shared the content of the 'poem' … and she did not pick up on a specific threat. She suggested a referral to Cook (Counseling Center) during your meeting. I also spoke with Frances Keene, Judicial Affairs director and she agrees with your plan." Dean then asserted, "I would make it clear to him (Cho) that any similar behavior in the future will be referred."

Ms. Keene later told the Governor's Review Panel that she would have needed something in writing to initiate an investigation into Cho's disorderly conduct. She said she never received a written request, which she contends should have come from the English Department. That may be technically true, but it is hard to believe that a person in Ms. Keene's position would be so void of common sense that she did not follow up on the situation. The fact that a professor was threatening to resign from fear for her life and the welfare of her students, and nothing was done because of a lack of a sheet of paper, is astounding. When someone fears for her or his life, is it too much to expect appropriate university officials to monitor the situation?

Ms. Keene did tell the review panel that she "recalled" that concern for Cho was brought up to the university's Care Team. She indicated that Care Team members were briefed on the situation and told that Professors Roy and Giovanni wanted to proceed with a class change to address the matter. She also recalled that the perception of the team was that the situation was taken care of and Cho was not discussed again. The Care Team did not refer Cho to the Cook Counseling Center.

Cho agreed to meet with Professor Roy, answering her email request with an angry two-page letter criticizing Professor Giovanni. Roy asked a friend and fellow English professor, Cheryl Ruggiero, to be present at the meeting and to take notes. When Cho arrived, he was wearing dark sunglasses, presenting the image that had gotten him into trouble in Giovanni's class. Roy, just as Giovanni, asked Cho to remove his glasses. He complied, but only after a lengthy pause. Throughout the meeting Cho was quiet and took a long time to answer questions.

In the final analysis, Roy was obliged to offer Cho an alternative to poetry class, and that alternative was for her to tutor him. Twice during the meeting Roy asked Cho to talk to a counselor, saying she would be happy to recommend one. He hesitated to answer, but finally said, "Sure."

One month after meeting with Cho, Roy wrote to Associate Dean Mary Ann Lewis, Liberal Arts and Human Sciences, saying that the private tutoring sessions were going well. Roy noted however, that Cho's writing was riddled with images of shooting and harming people. According to Roy, he was angered by people in authority and also angered by their behavior. Roy asserted that she remained "very worried" about Cho and noted that he continued to wear reflective sunglasses during the tutoring sessions. Roy continued to urge him to seek counseling. Roy also noted that she was very impressed with his writing—he ended up getting an "A."

Aggressive Behavior

Cho's behavior abnormalities were becoming apparent in other venues and came to the attention of the Virginia Tech Police Department (VTPD)—specifically, his unwanted attention toward female students.

On November 27, 2005, the VTPD received a complaint from a female student on the fourth floor of West Ambler Johnston Hall about Cho's unwarranted attentions. He had sent disturbing text messages to the female student, and at one point went to her room wearing sunglasses and a hat pulled down over his face. He apparently told her, "I am the question mark." According to the police incident report, Cho was warned not to bother the young woman anymore and was told the incident would be turned over to Judicial Affairs. But still university officials remained passive.

Keene, who was already aware of Cho's aberrant behavior in Giovanni's class, indicated that she received no communications from the female students who had complained about Cho. The assistant director for Judicial Affairs, Rohsaan Settle, received an email on December 6th advising her of Cho's "odd behavior" and "stalking." *The Addendum* does not indicate who sent this email.

The policy of Keene's office is to contact students who have been threatened and advise them of their rights. But, one of the complaining female students told the Review Panel that she was never contacted and there is no record the others were contacted. I could not help but wonder if having a policy and acting on that policy are worlds apart at Virginia Tech.

By the fall of 2005, Cho had moved back on campus and into a dormitory. It did not take long for his fellow students to notice his odd behavior. Before long, one of Cho's roommates and another suitemate found a large knife in Cho's desk and threw it out. Cho, according to the Resident Advisor, "… was strange, and got stranger." The warning signs were becoming more and more apparent.

Three days after the West Ambler Johnston incident on November 27th, Cho apparently took Professor Roy's advice. He phoned the Cook Counseling Center at 9:45 a.m. on November 30th. He spoke with Maisha Smith, a licensed professional counselor.

Smith conducted a telephone triage with Cho, gathering pertinent information. Ms. Smith has no recollection of her conversation with Cho and her notes, part of Cho's medical records, were lost for more than two years.

Cho requested an appointment with Cathye Betzel, a licensed clinical psychologist. Betzel had been recommended by Roy. An appointment was set for 2:00 p.m. on December 12th, but Cho failed to appear. He phoned the counseling center at 4:00 p.m. and was triaged over the phone. According to the Center's record, Cho was triaged a second time that day at 4:45 p.m. by Betzel. Betzel, however, told the Review Panel she has no memory of the brief triage. Written documentation of the triage went missing with Cho's medical records and was only belatedly discovered in the summer of 2009—more than two years after the shooting. Once again pertinent documents disappeared.

The Review Panel report indicates that the ticket completed to indicate the type of contact made with a client shows a telephone appointment was kept and that no diagnosis was made. No referral was made for follow-up services. The Review Panel report does not indicate who filled out the ticket.

Betzel does remember that she had a conversation with Professor Roy about a student whose name she does not recall, but believes it was Cho. The date of that conversation is not known and any written record of the conversation, which should have been part of Cho's file, is missing.

As with so much of the bookkeeping at the Cook Counseling Center, their paper work seems to come and go.

I do not accuse anyone at the Cook Counseling Center of destroying documents or attempting to hide information, but what is the explanation for all the missing records? We now know that the former head of the Cook Counseling Center accidently took Cho's records home with him. By the time those records were discovered, the families were on the verge of settling with the school and The Review Panel Report was essentially done. The Governor's blue ribbon panel never tackled the problem of the missing documents—other than noting their absence.

Cho's threatening behavior continued through 2005. On December 12th, the Virginia Tech Police Department received another complaint from a female student. This time it was from a resident at East Campbell Hall. The young woman knew Cho through one of his suitemates.

On one occasion, when Cho was in the young woman's room, he pulled out a knife and stabbed the carpet. The student no longer saw Cho, but she received instant messages that she believed were from him. The messages were not threatening, but were self-deprecating. She replied asking if the messages were from Cho and the answer she got back was, "I do not know who I am."

At one point she found a note with a quote from *Romeo and Juliet* on the erase board outside her room door reading:

> *By a name*
> *I know not how to tell thee who I am*
> *My name, dear saint is hateful to myself*

Because it is an enemy to thee
Had I written, I would tear the word

Concerned, the young woman talked to her father, saying she believed Cho was behind the message. Her father, equally concerned, talked to the local Christiansburg police (Christiansburg is adjacent to Blacksburg) who advised that campus police be informed.

On December 13th, the campus police, for the second time in a month, met with Cho and instructed him not to have contact with the young woman. No charges were filed. The student later told the Review Panel that no one informed her of her rights to file a complaint with Judicial Affairs.

St. Albans Behavioral Health Center for the Carilion New River Valley Medical Center

Police returned the same day, around 7:00 p.m. to interview Cho. This time, the officers took Cho to the campus police headquarters for further assessment and around 8:15 p.m. a licensed clinical social worker for the New River Valley Community Services Board conducted a pre-screen evaluation.

The social worker interviewed Cho and a police officer then spoke with both of Cho's roommates. She filled out a five-page Uniform Pre-Admission Screening Form. She checked the boxes indicating that Cho was mentally ill, was an imminent danger to self or others, and was not willing to be treated voluntarily. The social worker found a bed at the St. Albans Behavioral Health Center of the Carilion New River Valley Medical Center and contacted the magistrate to request a temporary detention order.

The detention order was issued and at 10:12 p.m. the police transported Cho to St. Albans, where he was admitted at 11:00 p.m. Upon admission, Cho was diagnosed with mood disorder, "NOS," meaning non-specific. Cho denied any past history of violence but did volunteer that he had access to firearms. He was not on any medication, but was given Ativan for anxiety.

The next morning, December 14, 2005, Cho met with a Clinical Support Representative, at 6:30 a.m. The representative informed him about his upcoming hearing to determine the state of his mental stability. There is no record that anyone at St. Albans contacted the social worker who had diagnosed Cho as a danger to himself or others.

At 7:00 a.m. Cho was taken to a meeting with Roy Crouse, a licensed clinical psychologist, who conducted an independent evaluation. Crouse did not have access to Cho's medical records. Crouse, however, did have access to the prescreening report containing information from people who knew Cho well and assessed him to be a danger to himself and others. The psychologist reviewed the prescreening report, but because of the early hour, no hospital records were available. Furthermore, he did not speak with—or apparently try to speak to—the attending psychiatrist who had not yet seen Cho. Crouse's meeting with Cho lasted a quarter of an hour.

Based on this fragmentary information, Crouse then completed the evaluation form certifying that Cho "is mentally ill; that he does not represent a danger to himself or others." There is nothing in the records that we can find to explain why the St. Albans psychologist, who spent less time with Cho than the pre-screener, disagreed with the initial diagnosis that Cho was a danger. But, in a scant 15 minutes, and without getting further explanation of the initial findings, he overrode the pre-screener and indicated Cho was not a threat. Curiously, knowing that the pre-screener had described Cho as a threat, Crouse checked the box on the form indicating Cho had access to guns.

The checked box for access to guns was later described as having been in done in error and therefore was discarded as a mistake. But, there is no evidence that the checked box was a mistake and the psychiatrist certainly had no evidence of a mistake when he interviewed Cho. That checked box, coupled with the diagnosis that Cho was a threat to himself and others, should have been a huge red flag signaling the seriousness of the situation at hand. But instead, the warning signs were ignored. Why ignore that one entry? Why discredit just one entry? If one entry is wrong, what made the psychiatrist think there were not other errors on the report? The so-called "mistake" excuse appears to be a Monday-morning cover-your-rear-end, for a colossal error in judgment.

Cho was then taken to a commitment hearing. Shortly before the hearing the attending psychiatrist (*The Addendum* does not specifically give a name, but presumably it was Dr. Jasdeep Miglani, MD) evaluated Cho. The psychiatrist later said he found nothing remarkable about Cho and did not "discern dangerousness" in him. He apparently did not seek to resolve the discrepancy between the pre-screener and the psychologist over whether or not Cho was a threat. His assessment was that Cho was not a threat to himself or others, and he suggested that Cho be treated as an outpatient. The psychiatrist later told the Review Panel that his conclusion was based on Cho's denying drug or alcohol problems, or any previous mental health treatment.

The psychiatrist acknowledged that he did not gather any collateral information or any information to refute the pre-screeners contention that Cho was a threat. In other words, he made his decision without taking the time to consult the person who probably knew the most about the true depth of Cho's illness. He also accepted, without question, Cho's denial of any previous mental health care.

St. Albans's handling of Cho raises serious questions about professionalism. Nowhere is there any reference about a detailed tool used to evaluate Cho's mental status. Cho came in with a diagnosis of mood disorder and left with no new diagnosis and no prescribed medication. In sum, Cho was admitted at night, had an initial history and physical (there is no mention of a psychological examination), was medicated with Ativan, and then was briefly evaluated the next morning by Roy Crouse, who did not have access to the information gathered the night before. Crouse apparently did not speak with Dr. Miglani, the attending psychiatrist.

The evidence at hand in the early morning of December 14, 2005, was that a dangerously mentally ill young man had been brought into St. Albans. The handling of Cho at St. Albans raises serious questions about the competency and quality of care and attention given Cho. There was no depth to what was done in examining Cho at St. Albans. He was not given a thorough evaluation, there was no extensive gathering of information, nor was there the development of a solid treatment plan for him. And, there was no follow-up to ensure that he got treatment—at that facility or elsewhere.

The psychiatrist indicated that he did not gather collateral information or information to refute the data obtained by the pre-screener on the basis of which the commitment was obtained, because what he did is standard practice and that privacy laws impede the gathering of collateral information. This is simply not true. If a person is a threat to himself or others, the laws do not impede gathering more information; the laws do not prevent a psychologist or psychiatrist from consulting parents when confronted with a student who is a threat to himself or others.

Some have said that "the system" let Cho down. But what is "the system?" The system is made up of the people who run it. There is no getting away from the reality that the medical professionals who saw Cho at St. Albans failed—they failed miserably and there is no way to sugar-coat that fact by calling it "a system failure."

To call what happened at St. Albans "a system failure" is purely a way of protecting people and preventing them from being held accountable.

*   *   *

As 2005 came to a close, Cho's family was in the dark about their son's deteriorating mental health. The troubled student's parents had consistently and persistently monitored their son's health. As they had taken actions to help him in the past, there is no reason to believe they would not have done the same again had they been told of the seriousness of the problem. The Governor's Review Panel asked Cho's parents what they would have done had they been informed of their son's behavior. They responded, "We would have taken him home and made him miss a semester to have this looked at ... but we just did not know ... about anything being wrong."

*   *   *

Cho was thus left to fend for himself. His parents knew nothing and those who did—for large part—kept it to themselves. Cho continued to descend into his non-communicative, paranoid world.

More Warning Signs

The problems continued in 2006 and more red flags went up, this time in Robert Hicok's Fiction Workshop. The violent content of Cho's stories, combined with his lack of communication, again raised concerns. Hicok consulted with Professor Roy about the problems he saw, but in the end decided to keep Cho in the class.

Hicok was not the only one to have problems with Cho that semester. Cho was also enrolled in Professor Carl Bean's Technical Writing course. Bean later told the Review Panel that Cho was always quiet, wore his hat down over his head and spoke softly. Bean also suggested that Cho got pleasure from learning how to "play the game—do as little as he needed to do to get by."

For one assignment in Hicok's class, Cho decided to write an objective real-time experience based on Macbeth and corresponding to serial killings. On April 17, 2006—one year to the day before Cho's murderous rage—Hicok talked with Cho after class, telling him the proposed subject was not acceptable. Hicok suggested that Cho drop the class. Cho, however, followed Hicok to his office and began arguing loudly that he did not want to drop the course. Hicok told him to leave and said he would not talk to Cho again until he was more composed. Cho later sent an email to Hicok saying he had dropped the class.

In the fall of 2006, Cho enrolled in Professor Ed Falco's playwriting workshop. The opening day of class, when the students were asked to introduce themselves, Cho got up and left before it was his turn. When Cho appeared for the second class, he was told he would have to participate—he did not respond. After the massacre, students from Falco's class were quoted in the press as saying Cho "was the kind of guy who might go on a rampage killing."

The warning signs, then, continued apace. Cho's roommate told the Review Panel that he barely knew him. They slept in the same room, but apparently hardly ever talked. The Resident Advisor in Harper Hall, where Cho lived, knew there were issues with Cho. She knew of his unwanted advances toward a female student, but she did not have any problems with him.

Cho also enrolled in Professor Lisa Norris's Advanced Fiction Workshop. Norris knew Cho, he had taken one of her courses on contemporary fiction. When he showed up wearing a ball cap pulled down over his face and making no eye contact, Norris was concerned and contacted the dean's office. According to the Review Panel Report, she wanted to know if he was ok and asked for someone to intervene on his behalf. We do not know what "intervene" means and the Review Panel Report does not explain the word.

What we know is that the English Department knew nothing about Cho's dealings with the police, nor did they know anything about his stalking behavior. Unequivocally, they should have been told.

Norris told Cho he would have to see her if he was to make it through the class. Norris believed that Cho had trouble communicating in both English and Korean and offered to help him get in touch with the Disability Services Office. After the meeting, Norris emailed Cho to repeat her offer to go with him to student counseling—he did not follow up on the offer.

Cho apparently finished the class with few problems, although he did not show up for the last two weeks and ended up with a B+ for the semester.

The spring semester of 2007, Cho continued to sink deeper and deeper into his word of isolation and darkness. He began to buy guns and ammunition. In February he bought a .22 caliber Walther P22 handgun online and a handgun from J-N-D Pawnbrokers in Blacksburg. In March he bought a 9 mm Glock 19 handgun and a box of 50 9mm full metal jacket practice rounds at Roanoke Firearms. Also in March, Cho bought two 10-round magazines for the Walther P22 on eBay. Later that month he purchased three additional 10-round magazines from another eBay seller.

And finally, on March 31st he bought additional ammunition magazines, ammunition, and a hunting knife from Wal-Mart and Dick's Sporting Goods. He bought the chains he used on Norris Hall's doors from Home Depot. There were, however, apparently no outward signs of the depths of his mental illness. And even if there had been, I believe it is highly improbable the school would have taken effective measures, given its track record.

Professional Negligence?

One of the victims' family members filed a complaint with the Virginia Department of Health Professionals, asking that Roy Crouse, the independent clinical psychologist who assessed Cho on the morning of December 14, 2005, and Maisha Smith, one of the counselors at the Cook

Counseling Center who triaged Cho, be investigated for possible professional wrongdoing. The investigation report, signed by Patricia Larimer, Deputy Director of the Virginia Board of Psychology, indicates there was not sufficient evidence to determine if a violation of law or regulations governing the practice of clinical psychology occurred.

But a simple reading of *The Addendum* indicates enough questionable, and possibly unprofessional, behavior on the part of medical professionals to warrant an investigation. Furthermore, if you read the regulations governing the practice of psychology put out by the Virginia Board of Psychology, it is fairly evident, even to a nonprofessional, that these regulations were broken. The regulations governing the practice of clinical psychology state the following:

1. *"Testing and measuring" which consists of the psychological evaluation or assessment of personal characteristics such as intelligence, abilities, interests, aptitudes, achievements, motives, personality dynamics, psychoeducational processes, neuropsychological functioning, or other attributes of individuals or groups.*

2. *"Diagnosis and treatment of mental and emotional disorders" which consists of the appropriate diagnosis of mental disorders according to standards of the profession and the ordering or providing treatments according to need. Treatment includes providing counseling, psychotherapy, marital/family therapy, group therapy, behavior therapy, psychoanalysis hypnosis, biofeedback, and other psychological interventions with the objective or personal goals, the treatment of alcoholism and substance abuse, disorders of habit or conduct, as well as of the psychological aspects of physical illness, pain, injury, or disability."*

The problem is that nowhere in Cho's medical records is there evidence that any part of the above was done. Indeed, medical professionals seemed content to handle Cho with brief phone calls, or at St. Albans with short, quarter-of-an-hour interviews. In fact, there is no way that Cho received any sort of diagnostic care at St. Albans. He was brought in late at night, given medication to treat insomnia, awakened at 6:30 a.m. and then given a 15-minute "evaluation." He later met with a psychiatrist for a short time.

Ms. Larimer signed the investigative report knowing the standards of the profession, yet she found no evidence of wrongdoing. Cho's medical history at Virginia Tech is riddled with sub-par care. The fact that so many documents and records dealing with Cho's treatment were either never created in the first place, went missing, or are still missing, should be of utmost concern.

When I received a copy of the complaint filed by the victim's family, I filed a Freedom of Information request with Virginia' s Department of Health Professions for a copy of the investigation that was done on Smith and Crouse. My request was turned down. I received two letters from the Department of Health Professions. The first cited a Virginia law that any "reports, information, or records received or maintained in connection with possible disciplinary proceedings, including any material received or developed by a board during an investigation or disciplinary proceeding, shall remain confidential." The second, signed by Patricia Larimer, the same Deputy Executive Director of the Virginia Board of Psychology who earlier had indicated there was not enough evidence to warrant an investigation, stated that she could "neither confirm nor deny the existence of complaints/investigations regarding Marisha Smith and Roy Crouse."

Both letters are disturbing, but the second raises the question as to whether an investigation was seriously considered.

Memory loss, possible missing patient records, and sloppy bookkeeping apparently are the hallmarks of the Cook Counseling Center and its employees. Look at the facts:

I.   Marisha Smith's records of her triage of Cho were missing for months;
II. Dr. Betzel's records of her triage of Cho were missing for months;
III. Cho's Cook Counseling Center records were missing for months;
IV. Dr. Betzel does not remember her conversation with Professor.

Roy about Cho, although Professor Roy remembers it quite well.

All these missing records are reminiscent of what happened at the Appalachian School of Law. Following that shooting, a school official went to one of the school offices and told a student working there to destroy records showing that the school was willing to "adjust" evidence relating to the law school's enrollment—specifically regarding the student status of the killer, Peter Odighizuwa. The student made copies of all the records, destroyed the originals, and then offered the copies to the lawyers who were handling the lawsuit against the school.

I am not saying that any records were intentionally destroyed at the Cook Counseling Center, but the multiple instances of misplaced or lost documents, coupled with memory loss, are suspicious.

The specters of conflict of interest and cover-up once again raise their heads; this time it is the State Board of Psychiatry investigating a state-licensed psychiatrist and counselor. The question that persists is: Can a truly objective analysis of the facts surrounding Cho's mental illness ever be produced and made public? The answer is, "Apparently not."

The Health Insurance and Portability and Accountability Act of 1996
And the Family Educational Rights and Privacy Act of 1974

As already noted, patient privacy and privacy laws have been cited numerous times as the reason for not sharing information about Cho. In fact, privacy laws contain many provisions that allow the sharing of information. The Health Insurance and Portability and Accountability Act of 1996 (HIPPA) and the Virginia law on medical information privacy is found in the Virginia Health Records Privacy Act (VHRPA). Both laws have provisions to share information. Specifically:

> *"Situations where privacy is out-weighed by certain other interests. For example, providers may sometimes disclose information about a person who presents an imminent threat to the health and safety of individuals and public safety. Providers can also disclose information to law enforcement in order to locate a fugitive or suspect. Providers also are authorized to disclose information when state law requires it."*

Let's look at Cho's commitment hearing for involuntary admission. A judicial officer made the determination that Cho would be committed to a mental institution for involuntary treatment. The records of the hearing were sealed but information about the hearing, including the patient's name as well as the time and place of the hearing, are publicly available. Therefore, there was no legal reason why Virginia Tech or its Police Department did not notify Cho's parents of their son's involuntary admission to a mental health facility.

For medical, school, or law enforcement officials to say that privacy laws stood in their way of notifying the Cho family is simply not true and represents ignorance of the law or incompetence—or both.

Now, look at the confusion surrounding school records. Privacy of educational records is mainly governed by the Family Educational Rights and Privacy Act of 1974 (FERPA). FERPA's rules favor privacy, but it contains special regulations for law enforcement and medical records. FERPA and state law govern restrictions on medical records. FERPA laws apply only to information in student records. Personal observations and conversations with students fall outside the law's purview. That means that professors and anyone else, who observed Cho's behavior and raised concerns, could have notified his parents.

Many other records fall outside the restrictions of FERPA. For example, when, in the fall of 2005, campus police received complaints from fellow student Jennifer Nelson about Cho's behavior, their records were part of the investigation of a potential crime. The police would have been within the law to notify Cho's parents.

A wide variety of law enforcement duties are not covered by privacy laws. For example, when transporting an individual, who is under temporary detention orders, to a mental health facility, the police were under no restrictions and could have reported what was going on to school officials and Cho's parents.

Finally, there is an emergency provision in FERPA that allows for the disclosure of educational records. "If the knowledge of such information is necessary to protect the health or safety of the student or other persons," then the information is releasable. HIPPA also contains a similar emergency provision. This is not just law; it is common sense.

It is surprising that before Cho's rampage school, medical, and law enforcement officials appear to have been obsessed with privacy. But, when Robert Miller, the head of the Cook Counseling Center, violated patient privacy by taking Cho's files home, these same officials just looked the other way.

When Cho's medical records were discovered in mid-July 2009 in Miller's home, then-Governor Timothy Kaine said he was perplexed over how Cho's mental-health files ended up in the personal files of the former director of Tech's Cook Counseling Center.

"Every bit of the lawyer in me . . . and the common sense in me, says nobody should have been able to walk out of a counseling center with these kind of mental-health records," Kaine said. "They should have stayed right there." The records were critical to the investigation of Cho's crime. "Certainly that aspect of the investigation — the discussion, what happened, … that is really critical," Kaine said.

Kaine added, " …I think the other critical piece is how he could remove those records. These are confidential records, that by my understanding cannot be legally removed — certainly not by someone who is a former employee." In other words, Miller apparently broke the law, and no one has ever followed up on that crime.

An editorial in *The Richmond Times-Dispatch* on July 26, 2009 put the fiasco surrounding Cho's medical records clearly and succinctly when the paper wrote:

"It strains credulity to think that files relating to the worst campus massacre in American history might simply have slipped the mind of the very person who had counseled the gunman. Not since the Rose law-firm billing

records went unfound [sic] for two years in the Clinton White House has there been such a remarkable lapse of memory.

"The performance of the Virginia Tech administration throughout this entire affair has not always inspired confidence, either. That university officials received Cho's miraculously rediscovered records late last Thursday, but did not inform the State Police and the governor until the following Monday, adds to a widespread sense that the Tech administration has been less than completely forthcoming."

*   *   *

Time and time again, faculty and staff at Virginia Tech raised concerns about Cho, but to no avail. Professor Lucinda Roy alone voiced her concerns about Cho with the Division of Student Affairs, the Cook Counseling Center, The Schiffert Health Center, the Virginia Tech Police, Department, and the College of Liberal Arts and Human Services—all for naught. The warning signs were numerous and glaring, Cho could have done little more than he did to alert people of his pending rampage— practically the only more obvious thing he could have done to alert people was to put up a neon sign announcing his intentions. The excuses are equally as numerous and just as glaring in the covering up of ignorance of the law, mediocre and incompetent medical care, and an astonishingly incredible lack of common sense.

CHAPTER IV

NORRIS HALL

*"Whenever there is news of a terrible shooting, I
wonder why America has so miserably failed to enact even
common-sense gun legislation."*

~Jon Meacham, Pulitzer-prize winning author,
executive vice president at Random House

It was 8:45 a.m. on April 16, 2007, nearly all of Virginia Tech went about business as usual. The police at West Ambler Johnston Hall had identified Karl Thornhill, Emily Hilscher's boyfriend, as a person of interest and they were focused on him. The Police Chief had characterized the double homicide as a case of domestic violence, even though he had never conducted a murder investigation before. The university's Policy Group, the only senior leadership body, with the capacity to issue an electronic warning to the campus, did not actually have the responsibility to do so, according to three different emergency procedures that were in effect. However, they had been in session since 8:25 a.m., knew that at least one student was dead and another was critically wounded. At 8:45 a.m., they were just beginning to compose a notice to the university community about the dormitory shootings. At this point, one hour and 35 minutes had passed since Emily Hilscher and Ryan Clark had been gunned down and the vast majority of the campus remained uninformed of the events that morning.

2007 **(April 16)** (around 7:15 a.m.) **Cho shot Ryan Christopher Clark (an RA whose room was next to Emily Hilscher's). Clark apparently came to investigate noises in Emily's room. Cho then shot Emily Hilscher who had sought refuge under her bed.** Both of the victims' wounds proved fatal. (Ryan died almost instantly, Emily died after being evacuated to a Roanoke trauma care hospital.) Cho exited the crime scene leaving bloody footprints and shell casings.

2007 **(April 16)** (7:17 a.m.) **Cho's access card was swiped at Harper Hall, which is near West Ambler Johnston and was Cho's dormitory. He went to his room to change out of his bloody clothing,** canceled his computer account, and made preparations for his rampage.

2007 **(April 16)** (8:50 a.m.) **First period classes ended.** The Policy Group members began composing a notice to the university about the shootings in West Ambler Johnston Hall. The Associate Vice President for University Relations, Larry Hincker, was unable to send the message at first due to technical difficulties with the alert system.

2007 **(April 16)** (8:52 a.m.) **Blacksburg Public Schools locked down until further information was available about the incident at Virginia Tech. The school superintendent notified the school board of this action by email. The Executive Director of Government Relations, Ralph Byers, directed that the doors to his office be locked.** His office was adjacent to the school President's suite, but the four doors to the President's suite remained open.

2007 **(April 16)** (9:00 a.m.-9:15 a.m.) **Virginia Tech Veterinary College locks down.**

2007 **(April 16)** (9:15 a.m.) **Second period classes began in Norris Hall.** Both police Emergency Response Teams are staged at the Blacksburg Police Department in anticipation of executing search warrants or making arrests.

2007 **(April 16)** (9:15 a.m.-9:30 a.m.) Cho was seen outside and then inside

Norris Hall (an engineering building) by several students. He was familiar with the building because one of his classes was there. **Cho chained the doors shut on three public entrances from the inside. No one reported seeing him. A faculty member found a bomb threat note attached to an inner door near one of the chained exterior doors. She gave the note to a janitor who hand carried it to the Engineering School dean's office on the third floor.** A Virginia Tech police captain joined the Policy Group as a police liaison and provided updates as information became available. He reported one gunman at large, possibly on foot.

2007 **(April 16)** (9:26 a.m.) **Virginia Tech administration sent email to campus staff, faculty, and students informing them of a dormitory shooting "incident." The message contained no specifics, no one was made aware that one student had been killed and another seriously wounded, and there was no hint that a killer might have been roaming the campus. The gravity of the situation and seriousness of the threat was played down.**

2007 **(April 16)** (about 9:30 a.m.)Radford University Police had received a request from the Blacksburg Police Department to look up Thornhill's class schedule and find him in class. Before they could do this, they got a second call that he had been stopped on the road.

2007 **(April 16)** (9:30 a.m.)The police passed information to the Policy Group that it was unlikely that Hilscher's boyfriend, Karl Thornhill, was the shooter (though he remained a person of interest).

2007 **(April 16)** (9:31 a.m.-9:48 a.m.)A Virginia State Police trooper arrive to help question Thornhill at the traffic stop, and a gunpowder residue test was performed and packaged for lab analysis. (There is no immediate result from this type of test in the field.)

2007 **(April 16)** (9:40 a.m.-9:51 a.m.) **Cho began shooting in room 206 in Norris Hall, where a graduate engineering class in Advanced Hydrology was underway. Cho killed Professor**

G.V. Loganathan. He killed 9 students and wounded 3 others. There were a total of 13 students in the class. Cho went across the hall to room 207 and entered an elementary German class. He shot and killed the instructor, Christopher James Bishop, and then turned his gun on the students in the front row, where Michael Pohle, Jr. and Nicole White were seated next to each other. He then went down the aisle and methodically shot others. Students in room 205, attending Haiyan Cheng's class on Issues In Scientific Computing, heard Cho's gunshots. (Cheng was a graduate assistant substituting for the professor that day.) The students barricaded the door and prevented Cho from entering despite the fact that he fired through the door. In room 211, Madame Jocelyne Couture-Nowak's French class, the students and instructor heard the gunfire. Colin Goddard called 911. A student told the teacher to put a desk in front of the door—which she did. Cho managed to push the door open. He again begins his methodical slaughter walking up and down the rows of students. Emily Haas picked up a cell phone and called the police, telling them to come quickly. Cho heard Haas and shot her twice in the head (she would survive). Heroically, Haas played dead and kept the cell phone hidden with the line open. Cho said nothing upon entering the room or during the shooting. (Three students who pretended to be dead survive.) Two students, Rachael Hill and Henry Lee, whom the police allowed to leave West Ambler Johnston Hall despite a lockdown, were killed. The Governor's Review Panel Report glossed over this critical point.

2007 **(April 16)** (9:41 a.m.) **The Blacksburg Police dispatcher received a call regarding the shooting at Norris Hall.** The dispatcher initially had difficulty understanding the location of the shooting. Once identified as being on campus, the call was transferred to the Virginia Tech Police Department (VTPD).

2007 **(April 16)** (9:42 a.m.) **The 911 call reporting shots fired at Norris Hall** reached the Virginia Tech Police Department. A message was sent to all county EMS units to staff and respond.

2007 **(April 16)** (9:45 a.m.) **The first police officers arrived at Norris Hall, a three-minute response time from their receiving the call.** Hearing shots, they paused briefly to check whether they were being fired upon, then rushed to one entrance, and then another but found the doors were chained shut. An attempt to shoot open the chain or lock on one door failed.

2007 **(April 16)** (about 9:45 a.m.) The police informed the school administration that there has been another shooting. Virginia Tech President Steger heard sounds like gunshots, and saw police running toward Norris Hall. **In the German class in room 207, two injured students and two uninjured students go the door and held the door shut with their feet and hands, keeping their bodies away. Within two minutes Cho returned. He beat on the door and opened it an inch and fired shots around the door handle, then gave up trying to get into the room. Cho returned to room 211, the French class, and went up one aisle and down another shooting people again. Cho shot Colin Goddard two more times. A janitor saw Cho in the hall on the second floor loading his gun; the janitor fled downstairs. Cho tried to enter room 204 where engineering professor Liviu Librescu was teaching mechanics. Professor Librescu braced his body against the door, yelling for students to head to the windows. He was shot through the door and killed, but his heroic action saved lives. Students pushed screens and jumped or dropped to the grass and bushes below. Ten students escaped this way. The next two students were shot. Cho again returned to room 206 (the Advanced Hydrology class) and shot more students.**

2007 **(April 16)** (9:50 a.m.) **Using a shotgun, police opened a Norris Hall entrance that led to the machine shop and that Cho had not been able to chain. These officers heard gunshots as they entered the building. The police immediately administration to all Virginia Tech email addresses that**

"A gunman is loose on campus. Stay in buildings until further notice. Stay away from all windows." Four outside loudspeakers broadcasted a similar message. Virginia Tech and Blacksburg police Emergency Response Teams (ERTs) arrived at Norris Hall, including one paramedic with each team.

2007 (April 16) (9:51 a.m.) Cho has returned to the French class in room 211 for the third time. He killed himself with a shot to the head just as police reached the second floor. Investigators believe that the shotgun blast, when the police entered the building, alerted Cho to their presence. Cho's shooting spree in Norris Hall lasted 11 minutes. He fired 174 rounds, and killed 30 people and wounded 17 others in Norris Hall before killing himself. The first team of officers began securing the second floor and aiding survivors from multiple classrooms. They also got a preliminary description of the suspected gunman, and tried to determine if there were additional gunmen.

2007 (April 16) (9:52 a.m.) The police cleared the second floor of Norris Hall. Two tactical medics attached to the ERTs, one medic from the Virginia Tech Rescue and one from Blacksburg Rescue, were allowed to enter to start their triage.

2007 (April 16) (9:53 a.m.) The 9:42 a.m. request for all EMT units was repeated.

2007 (April 16) (10:08 a.m.) A deceased male student was discovered by the police. The police suspected he was the gunman:

- No identification was found on the body.
- He appeared to have a self-inflicted gunshot wound to the head.
- He was found among his victims in classroom 211, the French class.
- Two weapons were found near his body.

2007 (April 16) (10:51 a.m.) All patients from Norris Hall had been transported to a hospital or moved to a minor treatment unit

2007 **(April 16)** (10:17 a.m.)**A third email from the school administration canceled all classes and advised people to stay where they were.**

2007 **(April 16)** (10:51 a.m.) **All patients from Norris Hall had been transported to a hospital or moved to a minor treatment unit.**

2007 **(April 16)** (10:52 a.m.) **A fourth email from the Virginia Tech administration warned of "a multiple shooting with multiple victims in Norris Hall," saying "the shooter is in custody" and that as a routine procedure police were searching for a second shooter.**

2007 **(April 16)** (10:57 a.m.)**A report of shots fired at the tennis courts near Cassell Coliseum proved false.**

2007 **(April 16)** (12:42 a.m.) **Virginia Tech President Charles Steger announced that the police were releasing people from buildings and that counseling centers were being established.**

The few who did know about the shooting were taking precautions. Sometime around 8:00 a.m., Virginia Tech's Center for Professional and Continuing Education locked down its doors.

President Steger and the university administration have gone on record saying that there was no way to predict that the double homicide that morning was going to lead to further violence. That argument might be believable, if we accept that assuming the murder was "domestic" or "targeted" was reasonable, and that being "domestic" made further violence less likely than in any other murder. But that is simply not true. According to the International Association of Chiefs of Police, between 1996 and 2009, 771 law enforcement officers were murdered in the line of duty. Of that figure, 106 were killed responding to domestic violence calls. To say that a murderer is less violent when the motive is a domestic dispute, rather than criminal activity is simply false. Murderers are murderers. Once they have killed there is absolutely no reason to believe they are less violent.

Indeed, on April 16, 2007, before the morning was over, Cho would act out a script he wrote in Professor Ed Falco's playwriting class the previous fall. In that script, a young man who hates the students at his school plans to kill them and himself. Falco was so upset with what he read that he brought Cho's script to the attention of two English Department colleagues, Professor Lucinda Roy and Lisa Norris. Both told Falco of their concerns about Cho and the fact that they had alerted Associate Dean Mary Ann Lewis to Cho and his writings. Who can accept the assertion that Cho's rampage was unpredictable, particularly when he had already describe his plans in writing?

Collective Ignorance and Communication Delays

In the eleven years preceding the spring of 2007, there had been 39 school shootings in this country. With all the inquiries and investigations following those shootings, it is hard to believe that Virginia Tech was so oblivious to the familiar warning signs. Furthermore, the shooting at the Appalachian School of Law, on January 16, 2002 was a scant 130 miles away. The parallels—including the warnings and the killers' profiles—between those two shootings are alarming. It is evident that the administration of Virginia Tech learned nothing from these tragedies.

On April 16, 2007, first-period classes were coming to an end at 8:50 a.m., just five minutes after Ralph Byers, Virginia Tech's Director of Public Relations and Virginia Tech Policy Group member, sent an email to a colleague in Richmond (for transmittal to the Governor) that one student was dead and another seriously wounded. According to The Governor's Review Panel Report—*The Addendum*, Byers wrote, "Gunman on the loose," adding, "this is not releasable yet." Four minutes later, *The Addendum* quotes Byers reminding a Richmond colleague, "just try to make sure it (news of the shooting) doesn't get out." And indeed it had not gotten out, and it would not get out for another half hour. At that time, only those in the administration's inner circle knew that there was the possibility of a gunman on campus.

Cho had returned to his room in Harper Hall and no one noticed his blood-spattered clothes. The campus at large had no information about the shooting at West Ambler Johnston Hall and no reason to be looking for a murderer on campus. Cho changed his clothes and prepared to mail a rambling diatribe to NBC News in New York.

Sometime around 8:50 a.m., the Associate Vice President for University Relations, Larry Hincker, allegedly tried to send a message through the alert system but couldn't due to technical difficulties. Earlier, Hincker had prepared a draft message with specific details of what had happened, which the Policy Group reviewed and vetoed before 8:50 a.m.

At 8:50 a.m., as the Policy Group sluggishly worked on a notice, the Blacksburg public schools locked down. Approximately two minute later, at 8:52 a.m. (according to trial testimony), Ralph Byers—Tech PR Director and a Policy Group member—ordered that the doors to his office be locked. His office is adjacent to school President Steger's office suite where doors remained unlocked.

As the Policy Group met and deliberated in the Burruss Hall boardroom, the Virginia Tech Veterinary College locked its doors. The Virginia Tech trash collection and bank deposits were cancelled just about the time that second-period classes began on the campus—including Norris Hall—and still there was no hint among the general faculty and student body of anything wrong, still no warning. There is no evidence of what the Policy Group was talking about, but clearly by 8:50 a.m. at least one message had been drafted—and vetoed. No adequate explanation has been given as to why it was not sent out.

Back in his room, Cho cancelled his computer account and made final preparations for his mass murder.

At 9:01 a.m., four minutes before the start of the second period, Cho went to the Blacksburg post office and mailed a package to New York. There is no mention in the Governor's Review Panel Report as to whether he had his weapons with him. The report does say however, that a professor recognized Cho and described him as looking "frightened." The package contained pictures of Cho with weapons as well as a rambling 1,800-word diatribe expressing rage, resentment and a desire to get even with unnamed oppressors.

At 9:05 a.m., second-period classes began at Virginia Tech, and the Policy Group continued to hesitate on the substance of the message.

For Colin Goddard, April 16, 2007, was something of an unusual morning. He moved about slowly, spending time getting organized for the day and texting fellow student Kristina Anderson, who was in his French class. He had made arrangements to take her to class, but was running late when he picked Kristina up and by the time they got to Norris Hall, the class had started. They debated whether to skip class, but finally decided to go in. It was now about 9:08 a.m.

Sometime between 9:15 and 9:30 a.m., Cho walked unobserved to Norris Hall, a gray stone engineering building in the middle of campus. It stands next to Burruss Hall, where President Steger and much of the school's senior administration have offices. Cho was carrying two handguns; almost 400 rounds of ammunition most of it in rapid-loading magazines; a knife; heavy chains; padlocks; and a hammer. Silently and without notice, from inside Norris Hall, he chained shut some of the doors many of the students used to enter and exit the building.

Shortly after the doors were chained, a faculty member found a bomb threat attached to an interior door. She gave the note to a janitor, asking him to take it to the office of the dean of the Engineering School on the third floor. According to the Governor's Review Panel Report, this was contrary to university instructions, which specify that all bomb threats be reported immediately to the police. The standard practice at Virginia Tech, when there is a bomb threat, is to send officers to the threatened building and immediately evacuate it. Had the bomb threat been reported immediately, the campus police would probably have arrived at Norris Hall sooner. Someone in the dean's office was just preparing to call the police when the shooting started.

Other students saw the doors chained closed but did nothing. One young woman left the building for a brief time and when she returned was unable to enter. The door was chained from the inside and she thought it had been locked for some reason associated with the construction nearby. She climbed through a window to get to her first-floor destination— apparently without telling anyone what she saw.

Around 9:20 a.m., Virginia Tech Police Department Captain Joe Alberts arrived at the Policy Group meeting in Burruss Hall to act as law enforcement liaison, per order of Chief Wendell Finchum. He updated the attendees on the situation, telling them that a gunman was at large and possibly on foot.

Finally, after deliberating for an hour, at 9:26 a.m., and only two minutes after the police had stopped Karl Thornhill on Prices Fork Road at the entrance to the campus, the Virginia Tech administration sent an email to the campus staff, faculty, and students informing them of a dormitory shooting "incident." As noted earlier, the message contained no specifics, no one was made aware that one student had been killed and another seriously wounded, and there was no hint that a killer might have been roaming the campus. A subsequent press release, and all initial timelines, state that all students [were] notified of homicide. That is simply not true. Four minutes later, at 9:30 a.m., the Governor's Review Panel Report writes that Captain Alberts told the Policy Group that Emily Hirscher's boyfriend, Karl Thornhill, was probably not the killer.

At Norris Hall, sometime around 9:30 a.m., Colin Goddard remembered a strange and disturbing thought after Rachael Hill, one of the best students in the class, came in and sat down in the front row. He wondered why she had come in when the class was nearly half over. She told the students seated near her that there had been a shooting in her dorm and the building was locked down, but she and another student, Henry Lee, had argued they had to go to class and were finally allowed to leave the dorm. Colin remembers thinking, "Wow, a shooting on campus and we know nothing about it."

The Norris Hall Executions

At 9:40 a.m., fourteen minutes after the email about the dormitory shooting went out, Cho began his eleven-minute bloodbath at Norris Hall.

Cho apparently walked around Norris Hall's second floor, peering into several classrooms before picking his victims. For reasons known only to Cho, he selected and first entered room 206, where a graduate engineering class, taught by Professor G.V. Loganthan, was in progress. He immediately killed Loganathan. Of the 13 students in the room, Cho killed nine and wounded two—only two students survive uninjured. The class was so paralyzed with horror that no one called the police.

Just moments before Cho entered Madame Jocelyne Couture-Nowak's French class in room 211, Henry Lee saw the notice of the dormitory shooting on his computer. He apparently said something and both Ross Alameddine and Emily Haas started looking over Henry's shoulder.

The gunfire was heard in other classrooms, but practically no one recognized the sounds. Sometime around 9:40 a.m. Colin Goddard, in room 211, vividly remembers hearing loud bangs. Madame Jocelyne Couture-Nowak, the French instructor, stopped momentarily, and her face took on a puzzled expression. All semester the class had heard construction noises coming from next door. That seemed to be the answer and the class resumed.

A moment later, however, they heard more loud bangs, this time they were clearly coming from within Norris Hall. Madame Couture-Nowak stopped again. She went to the door, opened it and peered into the hall. She turned around, her face dropped, and she told everyone to get under his or her desk. She asked someone to dial 911. Colin was apparently the first to do so. The emergency number his Nextel cell phone dialed, however, did not connect him with the local Blacksburg emergency services. It took him several moments to get the person on the other end of the line to understand where he was and what was going on. Only then was the call transferred to the Blacksburg Police Department. Goddard's call was first word of what was taking place. By 9:42 a.m. other calls were coming in from other classrooms; some of these went to the Virginia Tech Police Department.

Meanwhile, Cho had walked across the hall to room 207, where Christopher James Bishop's German class was in progress. Cho shot and killed the instructor first. He then turned his weapons on the students sitting at the front of the class. He methodically walked up and down the aisle shooting students in cold blood. Cho slaughtered four students, including Nicole White and Michael Pohle, Jr., and wounded six more in room 207.

The students in room 205, Haiyan Cheng's class in Issues in Scientific Computing, heard Cho's weapons. They quickly barricaded the door to prevent him from entering. Cho fired through the door, but was never able to enter the classroom.

Further down the hall in room 211, Couture-Nowak's class, having heard the shots and called 911, tried without success to barricade the door with the instructor's table. At that point, bullets began coming through the door. Cho pushed his way in and the murderous rampage continued. He shot Couture-Nowak first and then turned his weapons on the class.

Colin looked toward the front of the class from under his desk and could see boots, khaki pants, a white shirt and holsters. At first it looked as if the person was exiting the classroom. Colin thought it was the police who had somehow climbed up the side of the building and come in through the window.

Instead of exiting however, the figure started walking down the rows of seated students. He first started down Colin's row. Colin was one of the last in the row. He tried to play dead—there was no place to go. The windows opened outward and escape was awkward if not impossible. He could hear Cho moving and the constant, repetitious gunfire.

Then Colin felt something; it was as if someone had kicked his leg. There was a sharp stinging, then numbness and a warm feeling in his leg. He realized he had been shot. Colin had been in disbelief up to that point. Cho, the shootings, the whole situation were surreal. But now reality was setting in. He remembers hearing more gunshots. He knew he had been hit but he felt no pain.

Now, fully aware of the magnitude of what was happening, Colin threw his cell phone away. It was still on and he wanted to get it away from him in case Cho heard it. The phone landed near Emily Haas who hid it in her hair and heroically stayed on the line.

Colin is not sure when, but Cho left the room. He did not see Cho leave but heard him. Cho headed back to room 207, the German class. But by now two uninjured students had run to the door and using their feet and hands held it shut in case Cho returned. Finding the door blocked he beat on it and managed to pry it open just enough to fire several shots into the room. Unable to gain entry, Cho went back to Madame Couture-Nowak's French class.

There, Cho resumed his methodical march up and down the aisles, firing into the dead and wounded. Colin was shot again. He remembers hearing gurgling noises as his fellow students struggle to stay alive, but he did not look up—he continued to play dead. Once again Cho left room 211 looking for more victims.

At some point during the rampage Cho went to classroom 204 where engineering Professor Liviu Librescu (a survivor of the holocaust) knew the sounds of gunfire immediately. He had braced himself against the door to hold it closed and yelled to his students to head for the windows. The students pushed out screens and jumped to the bushes and ground below. Ten of the sixteen students in Librescu's class escaped unharmed. The next two to try and get out were shot and Professor Librescu was fatally shot through the door. Professor Librescu sacrificed his life for others; his heroism prevented further carnage. A total of four students in his solid mechanics class were shot, one fatally.

The Governor's Review Panel Report erroneously has Cho going to Librescu's class after his last shooting rampage in the French class. That is impossible. Cho committed suicide in the French class. The killings in Librescu's class, therefore, must have taken place earlier. This timeline mistake is a critical error, raising questions about the professionalism and thoroughness of both the Review Panel and TriData, the firm hired to write the report. See Chapter V for a detailed discussion and analysis of the numerous errors, inconsistencies, and flaws in the Governor's Review Panel report.

It is not clear where Cho had gone, but he was not through with room 211. He came back a third time and resumed his murderous march. Again Colin Goddard became a target; he felt a shot graze his chest and enter his armpit. The bullet exited through his upper shoulder. The force of the bullet turned him over. Colin Goddard was then shot a fourth time—this time in the right hip.

Colin could hear the police outside as they tried to get in the building. He first heard them yelling and then a deep boom of a shotgun blast. Then he could hear the police moving about in the building both above and below where he was as they began clearing rooms. Next, Colin heard one last shot, Cho's suicide.

Unlike the double homicide some two and a half hours earlier, the police, in this instance, knew what they were dealing with and acted accordingly. They had learned from Columbine. They did not hesitate; they broke in. At Norris Hall, in contrast to West Ambler Johnston, the police conducted themselves in exemplary fashion, applying the lessons learned from previous school shootings. Their actions brought Cho's rampage to an abrupt end—his suicide at around 9:51 a.m. The police undoubtedly prevented more killings through their quick, professional assault on Norris Hall.

Later, one of the officers who participated in the storming of Norris Hall walked the Goddard family through the crime scene and explained the police's actions. The shotgun blast that Colin had heard had blown off the lock on a service door to a lab on the west end of Norris Hall. The police had entered and then gone into an inner corridor, some going up to the second floor, others moving along the first-floor corridor. The police had secured the second floor by posting officers at each end of the corridor, while others went to the third floor.

At that point, Colin could hear the police moving about, but lay still. There was a gap between Cho's last shot and the arrival of the police; Colin, not knowing Cho was dead, feared that all was quiet because Cho was waiting for the police and there would be a shootout.

Emily Haas, who was wounded, had hidden Colin's cell phone in her hair and kept the line open. After the shooting stopped she kept asking the dispatcher, "Where are the police? … What is taking so long … People are hurt. We need help …"

When the police did come to room 211, Colin could hear them trying to push the door of the classroom open, but the bodies of Madame Couture-Novak and Henry Lee blocked their entrance. The police called for help to get in. By now Colin had crawled closer to Kristina, who was also seriously wounded but would survive, and they were holding hands. He remembers thinking, 'Help from *us*? You are here to *help us*.' At the time Colin did not know it, but eleven of his classmates were dead, four others were wounded, and only one survived unscathed.

Finally, the dispatcher responded to Emily Haas saying, "The police are at the door." At that point, Emily went to the door to push a body out of the way. The police arrived at room 211 sometime around 10:08 a.m., the time given for their discovery of Cho's body at the front of the French class. The police immediately took Emily outside where she was given emergency medical treatment.

Colin remembers putting his hand up as the police entered to signal where he was and that he was alive. He could see the police and remembers the startled, almost shocked, look on the officers' faces; he could see they were "on edge"—and the gruesome scene they found probably haunts those officers to this day. The first thing he heard after the police entered the room was, "Shooter down."

Cho ended his rage at approximately 9:51 a.m. by shooting himself in the head. (By this point, the Policy Group was aware of the mass shootings, but the Review Panel Report did not specify the precise time they were told. They were in Burruss Hall across from Norris and probably didn't have to be told a shooting was taking place.) Within a nine-to-eleven-minute shooting spree, Cho murdered 25 students and five faculty members. He had coldly and systematically walked up and down the second-floor corridor of Norris Hall killing at will. He entered most of the classrooms more than once. He fired from the doorway or walked around inside the rooms. To quote the Governor's Review Panel Report, "It was very close range. Students had little place to hide other than behind the desks. By taking a few paces inside he could shoot almost anyone in the classroom who was not behind a piece of overturned furniture." They were execution-style killings.

At least 17 students were shot and survived, and six more were injured jumping out of windows. Cho expended at least 174 bullets from two semiautomatic guns—his 9mm Glock and his .22 caliber Walther. Most of his shots were fired at point-blank range, making his slaughter the worst school shooting in this nation's history. The police found 17 empty magazines, each capable of holding 10-15 bullets. Ammunition recovered included 203 live cartridges, 122 for the Glock and another 81 for the Walther.

Aftermath

Colin Goddard knew he was wounded, but he never thought he was going to die. He simply could not believe what was happening. It was all some sort of nightmare, he would wake up and everything would be OK. But he was not asleep, he was awake. It was not a nightmare, and he was not OK.

He remembers hearing the police say, "Put a red tag here, a yellow one here, a black tag here." He was in a daze.

The police dragged Colin by the arms out into the hallway. They also got Kristina out and in the hall the police checked both of them. Colin could see Kristina look as if she were about to go to sleep and could hear the police ask her questions-"What is your name? What is your major?"-anything to keep her awake. The police kept calling her by the wrong name—Kristen, Christine—until Colin yelled out, "Her name is Kristina!"

The police asked him if he could walk and he said, "No." Four officers picked Colin up, one under each limb and carried him down the steps, out the front door and onto the lawn. Two officers carried Kristina outside. There they cut off his shirt and jeans to inspect his injuries. It was lightly snowing and freezing cold. Colin kept yelling for a blanket and finally got one. It was during these moments that someone on the other side of campus snapped a photo that would make the front page of the newspapers the next day.

He could hear the police saying they were trying to land a helicopter right outside the building, but due to bad weather, were unable to do so. So they brought an ambulance over the curb and onto the lawn and loaded him and another wounded student, Garrett Evans inside. As Colin was one of the last survivors to be removed from the building, the local hospital, Montgomery General, was already full. They were taken to the hospital in neighboring Radford, Virginia. As they began driving, that is when the shock and numbness of the adrenaline began to wear off and the pain began to set in. He thought they must have been going over 100mph on the shoulder as Colin was bouncing up and down on the medical table. He yelled and screamed for the driver to stop or slow down.

Colin was immediately taken to the emergency room. His memory is vague, but he does recall seeing people everywhere, several of whom began working on him. He remembers saying to the surgeon humorously, "Are all these people really necessary?"

The doctors asked for Colin's parent's phone number to let them know he was under their care. As his parents recently moved into a new home, Colin hadn't memorized it yet and his cell phone was back at the crime scene. He told them to Google his mother's organization's name to get her number. They got his mother on the phone and her first words were, "Colin, what did you do?" His response, "Nothing Mom, I have been shot, I'm gonna be OK, but please get down here quickly."

Colin was lucky, and he is OK with that. When the doctors realized that no organs or arteries were hit, they were able to give him painkillers. He would have to have surgery on his leg the next day to implant a titanium rod down the center of his left femur in order to stabilize the leg and allow him to walk properly again. He was able to leave the hospital in a wheelchair in just six days. His many surgeries and road to recovery were just beginning. A young man of exceptional fortitude and determination, he wanted to attend the memorial service for his slain professor some two days later.

Colin says he made the right choice by choosing to begin his recovery in Blacksburg. He went back to his apartment when he got out of hospital, and back to his friends. To have gone to his parents' home in Richmond (the family had just moved to Virginia from Atlanta) would not have helped. He went back to the environment he knew and loved—Virginia Tech. Talking about the shooting—especially in the first few weeks—was beneficial.

And, after returning to school, the group therapy sessions set up by Tech were especially helpful. Everyone had to say what he/she remembered. Some could remember minute details, others next to nothing, but hearing those eleven minutes retold from other perspectives helped Colin and others put their own timelines together.

There were six or seven group therapy sessions. The last was a private session and the counselor told Colin he was expressing classic post-traumatic stress symptoms. That was somewhat shocking for Colin, who thought he was doing well in his return to school. The office of Recovery and Support, set up by Tech, was valuable in Colin's recovery process as well. Jay Poole headed the office, and about once a month Poole hosted a dinner at his house for the victims to get together. This was very beneficial for survivors to finally to meet each other in private and to get to know one another, and actually become friends in may cases.

For Colin, going back to Tech to finish his last year was the right thing to do. Everyone expected him and most of the other survivors to transfer schools. But staying helped him face the aftermath of the tragedy. Colin is very proud to report that all the wounded students eventually went back and got their degrees. By going back, he said, "We didn't allow Cho to take that (their education and their future) away from us."

Colin has had to have follow-up surgery despite the initial diagnosis doctors telling him that all the bullet fragments they left would solidify themselves permanently. Three years after the shooting he had to have a bullet fragment removed from his hip. Four bullets entered his body and only one left. He still has the shattered bullets in his right hip, left upper thigh, and left knee. The physical scars are not noticeable, and when you meet and talk with him you realize how well he is doing in overcoming the emotional and psychological scars.

When I asked Colin what he would like this book to do, he said, "I would like to believe that the school had the best intentions that morning, but I am afraid the book will not show that. It is already clear to me that better decisions could have been made on April 16th. Also, after the shooting, the families could, and should, have been made to feel that they were the top priority of school officials—but they were not. It is my hope that the book will show that if similar events happen, the same decisions would not be made. For example: The decision not to notify the students immediately. And the unexplainable decisions of the school in not having representatives visit the injured and their family members. It is my hope that the book will show that if similar events happen on campus, the same decisions of April 16, 2007 will not be made again.

"The decision makers that morning should have made different decisions. That needs to be made clear.

"What bothers me is that school officials were worried about saying something, anything, because of liability. Just say you are sorry, you screwed up, and you should have done things differently. Speak to us as human beings with compassion—with feeling. Speak the truth as decent human beings. If they had done that there might never have been the lawsuit."

Colin Goddard is an exceptional young man. He is not bitter he is determined. He has devoted his life to the memory of his 32 fellow students who perished that day. He now works for the Brady Campaign to Prevent Gun Violence, tirelessly trying to help make our society safer, and to help keep guns out of the hands of those who are a danger to themselves or others. If you can say anything good has come out of Cho's diabolical act, it is the courage and will of Colin Goddard and all the survivors to go on with their lives and not to let Cho take away their bright and promising futures.

Heroes

There were so many heroes in Norris Hall on April 16, 2007; we will never know all their acts of heroism, but we do know a few. There was Professor Liviu Librescu, a holocaust survivor who, using his body, barricaded the door to his classroom, sacrificing his life to give students a chance to open windows and escape. Then, there was Emily Haas, who despite being shot twice in the head, kept a cell phone line open urging the police to act quickly.

No talk of heroes would be complete without a discussion of the first responders. Their prompt response undoubtedly saved lives and prevented an even worse massacre at Norris Hall. Indeed, there were 46 people on the third floor of Norris Hall and had Cho not been stopped so quickly, it is likely he would have turned his murderous rage on them.

The police had learned lessons from Columbine and the training they received paid huge dividends on April 16, 2007 at Norris Hall. Both the Blacksburg Police Tactical Team (SWAT) and the Virginia Tech Tactical Team (SWAT) performed in exemplary fashion.

When the police arrived, they thought they were being fired at by the shooter; bullets were coming out of a classroom window. In fact, the bullets were Cho firing at students and faculty. The police knew not to wait when there is an active shooter and putting their personal safety at risk, they blew open a door to Norris Hall and went in. The sound of the police's entry alerted Cho to their presence and within moments he committed suicide.

Once inside the Tactical Teams (SWAT) spread out and began searching rooms. The carnage they found was so great they could not believe there was only one shooter. On the second floor they found 13 partially spent magazines on the floor.

Virginia State Police Trooper Gary Chafin was among the first to enter Norris Hall, right behind the Tactical Teams. What he found defies description—it serves no purpose for me to go into gruesome detail about the scene that confronted Chafin and his fellow police officers. It is enough to say that Chafin, a state police officer with three college-age children of his own, found wounded and dead young people everywhere. His heart was broken and he will take that sight with him to his grave.

Chafin helped secure room 211, Madame Couture-Nowak's French class. He found Cho's body at the front of the class where he had committed suicide. Nearby, with his arms stretched out as if to stop an intruder, was the body of Virginia Tech Cadet Matthew La Porte. Matthew's eyes were closed. He had eight bullet entry wounds—fingers, thumb, arms and shoulders, and to the front of his head. He apparently was repeatedly shot while moving forward and trying to charge Cho.

It was obvious that Matthew, in an act of heroism, had tried to stop Cho. But Chafin was so moved by what he saw that instinctively he knelt by Matthew and whispered in his ear, "What were you trying to do?" Chafin, as the other officers present, knew Matthew had tried to stop Cho, but the state trooper could not help but ask his question—almost as in disbelief.

Chafin looked around the carnage in dismay, trying to come to grips with the sight in front of him. His eyes fell on a female student who lay dead by her desk, her eyes were open in haunting disbelief. Again, Chafin could not help himself. He knelt in front of her and overcome with grief, he said in a soft voice, "I'm sorry."

All the police who came to Norris Hall would ask themselves over and over again, "What if?" "What if we would have gotten here earlier?" "We got here as fast as we could, and look what happened." But they came in remarkable speed. It would not have been humanly impossible to get there any sooner, but they still ask, "What if?" And they ask that question to this day.

Sometime around 10:45 a.m. the students' cell phones started ringing, frantic parents trying to reach their children. At first Chafin thought one or more of the students might be alive and had activated his or her phone to get help. But when he walked over to one of the ringing phones he saw a message, "Baby, phone home now! Mom." Grimly, Chafin told his fellow officers not to look at the phone messages—it was just too overwhelming. Throughout the day the cell phones in Norris Hall rang while the police stood guard over the terrible sight, each ring tearing at every fiber of the officers' souls.

Trooper Chafin was so moved by Matthew's heroism that he wrote the La Porte family. Drawing on scripture, the state trooper tried to give the La Porte's some solace. He told them Matthew was on the move against the enemy, he might as well have been killed in the line of duty at Gettysburg or Guadalcanal.

The La Porte family and trooper Chafin have established a strong bond, helping each other heal. Chafin has had reoccurring dreams of Matthew. In one, he was in a field of gently waving wheat, much like the last scene of the "Gladiator" in the Elysian Fields. In the dream Matthew is walking toward trooper Chafin asking him what is wrong. Chafin responds, "I see death coming up the hill." Matthew responds, "Not now, it is not your time. Don't worry about me, I have been completed."

Trooper Chafin and the La Portes talk frequently and when the La Portes come to Blacksburg they get together. Chafin, who is a Baptist, joins the La Portes for Mass at the Catholic Church. Chafin and the La Portes have established a life-long bond based on Matthew's courage and gallantry.

Barbara La Porte believes that Matthew has embraced our Lord and Trooper Chafin has tried to help comfort the family saying, "Matthew is fine up there among the stars."

Gift of God

The family of Matthew Joseph La Porte has found solace in their Catholic faith; their religion has given them strength. Matthew's parents and his sister Priscilla made a conscientious effort not to be angry, but the journey back to some semblance of normalcy has been hard, painful, and difficult. And, more than five years after the shootings, they still struggle—they still cry. The family, like almost all of the Tech families, sought counseling which has helped them deal with their loss.

A family whose child survived sent the La Portes a letter thanking them for Matthew's heroism because it helped save their daughter's life. At his funeral a friend of Matthew's told his sister, Priscilla, that her brother had recently discussed Columbine, saying that he "would do something" to try and stop the shooting. To quote Priscilla, "I don't know where his strength came from, but he was incredible. My heart swells with pride."

Priscilla La Porte remembers her brother vividly—his memory will always be with her. Matthew was two years older and the type of big brother every young woman should have. He was kind. Matthew was funny, and especially enjoyed making his sister laugh.

When Priscilla remembers about Matthew she thinks about his determination. Once Matthew, a Political Science student from Dumont, New Jersey, set his mind to something, there was no stopping him. He would move heaven and earth to get something done or to achieve a goal. Matthew was quiet; he didn't talk a lot. Not because he was shy, but because he was a thinker. He was so very, very special to his sister and to his parents. The memory of this fine, exemplary young man is bittersweet.

Despite the comfort of the church, despite the counseling, Priscilla feels the intensity of the loss every bit today as she did on April 16, 2007. "It is as if I (exist) without my arms and legs—you simply cannot forget. It will be with me forever. He was such an important part of me, and I lost something that was meant to be in my life forever."

Matthew La Porte was buried with full military honor.

CHAPTER V

THE DEFINING MOMENT

"Lying is done with words and also with silence."
~ Adrienne Rich, American poet, essayist, feminist

In my conversations with Michael Pohle, whose son, Michael Pohle, Jr., was killed in German class, I told him of my family's experience in hopes that it might help prepare him for what lay ahead for not only the Pohle family, but all Virginia Tech families. I feared that they would all eventually come to the same defining moment my family and I had as we attempted to find closure after the Appalachian School of Law shootings. Angela Dales, the mother of our oldest grandchild, had been killed in that shooting, and yet we had to play detectives ourselves in order to find out any of the details related to her death.

Sheila Tolliver, the Commonwealth's Attorney, had agreed to arrange a meeting for us with the police to try and answer some of our questions about Angie's death. Angie's father was especially upset because no one had ever taken the time to tell him some of the particulars—details that mean so much to the family. Who took Angie to the hospital? Where did she die? These are not earth shaking or accusatory questions they are simple details that help families heal by reconstructing the last moments of their child's life. These were the kinds of details that many of the Virginia Tech families wanted.

What took place during the meeting was not only disconcerting, but it was alarming in terms of uncovering significant shortcomings in the criminal investigative procedures associated with the law school shootings.

We gathered in Tolliver's office. Three state highway patrolmen were also there, John Santolla, Walt Parker, and Ashley Hagy. The three police officers were unable or unwilling to answer most of our questions or even give us something as simple as a timeline. In fact, the timeline is the foundation upon which much of the investigation rests. The parallels here with the Virginia Tech investigation are so close that one has to realize that this is a standard strategy for any organization that feels threatened: information is power, so don't give it out.

All the Tech families would find out that a flawed timeline plays a critical role in covering up facts and evidence. Just as in the case of the Appalachian School of Law, the Virginia Tech families would discover that there was a lack of sound crime scene and investigative practices at the murder scene. In the case of Virginia Tech, as I have discussed, this apparent malfeasance in investigating Cho's first shooting would lead to many more deaths.

In addition to bureaucratic obstructionism, I cautioned Michael to be prepared for open hostility. It was another ingredient that made the meeting in Ms. Tollivers's office our defining moment. From the outset, Officer Parker appeared to take an instant dislike to me. From the moment he entered the room, it was apparent that Officer Parker's idea of answering questions that he found distasteful, involved the use of verbal abuse or sarcasm. He challenged why he was there, why any of them were there. I felt that the only thing limiting his abusive behavior was the presence of the Commonwealth's Attorney. He even lashed out at our "lawsuit" which was an especially odd assertion because at that time there was no lawsuit against the Appalachian School of Law.

That anticipation of the lawsuit and the need to control information and opinions about the shootings would also come into play in the interactions between the Virginia Tech administration and the victims of the Cho shooting spree. One has to ask if there was not a bit of self-fulfilling prophesy at work here: two schools tried so hard to control the information about the respective shootings so that they could not be held accountable and sued.

The reality of what we faced began to sink in—a cover up.

The above is an abbreviated version of our story that was shared with Michael Pohle. What follows is his experience, as well as the Goddards, whose son was wounded in the massacre, and the Whites whose daughter died.

* * *

2007 (April 15)   Mike and Tricia White drove to Charlottesville, Virginia to meet and pick up their son Evan, who had spent the previous week visiting his sister, Nicole, a student at Virginia Tech.

2007 (April 16)   (circa 9:00 a.m.) Andy Goddard's mother-in-law was watching CNN and hears about shootings at Virginia Tech in a dormitory. Andy told her not to worry, Colin lives off campus.

2007 (April 16)   (circa 10:30 a.m.) The secretary to Andy's wife, Anne, called him after she saw cell phone footage of the shooting; Anne, was in a meeting and Andy told her secretary not to interrupt his wife. Andy said he would call Colin's cell phone and as soon as he found out that Colin was ok he would call back. Andy's mother-in-law tells Andy, "They are still shooting."

2007 (April 16)   (8:15-11:00 a.m.) Tricia White was at work early in Tidewater Virginia. Around 8:15 a.m. she received a call from her brother in North Carolina saying there has been a shooting at Virginia Tech. Less than two hours later, around 10:00 a.m., her brother called again to say there had been more shootings, this time in an engineering building. Tricia began calling Nicole's cell phone around 9:00 a.m., but did not want to call and worry her husband, Mike, until she had talked to Nicole. By 11:00 a.m. when she still could not contact Nicole, she called Mike.

2007 (April 16)   (11:45 a.m.) Michael Pohle went to lunch with co-workers. TV sets in the restaurant were carrying live coverage of the shootings. Michael went outside and tried several times to reach his son on his cell phone, but there was no answer.

2007 (April 16)   (noon) Andy Goddard has not heard from his son, Colin, so he called his wife who was on the phone to the hospital. Andy held on the line until his wife was off the phone and then found out that Colin had been wounded.

2007 (April 16)   Anne Goddard told her husband that a board member of her firm has offered his private plane; a staff member drove Anne home. The Goddard's went to their daughter's school and picked Emma up. From there they drove to the airport.

2007 (April 16)   (12:30 a.m.) Michael Pohle called his boss and told her he was leaving for Blacksburg (this was Pohle's second week on a new job). He then called home and told his wife he was heading directly to Virginia Tech and not coming home.

2007 (April 16)   (1:30 p.m.) After repeated unsuccessful attempts to reach Nicole and hospitals in the Blacksburg area, Tricia left for home to meet Mike. At home, the Whites still did not know that the German class had been the site of one of the shootings. A family friend who knew about the German class came over and without telling them the specifics, told the Whites to pack and that her husband would drive them to Blacksburg.

2007 (April 16)   (circa 1:45 p.m.) The Goddard's took off for Blacksburg and arrived some 45- 50 minutes later. Upon arrival, they spent a few minutes talking to the police and used a rental car to drive to the hospital.

2007 (April 16)   (3:00 p.m.) The Goddard's arrived at the hospital.

2007 (April 16)   (afternoon) Colin's friends tracked down his location and arrived at the hospital. No one from Virginia Tech was present or contacted the Goddards.

2007 (April 16)   Mike Pohle's daughter, Nikki (a student at West Virginia University) heard about the shootings at Tech. Unable to reach her brother, she started the five and a half hour drive to Blacksburg. Nikki and her father were in constant cell phone communication. She arrived in Blacksburg at approximately 4:30 p.m., two hours ahead of her father. Michael was also in cell phone contact with his son's friends, trying to find something out about Michael, Jr.

2007 (April 16)   (6:30 p.m.) Michael Pohle arrived in Blacksburg and went directly to the Inn at Virginia Tech and the Skelton Convention Center where he joined his daughter, Nikki.

2007 (April 16)   (7:30 p.m.) Michael Pohle had his first contact with someone from the school, a counselor hired by the school. Around 8:00 p.m. Pohle talked with a police officer who basically said he had no information.

2007 (April 16)   (Evening) Two professors' wives took the initiative and arrived at the hospital where Colin was being treated. They did not represent the school. Andy Goddard asked them to convey to the school that he would like a formal contact.

2007 (April 16)   (11:00 p.m.) Virginia Tech Police Chief Flinchum and someone from the medical examiner's office arrived and told Michael Pohle and Nikki that Michael, Jr. was dead. Pohle called home to break the news to his wife, Teresa. The family priest and friends had gathered at the Pohle home and were there to aid and comfort Teresa and the Pohle's other son, Sean.

2007 (April 16)   (11:30 p.m.) Nicole White's boy friend arrived and told the Whites that she was in the German class. There was still no word of her fate.

2007 (April 17)   (Early morning) Andy Goddard, after asking the hospital director several times the day before if anyone from Virginia Tech had contacted the hospital, asked the hospital director to call the school to set up a contact or communication point.

2007 (April 17)   (3:30 a.m.) Police told the Whites there would be no more information that night.

2007 (April 17)   (4:00 a.m.) Tricia White's brothers, Mark and Tom Gallagher, arrived at Virginia Tech.

2007 (April 17)   (circa 11:00 a.m.) A representative from Virginia Tech, a female doctor, and the police came to the White's room to break the news, Nicole was gone.

2007 (April 18)   (circa 10:00 a.m.) Andy Goddard heard that the school officials believed they were not allowed to come to the hospital because of privacy issues.

2007 (April 18)   (mid morning) Andy Goddard phoned the school and asked when a school representative would come to the hospital and was told no one would be coming. The school official told Goddard that Virginia Tech did not know the names of the wounded or where they were being treated—more than two days after the shootings and despite the fact that the school had class rosters. Adding insult to injury, the school official asked Andy if he would go around to the hospitals and collect the names and locations of the wounded and give that information to Tech. A livid Andy Goddard said, "No!"

2007 (April 18)   (1:00 p.m.) Michael Pohle and Nikki had spent their time in Blacksburg in Mike's apartment, crying and grieving. Sometime around 1:00 p.m. they began the arduous trip home to New Jersey.

2007 (April 19)   (2:30 p.m.) The Whites left Blacksburg and begin the long, painful trip home.

2007 (April 20)   For the first time, the Goddards met with the person assigned to be their liaison with the school.

2007 (Rest of April) Andy Goddard stayed with Colin in his apartment to help his son get back on his feet. He asked school officials if there was a way to contact the families of those injured. He is told "no."

2007 (Early May) Back in Richmond, Andy Goddard again asked school officials if there was a way to contact the families of those injured and the families of those killed. School officials offered to take his contact information and give it to the families. He was also told that the families of the deceased did not want to talk to the families of the survivors. *Andy would later find out that his contact information was never given to anyone and that some of the families of the deceased did want to talk to the families of the survivors. The school had lied.*

The Pohles

According to Michael, "One of the questions posed to me during the early idea stages of this book was whether there was a critical moment, or event, that crystallized in my mind that we were not being told the truth about how our son was killed. From the beginning of the formal investigation of the killings, which began almost immediately following the shootings, a number of the families believed strongly that we should have had representation on the special panel appointed by then-Governor Tim Kaine to ensure no stone would be unturned. Not only did he reject our requests, we were not allowed to see, nor evaluate, the inventory of information available to the panel, their legal and investigative support resources, or law enforcement. Simply put, given that Virginia Tech is a state institution we faced a situation of the state investigating itself and the families were left on the outside.

"On August 30, 2007, then-Governor Kaine held a press conference where he publicly released the formal report of findings of the panel that had investigated the events of Virginia Tech. (the Governor's Review Panel Report—*The Addendum*—is analyzed in Chapter VI.) This report contained hundreds of pages of information and my family, and others, spent many days going through it to learn all we could. It was our bible, and the "facts" contained in that document remained unchanged for the next 14 months, until October of 2008.

"Prior to October of 2008, and not long after my son, Mike Jr., had been killed, my family, as well as other families, retained counsel to preserve our legal rights. In our case, we were one of 20 families represented by the same firm. Among the numerous meetings held between our attorneys and the state that began in the fall, there is one of particular significance. It involved a meeting that was held in February 2008, one month before details of a proposed settlement agreement were presented to the families. The purpose of the meeting was for Virginia Tech Police Chief Wendell Flinchum to present details of the Virginia Tech shootings to the attorneys representing the families.

"Following that meeting, our attorney sent an email that described what had transpired, and his thoughts. In the message, our attorney began by stating that attendees were required to sign a confidentiality agreement, but, they were free to share information with their clients. The rest of the email went on to describe our attorney's input from the meeting, in which he stated he learned "nothing earth shattering" and made no mention about potential errors, missing information, or issues with what had been published in the Governor's Review Panel Report. Less than one month later, the families were presented with a settlement offer that our attorneys strongly urged the families to approve. What is relevant is the fact that a settlement was ultimately signed between the state of Virginia and all but two of the families in April of 2008, and approved by a judge two months later, in June.

"One of the conditions of that settlement was that the families would, for the first time, have face-to-face meetings with representatives from law enforcement directly involved in the shootings, members of the Virginia Tech administration, and two meetings with then-Governor Timothy Kaine who sponsored the formal investigation of April 16th. These meetings were vital because they would provide a forum for families to ask questions of, and seek answers from, many of the key participants. These discussions were also significant for my family because we were becoming more suspicious after hearing that Virginia Tech was being investigated for potential Clery Act violations and that at least one, or two buildings had locked down after hearing of the shootings.

"The first of these family meetings was held on Saturday, October 16, 2008 with various members of law enforcement. The location was the Department of Transportation offices in Northern Virginia. I remember that when I pulled up to the parking lot entrance there was a Virginia State trooper who checked my identification before allowing me to park, and I could see that the other entrances were guarded as well. After parking, I went into the building and saw additional state police officers directing the families to one of the main conference rooms. The families, of which there were about 20, were seated in chairs around some tables.

"Larry Roberts, then Chief Counsel to Governor Kaine, facilitated the meeting. The presenter was Wendell Flinchum, Chief of the Virginia Tech Police Department. Other law enforcement personnel involved on the campus joined him that day. I also noticed that sitting in the back of the room was another gentleman taking notes. I did not recognize him. I only found out years later that he was actually Peter Messitt, Assistant Attorney General for the state of Virginia who was a defense lawyer at the jury trial in March 2012. After Roberts gave a few opening comments, the presentation opened with Chief Flinchum saying that he was going to discuss details concerning the shootings, which included information that he had presented to the Governor's panel during their investigation in 2007. He proceeded through the series of events of the morning of April 16th, and when they occurred. Questions were raised by a number of families because we wanted to know as many details as we could. We anticipated that we would hear facts that were never documented in the original panel report, or disclosed at a later date. For example, what did the police find at the crime scene?

"We listened as Chief Flinchum described the scene of the initial shootings at the West Ambler Johnston dorm (a.k.a West AJ) and that when he arrived he learned that there was no weapon found, there was/were no suspect(s), there were no witnesses, and there were bloody footprints leaving the area. We were amazed because we simply could not understand how anyone could take that information and reach the conclusion that there was no longer any potential danger to the campus. The chief then provided additional details relative to the timing of events and actions being taken, which included interviewing people in search of leads.

"Experts will tell you that one of the most critical elements of any criminal investigation is an accurate timeline of events. That is the cornerstone from which further analyses and conclusions can be drawn when evaluating what was happening based on the crime scene specifics and other evidence. As far as the Virginia Tech tragedy is concerned, the timeline of events was particularly important because of the fact that there were actually two shootings, with a time delay of just over two hours between the first and second attacks. The accuracy of the timeline was central in determining what actions were being taken, or not, and the significance of those actions, especially because nothing was known about the shooter when police, and others, had arrived at the West AJ dormitory early that morning and began processing the crime scene.

"The families were well aware that the original panel report stated that law enforcement had begun their pursuit of a "person of interest" at 8:00 a.m. based on their interview of the female victim's roommate, which the report erroneously asserted began at 7:30 am. This was the baseline that would connect other actions. It was during this phase of his presentation when the Chief made a statement that stunned us all. We almost missed it at first because Flinchum spoke in an almost monotone voice, without expression. As he was talking about the timeline he stated that the interview of the witness, Hilscher's roommate (Heather Haugh) that had led police to the "person of interest" began at 8:16 am. My hand immediately went up because I knew that the official report specifically stated that interview had begun at 7:30 am. I asked the chief, "Are you saying the 7:30 a.m. time in the panel report is wrong?" His reply was a simple, "Yes." We could not believe what we were hearing. That lie was allowed to remain uncorrected for 14 months after the original panel report was published. I then realized that given this new start time for the interview, it was not humanly possible to have identified, or begin searching for, any person of interest until long after 8 a.m. The fact that Chief Flinchum and other school officials knew of this critical error before the Review Panel Report was published makes them guilty of lies of omission.

"To appreciate the significance of this new information one has to understand the period between the first and second shootings. At around 7:15 a.m., the killer shot his first two victims in the West Ambler Johnston dormitory. By 7:30 a.m. Virginia Tech police and emergency personnel were at the scene. By 8:00 a.m. Chief Flinchum had been notified of the shootings, had been at the scene where the investigation was underway, and had communicated with the office of his superior to report what was happening. At 8:11a.m., the Chief spoke via cell phone to University President Charles Steger about the situation. At 8:25 a.m. President Steger and senior policy officials convened to discuss what to do. It was not until 9:26 a.m. that a message went out to the campus concerning a "shooting incident." No specific details were provided in the message. At 9:40 a.m., the same person began methodically killing 30 additional people.

"What this also means was that between 7:30 a.m. and 8:25 a.m. all that was known about the situation was that there was no weapon found, there were no witnesses, there were bloody footprints leaving the scene, and no suspect or person of interest had been identified. Senior leaders of the Virginia Tech administration began their meeting faced with the reality of a gunman whose location, and intentions, were unknown. There were no campus wide warnings issued by the police, there were no campus wide alerts issued to students and faculty, there were no alarms turned on, there were no sirens. There were, however, students and staff soon to be making their way toward Norris Hall where classes would begin at 9:05 a.m. completely unaware of what was soon to happen to them. Thus it was not until 9:26 a.m. after another hour had passed, that the electronic alert message was issued by the administration; however, it was non-specific relative to what had had happened in the dormitory, rendering it ineffective. At 9:40 a.m., the killer began his second, much larger, rampage in Norris Hall where our son was gunned down.

"Immediately following the meeting, we shared what we had learned with reporters outside the building. The news of this serious error, this lie, was published in a major article by the Richmond Times Dispatch and picked up by the national media. In the article, retired Virginia State Police Superintendent Gerald Massengill, who led Governor Tim Kaine's investigation of the massacre, was quoted as saying, "*If they didn't have a suspect or a person of interest for another 45 minutes or an hour, I think that would have put a different light on things.*"

"During the long drive home to New Jersey following that meeting I began to ask myself why Virginia Tech officials had lied to the Governor's panel and what else might be wrong. Between that meeting, and the family meeting the following month with President Steger and members of the school administration, my thinking took a more frightening turn. Was it possible that the investigating panel and their well-compensated investigative team, as well as others, actually had the correct information in their possession yet intentionally elected not to disclose it in their public report because of legal concerns and to protect the school? Was this a collaborative effort to keep the truth from the families? In the months that followed it became apparent that it was impossible that Col. Massengill and the investigative team did not know that the timeline of events they published in August of 2007 was wrong, yet not a single member of the panel, a single school official, not anyone from the Governor's or Attorney General's offices, or even our own attorney had done anything about the errors. Everyone waited until after a legal settlement had been reached to correct the critical error in the timeline.

"In addition to sharing what we had learned at the meeting with my wife, Teresa, I also shared it with my father. Although he never admitted it, Mike's death devastated 'Pop-pop' as he was called. Dad spent his career in the military and had served during the Korean and Viet Nam wars and rarely showed emotion. When Mike was killed Dad had been living in New Jersey near our home. My mother had died a few years earlier. 'Pop-pop' was special to Mike, and they had a strong relationship. Unfortunately, Mike never got to meet his maternal grandfather, "T.W.," who was a career member of the Marine Corps and had served in Viet Nam and the Middle East. This was because less than two weeks after Mike was born, in October of 1983, "T.W." was killed in the suicide bombing of the Marine barracks in Beirut, Lebanon.

"Following Mike's death there was noticeable change in my father. He had always stressed to everyone to work hard, be strong, and move forward. He would constantly ask about what was going on and what information we had about Virginia Tech. He also would tell me that we were being told the truth by officials and it was not healthy to suspect them. That was his military background speaking because he was used to the "chain of command" stating what the facts were, and that was it. That is not meant as a criticism, it was just the way he was. Once I shared the details of what had been learned with him following the meeting I had just attended, as well as the meeting with school officials held one month later, you could see that he realized the deception. From then on, it appeared that things didn't matter to him much anymore; whenever we would be alone talking he would say he was glad he wouldn't be around much longer because people just don't care about responsibility, honor, and duty. In December of 2008, two months following the first family meeting after the settlement approval, Dad died peacefully in his sleep, still proud—but a hurt man.

"For me, my defining moment came in two parts. The first was when I learned I was being intentionally lied to by people sworn to be truthful. The second was when I saw the strongest man I had ever know simply lose his will to live as well as his faith in what he had believed about people and honor. That is also when I came to believe, as I do to this day, that the investigation of my son's death at Virginia Tech in April 2007 incorporated lies and omitted key facts. These were not simple mistakes caused by time constraints imposed on the panel by the Governor, or the lack of experience and skill of those involved in researching and analyzing; they were intentional errors to hide the truth about one of the worst school mass killings in history. Based on what we have learned then and since, I believe that this was a carefully orchestrated plan of deception and silence to minimize the potential for legal actions against Virginia Tech and the state."

The Goddards

For the Goddard family, the realization that something was amiss, that Virginia Tech was hiding something, came early—in the hours and days immediately following the shooting.

Unlike school officials such as Associate Vice President for University Relations Lawrence Hincker, whose memory repeatedly failed him on the witness stand during the Pryde and Petersen families' trial against Virginia Tech, Andy Goddard remembers Monday April 16, 2007 in vivid, painful detail. He was at home that day getting ready to take his mother-in-law to the train to return home to New Jersey. When the news of the double shootings at West Ambler Johnston Hall came over the television he told his mother-in-law not to worry, that Colin lives off campus in an apartment. But as the news of the Tech tragedy grew steadily worse, Andy's concern for Colin's safety turned to fear and then to panic. He tried to console himself by saying what are the odds? On a campus that big, what are the odds Colin had been shot?

He clearly recalls phoning his wife's office only to be told she was on another line talking to Colin, who had been shot. All they knew was that he was in the hospital, was wounded, and apparently would recover. It was not until they got to the hospital and talked to the doctors that the Goddards found out their son had been shot four times and had five wounds—the fifth wound being where a bullet had exited Colin's body.

The hospital Colin had been taken to was not far from the school. As Andy Goddard sat watching his son struggle to deal with his life-threatening wounds, he waited for someone from the school to contact him. But no one came. This absence on the first day, the day of the shooting, was not hard to explain. Andy told himself school officials were busy with the families of the deceased—as they should be. But months later when Andy met with some of the families of the deceased he was shocked to find out they had not been the main focus of the school administration's attention either. By that afternoon Colin's friends had found where he was and were at the hospital. Andy could not help but think if students could find Colin certainly the school could—surely someone from the school would show up soon. He waited that evening, yet no one appeared and the school made no attempt to contact the Goddard family or inquire about Colin's condition.

Two professors' wives did come to the hospital, but it was on their own initiative. As sympathetic and kind as their gesture was, the two women did not represent the school and had no authority to open up a line of communication. Their presence only underscored the school's inaction and increasingly obvious indifference.

On Tuesday, still no contact with the school, but again, Andy assumed they were busy with the families of the dead. As the day progressed, there was no sign of anyone from Virginia Tech—no administrators, no counselors, no faculty, no one. Andy had sent messages through the hospital director and the two faculty wives, asking them to relay his concerns directly to Tech officials. But still there was no word or inquiry from the school, there was no contact point, and no school official came to the hospital or made any attempt to inquire about Colin.

For Andy Goddard, an engineer, when something is broken you spend time analyzing the problem and find out what went wrong and what needs to be done to fix it. Usually disasters, such as what occurred at Virginia Tech, are caused by many small things going wrong and by those things coming together with tragic consequences—a confluence of mistakes, missed signals, and sometimes negligence. Andy wanted answers and it did not take him long to realize school officials did not want to talk. Tech officials wanted minimal contact with the families of the dead and wounded; clearly, he thought, someone had gotten to Tech and told them not to talk.

By now Andy was not just annoyed, he was angry. He would later find out that the school had contacted none of the families of the wounded and that even three days after the shooting, the school did not know the names of the wounded, where they had been taken, or their conditions. It was as if once the injured were taken off the campus, the school had no responsibility or interest in them.

On Wednesday, as Colin was taken to surgery, there was still no official contact with the school. Again Andy turned to the hospital director to help open a line of communication to Tech, but once more the school did not respond.

An increasingly agitated Andy then went to the phone, called the school and asked when a school representative would appear at the hospital. The response was that nobody could come because of privacy issues, and they would not be allowed in unless they were family. The excuse was out and out false. President Steger did visit at least one wounded student after hours when the parents were not present. Furthermore, the school official added that Tech did not know names of those in the hospital, much less what hospitals the wounded were in or their conditions. Andy was furious. He wanted to blurt out, but did not, "For god's sake, Tech has class rosters, the school knows the names of the dead and yet days after the shooting claims to have no idea who the wounded are, where they are, or their condition."

Adding insult to injury, the school official asked Andy to go around the hospital and gather the names of the other injured and then report that back to him. A livid Andy Goddard refused.

At this point Andy lost his temper and demanded that someone representing the school administration come to the hospital. He said he would be at the front door waiting for someone to show up. And wait he did. While Colin lay in the recovery room, Andy Goddard stood for hours at the front door of the hospital, but no one came. What Andy wanted was a contact point, a name or a number to call; he didn't want answers, he didn't want apologies, he just wanted a line of communication with school officials. He wanted contact with the people who had been responsible for his son's education right up to the point when he was loaded into an ambulance and driven away. Those people, however, appeared to have washed their hands of Colin Goddard once he was taken to the hospital.

Finally, late in the day some nurses from Tech did appear. By then Andy had no patience, he could only respond, "What we want is an administrator—we have nurses! Has someone told Tech not to find out information, or does the school just not care?" Andy realized that Tech was a big school, and this was a crisis, but it stretched all credibility to think that a school the size of Tech could not find four administrators to send, one each, to the four hospitals where the wounded were being cared for.

Andy Goddard's suspicion of obstruction grew. It was becoming clear; Tech was trying to hide something. It was at that point that Andy realized that Tech had embarked on a campaign to cover up and hide incompetence and bureaucratic inertia. He believed there could be only one explanation for the school's lack of responsiveness; Virginia Tech had played a role in Cho's massacre. It remained to be seen just what that role was, but as the evidence and facts surfaced over the succeeding weeks and months, not only would the school's complicity in enabling Cho to carry out his massacre become clear, but evidence of the lengths to which the Steger administration would go to cover up the school's negligence would become glaringly apparent.

Upon reflection, Andy realized how naïve he had been. He had thought that everyone was in this together; they were all victims—the school and the families. He was finding out just how wrong he was.

The school did finally assign a liaison person, and she contacted the Goddards on Friday, April 20th.

Andy stayed in Blacksburg, in Colin's apartment to help him get back on his feet. After a couple of weeks he asked if he could contact the families of the deceased, or just be given the names, he was told no. Andy was told those families did not want to talk. Andy soon found out that was a lie. Just as he was trying to get the names and contact numbers for the families of the wounded, Joe Samaha, whose daughter had been murdered, was trying to do the same for those whose children and loved ones had been killed. Samaha was also intent on contacting the families of those who survived. The school apparently wanted the families to have as little contact with each other as possible. Tech officials did not want the families talking to each other and comparing notes. Their strategy appeared to be to divide and conquer.

When he got back to Richmond, some three weeks later, Andy again raised the subject of contacting the families of the injured and those killed. The school offered to take the Goddards' contact information and give it to other families, who could then decide if they wanted to talk to the Goddards. That was the last Andy Goddard would hear on the subject and none of the families he later talked with remember ever being offered the contact information. Clearly the school had lied.

Again, Andy Goddard took the initiative. He went through press reports and collected the names of the families of the dead and wounded. It took him three or four weeks to draw up a master list of family names and to make his first contact with other families. One by one he began contacting other families and one by one he found them all eager to talk. Andy contacted Joe Samaha and found that he and others were not only anxious, but eager to talk to the families of the survivors. The picture was clear that school officials had lied when they said the families of the deceased did not want to talk to the families of the survivors. There could be no doubt Virginia Tech was hiding something and had been willing to lie to attempt to keep the families apart.

For the Goddards then, the defining moment came soon after arriving in Blacksburg—within the first 24 hours. The school's lack of willingness to send a representative to the hospital alerted Andy Goddard to some sort of nefarious activity on the part of the Steger administration, a suspicion that was confirmed when Andy Goddard found out he had been lied to about the families of the dead not wanting to talk to the families of the wounded.

Where Is Nicole?

For Tricia and Michael White, who lost their daughter Nicole in Christopher James Bishop's German class, the morning of April 16th started much as any other Monday in Tidewater Virginia, with the two heading off to their respective jobs. By the end of the day, however, their oldest child would be dead and they would realize they were not being told the truth about how it happened.

In the early hours of that spring morning however, death was the furthest thing from their minds. Both were reflecting on the wonderful weekend they had spent with their two children—Evan and his older sister Nicole. The previous week Evan had been on school vacation and had spent it with his older sister on the Hokie campus. The two were very close. Evan's best friend was his tall vivacious redheaded sister. Evan reveled in the time he spent with Nicole, and his days with his sister at Tech were special. He went to many of her classes and hung out with his older sister's friends.

On Sunday the 15th Tricia and Mike White drove half way to Blacksburg, to Charlottesville, to meet Nicole and Evan. They ate at Applebee's and throughout the meal Nicole could not stop talking about her future and how much she enjoyed her classes. She especially enjoyed Christopher James Bishop's German class. This was the second time Nicole had been in one of the charismatic young instructor's classes. In fact, she should not have been in that German class; it was closed when she tried to enroll. But Nicole would not be denied, she insisted on being in Bishop's class and finally convinced him to accept her as a "forced add."

Christopher James Bishop was the first to be gunned down when Cho entered the German class in room 207. Ironically, had Cho's murderous rage taken place a week earlier Evan would probably have been in the German class and the Whites might have lost both their children.

Sometime shortly after Tricia arrived at work on the morning of the 16th, her brother called from Greensboro, North Carolina to tell her that two people had been killed in a dormitory on the Virginia Tech campus. Her first reaction was concern tempered by the fact that Virginia Tech is huge, with around 30,000 students, faculty, and staff. She asked him to keep her posted.

When her brother called back around an hour and a half or so later to say there had been more shootings and multiple deaths her concern became fear. She learned that this time the deaths were in an engineering building. At that point, Tricia did not know Nicole's schedule or if she had any classes in the engineering building, but she immediately tried to reach her daughter by cell phone and texting—but there was no response.

Alarmed, she called her father in New York and asked him to watch the TV and keep her posted. Her father called back in just a few moments and said, "This is not looking good." She then called Nicole's roommate who confirmed that Nicole's German class was in the engineering building, Norris Hall. In a near panic she called her husband, Mike, who himself had just heard about the shootings. He too had not heard anything from Nicole. They agreed to meet at home and then go to Blacksburg.

By now Tricia's whole office was aware of the situation, all work had come to a halt and everyone was glued to the news. Tricia's boss told her she needed to go home; she needed to get to Blacksburg.

A co-worker drove Tricia White home—she was too upset and frightened to drive. All the way she kept denying that her daughter was or could be a victim. When she arrived at their suburban home in Smithfield, Virginia, Mike was waiting for her. The two deliberated about going to Tech, but what if they were to miss Nicole's phone call telling them she was all right? They monitored the news and Mike saw TV coverage of someone with red hair being carried out of Norris Hall. At that point he said, "We have to go; we have to go now."

Before leaving they called the local Smithfield police to tell them where they would be and how to reach them in case they had any news of their daughter. They also left a message on their home phone answering machine telling Nicole or anyone who phoned that they were headed for Blacksburg—Tricia left her cell phone number on the message. Reporters called the White's home and later used that cell phone number to harass the Whites.

A friend drove Tricia, Mike, and Evan to Blacksburg. The day was dark and rainy. All the way Mike kept saying to himself, "God you are in control now." He hoped against hope that God would hear him and Nicole would be spared, but inside he had a sinking feeling she was gone. He had a terrible, terrible stifling feeling that he was in the midst of a life-changing event, something from which he might never fully recover. It was suffocating him.

When the Whites got to the campus, they went immediately to the Inn at Virginia Tech and Skelton Conference Center, which had been set up as the focal point for dealing with the crisis. At the reception desk Tricia identified herself and asked to see Nicole. The person behind the reception desk checked some papers and then said, "Please follow us."

They were taken to a bank of elevators.

Both Tricia and Mike remember the elevator door opening and a man emerged sobbing. Tricia remembers saying, "Please don't take me there. Don't take me to where he was; don't take me there."

But the Whites were taken there, they were taken to a small room with a table and aluminum chairs. By now, both were in a state of near panic. Neither one can remember how many people were in the room or who they were other than a female doctor.

Tricia kept repeating louder and louder, "Where is someone from Virginia Tech?" They would soon learn, just as the Goddards and the Pohles were learning, that the "someones" from Virginia Tech would be few and far between. And when the "someone" did come, he was ill equipped to deal with them and the situation.

Mike remembers people trying to calm Tricia down. Nicole's boyfriend arrived and confirmed that she was in the German class where the shootings took place. A doctor who was present kept trying to reassure Tricia saying, "Maybe she is dazed, traumatized and walking around. Maybe she is with friends seeking comfort." The doctor said she would call hospitals to see if there was any word about Nicole.

Tricia and Mike had the sinking feeling that the doctor was just stalling for time and trying to make it look as if something was being done. Deep inside they both knew Nicole was gone, and they knew that everyone in the room knew that. They felt they were being lied to. They would continue to feel that way for months, and feel that way to this day.

Tricia kept getting louder and louder and said if no one had any answers she would go to Norris Hall. She would go there; she would find Nicole. Someone in the room dissuaded her—they don't remember whom—saying the authorities would not allow anyone into the crime scene. Late that night, Mark McNamee, the Provost, came in, but had next to nothing to say of any value. Captain Chumley of the Virginia State Police then volunteered that there would be no answers that night and suggested they try to get some sleep.

The Whites were taken to a room in the Inn with one king-sized bed for the three of them. It was around 11:30p. m.. About one half-hour later, Tricia's two brothers, Mark Gallagher and Tom Gallagher, arrived and all five stayed in the same room. They would doze briefly, but no one could sleep. Even if they could have slept, there were interruptions. Several times throughout the night, in a callous disregard for the anxiety the family was experiencing, reporters called Tricia's cell phone asking about their daughter.

Throughout those first hours on April 16th, as the dead were being identified, the families—including the Whites and Pohles—frantically kept trying to reach their children on cell phones. The result was a macabre sound of the dead students' and faculty members' cell phones ringing, echoing through the empty corridors of Norris Hall. The smell of gunpowder and death hung in the air. The sound was a pall hanging over the bodies of two beautiful young people, Michael Pohle and Nicole White. Michael had died apparently in a vain effort to shield Nicole White from multiple bullets that tore life from the vivacious, spirited young woman. The two students lay together in death's embrace, an embrace that would unite the Pohle and White families forever.

On the morning of April 17th, the Whites were put in a different room. By 10:30 a.m. there was still no word about Nicole. Tricia's sister, Kathleen Field, had now arrived, as had their minister and their church's youth pastor. Sometime around 11:00 a.m. the female doctor who had been with them the night before, Provost McNamee, and the police came in the room with the terrible news that Nicole was dead. She had been shot multiple times, including once in the head.

There are no words to describe the impact. The three cried with the depth and intensity that can only be brought about by the death of a child and a beloved sister.

The Whites were on an emotional roller coaster, all the time crying harder than they had ever cried in their lives. Mike kept saying to himself, "This is not fair." His grief was overpowering, he was grasping for air and felt guilt as he kept asking, "God, why couldn't this have been someone else? Why a child that is going down the right path? She was doing all the right things."

For the Whites, much of the rest of that day was lost in a tidal wave of incredible emotional pain. They do remember a meeting for the families with school President Steger late that morning, but there was nothing Steger could say or do that could give them solace. They remember a contrite school president responded to a question from a father whose daughter was among the victims. The man asked, "Who is in charge?" To which Steger responded, "I am." Then, to the father's follow-up question, "Who is responsible for all this," Steger hesitatingly and reluctantly said, "I am," an answer he would begin to deny and retreat from almost immediately.

The school sent the manager of the school cafeteria to be the official liaison with the Whites. Nicole had worked at the cafeteria and he knew her quite well. The problem was he too was traumatized and ill equipped to answer their questions. Every time they would ask something, he would go away to find the answer. This was not his fault; it was just another example of the school's poor handling of the families. When the Whites complained, Tech named someone from the Office of Admissions, but even the resulting interaction, while better, was superficial and lacking.

The police explained the delay in identifying Nicole was because she apparently had someone else's identification in her hand. The Whites remember the doctor theorizing that Nicole, who was a medic, was trying to help someone and therefore had that person's I.D. in her hand. But, as with so much the Whites were told, this explanation simply did not make sense from the position of the bodies. And indeed one of the investigating police officers later told the Whites that he doubted that story because Nicole's wounds were so severe, particularly the head wound, she would not have been able to help anyone. The inaccuracies just kept coming.

The Whites were told there would have to be an autopsy. Nicole was an organ donor, but the police said that would not be allowed because this was a crime scene. Was this a fabrication or riding roughshod over family wishes—or both? Was this a lie? When Angela Dales was killed at the

Appalachian School of Law five years earlier, her organs had been donated and that was a crime scene.

There were more frustrations, more delays and more meaningless meetings. The police were still not satisfied with the identification of Nicole and wanted more. They wanted fingerprints. Tricia's two bothers found and took the police to their niece's car and gave law enforcement officers access to Nicole's apartment in order to take the prints they needed.

By Thursday, most of the families had left. But the Whites were still waiting; they were waiting for Nicole's body to be released. The Whites would not leave the campus without their daughter; there had been enough double-talk, they wanted Nicole. There seemed to be no one who could tell them when they would get their daughter. The inability or unwillingness to provide families with access to accurate information shaped the defining moment for yet another family.

The Whites had been the last of the victims' families to arrive on campus; they would be the last to leave.

*   *   *

Truth is the one thing that the families of the victims of these school shootings need more than anything else. They need to know what was their loved one was doing or saying before he or she was gunned down. The families need to know things such as who found my child, where was he or she taken, was anything done to try and save him or her. They need to know every little detail. I am not sure why, but it helps the surviving family members if they are able to reconstruct the last few moments of their loved one's life.

Truth, however, is rarely what the families get. In the case of Virginia Tech, the dishonesty that the Pohles, Goddards, and Whites encountered would only grow. The recognition of the fact was the defining moment. It was not bad enough that their children had been wounded or killed—they were being lied to. With the power and pocket book of the state of Virginia, school officials and politicians almost immediately embarked on what has to be one of the most expensive and widespread cover ups in academic history. It is this cover up, and how the families fought against it, that I will explore throughout the rest of the book—beginning with the Governor's Review Panel Report.

CHAPTER VI

THE GOVERNOR'S REVIEW PANEL REPORT

(AND TRIDATA, THE HIRED GUN)

*"The right to search for the truth implies also a duty; one
must not conceal any part of what one has recognized to be the truth."*
~Albert Einstein, German-born theoretical physicist

"I know of no formula for evil that is surer than sloppy research ... ,"
~Sherman Kent, World War II intelligence officer and
the father of U.S. modern intelligence analysis

By the time it was done, the Governor's Review Panel Report (*The Addendum*) on the shooting rampage at Virginia Tech cost the taxpayers around three-quarters of a million dollars. In the final analysis the document is a testimony to the willingness of a large number of Virginians in positions of trust to engage in half-truths and even lies to protect their careers and thwart legal action. The report is specious—it is, in many respects, impotent. On the surface it looks good; the goals, as laid out by the governor, are excellent. But upon close examination, the report is stunningly flawed. Some of the most damning evidence against Virginia Tech, Virginia law enforcement officials, and the politicians in Richmond is missing in the error-ridden report's content and in the circumstances surrounding its writing. Furthermore, the report writers were at the mercy of Virginia Tech for much of their information. For example, school officials insisted that they had to clear all those speaking to the panel. No one would accept a suspect who had veto power over who the police could interview on a case, but somehow this arrangement was accepted when the review panel was set up.

2007 **(April 19) Governor Kaine appointed an independent Virginia Tech Review Panel to review the shootings.** The panel was headed by retired Virginia State Police Superintendent Colonel Gerald Massengill.

2007 **(August 30)** Governor Kaine held a press conference where he publicly released the review panel's findings. **The initial report was written by Arlington, Virginia-based TriData and cost over $600,000.**

2008 **(June 7)** Judge Theodore J. Markov approved a settlement of $11 million against the state of Virginia.

2008 **(October 16)** The first of a series of meetings between the victims' families and school officials/politicians is held. Virginia Tech Chief of Police Wendell Flinchum is the main presenter. **Flinchum admits to the families that a "person of interest" was not identified until after the interview with Heather Haugh began at 8:16 am—not at 7:30 am as stated in the Governor's Review Panel Report. The admission of this critical error came** *after the families settled with the state* **and would not be corrected for another 14 months in the revised Review Panel Report—** *The Addendum.*

2008 **(November 22-23)** The second meeting covered two days and was with school president, Charles Steger, and members of his administration. President Steger entered and exited the meeting through a side door. At no time did Steger mingle with the families. At no time did Steger or a member of his administration say they did anything wrong or that they would have done anything differently. **For the first time, the specific wording of the school's timely warning procedure was read. Sitting in the back of the room was Peter Messitt, Assistant Attorney General for Virginia,**

> who would be the state's lead attorney for the state in Pryde/Peterson trial against the state in March 2012. Governor Kaine did not respond or commit to anything other than to say he was open to fixing the report.
>
> 2009 **(November)** A revised report was published, but it too contained errors.
>
> 2009 **(December)** A second and last revision of the Governor's Review Panel Report is issued. But that report also contained errors. **TriData was paid an additional $75,000 for the two revisions which were largely based on the investigative work of the victims' families and the news media. Apparently the state had no clause in its contract with TriData to fix errors at no cost.**
>
> 2011 **(March 11) The Department of Education fined Virginia Tech $55,000** for waiting too long to notify the campus community following the initial double homicide at West Ambler Johnston Hall. Virginia Tech appealed the ruling and the fine.
>
> 2012 **(March 29)** Department of Education Administrative Judge Canellos overturns the $55,000 fine against Virginia Tech.
>
> 2012 **(September 1)** Secretary of Education Arne Duncan overrules Judge Canellos and reinstates a fine against Virginia Tech of $27,500.

Some might say that small errors and inconsistencies creep in to any large work; however, the report has a basic flaw that is so serious that it undermines the credibility of much of the document and the people who wrote it. This flaw, in and of itself, is a testimony to the lack of thoroughness and professionalism in the document's research and writing. The flaw is so fundamentally important to the investigation that leaving it uncorrected puts into question whether any investigation was done by TriData at all. The flaw shows that TriData was not able to even simply record what multiple witnesses reported: the location and time that the killer, Seung Hui Cho, committed suicide.

Survivors were in the room when Cho committed suicide in the front of the French class, right after he heard the police use a shotgun to blast open the lock of a Norris Hall entrance.

Here are excerpts from the Governor's Review Panel Report 9:45 a.m. timeline entry. "Cho returns to room 211, the French class, and goes up one aisle and down another, shooting people again. Cho shoots Goddard two more times. ... Cho (then) tries to enter room 204 where Liviu Librescu is teaching Mechanics. Professor Librescu braces his body against the door yelling for students to head for the windows. He is shot through the door. Students push out screens and jump or drop to grass or bushes below the window. Ten students escape this way. The next two students trying to escape are shot. Cho returns again to room 206 (the graduate engineering class in Advanced Hydraulics) and shoots more students."

The 9:51 a.m. entry reads: "Cho shoots himself in the head just as the police reach the second floor. ..." The timeline is botched up. Cho *did not* leave the French class and go to rooms 204 and 206. Cho was in those rooms *before* he committed suicide in room 211.

A timeline is the most important part of any crime scene analysis. Indeed, all analyses flows from the time-sequence of events. Not knowing where the killer committed suicide implies either incompetence or purposeful blurring of facts, and could indicate an effort to make the report less useful to those who would seek to analyze the crime independently. This error in the Governor's Review Panel Report is critical and casts serious doubt on the report as a whole.

Here is another example of a flaw in the timeline. This one, being an error of omission, seems even more likely to be an attempt on the part of TriData to keep their clients, Virginia Tech and the state of Virginia, out of trouble:

April 16, 2007: 8:16 a.m.-9:24 a.m.: Police allow students in West Ambler Johnston Hall to leave; some go to 9:00 a.m. classes in Norris Hall. *(The timeline does not specify that students Henry Lee and Rachael Hill were allowed to leave West Ambler Johnston Hall for their 9:05 a.m. class French class in Norris Hall where they were shot and killed. The school's failure to lockdown West Ambler Johnston Hall and the deaths of Lee and Hill are critical in making a judgment about the school's reaction to the shooting—a lockdown would have saved those two lives.)*

If the above error was not serious enough to cast doubt on the report's accuracy, stop to think that when it was first published in August 2007. The errors in the initial version were so glaring and the outcry in the media and from the victims' families so great, that the report was revised— twice. The first revision was published in November of 2009 and the second revision in December of 2009. Even the second revision, *The Addendum*, did not correct all the mistakes.

The extent and magnitude of the flaws in the initial report were so serious that Governor Kaine had no choice but to go back to TriData to fix the problems. The "fix" was based primarily on the work of the victims' families—to my knowledge TriData caught none of the errors. To reiterate, the $75,000 was given to the firm to make corrections based on the work others had done. None of these errors seems to have inspired the company to go back and do their own research or fact checking. As far as I can tell, TriData was adept at printing what was handed to them, but less adept at looking at the evidence with a critical eye.

Putting it bluntly, the company that did substandard work in the first place, was then rewarded with another fee to fix what they screwed up. If the first report wasn't accurate, then TriData ought to have been fined, not rewarded with more money. But that argument assumes that TriData was not doing exactly what it had been paid to do. You have to ask yourself, "Was TriData the hired gun to shoot down truth and accountability?"

The report, even with the revisions, will probably go down in history as a poorly researched, poorly analyzed, and poorly written document. What a shame. Even in the best light, the report can only be seen as a missed opportunity to do something to help prevent school shootings. For example, the Review Panel Report does not address problems central to the causes behind the shooting and shies away from making the tough recommendations needed to get at the heart of the problem and prevent future shootings on school grounds. In the final analysis, the reader is left with the impression that the incentive to produce a candid and objective report was low.

$*$ $*$ $*$

The process of producing the report was flawed at every turn. TriData was apparently chosen because it had done a report for the Department of Homeland Security on Columbine. The problem is the Columbine report is something very different. The first two sentences on page one of TriData's Columbine report make that clear. "This report is an analysis of the fire service and emergency medical services (EMS) operations and the overall response to the assault on Columbine High School at Littleton, Colorado, on April 20, 1999. Incident command, special operations, and mass casualty emergency medical services are featured." TriData's work at Columbine was *not* an analysis of the crime itself.

The Virginia Tech report was *never* meant to be an analysis of the fire service and emergency medical services. The Virginia Tech report was intended to be a far broader document—an analysis of the worst campus shooting in this nation's history. The following is a direct quote from *The Addendum*—the name given the final version of the Governor's Review

Panel Report on Virginia Tech. The quote is taken from Governor Kaine's executive order directing the panel to accomplish the following:

1. "Conduct a review of how Seung Hui Cho committed these 32 murders and multiple additional woundings, including without limitation how he obtained his firearms and ammunition, and learn what can be learned about what caused him to commit these acts of violence."

2. "Conduct a review of Seung Hui Cho's psychological condition and behavioral issues prior to and at the time of the shootings, what behavioral aberrations or potential warning signs were observed by students, faculty and/or staff at Westfield High School and Virginia Tech. This inquiry should include the response taken by Virginia Tech and others to note psychological and behavioral issues, Seung Hui Cho's interaction with the mental health delivery system, including without limitation judicial intervention, access to services, and communication between the mental health services system and Virginia Tech. It should also include a review of educational, medical, and judicial records documenting his condition, the services rendered to him, and his commitment hearing."

3. "Conduct a review of the timeline of events from the time that Seung Hui Cho entered West Ambler Johnston Dormitory until his death in Norris Hall. Such review shall include an assessment of the response to the first murders and efforts to stop the Norris Hall murders once they began."

4. "Conduct a review of the response of the Commonwealth, all of its agencies, and relevant local and private providers following the death of Seung Hui Cho for the purpose of providing recommendations for the improvement of the Commonwealth's response in similar emergency situations. Such review shall include an assessment of the emergency medical response provided for the injured and wounded, the conduct of post-mortem examinations and release of remains, on-campus actions following the tragedy, and the services and counseling offered to the victims, the victims' families,

and those affected by the incident. In so doing, the Review Panel shall to the extent required by federal or state law: (i) protect the confidentiality of any individual's or family member's personal or health information; and (ii) make public or publish information and findings only in summary or aggregate form without identifying personal or health information related to any individual or family member unless authorization is obtained from an individual or family member that specifically permits the Review Panel to disclose that person's personal or health information."

5. "Conduct other inquiries as may be appropriate in the Review Panel's discretion other- wise consistent with its mission and authority as provided herein."

6. "Based on these inquiries, make recommendations on appropriate measures that can be taken to improve the laws, policies, procedures, systems and institutions of the Commonwealth and the operation of public safety agencies, medical facilities, local agencies, private providers, universities, and mental health services delivery system."

In other words, the Review Panel was tasked to review the events, assess actions taken and not taken, identify lessons learned, and propose alternatives for the future. The panel was intended to review Cho's history and interaction with the mental health and legal systems and of his gun purchases. "The Review Panel was also asked to review the emergency response by all parties (law enforcement officials, university officials, medical responders and hospital care providers, and the Medical Examiner). Finally, the Review Panel reviewed the aftermath—the university's approach to helping families, survivors, students, and staff as they dealt with the mental trauma and the approach to helping the university heal itself and function again."

But if you look at the credentials of the head of TriData, Philip Schaenman, you find a man whose background is limited and does not include much in terms of the requirements as laid out by Governor Kaine. If you google Schaenman, one of the entries is entitled: "Fireman, Philip Schaenman." His background includes fire administration and he is "known to the fire community for leading studies and research on first responder issues," according to the Web site for TriData, whose products include titles such as "Fire in the United States" and "International Concepts in

Fire Protection." The question is, do you send a fireman to analyze mass murder? You certainly don't send a policeman to analyze or put out a fire.

Indeed, the Columbine report is a better report than TriData's effort on Virginia Tech, probably because it deals with an area that TriData knows something about—emergency responses by fire and medical services. The Columbine report never analyzes the warning signs or the actions of people in positions of authority prior to April 20, 1999, which was one of the principal mandates at Virginia Tech.

That said, there are sections of the Columbine report that do pertain to the Virginia Tech tragedy. Inexplicably, though, these sections are not sufficiently developed in the Tech report. For example, the Columbine report repeatedly refers to the importance of the Incident Command System (ICS) in responding to a crisis. While the Columbine report refers to ICS with reference to fire service personnel managing major incidents and crises, a major flaw at Virginia Tech was the poor management at the ICS-equivalent level. Given the emphasis on the role of the ICS in the Columbine report, it is puzzling why TriData did not put greater emphasis on that aspect of the Virginia Tech report. There was mismanagement and poor decision-making on the part of Tech's command structure after the double homicide at West Ambler Johnston—of that there is no doubt. This mismanagement contributed to the murder of 30 more people at Norris Hall nearly two and one-half hours later. TriData never addresses this critical point, but both the Department of Education and a jury in Montgomery County, Virginia found Virginia Tech to be negligent.

The problem with the Virginia Tech report may, in fact, not be so much TriData, but then-Governor Kaine and then-Attorney General McDonnell. They apparently did not fully check out options other than TriData. For example, a far better model for the state of Virginia to follow would have been the 174-page report produced at the behest of Colorado Governor Bill Owens.

To begin with, the state of Colorado did not pay a private consulting firm that does business with Colorado to write the "official" report of the Columbine tragedy—thereby removing the specter of conflict of interest that hangs over TriData's Virginia Tech report. The Governor's Columbine Review Commission, members of which were not paid, was tasked with "the responsibility for writing, editing and assembling the Commission report for public release."

The first section of the first chapter of the Colorado report is entitled, "Investigative Obstructions Encountered by the Commission." The Colorado Governor, the report asserts, "… anticipated that it (the commission) would receive full cooperation from all governmental agencies that responded or were involved in the events surrounding the deadly assault made at Columbine High School on April 20, 1999. As a consequence, the Commission was not empowered to issue subpoenas ..."

The report then goes on to describe a litany of obstructionist behavior—much of which was repeated in Virginia. The Colorado report describes officers providing the Commission with only a "minimal description" of the Sheriff's response to the events at Columbine High School."

The Colorado report is hard-hitting in describing the lack of cooperation and is spelled out in pages seven and eight of the report:

"Although data bearing on the assaults perpetrated by Klebold and Harris at Columbine High School, including the pre-massacre tapes obtained by the Sheriff's office during its later investigations, were made available to *Time Magazine*, local news media and other groups and individuals, Sheriff John Stone repeatedly denied the Commission access to those materials, on the ground that civil litigation was pending against the sheriff and other Jefferson County Officials, commenced by victims and their families; it has been asserted that several of the defendants would be prejudiced in the course of that litigation were they to provide the data sought by the Commission. Throughout the course of the Commission's work, Sheriff Stone and the Jefferson County Sheriff's Office have been singularly uncooperative in assisting the Commission in obtaining the factual information it required, and thereby forced the Commission to acquire its facts through a series of hearings and in the course of a lengthy investigation. In short, the Commission has been unable to garner significant testimony and other relevant data from Sheriff Stone and the Sheriff's Office, the principal law enforcement agency in Jefferson County. When the Governor assigned the Commission its duties, he did not anticipate that information would be withheld which would assist the Commission in completing an accurate and analytical review of the events at Columbine on April 20, 1999, so that the requested recommendations could be made to the Governor."

Compare the Colorado report's handling of lack of cooperation on the part of law enforcement with the way TriData touched on the same subject.

"... due to the sensitive nature of portions of the law enforcement investigatory records and due to law enforcement's concerns about not setting a precedent with regard to the release of raw information from investigation files, the panel received extensive briefings and summaries from law enforcement officials about their investigations rather than reviewing those files directly. ..."

The Addendum asserts that Cho should not have been allowed to buy a gun, yet his name was not on the list prohibiting gun sales. Whose responsibility is it to put those names on the list? Law enforcement. The panel was never allowed to look at the actual documents pertaining to this vital aspect of the case.

Page seven of *The Addendum*, addresses this point glossing over the obstructionism:

"Finally, with respect to Cho's firearms purchases, the Virginia State Police, the ATF, and the gun dealers each declined to provide the panel with copies of the applications Cho completed when he bought his weapons or of other records relating to any background check that may have occurred in connection with those purchases. The Virginia State Police, however, did describe the contents of Cho's gun purchase applications to members of the panel and its staff."

Then-Governor Kaine and then-Attorney General McDonnell bought this obstructionism hook, line, and sinker. They never said a word.

When TriData's initial report was presented to Governor Kaine in late August 2007, at a cost of over $600,000 the problems with the document were readily apparent. The number of revisions, clarifications, and additions to the timeline alone was, by my count, over 20. That number adds to the indictment of the initial report.

The state was apparently in such a hurry to get the report out, that it made no provision for errors, omissions, and corrections. This glaring oversight by then-Governor Kaine and then-Attorney General McDonnell (and their legal staffs) may be explained by the cozy relationship that exists between the state and TriData. TriData was already doing business with Virginia when it was hired to write the Virginia Tech report. The conflict of interest is readily apparent—the state of Virginia hired a company that already relied on part of its income coming from contracts with the state, to write a report analyzing whether or not the state's largest university was in any way at fault (and thereby liable) in the massacre on April 16, 2007. It is stupefying that two career lawyers, then-Governor Kaine and then-Attorney General McDonnell, did not see this point.

Remember, TriData has had at least one other contract with the state of Virginia and probably will be bidding for more. Did Governor Kaine's office look at other qualified individuals or firms? Or, did Virginia's government go with a firm with whom the state already had business relations and on whom the state could count to come up with the right analysis?

For their part, it is hard to believe that TriData would want to kill the cash-cow (Virginia) by writing a critical report. Indeed, a report that would seem to exonerate the state's largest university and the school's president from any wrong-doing might endear TriData to the power elite in Richmond. Even if TriData had not previously done business with the state, they might have been angling for future contracts. Then-Governor Kaine and then-Attorney General McDonnell should have bent over backwards to ensure there was no cloud of suspicion hanging over the firm the state chose to write the Virginia Tech report. That they did not, and in fact paid yet more money for corrections to a report that should have been above reproach the first time, gives the worst possible impression.

*   *   *

TriData must have thought it hit the jackpot when it got the Virginia Tech contract. Take a look at the *hourly rates* the state was willing to pay the company. The figures are taken from an August 17, 2009 letter from Mark E. Rubin, Counselor for the Governor, to Philip Schaeman, President of TriData. When you look at the letter you see that the name Philip Schaeman is crossed out and "Phil" is written in by hand—implying a degree of familiarity between Rubin and Schaeman. The seriousness of the issue at hand and the magnitude of the crime, coupled with the fact that hundreds of thousands of taxpayers' dollars were being spent, dictated professional correspondence—not casualness. Here is the pay scale:

"TriData's fee . . . will be based upon the applicable standard government hourly rates for TriData personnel performing the services as follows:

- Corporate Program Director $230.00
- Deputy Program Director $150.00
- Senior Program Specialist $ 86.00
- Program Specialist $ 55.00
- Intern $ 40.00
- Senior Communications & Media Specialist $125.00
- Senior Public Safety specialist $137.00
- Public Safety Specialist $ 80.00
- Senior Specialty Consultant $323.00"

It is a generally accepted legal principle that when money exchanges hands in a business relationship, the person or organization receiving the money owes primary allegiance to the person or organization paying the money. Indeed, the original letter to TriData, dated April 26, 2007, cited the company's past working relationship with the chairman of the panel, Col. Gerald Massengill, as reason for hiring TriData.

The breakdown of expenses paid to TriData is troubling. For example, what is a "Senior Communications & Media Specialist?" Isn't that a public relations officer? Why did TriData need to pay a public relations person $125.00 an hour and only pay a "Public Safety Specialist" $80.00 an hour? The report is all about public safety on our campuses, yet TriData and the state of Virginia apparently were willing to spend more on a spin-doctor than on a safety expert.

The letter lists a total of nine categories of TriData officers who will be involved in the report. The rate of pay is highly questionable. For example, the Corporate Program Director was being paid $230.00 an hour. Why was someone called a "Senior Specialty Consultant" being paid $323.00 and just what is a "Senior Specialty Consultant?" Did the state agree to such a pay scale without asking for an explanation of who was getting this money and what specifically he or she would do to earn the money?

The Addendum never really addresses the question of responsibility and accountability. Indeed, TriData makes just enough revisions to give them the fig leaf of being able to say, "We listened to the families; we made revisions." Did they really? Ok, let's lift up the fig leaf and take a look at one of the revisions.

In fact, the panel seemed to go off on tangents and interviewed at least one expert who added little insight to *gun violence on campuses and school grounds*. Dr. Jerald Kay is a case in point. Here is the explanation for including Dr. Kay in the report:

"The panel heard a presentation from Dr. Jerald Kay, the chair of the committee on college mental health of the American Psychiatric Association about the large percentage of college students who binge drink each year (about 44 percent), and the surprisingly large percentage of students who claim they thought about suicide (10 percent). College years are full of academic and social stress. The probability of dying from a shooting on campus is smaller than the probability of dying from auto accidents, falls, or alcohol and drug overdoses."

Even with this explanation, the relevancy of the testimony of Dr. Jerald Kay on the frequency of shootings on campus is especially puzzling. What was the purpose of interviewing him? Were his words an attempt to downplay the seriousness of the Virginia Tech shootings in light of other dangers to students such as drunk driving? Here is TriData's excuse for including Kay's words:

"The Review Panel invited Dr. Kay's presentation for two reasons: First to consider the risk from guns as part of the larger picture of campus emergency planning. The Review Panel wanted colleges and universities to consider, as part of emergency planning, the whole range of threats and their likelihood, not just guns. Second, this testimony was of interest as part of the discussion of whether guns should be allowed to be carried on campuses. The frequency and nature of shootings on campus was very relevant to the deliberations of the Review Panel in making recommendations regarding these issues. It also was relevant in understanding the risk of a further shooting faced by the Policy Group after the double homicide."

1. Nowhere does the report state that Dr. Kay says anything about guns as part of emergency planning.
2. If the frequency and nature of shootings on campus was relevant to the Review Panel deliberations, why is Dr. Kay not quoted on the subject?
3. What insight did Dr. Kay provide on understanding the risk of a further shooting faced by the Policy Group after the double homicide?

Is TriData trying to tell us that binge drinking played a role in the killings at Virginia Tech? As for the sentence: "The probability of dying from a shooting on a campus is smaller than the probability of dying from auto accidents, falls, or alcohol and drug overdose." What possible reason could there be for this sentence in the report other than to downplay the significance of gun violence on campuses?

TriData's response is that they wanted colleges and universities to examine the whole range of threats. Fine, but that was not the Panel's overwhelming priority and responsibility, nor was it the duty to emphasize those threats at the expense of analyzing the Virginia Tech shootings. There is nothing in the Panel's mission statement telling them to go into a broader range of campus threats. Here is the Review Panel's Mission Statement:

> "The Panel's mission is to provide an independent, thorough, and objective incident review of this tragic event, including a review of educational laws, policies, and institutions, the public safety and health care procedures and responses and the mental health delivery system. With respect to these areas of review, the Panel should focus on what went right, what went wrong, what practices should be considered best practices, and what practices are in need of improvement. This review should include examination of information contained in academic, health and court records and by information obtained through interviews with knowledgeable individuals. Once that factual narrative is in place and questions have been answered, the Panel should offer recommendations for improvement in light of those facts and circumstances."

Are we saying the interview was worthless? Not necessarily, although it is hard to tell when exact quotes are not included in the text. What we are saying is that the inclusion of Dr. Kay was a misplaced band-aid attempting to cover the massive gaps left by some notable absences. The Panel interviewed Dr. Jerald Kay, but look at the list of key individuals they did not interview:

1. Dr. Robert Miller, the director of the Cook Counseling Center at the time Cho was taken to Carilion St. Albans Psychiatric Hospital. He was the man who "accidently" took Cho's medical records home, meaning those records were not available to the Review Panel nor to the families before they settled with the state.

2. Kim O'Rourke and Lisa Wilkes, both of whom took notes at the Policy Group meeting the morning of April 16, 2007. Those notes indicate the police on the scene at West Ambler Johnston Hall advised there was no need to warn the campus. The police liaison with the Policy Group during this time was Virginia Tech Police Chief Wendell Flinchum.

3. Heather Haugh, the roommate of murdered student Emily Hilscher. Haugh was the one who identified Hilsher's boyfriend, Karl Thornhill. An interview of Haugh would have pinned down the time Thornhill was identified as a person of interest.

4. Karl Thornhill, Emily Hilscher's boyfriend, was never interviewed by the panel.

5. Ralph Byers, a participant in the Policy Group, who at 8:45 a.m. sent an email to Laura Fornash in Richmond telling her not to release details of the shooting.

For those who say the families should now move on, we ask, "How can anyone move on when their child has been gunned down and there is a cover-up? How can anyone move on when he or she knows that there are lies of omission dealing with the death of a child?" I want to ask then-Governor Kaine, then-Attorney General McDonnell, Virginia Tech President Charles Steger, Virginia Tech Chief of Police Wendell Flinchum, and members of the Virginia Tech school administration, the review panel, and the people at TriData, "Did you really read the Review Panel's Report? If you did, why did you remain silent about this incredibly flawed document?"

Many of the original report's flaws stem from decisions made before a word of it was written. In the first place, the idea of a state-sponsored panel investigating a state institution is a conflict of interest—I have said that before, but it bears repeating. That conflict of interest probably explains why the report does not hold anyone accountable for anything. Furthermore, from the outset, the credibility of the Review Panel and their report was undermined because of the failure of the review panel to have subpoena power (just as in the case of Colorado) and the inability of the panel to have people interviewed under oath. The justification for hiring TriData was their experience with the Columbine shooting, so surely someone should have been aware enough to learn the lessons that the Columbine report stated so clearly that in the wake of tragedy, people will try to protect themselves from blame. Without the power to subpoena, the review panel simply had no teeth.

The systemic flaws in the panel itself play out in the Virginia Tech report. There appear to be eight major failings:

First, the report did not address issues such as identifying mistakes in judgment and the individuals who should be held accountable for their actions or inactions. Indeed, the report is an exercise in avoiding accountability and legal liability.

Second, the panel itself, which investigated the tragedy and wrote the report, is a prime example of conflict of interest. A state panel examining the behavior of state employees and a state organization cannot be completely objective. To even suggest that the panel was completely objective is sheer folly—particularly when the state was so well represented and not one member of the victims' families was a panel member. Instead, there is the state-selected family representative and spokesperson on the panel—again, a conflict of interest that is not conducive to impartiality.

Third, several key players did not fully cooperate with the review panel. This lack of cooperation is both disheartening and puzzling. Specifically, the Virginia State Police, the ATF, and the gun dealers "declined to provide the panel with copies of the applications" Seung Hui Cho completed when he bought the weapons that would eventually kill over thirty innocent people. The report notes that "the Virginia State Police ... did describe the contents of Cho's gun purchase applications to members of the panel and its staff." The state police's willingness to "describe" is a limp attempt to explain their failure to fully cooperate and provide the panel with documents related to the shootings and is a major flaw in the report—it is inexcusable.

Fourth, the report repeatedly falls back on passive voice sentences that obscure who did what and when; who knew what and when; and who acted and didn't act. The authors of the report carefully chose their words in order not to identify any individual by name.

Fifth, the panel was impeded in its work by the FOIA rules that did not allow more than two members to meet together or speak by phone without it being considered a public meeting. This is bureaucracy at its worst. The report needs to be more specific in detailing the problems this bureaucratic obstacle presented.

Sixth, the report sugar-coats glaring errors and problems: for example, on page 10, the report talks about its findings and recommendations being of two different kinds: "What was done well," and "what could have been done better." The report should talk about people in positions of authority <u>failing</u> to do their jobs.

Seventh, the report appears to make excuses for the decision of the university's Policy Group not to put out a campus-wide alert following the discovery of the first two bodies. But the previous August, the university had put out an alert that a convict named William Morva had escaped from a nearby prison and killed a law enforcement officer and a guard. The alert indicated that the murderer was on the loose and could be on campus. The university set its own standard in August of 2006 by issuing that alert, and then violated that standard in April 2007. The report skirts this critical point.

Eighth, a former head of the state police should not have chaired the panel. Here again is another example of a conflict of interest. The result appears to have been a downplaying of the mistakes made by the police on the day of the shooting—and probably mistakes they made in not placing Cho's name on the list of those people prohibited from buying guns.

In connection with systemic flaw eight, the report says that the police *may* have made an error in reaching the premature conclusion that their initial lead (following the discovery of the first two shooting victims) was a good one and that the person of interest was probably not on campus. *May* have made an error? They *did make a very serious error* by jumping to a premature conclusion and giving the wrong impression to school officials. I have examined in detail this fatal mistake in Chapter II.

In sum, the report fails to do its job in critical areas; it is bland, and raises no real red flags. The report is the equivalent of reading a book with no thesis. The recommendations indicate this or that "should" be done. The "shoulds" relate to such things as analyzing, training, complying with this or that act, police being members of panels, and so on and so forth. Yes, these "shoulds" need to be done. But, nowhere does the report say that individuals must (or even should) be held accountable for their actions or inactions; that organizations and individuals must be held accountable when they break their own standards and it results in over 30 lives being lost.

The report, then, falls short of what it needed to do: make clear that everyone in a position of responsibility must be held to the highest standards of safety, and that failure to meet those standards will result in stiff penalties. Instead, the reader is left wandering from page to page in an effort to tie ends together and make his or her own conclusions.

There are structural flaws in the report centering on the *Key Findings and Recommendations*. Most people who look at a report this size will only read those two parts. Professional writers are taught to put one or both of these sections at the beginning of the chapters or the report itself because it is a well-known principle among professional writers that the Key Findings and Recommendations are the meat. By placing them at the end, and by watering them down, the writers are weakening the significance of the key findings and recommendations. In other words, the report is written more as an on-going investigative report, rather than an analysis of a major crime. TriData Corporation employs professional writers who presumably know this.

Now, let's take a look at the specifics that typify errors found throughout the report. A major concern is the apparent selection of words in the report to downplay failings and mistakes. For example, the topic sentence on page 18 in the paragraph in the middle of the page needs to be replaced:

Original Sentence	Reasons for Replacing	My Replacement Sentences
"Shootings at universities are rare events, an average of 16 a year across 4,000 institutions."	Reason: To correct the report's downplaying of the seriousness of the threat and to be factually correct. Site: The Journal of College and University Law, a peer-reviewed journal published by the Notre Dame Law School, Professor Helen de Haven, "The Elephant in the Ivory Tower: Rampages in Higher Education and the Case for Institutional Liability," —the citation for the article is 35 JC&UL 503, 2009.	"Shootings at universities are becoming more and more frequent and now average 16 a year across 4,000 institutions. Even before the rampage at Virginia Tech, a growing body of legal opinion held that the nation's colleges and universities have a legal and moral responsibility to protect students, faculty and staff."

Another example is found on page 52—here, **The Key Findings** need to be rewritten to accurately reflect the magnitude of the school's failings. These failings are documented on pages 46 through 52:

Original Sentence	Reasons for Replacing	My Replacement Sentences
"The lack of information sharing among academic, administrative, and public safety entities at Virginia Tech and the students who had raised concerns about Cho, contributed to the failure to see the big picture."	Reason: vague language, inaccurate reflection of the magnitude of the failings and over use of platitudes such as "big picture."	The numerous failings of Virginia Tech to respond to warning signs that Cho was a serious threat to himself and others should not, and cannot, be glossed over. Members of the school administration and campus police failed to heed the warnings and take the initiative to head-off what became the nation's worst school shooting. There were at least five complaints about Cho's threatening behavior that reached the ears of campus police and or school administrators. Overly strict, and at times incorrect, interpretations of federal and state privacy laws combined with bureaucratic ineptitude to make the shooting rampage possible.

There are also discrepancies in logic and reasoning that need to be reconciled. For example on page 43 the reader will no doubt be confused over what constitutes a threat. In the left hand column, first full paragraph, third sentence through the end of the paragraph reads: "She (Dr. Giovanni) contacted the head of the English Department, Dr. Roy, about Cho and warned that if he were not removed from her class, she would resign. He was not just a difficult student, she related, he was not working at all. Dr. Giovanni was offered security, but declined saying she did not want him back in class period. She saw him once on campus after that and he just stared at the ground." Here is the problem: if a professor is threatening to resign because she feels threatened, then Frances Keene, Judicial Affairs director, needs to give a better explanation of why Cho's threatening behavior was not actionable under the abusive conduct-threats.

In fact, all of page 43 is confusing and is intellectual mumbo-jumbo—it may have been intentionally written that way to hide the shortcomings and failures of the school to act.

The report's excessive use of passive voice sentences appears to be intentional and meant to obscure. Passive voice sentences are the preferred sentences of members of the legal profession because they allow for greater courtroom interpretation and argumentation. In an historical document such as this, passive voice sentences should not be used, unless the writer has no other choice.

Let's take a look at a couple of examples. Look at page 43 and how the passive voice is intended to hide who knew what: "However, it is known that the university did not contact the family to ascertain the veracity of home town follow-up for counseling and medication management." Known by whom? Was the individual or department responsible for this failure ever questioned?

Professor Lucinda Roy, in her book *No Right to Remain Silent*, gives an excellent example of passive voice sentences obscuring information. When referring to Vice Provost of Student Affairs David Ford's statement to the panel on May 21, 2007, she writes, "As Ford revealed in his prepared statement, the president and the Policy Group were advised by the police that a suspect was being tracked—slain student Emily Hilscher's boyfriend." The prepared statement reads:

*"Information continued **to be received** through frequent telephone conversations with Virginia Tech police on the scene. The Policy Group **was informed** that the residence hall was being secured by Virginia Tech police, and students within the hall **were notified** and asked to remain in their rooms for their safety. We **were further informed** that the room containing the gunshot victims **was immediately secured** for evidence collection, and Virginia Tech police began questioning hall residents and*

identifying potential witnesses. In the preliminary stages of the investigation, it appeared to be an isolated incident, possibly domestic in nature." (Pages 81 and 82 of the Review Panel Report.)

Roy then adds, "When the passive voice is used in sentence construction it is hard to pin down who the subject is… Usually teachers of writing try to dissuade students from using the passive voice construction because it tends to result in accounts that lack specificity and removes a subject from his or her own action, as it does in this case."

The TriData Corporation specializes in report writing—they knew exactly what they were doing. TriData may have been following instructions, or did not want to be too specific and alienate the state of Virginia, a state that might hire them again.

Look at the section on page 82 entitled "Decision Not To Cancel Classes or Lock Down:"

"… Most police chiefs consulted in this review believe that a lockdown was not feasible."

This statement is clearly intended to make excuses for a bad decision not to act. My questions are how many police chiefs were asked, and how many said the school should be locked down? This assertion that police chiefs consulted "believed a lockdown was not possible" clearly indicates the police chiefs were cherry picked to ensure responses favorable to the school's inaction. In my talks with campus security representatives from colleges and universities, 100% said the school should have been locked down. The sentence also runs counter to the school's own past practices— do I have to cite the Morva incident again? In that case, the school didn't believe the killer was on the campus, yet it locked down.

On the next page (83) the excuses continue: "In the Morva incident, when the school was closed, it took over an hour and half for traffic to clear despite trying to stage the evacuation." An hour and a half is a small price to pay to save 30 lives.

The paragraphs on law enforcement records are especially disturbing.

On pages 63 and 64 your will find, "Law enforcement agencies must disclose certain information to anyone who requests it. They must disclose basic information about felony crimes: the date, location, general description of the crime, and name of the investigating officer. Law enforcement agencies also have to release the name and address of anyone arrested and charged with any type of crime. All records about non-criminal incidents are available upon request. When they disclose non-criminal incident records, law enforcement agencies must withhold personally-identifying information such as names, addresses, and social security numbers.

" ... Most of the detailed information about criminal activity is contained in law enforcement investigative files. Under Virginia's Freedom of Information Act, law enforcement agencies are *allowed* to keep these records confidential. The law also gives agencies the discretion to release the records. However, law enforcement agencies across the state typically have a policy against disclosing such records."

Many actions may be legal, such as withholding vital information in the nation's worst school shooting, but to do so is morally and ethically repugnant. *The panel should have made that point.* Furthermore, the police, in order to remove any suspicion that they did not do their job in connection with Cho's purchase of weapons, should have willingly released all documents.

Chapter VI of *The Addendum*, "Gun Purchases And Campus Policies" is important and unfortunately, it is also a disappointment. Perhaps nowhere else in the report is it as evident as it is on these pages that the panel members did not want to address critically sensitive issues.

Please take a look at page 71—"In investigating the role firearms played in the events of April 16, 2007, the panel encountered strong feelings and heated debate from the public. The panel's investigation focused on two areas: Cho's purchase of firearms and ammunition, and campus policies toward firearms. The panel recognized the deep divisions in American society regarding the ready availability of rapid fire weapons and high capacity magazines, but this issue was beyond the scope of this review." This borders on stating the obvious; how does it help? This paragraph should be dropped.

For example, on page 71 you will find, "Cho was not legally authorized to purchase his firearms, but was easily able to do so. Gun purchasers in Virginia must qualify to buy a firearm under both federal and state law. Federal law disqualified Cho from purchasing or possessing a firearm. The federal Gun Control Act, originally passed in 1968, prohibits gun purchases by anyone who has 'been adjudicated as a mental defective or who has been committed to a mental institution.' Federal regulations interpreting the act define 'adjudicated as a mental defective' as '(a) determination by a court, board, commission, or other lawful authority that a person, as a result of ... mental illness...is a danger to himself or to others.' Cho was found to be a danger to himself by a special justice of the Montgomery County General District Court on December 14, 2005. Therefore, under federal law, Cho could not purchase a firearm.

"The legal status of Cho's gun purchase under Virginia law is less clear. Like federal law, Virginia law also prohibits persons who have been adjudicated incompetent or committed to mental institutions from purchasing firearms. However, Virginia law defines the terms differently. It defines incompetency by referring to the section of Virginia Code for declaring a person incapable of caring for himself or herself. It does not specify that a person who had been found to be a danger to self or others is 'incompetent.' Because he had not been declared unable to care for himself, it does not appear that Cho was disqualified under this provision of Virginia law." The report should have done a better job of reconciling Cho's legal status to buy a gun. First the report says "under federal law, Cho could not have purchased firearms." Then it implies that there are exceptions under Virginia law. When you read the following, perhaps the reason for this lack of clarity becomes clearer.

On page 72 the issue of whether Cho should have been able to buy a gun is blurred. "This uncertainty in Virginia law carries over into the system for conducting a firearms background check. In general, nationally, before purchasing a gun from a dealer a person must go through a background check. A government agency (which government agency?) runs the name of the potential buyer through the databases of people who are disqualified from purchasing guns. If the potential purchaser is in the databases, the transaction is stopped. If not, the dealer is instructed to proceed with the sale. The agency performing the check varies by state. Some states rely on the federal government to conduct the checks. In other states, such as Virginia, the state conducts the check of both federal and state databases. In Virginia the task is given to the state police." Did the police not do their job? The report never even attempts to address that point.

Again, on page 72—"In Virginia, the Central Criminal Records Exchange (CCRE), a division of the state police is tasked with gathering criminal records and other court information that is used for the background checks. Information on mental health commitments orders 'for involuntary admission to a facility' is supposed to be sent to the CCRE by the court clerk (Was this done?) who must send all copies of the orders along with a copy of form SP 237 that provides basic information about the person who is the subject of the court order. (Was this done?) As currently drafted, the law only requires a clerk to certify a form and does not specify who should complete the form. Because of the lack of clarity in some jurisdictions (Which jurisdictions—the one where Cho bought his firearms?) it was reported to the panel that clerks in some jurisdictions do not send the information unless they receive a completed form. Recommendations to improve this aspect of the law were given in Chapter IV."

The lack of clarity continues on page 73, "The state police did not permit the panel to view copies of the forms in their investigation but indicated that Cho answered "no" to this question (Have you ever been adjudicated mentally defective, which includes having been adjudicated incompetent to manage your own affairs?) or have you ever been committed to a mental institution? It is impossible to know whether Cho understood the proper response was "yes" and whether his answers were mistakes or deliberate falsifications. In any event, the fact remains that Cho, a person disqualified from purchasing firearms, was readily able to obtain them."

Then on page 74 the reader is told, "Federal law prohibited Cho from purchasing ammunition." So, was the law broken? If so, why was no one held accountable?

The Key Findings on gun ownership and gun rights are weak and clearly represent the timidity of the panel when confronting a politically sensitive issue: gun ownership and guns rights. Indeed, the Key Findings are so weak as to be meaningless.

Now, look at page 75—The second paragraph of the Key Findings simply states the obvious, again an indication of the panel's timidity and lack of dedication to tackling difficult issues.

Original Sentences	Reasons for Replacing	My Replacement Sentence
Cho was able to kill 31 people including himself at Norris Hall in about 10 minutes with the semiautomatic handguns at his disposal. Having the ammunition in large capacity magazines facilitated his killing spree.	It simply restates the obvious and adds nothing to the findings.	Cho's ability to kill 33 people, including himself, is a clear indication of a systemic problem that permeates Virginia's legal and law enforcement system when it comes to keeping guns out of the hands of those who are a danger to themselves and others.

On the same page, the third and final paragraph of the Key Findings needs to be completely rewritten:

Original Sentences	Reasons for Replacing	My Replacement Sentences
There is confusion on the part of universities as to what their rights are for setting policy regarding	It does not address Virginia Tech specifically, and is in fact far too general in every	Virginia Tech has one of the tougher policy constraints among Virginia schools concerning possessing guns on campus, yet this did not prevent the killings on April 16, 2007. Moreover, there is confusion on the part of universities in Virginia as to what their rights are for

guns on campus.	respect.	setting policy regarding guns on campus. The panel finds this confusion to be a major weakness in improving campus safety. Moreover, the panel finds that no matter what the policies are, if organizations responsible for keeping guns out of the hands of those who are a danger to themselves or others do not do their job, campus security is seriously undermined. This is evident by the failure to have Cho's name on the list prohibiting him from purchasing weapons.

Time and time again, the report soft-pedals the mistakes made by the police. Look at the reference to the double homicide at West Ambler Johnston Hall on page 79: "... the police may have made an error in reaching a premature conclusion that their initial lead was a good one, or at least in conveying that impression to the Virginia Tech administration." *The word "may" needs to be dropped—it <u>was</u> a mistake.*

The Governor's Review Panel Report, *The Addendum,* failed in so many ways; from a flawed timeline, to critical omissions, to its failure to assign accountability, the report shied away from what needed to be done: uncover the truth.

As long as no consequences are assigned, as long as there are no public reprimands, the job remains unfinished. As a consequence, our schools are not as safe as they need to be. It is nothing short of a tragedy that an opportunity has been lost to make a difference, to find some sort of meaning in a horrific crime. As long as people are not held responsible for their actions or inactions, nothing meaningful will be done to protect our campuses.

Many of the actions taken or reasons for not taking actions following the double homicide at West Ambler Johnston Hall were based on pure conjecture.

The Governor's Review Panel Report represents a singular lack of courage and ethical behavior on the part of politicians on both sides of the aisle; a lack of courage to get at the root of the problem of school shootings, and a lack of willingness to find the truth about the shooting at Virginia Tech. Then-Governor Kaine and then-Attorney General McDonnell both turned blind eyes toward the fictitious timelines concerning "a person of interest" and ignored the TriData conflict of interest. Both men are lawyers. It stretches credibility to the limits to give them a pass on these oversights. As a result of these two men's inaction, they will, at best, go down in the annals of Virginia history as politicians of monumental smallness.

Kaine and McDonnell sat by as words were used to disguise the truth; it is as if they were complicit in a strategy to investigate without repercussions. Hindsight makes it appear that from the outset Kaine, McDonnell, and other Virginians in positions of authority were bent on marginalizing the truth and ensuring that no one would be held accountable for gross negligence and incompetence.

After extensive reviews of the facts surrounding the events of April 16, 2007, you get the impression people involved in the early response to the shootings were in over their heads. They didn't know what to do, what to look for, or how to respond correctly to the shooting crisis. None of that is specifically addressed in *The Addendum*.

Virginia taxpayers were billed over three-quarters of a million dollars for the nefarious conclusions contained in the state's "official report" on the Virginia Tech shootings—a report that is a blatant attempt to manipulate history and reality.

CHAPTER VII

DID VIRGINIA TECH BREAK THE LAW?

*"The promise given was a necessity of the past:
the word broken is a necessity of the present."*
~Niccolo Machiavelli, Italian historian, politician, diplomat

The above quote is central to the case against Virginia Tech, particularly in examining the actions of school and law enforcement personnel after the double homicide at 7:15 a.m. The school's nearly two and one-half hour delay in notifying the campus of the killings raised the legal question, did Virginia Tech break the law by violating the Clery Act?

The Clery Act is named for Jeanne Clery, a 19-year old Lehigh University student who was raped and murdered in her campus residence hall in 1986. Clery's parents found out that students had not been warned about 38 violent crimes on the Lehigh campus in the three years before their daughter's murder, and helped persuade congress to pass a law making it mandatory to warn students of violent crimes on campus grounds. Violation of the Clery Act can result in a loss of federal funds for any school, fines or both.

With so much at stake, we need to have an understanding of the parameters of the Clery Act, and we also must look at the legal precedents. In other words, when and under what circumstances has it been found that the Clery Act was violated?

The Clery Act encompasses requirements for many aspects of campus security including the reporting and tracking of several types of crimes, starting with murder and going on to include vandalism and hate crimes. The part that concerns us here has to do with notifying the campus population of the occurrence of crimes included on the mandatory reporting list.

2007 **(April 13)**	There were four bomb threats on the Virginia Tech campus.
2007 **(April 16)**	Seung Hui Cho killed 32 students and faculty members at Virginia Tech on two campus locations. He also wounded at least 17 others before killing himself. (See Chapters II and III for a detailed timeline of the killings.)
2007 **(April 17)**	Virginia Tech hires Firestorm, a crisis management firm. The company brought in grief counselor, Dr. Ralph Diner. **Billing records for Diner's time show he did next to no counseling of the victims' and their families. The official billings records show that he only met with the mothers of two of the victims. He did, however, spend a great deal of time on public relations matters. He also found time to meet with department heads, faculty, the bookstore staff, deans, and alumni to provide grief support.** Firestorm was used for 10 days.
2007 **(May 29)**	Virginia Tech signed a contract with one of the largest U.S. public relations firms, Burson-Marsteller, to spin the tragedy to the school's benefit.
2007 **(August)**	The victims' families meet with attorney Kenneth Feinberg, who was handling the

	Hokie Spirit Memorial Fund. Some of the families **believed Feinberg was evasive in answering their questions, and several families left the meeting with the distinct impression they were being manipulated.**
2007 **(August 30)**	Governor Kaine held a press conference where he publicly released the Review Panel's findings. The report was riddled with errors and critical omissions. The resulting outcry from the media and the victims' families resulted in a major review and corrections. **The report was written by Arlington, Virginia-based TriData and cost over $600,000.**
2008 **(June 7)**	Judge Theodore J. Markov approved a settlement of $11 million against the state of Virginia.
2008 **(October 16)**	The first of a series of meetings between the victims' families and school officials/ politicians was held. Virginia Tech Chief of Police Wendell Flinchum was the main presenter. **Flinchum admitted to the families that a "person of interest" was not identified until after the interview with Heather Haugh began at 8:16 a.m.—not at 7:30 a.m. as stated in the Governor's Review Panel Report. The admission of this critical error came** *after the families settled with the state* **and would not be officially corrected for another 14 months in the revised Review Panel Report—***The Addendum.*

2008 **(November22-23)**	The second meeting covered two days and was with school president, Charles Steger, and members of his administration. President Steger entered and exited the meeting through a side door. At no time did Steger mingle with the families. At no time did Steger or a member of his administration say they did anything wrong or that they would have done anything differently. **For the first time, the specific wording of the school's timely warning procedure was read. Sitting in the back of the room was Peter Messitt, Assistant Attorney General for Virginia, who would be the state's lead attorney for the state in the Pryde/Peterson trial against the state in March 2012. Governor Kaine did not respond or commit to anything other than to say he was open to fixing the report.**
2009 **(November)**	A second revision of the Governor's Review Panel Report was published, but it too contained errors.
2009 **(December)**	A third and last revision of the Governor's Review Panel Report was issued. But that report also contains errors. **TriData was paid an additional $75,000 for the two revisions which were largely based on the investigative work of the victims' families and the news media. Apparently the state had no clause in its contract with TriData to fix errors at no cost.**
2010 **(December 9)**	**The Department of Education fined**

	Virginia Tech **$55,000** for waiting too long to notify the campus community following the initial double homicide at West Ambler Johnston Hall. Virginia Tech appealed the ruling and the fine.
2012 **(March 29)**	Department of Education Administrative Judge Canellos overturned the $55,000 fine against Virginia Tech.
2012 **(September 1)**	Secretary of Education Arne Duncan overruled Judge Canellos and reinstates a fine against Virginia Tech at a lower amount: $27,500.
2012 **(March)**	A jury found Virginia Tech guilty of negligence in failing to warn the campus after the double homicide at West Ambler Johnston Hall, awarding the Pryde and Peterson families $4 million in damages. The amount was later reduced to $100,000 each, the maximum allowed under Virginia law.
2013 **(February)**	A panel of three judges ruled that the Virginia Supreme Court can hear Virginia Tech's appeal of the verdict against the school in the Pryde/Peterson jury trial.

The following description of the notification requirements of the Clery Act comes from www.securityoncampus.org. the Web site for the Clery Center for Security On Campus.

Issue timely warnings about Clery Act crimes that pose a serious or ongoing threat to students and employees. Institutions must provide timely warnings in a manner likely to reach all members of the campus community. This mandate has been part of the Clery Act since its inception in 1990. Timely warnings are limited to those crimes an institution is required to report and include in its ASR [Annual Security Report]. There are differences between what constitutes a timely warning and an emergency notification; however both systems are in place to safeguard students and campus employees.

Devise an emergency response, notification and testing policy. Institutions are required to inform the campus community about a "significant emergency or dangerous situation involving an immediate threat to the health or safety of students or employees occurring on the campus." An emergency response expands the definition of timely warning as it includes both Clery Act crimes and other types of emergencies (i.e., a fire or infectious disease outbreak). Colleges and universities with and without on-campus residential facilities must have emergency response and evacuation procedures in place. Institutions are mandated to disclose a summary of these procedures in place. Institutions are mandated to disclose a summary of these procedures in their ASR. Additionally, a compliance requires one test of the emergency response procedures annually and policies for publicizing those procedures in conjunction with the annual test.

It is clear from this reading of the law that not only are warnings of a murder by an unknown, and at large, gunman required, but they should also be "timely." It is behind the definition of "timely" that Virginia Tech's administration decided to hide. But before we examine Tech's "timely" excuse, let's look at some schools that have been found guilty of violating the Clery Act.

The case against Eastern Michigan University is the highest fine imposed on an institution. The school was fined $357,500 for failing to warn the campus of a 2006 student's assault and death.

Eastern Michigan University student Laura Dickinson was murdered by a fellow student on December 13, 2006. Dickinson was found in her room four days after her murder. She was naked, a pillow over her head, and there were traces of semen on one leg. The police later said there was "no reason to suspect foul play." The school therefore did not issue a warning. Ten weeks later, however, student Orange Taylor III was arrested and charged with Dickinson's murder. It just so happened that Taylor's arrest occurred on the first day that students could not withdraw from classes and housing and receive a full refund.

After a thorough investigation, the school was found in violation of the Clery Act for not notifying students of the danger. School President

John A. Fallon was fired; no reason was given for his termination, but the press reported it was for his apparent role in the cover up. Cindy Hall, the Director of Public Safety and Chief of Police were both relieved of their jobs.

On December 13, 2007, the school settled with Laura Dickinson's family for $2.5 million. The school did not admit any guilt. Orange Taylor III was convicted of first-degree murder and sexual assault. He was sentenced to life in prison on May 8, 2008.

There is a parallel between Eastern Michigan and Virginia Tech. That parallel is the failure of a school and police officials to warn a campus when confronted with a student homicide. Yes, the lengths of the delays were completely different, but in both cases the schools trivialized a homicide in order to delay a campus-wide notification. Whether you wait over two hours or over two months to warn is irrelevant. The Clery Act calls for a warning to be given to the campus population when a murder occurs on that campus. It does not distinguish between murders by deranged gunmen, murders by rapists and murders caused by a supposed domestic dispute. If someone is found murdered on campus, an immediate warning is called for.

In the case of Virginia Tech, the argument as to whether the school violated the Clery Act has been heated and prolonged. The school's propaganda campaign has been effective and potent. Virginia Tech, coupled with its powerful allies in Richmond, has persuaded many alumni that it did nothing wrong. In fact, the school has carried out a well-orchestrated public relations campaign, arguing that you cannot be a proud and faithful Hokie and criticize the way the Steger administration handled the events of April 16, 2007.

I would argue that you cannot be a proud Hokie alumnus or alumna and *condone the Steger administration's lack of action on April 16, 2007*. For me, there is no doubt—Virginia Tech violated the law. And I am not alone in that opinion.

Never Kick a Soccer Player

For Dr. Diane Strollo and her family there is no doubt, Tech betrayed its students and faculty and violated the law.

Dr. Strollo was at home in suburban Pittsburgh on that frigid blustering April morning when her husband called to tell her there had been a shooting at Virginia Tech, and their daughter, Hilary, had been shot. Strollo was stunned. In a state of disbelief, Diane Strollo kept wondering, "How could she be shot on a Monday morning at college?"

Doctor Strollo vividly remembers getting a phone call from Dr. Dick Davis saying that he was taking Hilary into surgery for three gunshot wounds. By sheer luck and circumstance, considering the mayhem, the loss of so many Hokies, and the extent of her injuries, Hilary was rescued from Norris Hall in the second ambulance to leave the crime scene. Dr. Strollo was fortified by the fact that Hilary was rock steady, physically fit, and an avid soccer player. On the soccer field, kick her and she kicks back.

The news was at first incomprehensible and would become more so, particularly as the Strollos learned about the Virginia Tech leadership's anemic response to the first murders and the months of ignoring the warning signs leading up to Cho's actions. As the details began to emerge, the Strollos became more and more puzzled by Virginia Tech's handling of the initial shootings. In addition, they questioned how members of the school administration (for example – Kim O'Rourke and Edward Spencer) could notify their own loved ones about the shooting, but not alert the entire campus and community.

The Strollo's son, Patrick, was a senior at Virginia Tech. He heard about the shootings, and he knew Hilary had class in Norris Hall. Fortuitously, one of Patrick's friends was a patient (not related to the shootings) in the emergency department of the Montgomery Regional Hospital when Hilary was transported in. The friend heard Hilary's name and called Patrick immediately to say his sister had been shot. Patrick, in turn, called his father.

The Strollos needed to get to Blacksburg immediately, but strong winds and bad weather had forced the cancellation of all flights out of Pittsburgh, so they drove—in record time. They could not think to pack suitcases, only to pick up their other daughter, Sara, and to get to Virginia Tech as quickly as possible.

Hilary was critically injured but survived. The first days in the intensive care unit were an emotional roller coaster, as were the surgeries yet to come. It took three days to discover the scope of who was lost or injured and to learn that the professor Hilary loved and admired, Madame Couture-Nowak, had died of her injuries while trying to protect her class. But by the end of the week, Dr. Strollo kept coming back to the discrepancy that more than two hours had lapsed between the initial shootings and the Norris Hall carnage. She was disturbed when she learned that the police allowed two students (Rachael Hill and Henry Lee), to leave West Ambler Johnston Hall to go French class in Norris Hall—only to be murdered there. Hill, the first to be struck down in French class, had arrived late. Hill had called her father on the way to Norris Hall to tell him that she was "okay."

As the details came into sharper focus, the same question kept eating away at the Strollos: how could the leadership of Virginia Tech not have issued a timely warning? The school knew two students were murdered and that there was an armed gunman at large. Dr. Strollo was mystified that the school had the time and technology to warn the campus but chose not to. Strollo would later find out that the school also chose not to immediately notify the families of the two deceased students. However, the school did notify Governor Timothy Kaine's office at 8:30 a.m., which was one hour and fifteen minutes before the carnage at Norris Hall. The Strollos kept thinking how odd it was, how curious to notify the governor but not your faculty and students.

Dr. Strollo knew her daughter and most students would have used caution had they been warned. In fact, because of the bomb threats on the campus and the closure of four academic building three days earlier, on April 13, 2007, Hilary had checked the Virginia Tech Web page at 9:00 a.m. on the 16th to see if Norris Hall was open. There was no mention of the 7:15 a.m. shootings, so she proceeded to class. The anger the Strollos felt began to grow as they realized the victims of Norris Hall did not have the advantage given to the families and loved ones of Dr. Steger and his Policy Group. Had there been an accurate and timely warning many lives might have been saved. In fact, several students who did not attend French class that fateful morning said they decided to miss class after hearing about a "shooting." It would seem the rumor saved them. How many more might have been saved by an official warning?

To this day, the Strollos ask, "Why would leadership hesitate to notify the campus of two unsolved murders on campus? For any campus security expert, April is a high profile month for terrorists. Based on the Branch Davidian fiasco in Waco, Texas on April 19, 1993, Timothy McVey executed the Oklahoma City bombing on the same day in 1995. In an effort to 'outdo' McVey, killers Eric Harris and Dylan Klebold carried out the Columbine High School massacre on April 20, 1999. (Their butchery was delayed one day by a glitch in obtaining munitions.) Virginia Tech gunman Cho referenced the Columbine killers in one of his recorded manifestos. April is also a high profile month for college administrations. Many families and potential students are visiting campus. Virginia Tech was already sullied by four bomb threats on April 13, 2007. The school knew that if there was a lot of publicity about two students who were murdered in a dorm, families might have questioned Virginia Tech's leadership and commitment to safety. Families might have sent their children elsewhere and Tech would have lost revenue and credibility."

Dr. Strollo commends the superintendent of the Montgomery County School District for her actions. When she heard via a police dispatcher that students were shot at Tech on April 16, 2007, she ordered the entire public school district into immediate lockdown at 8:52 a.m., almost one hour before the massacre at Norris Hall. What was her motivation? "Safety is our highest priority." This, according to Strollo, is someone who cares about her students and community.

The quick thinking of the superintendent has prompted Dr. Strollo to ask repeatedly, "Can someone nominate this woman for governor?"

As she reflects on that April day, Dr. Strollo tries to put the tragedy into perspective. "To notify our own loved ones in an emergency, that is human nature. To not notify the faculty, students, and community, what is that? At best, it is negligence or ineptitude. However, it is unconscionable when 'leadership' places the university's reputation and fundraising above campus safety."

The Strollos send their love and deepest respect to the families who lost a loved one and to all the survivors and their families. The Strollos are forever indebted to the Virginia Tech and Blacksburg area emergency responders, health care providers, and community.

The Grimes

For Suzanne Grimes, whose son Kevin Sterne survived the shooting, there is no doubt; not only did Tech break the law in failing to warn, but it mounted a campaign to use the tragedy for monetary gain.

Suzanne, just as the Strollos, lived near Pittsburgh in April 2007. On the 16th she was out shopping for Kevin's upcoming graduation. She wanted to do something special to honor her son's accomplishment. Sometime around 11:30 a.m., her sister in New Mexico reached Suzanne by cell phone and asked if she had heard about the shooting at Virginia Tech. She had not, and immediately went home. She tried first to reach her husband and then her son, but no such luck.

There was no answer on Kevin's cell phone, but she was not alarmed. Kevin's phone bill is part of the family's Verizon account, so Grimes printed the latest bill and began calling numbers identified with Kevin's phone. She also kept calling Kevin's number, but still no answer. One of the first numbers to answer was Kevin's roommate Joe. He had not heard about the shooting, but tried to reassure Suzanne that Kevin was ok. But, Joe added, "Kevin is usually home for lunch by now, and he is not here."

Suzanne persisted. The next number to answer was Kevin's good friend Marcus. This time the tone was somber. Marcus said Kevin was in the building where the shootings had taken place and there was a good chance he had been shot. Suzanne tried to reassure a badly shaken Marcus that everything would be all right, but when she hung up the phone she started crying uncontrollably.

An emotionally distraught Suzanne finally got through to her husband who said he would be right home. They would leave for Blacksburg immediately. Suzanne did not stop to pack, she just kept calling and calling: first Kevin's number and then the school or a number on the phone bill list, then Kevin. She kept the routine up. Suzanne finally reached someone who said she was on President Steger's staff—possibly his secretary. She doesn't remember the woman's name, all she remembers are her words, "We don't know what is going on."

Now frantic, Suzanne called the Virginia Tech police asking about her son. They had no information and told her to call the state police, who in turn told her to phone the Blacksburg police. Around and around the phone calls went. She kept getting the same people, none of whom could tell her anything. Her emotions were now raw. Each time she reached the police she could hear the growing panic in their voices.

Suzanne had been working on a graduation poster for Kevin. The poster lay on the table near the phone and included pictures of Kevin as a child. Every time she looked over at her unfinished work she broke down sobbing.

All of a sudden her fright exploded. Suppose Kevin is hiding from the killer, his phone is on and her phone calls alert the killer to her son's hiding place? Suppose the killer finds Kevin because of what she is doing and kills him? The fright was crippling; the emotional pain was excruciating.

From that point on she concentrated on phoning the police. At one point she was told she should call the morgue. She did, but again, no word—no answers.

By 1:30 p.m. the Grimes were speeding toward Blacksburg. Suzanne was beside herself; she was on the phone one call after another. She just kept dialing one number after another, hoping against hope she would hear Kevin was not hurt or worse yet, dead.

Sometime around 4:30 p.m. she got through to the Montgomery Regional Hospital. The hospital spokesperson said they had a survivor named Kevin, but could not say whether it was her son. At that point Suzanne reached one of Kevin's friends who had gone to the hospital. The friend could not tell the Grimes anything specific, but said if you have a picture of him on your phone, send it to me and I will give it to the hospital officials. Suzanne found a picture, and sent it. The photo was taken into the operating room, and moments later Suzanne was told the survivor was her son. Suzanne remembers, "We were afraid to believe it was him, we were still skeptical. There are no words to describe the relief." By now Suzanne was an emotional wreck; she was physically and emotionally exhausted. She was told that as soon as Kevin was awake they would have him call.

Grimes found out that her son had been the last survivor to be removed from Norris Hall. It had taken 51 minutes to get him to Montgomery Regional Hospital. She would also come to know that Kevin used skills he had learned in the Boy Scouts to stem the hemorrhaging in his leg and save his life.

There are no words in the English language to describe her feelings when she heard her son's voice. When Kevin called, Suzanne could tell he was on heavy medication; she would later find out it was morphine. His voice sounded so good, it sounded so sweet even though the painkillers had taken their toll. When the hospital doctor called his first words were, "I have saved his life, I am not sure I can save his leg." Kevin, just as Hilary Strollo, had lost over two-thirds of his blood. Fortunately, the doctor did save Kevin's leg and through the young man's grit and determination, he walked across the stage to get his graduation diploma that spring. Kevin's action was the true embodiment of the Hokie spirit.

For the Grimes, once in Blacksburg, it did not take long for them to realize something was amiss with the school. It was readily apparent to them—the school had something to hide. The first few days passed in something of a daze, but they quickly came to realize they were not being told the whole truth. They were plagued with questions about why the school failed to issue a timely warning. But no one could or would explain the school's actions and inactions on that fateful day.

The Grimes family managed to get the last available room at the Inn at Virginia Tech. Suzanne remembers the atmosphere as chaotic, bordering on mass hysteria. There were security checks everywhere. The Grimes were put at the end of the hall on the fourth floor—the floor where all the families of the dead were staying. Walking through that corridor was a terrible journey through unending grief and agony. Again Suzanne asked herself, why didn't the school warn there was a killer on the loose?

Again Grimes asked herself, why were these families being put though this excruciating pain when a warning would almost certainly have saved 30 lives and prevented 17 from being wounded? Why have all of us had to suffer this, when it could have been avoided?

At one point Suzanne bumped into Dr. Ralph Diner (see Chapter IX for an explanation of the role Diner appears to have actually played), the grief counselor hired by Firestorm the crisis management company used by Virginia Tech for ten days following the shootings. The two exchanged a few words and she only remembers Diner saying, "Tech has some issues."

Suzanne took a few phone calls, including one from the press. She was asked to fax a picture of her son for use in a newspaper article. No sooner did she comply with the request than she began thinking it was the wrong thing to do—suppose someone wanted to come back and kill Kevin.

Suzanne Grimes was entering a long period of fear and anxiety. For months and years she would be haunted by the thought that someone would still come and kill her son. As long as she stayed in Blacksburg, she felt relatively safe, because of the police and security presence. But once she returned to Pittsburgh, all the horror, shock, and fear came back with a vengeance. Back at home she locked all the doors and pulled all the shades. Her anxiety was so great that she had to go on medication. Again, she asked, "How could Tech not have warned there was a killer on the loose, how could they be so naïve to think that someone who had killed twice would not do it again?"

By July of 2007, Suzanne was beginning to make some progress toward regaining a degree of normalcy. It was at that time the Grimes received a phone call from the FBI office in Pittsburgh wanting to meet and talk with Kevin. The FBI agents wanted to hear, first hand, the account of the shootings. Kevin agreed and his mother accompanied him to the Bureau's office. As she listened to her son recount graphic detail after detail of Cho's methodical slaughter she felt she was going into shock. Kevin's words brought back anew the horror of what her son had gone through and survived. Her nightmares returned. The stress of what she had heard from her son's lips was so great that she had to remain on medication.

Suzanne Grimes would later find out that Tech President Charles Steger visited her son's hospital room, but only after his parents had left. For Suzanne, Steger's action was infuriating; it was the act of a coward. She could only say to herself, "How dare that man come into my son's hospital room when his parents were not there?"

In the weeks and months that followed, Grimes more and more believed the families were being manipulated. The school did assign a liaison officer to the family, but Grimes shared a feeling felt by many of the families—the main purpose of this liaison officer was to string the families along, to tell them as little as possible, and to try to prevent the families from talking to each other and to the press. This feeling was reinforced by the fact that the school, through the liaison officer, was often unresponsive to the Grimes' simplest requests and rarely answered questions.

Grimes also had the impression that Kenneth Feinberg, the noted U.S. attorney who handled, pro bono, the Hokie Spirit Memorial Fund (HSMF), was a central player in making sure the families were controlled. (I will examine the machinations surrounding the HSMF in Chapter X.) Suzanne Grimes vividly remembers a meeting in August 2007 with Feinberg concerning the HSMF. Time and time again during the meeting, she asked Feinberg pointed questions about how the money was being distributed. She found his answers vague and evasive.

Grimes also clearly remembers the way Feinberg had the families exit that meeting to keep them away from the press—he apparently wanted to be in complete control of the message concerning the millions of dollars that were flooding into the school. Feinberg was a key player in the distribution of the HSMF money and for some reason he could not, or would not, fully answer Suzanne Grimes's questions.

For the Pohle, Strollo, White, and Grimes families, there is no doubt, Virginia Tech not only violated the Clery Act, but the Steger administration violated common sense and good judgment. But don't take my word for it.

You, the reader, need to examine the legal aspects of the case against the school on the following pages and decide for yourself.

*   *   *

The case against Virginia Tech has gone back and forth in the legal system. On December 9, 2010, the Department of Education (DoE) issued findings that Tech did violate the law; Virginia Tech's appeal of those findings was rejected and the DoE fined the school $55,000 for failing to issue a timely warning after the double homicide at 7:15 a.m. on the morning of April 16, 2007.

The original fine is the maximum allowed. In issuing the decision, the DoE said, "While Tech's violations warrant a fine far in excess of what is currently permissible under the statute, the Department's fine authority is limited." Tech appealed the DoE decision and in March of 2012, DoE Administrative Judge Ernest C. Canellos ruled in the school's favor voiding the violation and striking the fine.

Take a moment and read excerpts from the original DoE's decision as spelled out in a letter to University President Charles Steger:

Dear Dr. Steger:

This letter is to inform you that the U.S. Department of Education (Department) intends to fine Virginia Polytechnic Institute and State University (Virginia Tech) $55,000 based on violations of statutory and regulatory requirements outlined below. This fine action is taken in accordance with the procedures that the Secretary of Education (Secretary) has established for assessing fines against institutions participating in any of the programs authorized under Title IV of the Higher Education Act of 1965 . . . ."

. . .

"The Clery Act and the Department's regulations require an institution to provide a timely warning to the campus community on certain crimes that are reported to campus security authorities or local police agencies and are considered by the institution to represent a threat to students and employees. . . . ."

. . .

During the morning of April 16, 2007, Seung Hui Cho, a student at Virginia Tech, shot Emily Hilscher in her dorm room at West Ambler Johnston (WAJ) residence hall. He then shot Ryan Christopher Clark, a Resident Advisor, in Ms. Hilscher's room. Both Ms. Hilscher and Mr. Clark were Virginia Tech students and both died from the wounds caused by the shootings. Although the Virginia Tech Policy Group met to plan how to notify the campus community of the dormitory shootings, it did not issue any notification until more than two hours after the shooting occurred. About 15 minutes after the Policy Group issued a notice of the shootings at WAJ to the campus community, Cho began shooting students and Virginia Tech staff in Norris Hall, a classroom building on the Virginia Tech campus. Ultimately, Cho murdered 32 people, wounded many more, and then took his own life."

...

"The Department is taking this fine action based on the findings in the FPRD, which concluded that Virginia Tech: (1) failed to provide a timely warning in response to the shootings and murders that occurred on April 16, 2007; and (2) did not comply with the timely warning policy it had disclosed to students and staff as part of the ASR [Annual Security Report all schools participating in the Higher Education Act of 1965, title IV, are required to prepare, publish and distribute every year]. Based on these violations of the Clery Act and the Department's regulations, the imposition of a fine is warranted. ... "

FAILURE TO PROVIDE TIMELY WARNING

"... all institutions participating in the Title IV, HEA programs must, in a manner that is timely and will aid in the prevention of similar crimes, provide a timely warning to the campus if certain crimes are reported to campus security authorities and are considered to represent a threat to students and employees. These crimes include the following: (1) criminal homicide (murder and manslaughter); (2) sex offenses (forcible and non-forcible); (3) robbery; (4) aggravated assault; (5) burglary; (6) motor vehicle theft; (7) arson; (8) liquor law, drug law and illegal weapons possession violations; and (9) hate crimes. The only exception to this requirement is if the crime is reported to a pastoral or professional counselor. ... ."

"... Virginia Tech failed to issue a timely warning to the campus community after the first two shootings occurred at the WAJ campus residence hall."

"On April 16, 2007, at about 7:15 a.m., Cho shot Ms. Hilscher and Mr. Clark in the WAJ residence hall on Virginia Tech's campus. ... The police chief also reported to President Steger that no weapon had been found and that bloody footprints were found, leading away from the crime scene. President Steger decided to convene the Virginia Tech Policy Group. At 8:25 a.m., the Policy Group convened to discuss the shootings and how to notify the campus community. The Policy Group issued an email to the campus community informing them of the shootings at WAJ at 9:26 a.m."

"The fact that the assailant had not been identified, a weapon had not been found at the scene and that bloody footprints led away from the bodies strongly indicated that the shooter was still at large, and posed an ongoing threat to the safety of the students, staff and others on the Virginia Tech campus. Because Virginia Tech failed to notify its students and staff of the initial shootings on a timely basis, thousands continued to travel on campus, without a warning of the events at WAJ."

" ... other institutions and individuals who had information regarding the shootings were taking action. At about 8:00 a.m., the Virginia Tech Office of Continuing and Professional Education (OCPE) locked down on its own after a family member notified an OCPE employee of the WAJ shootings. At 8:15 a.m., two senior

officials at Virginia Tech had conversations with family members in which they related the events at WAJ. In one conversation the official advised her son, a student at Virginia Tech, to go to class. In the other, the official arranged for extended babysitting. At 8:25 a.m., police cancelled bank deposit pickups. At 8:40 a.m., a Policy Group member notified the Governor's office of the double shooting. At 8:45 a.m., a Policy Group member e-mailed a Richmond colleague that one student had been killed and another critically wounded and stated 'gunman on the loose.' At 8:52 a.m., Blacksburg public schools locked down until more information became available about the incident. Also at about 8:52 a.m., the Executive Director of Government Relations at Virginia Tech, with an office adjacent to the President's suite, directed that the doors to his office be locked. Sometime between 9:00 and 9:15 a.m., the Virginia Tech Veterinary College locked down. At 9:05 am, trash pickup on campus was cancelled. ..."

"At 9:26 a.m., Virginia Tech first notified the campus community of the shootings at WAJ. The message was vague and only notified the community there had been a shooting on the campus. It did not mention that there had been a murder or that the killer had not been identified. The notice did not direct the community to take any safety measures. The message was not a timely warning as required by the HEA and the regulations."

...

"Between approximately 9:40 a.m. and 9:51 a.m. the gunman shot additional victims in Norris Hall before taking his own life. A second message was sent to the Virginia Tech community at 9:50 a.m. with a much more explicit warning. This message was not only sent to email and cell phones but was also broadcast on campus loudspeakers. At 10:17 a.m., approximately 26 minutes after the shootings at Norris Hall ended, a third message was sent to the community cancelling classes and advising everyone to remain in place."

"As discussed above, when individuals and organization received information about the events at WAJ, they were able to make their own decisions on how to react and on whether or not to take steps to protect themselves. Had an appropriate timely warning been sent earlier to the campus community, more individuals could have acted on the information and made decisions about their own safety."

"... As the Department has previously stated, a timely warning "should be issued as soon as the pertinent information is available because the intent of a timely warning is to alert the campus community of continuing threats ... thereby enabling community members to protect themselves. ..."

...

"While Virginia Tech's violations warrant a fine far in excess of what is currently permissible under the statute, the Department's fine authority is limited. The HEA authorizes the Department to impose a maximum fine of $27,500 per violation. As a result the Department is assessing the maximum statutory fine of $55,000. ..."

The letter was signed by Mary E. Gust, Director, Administrative Actions and Appeals Service Group.

Below are excerpts of Virginia Tech's response to the DoE decision with my critique of their words. To my thinking, the school's response is, unfortunately, an exercise in circular reasoning, double-talk, and a wholesale retreat from the truth.

The school's response begins with two pages of written remarks by Larry Hincker, associate vice president for university relations, and chief spokesperson for the school, dated May 18, 2010.

Hincker asserts: *"Virginia Tech appreciates the opportunity to respond to the Department of Education's preliminary report, especially given the factual inaccuracies about the events of April 16, 2007, that continue to be repeated and that are incorporated in the DoE's document. Notably, factual errors corrected in the most recent addendum to the Virginia Tech Review Panel Report were not corrected in DoE's preliminary findings, nor has Virginia Tech been accorded access to the administrative file for the purpose of responding to other factual misinformation on which DoE may have based its preliminary findings."*

I would note that Tech knew about the errors and omissions in the timeline before the DoE preliminary findings yet chose to say next to nothing about them until the school was ruled in violation of the law. Furthermore, the school knows there are still problems with the timeline: critical omissions that demonstrate that the school's failure to react promptly cost lives. The school remains silent on these points. Finally, it should also be noted that the inaccuracies in no way change the fact that the Virginia Tech administration failed to give a timely warning. If anything, it highlights how the Policy Group delayed giving out any kind of relevant or helpful information.

Hincker then goes on to state: *"From the beginning, we have been firmly committed to full transparency and to sharing lessons learned from this tragedy with the higher education community and beyond."*

Again, Hincker presents an incorrect, rosy picture of the school and its president. President Steger's policy of "full transparency" and "sharing lessons" from the beginning is simply not true. If you read Professor Lucinda Roy's book you will see that President Steger refused to meet directly with Roy—the faculty member who probably has the most first-hand information about Cho. Furthermore, other staff members appeared to be afraid to interact with Roy for fear of reprisals from the school administration. That is hardly an atmosphere that fosters "transparency" and "sharing lessons."

If Virginia Tech was devoted to "full transparency," why did the school pay a small fortune to a public relations firm to spin the tragedy? Less than six weeks after the shootings, on May 29, 2007, Virginia Tech signed a contract with one of this country's largest and most prestigious public relation firms—Burson-Marsteller—to handle publicity about the rampage. And no doubt, the intention was to put the school, President

Steger, and Chief Flinchum in the best light, by focusing public attention away from the administration's glaring mistakes in judgment and toward "the Hokie nation's" need to pull together and recover. (I examine Tech's relationship with Burson-Marsteller in detail in Chapter IX, "Denial and Deception.")

Perhaps the most damning part of Tech's response comes on the first page of the Introduction of its rebuttal: *"As part of the university response to the Department of Education's Program Review, Virginia Tech retained Delores A. Stafford who has over 26 years experience in law enforcement and the security industry, and who is a nationally recognized expert in the Clery Act to review both the DoE's Program Review Report and Virginia Tech policies, procedures and response on April 16, 2007."*

Virginia Tech neglects to tell the reader that the school paid Stafford $9,028.00 for that opinion, and awarded her a lucrative contract to teach two training courses. In addition, the school contracted with her to do an audit of all aspects of the school's adherence to the Clery Act. Clearly Ms. Stafford has profited quite well from her relationship with Virginia Tech. (I look more closely at the Virginia Tech-Delores Stafford relationship in Chapter VIII.)

Tech asserts in its defense, *"Neither DoE nor the Clery Act defines 'timely.' However, DoE's compliance guidelines illustrate 48 hours as an acceptable timely notification procedure. Other Clery guidelines as well as industry practices, call for notices to be released within several hours or days. The University actions were well within these guidelines and practices."*

Again, the reader is told only part of the story. The rebuttal fails to address the statements in the DoE letter pointing out that portions of the school took the initiative, warned and locked down within an hour of the double homicide at West Ambler Johnston Hall. Those actions were consistent with the Clery Act. Hincker also fails to mention that Tech took the initiative during the Morva incident several months earlier, when the killer wasn't even thought to be on the campus, and locked down.

The school claims that it is being held to unrealistic standards. *"It is inconsistent with regulatory process to hold Virginia Tech to standards that did not exist at the time or, as portions of this preliminary report do, to hold Virginia Tech to a new Clery Act standard that was developed after—and in response to—the tragic events that took place on our campus."*

Once again, key information is left out. There is no mention of the fact that while portions of the university were adhering to warning standards the university itself had set several months earlier, the main school administration was violating those standards.

Virginia Tech quotes the Federal Register 59 FR 22314-01 (Exhibit 2), as part of its appeal, writing:

"The Secretary (of Education) does not believe that a definition of 'timely reports' is necessary or warranted. Rather, the Secretary believes that timely reporting to the campus community for this purpose must be decided on a case-by-case basis in light of all the facts surrounding a crime, including factors such as the nature of the crime, the continuing danger to the campus community, and the possible risk of compromising law enforcement efforts. Campus security authorities should consult the local law enforcement agency for guidance on how and when to release 'timely reports' to the campus community."

This quote, however, far from helping the school appears to damn the Steger administration's actions. The double homicide at West Ambler Johnston Hall was not a routine campus crime. Two people were dead and there were bloody footprints leading away from the crime scene. A killer was on the loose. Because of the seriousness of the crime, the "case-by-case" evaluation demanded an immediate warning.

Tech asserts that immediately after the tragedy the school discussed with the Governor of Virginia the university's desire for a panel to be appointed to review the response to the events that occurred on April 16, 2007. Virginia Tech's President and Rector of the Virginia Polytechnic Institute and State University Board of Visitors sent an official request for a panel review to the Governor on April 19, 2007. The letter stated: 'Today we are writing to request that you appoint a panel to review the actions taken in response to the events that occurred on April 16, 2007, to include the actions of all agencies that responded that day. While we believe it would be most beneficial to have an independent review, we offer full assistance of all personnel and resources at Virginia Tech to assist a review committee."

The above sounds good, but the fact of the matter is that from the outset, the Steger administration tried to manipulate and spin the tragedy to the benefit of the school. Tech hired a public relations firm to do just that (See Chapter IX). The school engaged in heavy-handed tactics in dealing with the faculty—often insisting that an administration representative be on hand when faculty and staff met with panel members (see Lucinda Roy's book, *No Right to Remain Silent*). The net result was to intimidate and stifle the flow of information and evidence. Staff and faculty appear to have been afraid for their jobs because of the school's heavy-handed tactics.

Tech also asserts: *"In the 27 month period between Virginia Tech's response to the DoE's limited request for information and the issuance of the Program Review Report, the DoE has not at any time requested additional information or clarification from the university. However, the DoE continued to solicit information from the complainants until a month before issuance of the Program Review Report. Virginia Tech requested review of the DoE administrative file, but this request was denied.*

Therefore, Virginia Tech is unable to comment on the information (upon) which DoE relies, thereby jeopardizing Virginia Tech's ability to prepare a comprehensive response."

Virginia Tech does not have much room to cry foul when it comes to the flow of information. There is evidence that the school tried to keep the families of the deceased from communicating with the families of the survivors, and vice versa. Also, remember that Professor Lucinda Roy, one of the most knowledgeable faculty members about Cho and his problems, was denied access to President Steger. In her book she says Steger's office said he was too busy with the families to meet with her. But the family members I have talked to scratch their heads, asserting that he was too busy with other "things" to spend time with them. Indeed, as I have pointed out earlier in this chapter Steger appears to have intentionally waited until the parents were not at the children's bedside when he visited the hospitals. For Virginia Tech to complain about lack of communication doesn't hold much water.

Tech counters the DoE findings by arguing, *"The facts known at the time did not support a conclusion that any continuing threat existed and certainly did not indicate that any further act of violence was likely."*

It is with this statement that Virginia Tech's case most closely parallels Eastern Michigan University. There, a girl lay dead with a pillow over her face and semen on her thighs, and the police said they saw nothing suspicious. In this letter, Virginia Tech said that two students shot to death with no weapon found and bloody footprints leading away from the scene gave no indication that any further act of violence was likely.

In perhaps one of the weakest explanations for the school's inaction, Tech contends that *"there were no reported sightings of unusual activity on campus following the WAJ shooting, a person of interest was identified, and his vehicle was not on campus and he was believed to be off campus."*

The holes in this argument are big enough for the Virginia Tech band to march through. The school uses passive voice sentence construction to obscure. Who believed he was off campus? We need to talk to him or her to understand the basis for that belief. In fact, the police did make a quick sweep of the campus looking for Karl Thornhill's truck—some 15 or 20 minutes to cover a 2,600-acre campus. That was hardly a detailed search for "unusual activity on campus."

Tech asserts: "The (Governor's) Review Panel consulted with various police agencies (all of whom) opined that a lockdown for a campus like Virginia Tech was not feasible on the morning of April 16, 2007." What was so special about the morning that a lockdown was not possible? After all, a lockdown had been very successfully conducted several months earlier, as in the Morva case.

Virginia Tech challenges the DoE's assertions that evidence indicated the shooter was still at large and posed a clear and present danger to the campus community, and that since the person of interest was identified 46 minutes later than originally reported, having a suspect could not be used as an excuse for not sending out a warning." The school challenges these findings by writing, *"The evidence at the crime scene was presented as an act of targeted violence."*

The whole concept of targeted violence in connection with the West Ambler Johnston Hall shootings is puzzling. What evidence of targeted violence? As discussed in Chapter II, "Crime Scene Analysis 101," there was no such evidence. I challenge the whole idea of "targeted violence."

Tech asserts: *"Experience and training teach law enforcement officials, as conveyed by a representative of the Virginia State Police to the families, that perpetrators of a homicide will place time and distance between themselves and the location of the crime. All the evidence indicated that a crime of targeted violence had occurred, a person of interest had left the campus and there was not an ongoing threat. This was not the conclusion of one police department, but three independent agencies."*

Again, Virginia Tech engages in word games. The use of the word "will" is misleading. It implies that perpetrators always put distance between themselves and the crime scene. The correct word should be "sometimes." There is basis in fact in the saying, "the killer often returns to the scene of the crime." In fact, experience and training teach law enforcement professionals not to assume anything. Again, this is an attempt to justify wrong decisions. Police professionals are taught not to assume anything or rule out anything. *There was no evidence that this was a targeted homicide.* Tech accuses the DoE of applying current thinking to the situation on April 16, 2007, and then turns around and does exactly the same thing.

Virginia Tech argues that Cho's actions were not predictable. Well, that is not what the experts say. Take a look at the analysis of Virginia Tech's response to Cho's warning signs done by internationally known and respected mental health expert, Dr. Gerald Amada. Dr. Amada is the former director of the Mental Health Program, City College of San Francisco. He was speaking at the National Association for University and College Center Directors, on October 17, 2008.

> *"Even a cursory review of the events that led up to the massacre (at Virginia Tech), as delineated in the report of the governor's panel, indicates the university's abiding faith in three general approaches that it abortively used for dealing with his behavioral waywardness. (First), was to resiliently accommodate his strange and offensive behavior by, for example, arranging to have him individually tutored by a department chairperson, an arrangement that was evidently endorsed by the university's so-called care team, a diverse group of staff representing the Counseling Service, Residence Life, Legal Counsel, Judicial Affairs, and Student Life, that investigated the*

case of Mr. Cho and provided guidance to instructors who were struggling to deal with his misconduct. This accommodation of providing individual instruction was, please keep in mind, adopted after Mr. Cho's menacing presence in her class had caused an English instructor such terrible anguish that she threatened to resign."

"The (second) tack repeatedly taken by Cho's instructors and others was to prod, cajole and shoehorn him into psychotherapy; to the point that one instructor actually offered to chaperone him to the service. This particular tack of championing psychological treatment to Mr. Cho, although no doubt well-intentioned, should have been, in my view, recognized by someone at the university as terribly misguided and worse, doomed to fail with adverse consequences of some kind in its wake."

"The third (and most dangerous) tack taken by the university in dealing with Mr. Cho was to eschew using the disciplinary system of the school to admonish, warn and if necessary discipline him for his chronic and flagrant violations of the code of student conduct ... When Cho stalked (harassed), he was given a tempered warning by a police officer but no direct admonition or warning came from Judicial Affairs or a designated administrator with disciplinary authority, ordinarily the offices most responsible and effective in meting out discipline. When Mr. Cho took impermissible photographs of female students in the class, he was reported to a dean, who clearly stated in an email message to the instructor that Cho's behavior fell under the rubric of disorderly conduct, meaning, I would assume, that it should meet with some form of discipline. What was the response to this incident? The Judicial Affairs officer agrees with a plan to once again refer Cho to the counseling program, suggests nothing about the use of discipline and limits her remarks to (and I quote), "I would make it clear to him that any similar behavior in the future will be referred." Presumably, she means referred to the Judicial Affairs office or to counseling. Once again Cho walks away with impunity by not being held accountable for his misconduct. ... the university was fixated, it seems, on getting Mr. Cho repaired in the psychological service rather than on harnessing and correcting his disruptive and frightening behavior through the use of disciplinary measures. ..."

Dr. Amada also adds the following: *"In his book called* <u>Moral Mazes</u> *the author, sociologist Robert Jackal, points out that one of the greatest fears that plague corporate managers is that they will be caught in the wrong place at the wrong time and will not be able to outrun their mistakes when blame-times arrive."*

Amada then adds, *"Tech President Charles Steger and his administration were caught in the wrong place at the wrong time—clearly, the school is twisting and turning everyway possible to explain its failure to act decisively when confronted with Cho's threatening behavior."*

*   *   *

Finally, in challenging DoE, Tech asserts: *"Virginia Tech has overwhelmingly demonstrated that a finding by the DoE that there was a 'timely warning' violation is not supported by the evidence. The intent of 'timely warning' and the interpretation of timely warning proffered by DoE and those providing interpretation guidance to institutions of higher education did not consider a timely warning as an emergency notification."* Look at what else Tech asserts: "The guidance provided in *The Handbook for Campus Crime Reporting*, published in 2005 … is found in Chapter 5, page 62 and reads, "The issuing of a timely warning must be decided on a case-by-case basis in light of all the facts surrounding a crime, including factors such as the nature of the crime, the continuing danger to the campus community and the possible risk of compromising law enforcement efforts."

The problem is that the school's own words prove the case against Tech. Timely warnings should be decided on a case-by-case basis, depending on the nature of the crime and the continuing threat. How many times does Tech have to be reminded that two students were killed at WAJ and all evidence (bloody footprints) pointed to the fact that the killer was on the loose, on campus, and might strike again?

Ruling Overturned; Then Reinstated

Virginia Tech appealed the fine and on March 29, 2012, an administrative-law judge at DoE, Judge Ernest C. Canellos, overturned that ruling. A brief look at Judge Canellos's record in regards to the Clery Act shows just how lucky Virginia Tech was in getting Canellos to hear the appeal.

First, just weeks before his ruling on Virginia Tech, Canellos lowered a penalty levied against Washington State University for Clery Act violations from $82,000 to $15,000. Washington State misreported two sex-related crimes and had failed to provide complete statements about campus-crime reporting procedures in its annual compliance reporting.

Second is the case against Tarleton State University. The school was fined $137,500 for not providing "complete and accurate campus crime information in its crime report as required by the Jeanne Clery Disclosure of Campus Security Police and Campus Crime Statistics Act." On

September 21, 2010, Judge Canellos reduced the fine to $27,000—a mild slap on the wrist. Tarleton had failed to report, as required by law, 35 burglaries, 22 drug arrests, one robbery, and one referral for drug law violations.

On August 30, 2012, Secretary of Education Arne Duncan threw out Canellos's decision and reinstated the verdict. Duncan reduced the original $55,000 fine to $27,500.

No Warning; Thirty People Died

I would ask the following of those who say no laws were broken: If you know there was no suspect, no witness, no weapon, but there *were* bloody footprints leaving the crime scene, what would you think was possible as far as the shooter's location? How long would you wait to warn the campus?

Again, I remind you that Virginia Tech violated its own security standard set in August 2006. At that time, the school locked down when William Morva escaped from a nearby prison and killed a law enforcement officer and a guard. Virginia Tech locked down when there was a killer in the area, but in April 2007, the school took no action when all evidence pointed to the fact that another killer was actually on campus.

I would also ask: Do you find it acceptable that there was enough time for secret emails to be going to Richmond describing what was happening, but not to release information? How about the fact that trash and bank activities were stopped, phone calls were made by some Policy Group meeting attendees to their families about the shooting, various buildings and local schools were locked down, and even school and town SWAT teams were deployed. Yet only a few, select people on campus knew what had happened.

Finally, I would make one last point. Those who claim the Clery Act was not violated on April 16, 2007 often argue that the statute's main purpose is that crimes committed on college campuses are made public knowledge so that parents and students can factor that in when selecting a college. That is not true. One of the main purposes of the act is to ensure that faculty, staff, and students are warned about acts of violence on campus and can take precautionary measures. On the Virginia Tech campus that spring day in 2007, a clear warning was never given after the double homicide, precautions were not taken, and 30 people died who could have lived.

CHAPTER VIII

POLITICS IS THE ART OF KEEPING FROM PEOPLE THE THINGS THEY MOST NEED TO KNOW

*"... he who seeks to deceive will always find
someone who will allow himself to be deceived."*
~Niccolo Machiavelli, Italian historian, politician, diplomat

The response of officials at all levels to the shootings at Virginia Tech may go down as one of the most skillful and well-organized efforts to evade the truth in this nation's history. The school and politicians in Richmond knew that if the public were to become aware of the extent of the school's inept decisions and actions before, during, and after Cho's rampage, there would be hell to pay. Therefore, as much as possible, the public had to be kept in the dark about the incriminating evidence. The school, and state officials, needed to guide, control, and manipulate—whenever they could—what the public knew.

Tragically, Virginia Tech was not an isolated incident. There had been a devastating dress rehearsal for Virginia Tech's evasion of responsibility just a few years before in 2002, at the Appalachian School of Law in Grundy, Virginia.

Cho's rampage is especially unsettling for my family and me because Virginia Tech ignored the lessons from the Appalachian School of Law shooting. The parallels between the two shootings are staggering: mentally ill students whose penchant for violence was well known by the schools; inept school and law enforcement responses to the shootings that led to additional losses of life; and the unwillingness of school officials, law enforcement personnel, and politicians to be honest in dealing with the victims' families. These parallels dramatically underscore just how little the Steger administration had learned from Virginia's first shooting. Virginia Tech clearly wanted to keep that fact from the public's eye.

The Appalachian School of Law is less than 130 miles from Virginia Tech. For weeks and months after the law school shootings the media was filled with reports of killer Peter Odighizuwa's mental problems; the school president's belittling female faculty members' calls for campus security and the inept response of the school, law enforcement, and rescue officials on the day of the shooting. Virginia Tech would have to have been enclosed in a hermetically sealed container not to have been aware of what had happened at Grundy and the lessons to be learned from a school shooting less than three hours away a scant five years earlier.

There is no way to hide that the failure to heed the lessons of the law school shooting made the tragedy at Virginia Tech inevitable. And tragically now, because the school and others are trying to hide many of the facts and lessons of Virginia Tech more school shootings are certain to happen.

First and foremost, Virginia Tech needed plausible reasons to explain away its failure to act immediately following the double homicide. The school needed some sort of justification for its timidity in the face of a clear threat to the campus. Toward this end, Virginia Tech opened a multi-level campaign to give the appearance that the school had not only been victimized by Cho, but that the school could not be held responsible for allowing him the opportunity to go on his shooting rampage unhindered.

Enter Burson-Marsteller

Within a month of the shooting, the school hired one of the most powerful public relations firms in the U.S., Burson-Marsteller, to spin the tragedy to Tech's benefit, (I go into greater detail about Burson-Marsteller in Chapter IX, "Denial and Deception"). This spin-doctor team quickly developed the idea the school was as much a victim as those who had been killed or wounded. Indeed, the company did a training video with President Steger teaching him to answer media and public criticism that the school had not issued a campus-wide warning after the early morning double homicide—he was instructed not to apologize and to use such phrases as "the university grieves, too," and "the university is a victim, as well."

Burson-Marsteller was counting on the highly charged emotions following the rampage to carry their argument. The public was so horrified by the shootings that any argument that helped put the tragedy in the past fell on receptive ears. The slogan "Virginia Tech: Inventing the Future" was used to try and focus public attention away from the horror of the present. That slogan dovetailed with the feelings of the vast majority of the public who wanted to move on; who wanted to put the magnitude of this crime behind them. "Let the healing begin" became an emotional slogan to conceal the school's guilt and to cover up the fact that there could never be true healing unless the crime was thoroughly and completely analyzed. That analysis, however, school and elected officials were determined to prevent.

The school first adopted a code of silence. Simply put, if you don't talk about something, it cannot get into the public domain. As noted in an earlier chapter, the school had next to no contact with the injured and their families in the immediate aftermath of the shooting. Professor Roy, in her book *No Right to Remain Silent*, writes, "It therefore became necessary for the president [Charles Steger] and some members of his administration to construct an ethical framework on which a culture of silence could be rebuilt. The most convenient strategy was one that had been used before— i.e., a rigorous enforcement of state and federal laws related to student privacy." She goes on to note the irony in this solution as it was the same use of privacy laws that resulted in an inability by the university's care teams, faculty, and disciplinary board to share vital information about (or on) Cho that might have helped him receive proper treatment before the shooting. As I have discussed in Chapter III this was, both before and after the shooting, a complete misinterpretation of both the spirit and the letter of the law. However, it was this bogus and obstructive interpretation that the school chose to use during the investigation of the shooting. To assert the primacy of a dead criminal's right to privacy over the public's need to understand what led to his murderous rage seems ridiculous, but what else were the administration and campus police doing when they did not inform Cho's parents or the English department of Cho's incarceration at the St. Albans Behavioral Center for the Carilion New River Valley Medical Center?

But, silence was not enough; Tech needed more. The school needed a scholar, a respected academic to explain why the Steger administration could not have foreseen Cho's rampage. The Steger administration thought it had found the answer to its prayers in the writings of *New York Times* best-selling author, Nassim Taleb. Taleb's book, *The Black Swan*, deals with events that cannot be predicted. A "Black Swan" event can be positive or negative; it is "deemed highly improbable yet causes massive consequences." School officials, as they clamored to argue that April 16, 2007 was not foreseeable, were quick to call Cho's massacre a "Black Swan." The school used the "Black Swan" argument in rebutting the Department of Education's findings that Virginia Tech, by not issuing a warning immediately following the double homicide, had broken the law— the Clery Act.

If you read Taleb's book, he says that a "Black Swan" event has several characteristics. The most distinctive of which is that nothing in the past can point to its possibility. Here, the author cites a turkey that is fed lots of food for months on end, and then a few weeks before Thanksgiving, the farmer cuts off his head. For the turkey, nothing pointed to its imminent demise—the head-lopping was a total surprise; it was a "Black Swan."

Virginia Tech neglected to tell the public that Taleb also says that "some events can be rare and consequential, but somewhat predictable, particularly to those who are prepared for them and have the tools to understand them…" Taleb calls these events "near Black Swans." The events of April 16, 2007, clearly fall into that category. Furthermore, I would remind Virginia Tech that just because something is unlikely does not mean that it is not predictable. And, there was ample evidence that Cho might harm himself or others and the school found every excuse it could to avoid confronting those indications and doing something about them.

The school's use of the "Black Swan" defense is equivalent to intellectual dishonesty. What a shame that a great academic institution would stoop to such duplicitous measures. Rather than support the school's case, Tech's willingness to distort the "Black Swan" is an indication of just how bankrupt Virginia Tech's defense is. In fact, the school's readiness to misrepresent the "Black Swan," as it desperately grasped for excuses, only underscores the indefensible actions of the Steger administration.

Was Cho's rampage not foreseeable, was his mental illness not widely known to school officials? How many times does Virginia Tech have to be reminded of all the warning signs? Does the school really have to be told again that a judge ruled that Cho was an imminent danger to himself as a result of mental illness? Has the school forgotten that Cho's behavior toward women got him into trouble with campus police? Does the school not remember that in the fall of 2005, Cho's writings in Professor Nikki Giovanni's "Creative Writing: Poetry" class were so dark and menacing that students dropped out? What more evidence of prior knowledge does anyone need than the fact that Professor Giovanni contacted the Dean of the English department saying that unless Cho was removed from the class, she would resign?

Was the school not aware that Cho sent a very clear and vivid warning when he wrote a paper for a creative writing class concerning a young man who hated the students at his school and planned to kill them and himself?

No matter how much the Steger administration twists and turns, the facts are the facts. The school has a right to its own opinion, but not its own facts. Furthermore, Virginia Tech has no right to keep all the facts from the public. While some of you may argue that hindsight is 20-20, and therefore it is not fair to criticize or condemn Virginia Tech now for what took place on or before April 16, 2007, I would argue that hindsight is foresight—the signs were there and they were ignored. And, if we don't analyze and condemn wrong actions before the shooting, we will never learn.

The Expert Opinion

Another part of the school's campaign to pull the wool over the public's eyes was to find an expert on campus safety to say that Virginia Tech could not have foreseen the events of April 16, 2007. And that is what they did. Virginia Tech called upon Delores A. Stafford, President & CEO of D. Stafford & Associates and former police chief of George Washington University to write an opinion as to whether or not the school violated the Clery Act. Ms. Stafford is indeed a leading campus security expert with outstanding credentials. Her reputation is among the finest in the field of school security. I could devote a whole chapter to her distinguished career, most notably as Chief of Police for George Washington University. To quote from her biography, " ... she is a much sought after speaker, consultant, educator, expert witness, and instructor on campus security, campus safety and law enforcement related issues and on compliance with the Jeanne Clery Disclosure of Campus Security Policy and Campus Crime Statistics Act (The Clery Act) ... ."

The problem is that Virginia Tech paid big money for her opinion. In response to my Freedom of Information request, Bobbie Jean Norris, Special Assistant to the Associate Vice President, Virginia Tech, reported that Ms. Stafford was paid $9,028.00 for her opinion and then another $26,923.80 for Clery Act training, consulting, and an audit. No matter how sincere or well written the opinion is, the fact that Stafford took money for her expertise and subsequently got work from the university seriously undercuts the credibility of her words. It stretches the limits of credibility to believe that Virginia Tech would pay an expert thousands of dollars to write an opinion stating that the school broke the law.

It is also important to note the narrowness of Stafford's brief. She was not asked to write about the case overall, or about how the university could have done better; she was asked only if the University violated the Clery Act. Because this was a paid analysis, Stafford did not look outside the specifics of her brief. She did not have to lie or stretch the truth, she only had to do what she was paid to do, and not one bit more.

As you, the reader, well know, the heart of the problem is what the Virginia Tech administration was doing after the double homicide at West Ambler Johnston Hall. Why did it take over two hours for the school to issue a vaguely worded warning—just moments before Cho slaughtered 30 people at Norris Hall?

Here is the vague message the Policy Group sent out at 9:30 a.m. just 10 minutes before Cho began his rampage:

"A shooting incident [no mention of two people killed or that a murderer could be on the campus] occurred at West Ambler Johnston earlier this morning. Police are on the scene and are investigating. The university community is urged to be cautious and are asked to contact Virginia Tech Police if you observe anything suspicious or with information on the case. Contact Virginia Tech Police at 231-6411. Stay tuned to the www.vt.edu. We will post as soon as we have more information."

Stafford notes that the Clery Act does not give a timeframe for issuing the warning notice. She therefore argues that the letter of the law was not broken—what she does not say is that at best, Virginia Tech was doing the minimum acceptable under the Clery Act. Stafford admits 25 percent of the schools queried indicated that in 2006—a year before the Tech tragedy— they were issuing warnings within an hour of an incident. The fact that these schools were issuing warnings within an hour, following the guidelines of the Clery Act, undercuts the thrust of Stafford's argument because those schools were adhering to Clery Act standards.

Stafford's opinion is even more puzzling when you remember that President Steger admitted under oath that no one knew who the killer was or where he or she was, and that a school official sent an email to notify the governor of the events at West Ambler Johnston Hall, saying "gunman on the loose."

Stafford's analysis and justification for her conclusion appears to selectively pick facts. For starters, she does not address why parts of Virginia Tech took the initiative and locked down—in compliance with the Clery Act—yet the whole school did not. She never addresses the inconsistencies in Tech's response to the double homicides. Nor does she question the lack of evidence behind the police's initial assertion that the Clark and Hilscher murders were the result of a "domestic incident."

The bottom line is the fact that Stafford was paid big money to write an analysis saying Virginia Tech did not violate the law. This exchange of money raises serious questions about her objectivity. While I am sure there was nothing under the table in her financial dealings with the Steger administration, the fact remains that because Stafford was paid for her words, her opinion is not only tainted, but open to serious questions.

Excuses: Missing Information and Ignorance of the Law

Another perplexing problem centering on keeping information from both the public's eye and from the Governor's Review Panel centers on Cho's "lost" medical records. There is no evidence that Cho's medical records were intentionally lost, but their disappearance was certainly convenient from the school's point of view. The circumstances surrounding

Cho's missing medical records and then their discovery have a particularly unsavory odor. Indeed, all the hemming and hawing by individuals in positions of authority—following the discovery of Cho's medical records— brings into question the credibility of those who claim to search for truth in the aftermath of the shootings at Virginia Tech.

I fully agree with the *Richmond Times-Dispatch* when it wrote, "It strains credulity to think that files relating to the worst campus massacre in American history simply have slipped the mind of the very person (Robert Miller) who had counseled the gunman." Robert Miller, the former director of the school's counseling center, was in fact among several senior school officials who consulted with English department Chairwoman Lucinda Roy when she sought help for Cho after Professor Nikki Giovanni barred Cho from one of her writing classes.

Somehow Dr. Miller forgot that he had Cho's medical records. It is amazing that someone so absent-minded could ever have risen to be the head of the Cook Counseling Center. Just the fact that a patient's medical records were "accidently" removed from an office in the first place raises questions about his motive and professionalism.

What the records show is a lack of thoroughness in dealing with a deeply troubled student. This lack of thoroughness raises the specter of culpability on the part of some officials at the Cook Counseling Center. The records show that the Center had numerous opportunities to deal with Cho's mental instability and did nothing. For example, as early as 2005, a Counseling Center staff member described Cho as "troubled" and in need of follow-up counseling. That follow up did not take place. The legal question that will probably never be addressed (or answered) is whether or not the counseling center is liable for its lack of professionalism in handing Cho's records. What is clear is that both Dr. Miller's and the center's poor practices should have at least brought a review of their licenses.

School officials said that they were "dismayed" that the records were found in Miller's possession. It is one thing to express this emotion and another to act on it. In fact, if anything characterizes the reaction of people in positions of authority (school leaders and politicians) since the Virginia Tech tragedy of April 16, 2007, it is that they are long on words and short on action. I would have thought that the school would have been in the forefront of thoroughly examining the Cook Counseling Center and scrubbing it to remove any question of incompetence. Not only was the school quiet on the counseling center's conduct, but the Governor's Review Panel never interviewed Robert Miller.

Then there are the school's claims of ignorance of the law. If I recall correctly, Virginia Tech said it did not contact the Cho family about their son's odd and menacing behavior because of privacy issues. The same defense was given as reason for the various school components (who were aware of the problems Cho presented) for not communicating and consulting with each other. In fact, the school was wrong in all cases.

According to the U.S. Department of Justice and Human Services, there was plenty of support under the Health Information Privacy Act for notifying Cho's parents.

The Privacy Rule sets rules and limits on who can look at and receive your health information. To make sure that your health information is protected in a way that does not interfere with your health care, your information can be used ads shared:

1. *For your treatment and care coordination*
2. *To pay doctors and hospitals for your health care and to help run their business*
3. *With your family, relatives, friends, or others you identify who are involved in your health care or your health care bills, unless you object*
4. *To make sure doctors give good care and nursing homes are clean and safe*
5. *To protect the public's health, such as by reporting when the is in your area*
6. *To make required reports to the police such as reporting gunshot wounds*

As far as his school records go, there was no reason for his high school not to share information with Virginia Tech, and no justification for Virginia Tech to withhold information from the Governor's Review Panel. According the U.S. Department of Education, writing about the Family Education and Rights Privacy Act:

Generally, schools must have written permission from the parent or eligible student in order to release any information from a student's education record. However, FERPA allows schools to disclose those records, without consent to the following parties or under the following conditions (34 CFR 99.31):

1. *School officials with legitimate educational interest;*
2. *Other schools to which a student is transferring;*
3. *Specific officials for audit or evaluation purposes;*
4. *Appropriate parties in connection with financial aid to a student;*
5. *Organizations conducting certain studies for or on behalf of the school;*
6. *Accrediting organizations;*
7. *To comply with a judicial order or lawfully issued subpoena;*
8. *Appropriate officials in cases of health and safety emergencies; and*

9. State and local authorities, within a juvenile justice system pursuant to specific State law.

Clearly, in Cho's case, there should not have been any serious obstacles to health workers or university staff sharing information among themselves about his case. In fact this is reiterated on Virginia Tech's own Web site where it lists the rights to privacy that a student may expect with regard to academic records:

> *The right to consent to disclosures of personally identifiable information contained in the student's education records, except to the extent that FERPA authorizes disclosure without consent. One exception that permits disclosure without consent is disclosure to school officials with legitimate educational interests or concerns of health safety. A school official is a person employed by the university in an administrative, supervisor, academic or research, or support staff position (such as health staff); a person or company with whom the university has contracted (such as an attorney, auditor, or collection agent); a person serving on the Board of Visitors; or a student serving on an official committee, such as a disciplinary or grievance committee, or assisting another school official in performing his or her tasks. A school official has a legitimate educational interest if the official needs to review an education record in order to fulfill his or her professional responsibility.*

Privacy and the right to privacy seem to bounce around at Virginia Tech like a leaky balloon—sometimes privacy is respected, sometimes not. I am confused. To borrow a word that university officials used, I am "dismayed." Can there really be confusion about patients' privacy?

You have to wonder—how can one of this nation's best academic universities be so ignorant of the law?

The Attorney General of the Commonwealth of Virginia

Have laws been broken in the mishandling of Cho's medical records? The victims' families and the public in general have a right to know. And where better to find out than from the office of the Attorney General of the Commonwealth of Virginia? Common sense dictates that the Attorney General would not be part of keeping information from the public; certainly the Attorney General would leave no stone unturned to bring the facts to light. Just look at the mission statement of the office of the Virginia Attorney General:

The Office of the Attorney General is the Commonwealth's law firm. The office is charged with providing advice to state agencies and the Governor; serving as consumer counsel for the people of the Commonwealth; defending criminal convictions on appeal to ensure that justice is served; and defending the laws of the Commonwealth when they are challenged on constitutional grounds. In the carrying out of these obligations this office will adhere to the highest ethical standards, respect the traditions and precedents that have shaped our Commonwealth, and bring all legal resources to bear in order to protect the people, the customs, and the welfare of the Commonwealth of Virginia. As Virginia's law firm, the Office of Attorney General is dedicated to seeing to it that justice is served, wisdom is sought, and the right course of action is consistently taken. By faithfully serving Virginia and her people, this office strives to ensure that the Commonwealth will reach a future even brighter than its glorious past.

Where else, then, could justice be better served, wisdom sought, and the right course of action be consistently taken to ensure that a brighter future is guaranteed, than in the search for truth in two Virginia school shootings? And who better to bring all the facts into the open than the Virginia Attorney General?

Unfortunately, and sadly, that was not the case. We need to take a look at how the Virginia Attorney General's office has acted in response to both the murders at the Appalachian School of Law and Virginia Tech.

My interaction with the Attorney General's office goes back to July of 2004, when my family was trying to find the truth about the shootings at the Appalachian School of Law in Grundy, Virginia that killed the mother of my oldest grandchild. My experience was a huge disappointment.

As noted in an earlier chapter, Angela Dales had received a threatening email several months before she was murdered. The email was in clear violation of both state and federal laws. However, when Angela' family asked for details, the police refused to let the dead student's family look at the investigative report. The police did promise to the family to read its content and answer questions. Twelve years later the family is still waiting for that to happen.

Not satisfied, we hoped that then-Attorney General Jerry Kilgore would help us. What a great way for him "to better serve justice" particularly because he had issued the following statement after the law school shooting:

"It was with great sadness that I learned of the shootings that injured and killed innocent people at the Appalachian School of Law

in Grundy, Virginia. As natives of Southwest Virginia, my wife Marty and I extend our sympathies to the families and friends who lost loved ones in the senseless act."

"At the same time we experience these emotions, however, there is a clear sense among us all that as Virginians we cannot tolerate such acts of violence. Our institutions of higher learning are intended to be sanctuaries of education and self-improvement—not places of violence. Law abiding Virginians may rest assured that law enforcement authorities will identify whoever is responsible and our court system will see that justice is done."

Armed with the thought that we would find a sympathetic and responsive ear, I sent the following letter:

Virginia Attorney General Kilgore
900 E. Main Street
Richmond, VA. 23219

Sir:

On January 16, 2002, Angela Dales—the mother of my granddaughter—was shot and killed at the Appalachian School of Law. Nearly a year before the tragedy, she received a threatening e-mail. State Highway Patrolman Lambert, who investigated the e-mail, told the Dales and Cariens families that the police do not know who sent the e-mail, but that there is no link between the e-mail and the shooting. Mr. Lambert said we could not see the police report because it is "confidential," but that he would retrieve the report from the Richmond archives and answer any questions we have. This was never done.

We are asking the help of your office to:
1. *Explain why the police assert that there is no connection between the e-mail and the shooting when they do not know who wrote it.*
2. *Explain the justification for classifying the police report 'confidential.'*
3. *Explain the procedures we would have to take to get access to the police report.*
4. *Explain why officer Lambert never followed up on his promise to answer our questions.*

I am enclosing both a copy of the e-mail and copy of a notarized note authorizing me to act on behalf of Angela Dales parents—Sue and Danny Dales.

I look forward to hearing from you or a member of your staff.

Yours sincerely,

David Cariens, Jr.

When I sent the letter, I was not aware of the fact that one of the major financial supporters of the attorney general (and probably of his later unsuccessful run for governor), was on the board of the law school. But even had I known, I would not have been deterred—assuming that Attorney General Kilgore would "faithfully serve Virginia and her people." I was convinced that the attorney general would help, not only because of what he had said in public, but because he and his political party run on a platform of family values. What better way to live up to the family values platform than to help a school-shooting victim's family, a family in severe distress?

The following is the response I received from Kilgore's office:

Dear Mr. Cariens,

This office is in receipt of your letter with regard to the questions you have concerning the State Police investigation of (a) threatening email received by Angela Dales, the mother of your granddaughter. I am very sorry to hear that Angela's life was subsequently taken at the Appalachian School of Law.

I understand from your letter that you have been informed by the investigating officer that the author of the email is not known but there is no link between the email and the shooting. Please understand that the authority and jurisdiction of this Office are limited by statute. The Attorney General's Office functions primarily as a law firm for state government. In this capacity, it advises state officials and represents the various state agencies and departments.

Because this Office is not typically charged with the oversight of the investigatory functions of police and local prosecutors, it has no knowledge of the investigation of which you inquire. The proper functioning of our criminal justice system, however, necessitates that criminal investigations be kept confidential. This need is recognized in Virginia Freedom of Information Act ("VFOIA"), which excludes from its provisions, subject to the discretion of the custodian, "complaints, memoranda, correspondence and evidence relating to a criminal investigation or prosecution, other than criminal incident information." "Criminal incident information" consists of "a general description of the criminal activity reported, the date and general location the alleged crime was committed, the identity of the investigating officer, and a general description of any injuries suffered or property damaged or stolen." Please note that, under certain circumstances, even "criminal incident information" may be withheld under the VFOIA. Information on obtaining records from the State Police under the VFOIA is contained on their web site at www.vsp.state.va.us.

If you are dissatisfied with the manner in which the investigation was handled, or by the fact that the investigating officer did not follow up on his promise to answer your questions, you may file a complaint at any State Police Office or by calling the Internal Affairs Section at telephone number (804) 323-2383. Information on filing complaints can also be obtained at www.vsp.state.va.us/professionalstandards.htm.

Please understand this Office is prohibited from providing legal advice to private citizens and, consequently, nothing herein may be construed as such. You are of course, free to consult with any attorney engaged in private practice of law. I hope you will find this information helpful in obtaining answers to your questions. Thank you for expressing your concerns.

Sincerely,
James O. Towey
Assistant Attorney General

The response from the Attorney General's office, albeit polite, contains prime examples of the "double talk" victims and their families encounter in Virginia. First, Mr. Towey ignores the illogical aspect of the police saying they don't know who wrote the e-mail, but there is no connection to the law school murders. Second, Mr. Towey wrote that his office "is not typically charged with the oversight of investigatory functions of local police and local prosecutors, it has no knowledge of the investigation of which you inquire." The word "typical" tells me that the state's Attorney General's office does have the statutory powers to review local investigations. In fact, I cannot find anything in the statutes governing the functioning of the Attorney General's office that prohibits him from investigating the circumstances and investigations surrounding the e-mail. Furthermore, the shootings at the Appalachian School of Law were not "typical." The shootings were the worst to occur on school grounds in the state's history up to that time. If there are indications of incompetence in either the investigation surrounding the crime or in prosecuting the case against the killer, are we to believe that it is "*typical*" for the state's Attorney General to turn a blind eye to a miscarriage of justice?

Sadly, slightly more than five years later, the Virginia Tech massacre occurred, and while I had hoped to see changes in how information was shared with the public, the surviving victims, and the victims' families, what I saw was confusion over jurisdiction and an inconsistent approach to finding and considering evidence.

Nevertheless, given the magnitude of the Virginia Tech tragedy, surely the Attorney General of the State of Virginia would leave no stone unturned to help find the truth and help adopt measures designed to prevent a repetition of these atrocities. Certainly this time the public would find out the whole truth.

Unlike the Appalachian School of Law, the Attorney General's office did take an aggressive, no nonsense approach to the Tech tragedy. But unfortunately this assertiveness would be selective and aimed at protecting the state of Virginia, its institutions, and its employees. When confronted with violations of the law, the actions of the Attorney General's office would go back and forth between threats and stony silence. For example, point seven of the Governor's Review Panel Report's Key Findings states that "Cho purchased two guns in violation of federal law." One of those guns was purchased in Virginia, but the Virginia Attorney General never investigated this crime.

Lucinda Roy notes in her book that members of the school received a toughly worded memorandum from the Office of the Attorney General of the Commonwealth of Virginia, demanding cooperation from the English faculty in turning over their computer hard drives. Indeed, the no-nonsense tone of the memo took the English faculty by surprise. Professor Roy writes in her book, *No Right to Remain Silent:*

> "I was taken aback … when we received another memo, this time from the Office of the Attorney General of the Commonwealth of Virginia. The memo, dated July 10, 2007, bore the state's official seal and was signed by a person I had never heard of: Ron Forehand, chief, Education Section. [Ronald C. Forehand serves as the senior assistant attorney general in the Health, Education and Social Services Division in the state's attorney

general's office.] It was addressed to university counsel but its subject related to faculty in English who had lingering questions about the imaging of their hard drive. For those of us who had hoped that the administration would be responsive to our security concerns, the contents and tone of the memo were shocking. Ron Forehand made it clear that the punishment for non-compliance would be extreme:

"Employees who refuse access to Virginia Tech-owned electronic equipment for this data preservation project may be subject to a range of sanctions, to include discipline (including discharge) and denial of a defense by the Attorney General's office in the event litigation is filed as a result of April 16th."

"In the even (sic) an employee is not cooperative, I suggest that the university simply confiscate the equipment, take appropriate action in respect to copying, and then take appropriate personnel action against the resistant employee."

"I'd be happy to speak personally to any employee should that be necessary. Please know that you, the legal department, and the university have the full support of the Office of the Attorney General in your endeavors."

" … if Virginia Tech employees wish to be represented by the university attorneys, they must abide by their advice. The Tech administration can deny them representation, if it sees fit. The result of this arrangement at Virginia Tech was that free speech was severely curtailed, and advice for those outside the upper administration could be hard to come by." (Page 145, *No Right to Remain Silent*)

One wonders where this hard-hitting attitude was when Cho's medical records were reported lost. If you look closely at Forehand's words then maybe the silence on his part when it came to Cho's "lost" records is not too surprising. Indeed, the conflict of interest and complexity of the role played by the state's Attorney General in the Virginia Tech tragedy quickly became a cause for concern by many. Again, Professor Roy points that fact out when she cites Virginia Tech President Charles Steger's testimony to the Review Panel:

"In his introductory remarks, President Steger reminded the panel that the Virginia Tech attorney also serves as "Special Assistant Attorney General." This implied that the

Office of the Attorney General in Richmond was overseeing the entire procedure on behalf of the Commonwealth of Virginia, and reinforced the notion that whatever was said by the legal counsel had been approved by the state. In this tricky situation—i.e., a state-controlled system of education was being investigated by the state that controlled it—potential conflicts of interest could not be more apparent. Not only was one arm investigating another arm, the two legal offices—the state's and the university's—were, all the while, shaking hands. Although a full list of Policy Group participants has not been made public, university legal counsel was present on April 16. This means that the office responsible for representing all the administrators, faculty members, and staff at Virginia Tech was placed in the unenviable position of having to defend itself and its clients at the same time. I can't imagine how any attorney, however dedicated they may be, could manage this task." (Page 97, *No Right to Remain Silent*)

Professor Roy lays out a complicated set of conflicting interests—the problem of a state body, the Attorney General's office investigating a state organization, Virginia Tech; and the attorneys at Virginia Tech (part of the Attorney General's office) having the responsibility of defending their clients against their bosses at the Attorney General's office.

Despite the obvious conflicts of interest, it appeared in the case of Virginia Tech that, the Attorney General would be aggressive in getting to the bottom of crime. Therefore, I was surprised when nothing appeared in the news media to indicate any reaction from the Attorney General's office to Cho's missing medical files being found in Dr. Miller's home in the summer of 2009. Puzzled, I sent a Freedom of Information Request to the Attorney General's office on September 6, 2009, more than two months before the final version of the Governor's Review Panel Report (*The Addendum*) was released. I received the following response:

COMMONWEALTH of VIRGINIA
OFFICE OF THE ATTORNEY GENERAL

September 14, 2009

Mr. David S. Cariens, Jr.
Xxx Road
˙ Kilmarnock, Va. 22482

Dear Mr. Cariens:

This Office has received your e-mail of September 6, 2009 in which you make a request under the Freedom of Information Act ("FOIA"), Va. Code 2.2-3700 et seq., as follows:

Has the Attorney General or the Attorney General's office issued an opinion on the fact that the medical records of Seung Hui Cho had been removed from the school's counseling office and were in the home of Dr. Miller?

No opinion has been issued by this Office in this matter. Further, the Attorney General's Office represents and provides legal services to the agencies and institutions of Virginia's state government, including Virginia Tech in ending litigation arising out of the tragic massacre of April 16, 2007. It is the responsibility of locally elected Commonwealth's Attorneys to investigate and enforce the criminal laws of the Commonwealth that might apply in this situation.

Only public records, as opposed to information generally, are subject to the Freedom of Information Act. The health care records you refer to, thanks to the consent of Cho's family and administrator of his estate, have been made available by Virginia Tech and may be accessed at http://www.vtnews.edu/story607.php. A review of those documents reveals that they do not provide any information that is new or different from that which was available to the Governor's Review Panel.

Sincerely,

Jan Myer
FOIA Administrator

All of a sudden the tough, threatening tone of the Attorney General's memorandum to the Virginia Tech English Department was gone and instead, Ms. Myer tells me there is "no opinion." If it is the responsibility of the locally elected Commonwealth's Attorneys to investigate and enforce the criminal laws of the Commonwealth that might apply to the situation, why had the Attorney General's office played such an aggressive role in dealing with the school's English Department? Why be so vocal in dealing with the English Department and so silent with the Cook Counseling Center, unless you wanted to avoid drawing attention to the unprofessional handling—or lack of treatment—of Cho?

Finally, one has to question the Virginia Attorney General office's assertion that Cho's medical records "do not provide any information that is new or different from that which was available to the governor's Review Panel." That is simply not true:

1. Just having access to the medical records would have made the victims and the victims' families more confident in decisions they would have to make and course of action they should follow. If you recall, the Governor's Review Panel Report cited the missing records as a key gap in the investigation.

2. The records indicate that when triaged, Cho denied any suicidal tendencies. However, nowhere is there a reference to a medical professional's thorough evaluation of Cho. In a broader sense, I question whether these records are representative of acceptable record keeping policy for any professional in any facility providing medical services. If these records are an example of the quality of work done at the Cook Counseling Center, then they are evidence of serious problems in the Center's counseling.

3. The medical records contain curious hand-written comments: Counselor S. Lynch Conrad, dated 12/14/05: "Did not assess—student has had two previous triages in past 2 weeks—last 2 days ago." Is that a legitimate excuse for no triage? No it is not. In fact, I would argue that if a student has been triaged twice in a two-week period for possible suicidal tendencies, there is a real problem that demands attention. I would argue strongly that a third triage is exactly what is needed.

4. The fact that there are no supervisory signatures, as required, on the Cook Counseling Center

Triage records for Cho on December 12, 2005 and December 14, 2005, means that these documents could have been prepared or modified at any time up to the day they were found. The Triage record for November 11, 2005, has a supervisor's co-signature, dated December 1, 2005. The entry made on the last page was apparently done by Dr. Betzel on December 12th, but it is not co-signed. Subsequently, not only is the authenticity of those documents in doubt, I also question whether they are representative of acceptable record keeping policy for any professional in any facility providing medical services.

Seung Hui Cho's medical records bring into play the question of the professionalism and competency of the Cook Counseling Center and its staff as well as the foreseeability of his actions. That foreseeability is central to the whole investigation and analysis of the Virginia Tech massacre. The Cook Counseling Center records, then, do have a very direct bearing on the events of April 16, 2007.

The Addendum acknowledges the discovery of Cho's medical records and both the victims' families and Virginia Tech were given until September 2009 to submit any corrections or additions to the report. The medical records however, played a small role in the revision—the panel and the state apparently accepting the line argued by Ms. Myer that the records provided little new or different information from what was already known.

While the Attorney General's office cannot keep Cho's records from the public—they are available on the Internet—they are counting on the fact that few people will read them. If the Attorney General's office keeps repeating that there is nothing new in those records, then they are counting on the majority of people taking their words at face value and accepting Myer's words.

A number of years ago I attended a debate by the candidates running for the office of Virginia's Attorney General. In the question-and-answer segment I asked, "Why should the average voter be concerned about the Attorney General? What is it that the Attorney General does for the average citizen?" The answers from each candidate were convoluted, vague, and unsatisfactory. I now know why.

As long as law enforcement officials refuse to turn over documents central to finding out what led up to these tragedies, we will never learn from past mistakes. As long as officials spread half-truths and cover ups, carry on investigations without repercussions, the truth will never be known. As long as these people engage in their formidable and shrewd campaign of silence aimed at keeping the public in the dark, our schools will not be safe.

For the Pohle family the politicians, law enforcement personnel, and school officials cannot hide the harsh reality of what happened. And the attempts to hide the truth make the reality of what Cho did penetrate every fiber of their bodies, every aspect of their souls, shattering all hope of any return to some semblance of normalcy. To the Pohle's, Mike, their first child, was simply a great kid. They have so many wonderful memories of him that it would be impossible to write them all down.

Little Mike

Michael Pohle writes the following about his son: "Hopefully, you will be able to get a little glimpse into what life with him was all about once you read this.

"It seems like just yesterday that Mike was taken from us. His smile, infectious laugh, and compassion for others will always be part of our memories. We are blessed to have two beautiful children whom we love dearly and who are also gifts from God that we will cherish, and protect, for the rest of our lives. We will also, unfortunately, never be whole. It has been said that there is nothing as painful as the loss of a child. That is true. Part of your soul and your reason for being leaves with the death of a child. We will always have to live with an emptiness that is impossible to fill. At times, Mike's murder and his absence are very difficult on our remaining children. Nikki and Sean feel that they have to live up to the standard their dead brother set. No matter what you say to them, there is an expectation that cannot be fulfilled nor should it be. A tragedy like this can tear a family apart, but it is only as a family that we can continue on. Mike's death changed our family. It changes any family; but even with that we will continue to survive and love each other more each day.

"Mike faced some tough times growing up like every child does, but, never let life get him down for long. He always had a positive outlook. Growing up, he endured teasing and ridicule at a young age because of a speech problem, yet, he refused to let that define him. Teresa and I felt horrible at the way he was treated and like any parent tried to do whatever we could so that it would stop. Mike not only overcame his difficulties, he loved trying different things such as being in the Cub Scouts, playing the guitar, earning a black belt in karate, and playing sports. From elementary school through middle school he played soccer, basketball, baseball, and lacrosse. Once he entered high school he decided to try out for the football team, and stayed with that and lacrosse for the next four years. He continued to play lacrosse at Virginia Tech and truly loved that experience.

One of the things Mike was known for during his high school and college years, both in the classroom and on the field, was his drive to do his best and his commitment to his fellow students and his team.

"His compassion for others was reinforced for us the night prior to his funeral service at the wake we held so that people could come and pay their respects. We were in such awe at the hundreds of people who came to say goodbye. What touched us even more was the number of mothers and fathers who we had never known prior to the wake that actually thanked us for what Mike had done for their children. They told us stories of how their children had seemed so lost and alone in a high school of over 3,000 kids, yet, even though Mike didn't know them he reached out to their son or daughter because he remembered how alone he felt when he was the target of jokes and didn't feel like he had any friends. That touched our hearts so much and made us extremely proud even with our pain. That was the exact same behavior Mike took with him when he went to Virginia Tech.

"On April 16th, from the moment Mike's sister, Nikki, and I arrived in Blacksburg late in the afternoon after hearing of the mass shootings in the news and not being able to reach Mike, we desperately tried to get any information we could to find out where he was, without any success. As the hours passed, our fears grew and we started to think the unthinkable, but never gave up hope nor stopped trying to find him. Even in the chaos, with thousands of people moving about, you knew that some of those individuals walking around were also families trying to find their child just like us. In New Jersey, Mike's Aunt Liz and a number of our closest friends were at our home doing whatever they could to help my wife Teresa while praying that nothing had happened to him. Teresa had stayed home to keep us abreast of what was happening, and also with the expectation that Mike would call at any minute saying he was OK in a school of over 26,000 students. I called at different times to let Teresa know that we didn't know anything, both during the time I was driving and once I had arrived. It was not until around 11:00 p.m., while sitting in a room with Nikki and a group of Mike's friends at the hotel on Virginia Tech's campus, that we were told that Mike was dead. Our hearts stopped at that instant. I then moved to the most secluded section of the room we were in and called home to give Teresa the news.

"There are no words that can describe that moment in our lives. Our souls were ripped apart. I don't remember what was said, nor do I remember much of anything. The rest of the night was spent awake, crying and yelling, in Mike's apartment. Someone stayed with Teresa constantly and more friends, and our priest, came to the house starting the next morning.

"Mike was "big brother" to Nikki and his younger brother Sean. He was four years older than Nikki and ten years older than Sean. Mike watched over them and always made sure they were OK. He was protective of Nikki especially when it came to dating other boys and would make sure they knew he was watching over her. At times, she may not have seemed very pleased with her older brother getting involved in her social life, but, the reality was that she felt very good knowing that Mike would always be there for her. When she went off to college at West Virginia, Mike was still at Virginia Tech and they stayed in close contact with each other, constantly joking about who would win the football game between the two schools. The football rivalry was one of the many things they talked about. The last year that Virginia Tech and West Virginia played each other in football we decided it would be fun if our family met in Morgantown to be together and enjoy the game. I remember what a beautiful day it was and there were thousands of West Virginia fans all around us wearing their jerseys as we tailgated. Teresa and I were each wearing two shirts, one on top of the other. The outer shirt was West Virginia colors and the inner shirt was Virginia Tech colors. Mike, on the other hand, was walking through the crowd proudly wearing his Virginia Tech jersey and hat while chanting "Let's Go Hokies," all the while making sure he was staying real close to his sister who was wearing her West Virginia colors, but, trying to get as far from her brother as she could. Although one might think that what Mike was doing in the midst of thousands of loyal home team fans was a recipe for disaster, everyone realized that what was going on was all in good fun and enjoyed the moment. There were also times where Mike and Nikki would fight like cats and dogs, but, through it all they had a bond of love that was very strong. On April 16th, after hearing the news of the shootings and not being able to reach her brother at Tech, Nikki didn't think twice and immediately began to drive 5 ½ hours to Blacksburg to find him. There was no hesitation because it could involve Mike. She arrived in Blacksburg a couple hours ahead of me and kept us updated on her efforts to find him. Along with Mike's girlfriend Marcy, and his other friends, they began to contact the local hospitals in the area to see where he might be since he was nowhere to be found.

"Sean saw Mike as not only his mentor, but, actually thought of him as his hero. Given their age difference, Sean never really saw how Mike had been treated when he was very young, but, he was his biggest fan in high school. Sean loved going to Mike's games where he would see his brother on the field and his sister, a cheerleader, on the sidelines. Sean tried every sport that Mike had played, yet that was not where his real passion lay. Although Sean didn't realize it then, Mike was his biggest fan. One of many memorable moments in Sean's youth sports career happened during his first exposure to lacrosse. Sean was about seven years old and the referee for his game was not able to make it. To his surprise, his big brother Mike was asked if he would referee the game instead. Of course Mike said he would, but, the surprise that made us all laugh was that Mike had to blow the whistle for a foul and make Sean go to the penalty box for one minute. What was precious was watching Sean, again seven years old, walk up to Mike and look up at his big brother and ask him why he was putting his brother in the penalty box, to which Mike replied "I am so sorry Sean," gave him a hug, and they walked together to where Sean had to stand for his penalty time. When Sean was allowed back into the game the two of them hugged and everything was good. It was just a special moment. Mike and Sean were buddies. They would spend time together from watching cartoons to doing homework to just running around together."

*   *   *

When looking at the missteps at Virginia Tech, and the willingness of school officials to turn a blind eye toward the facts and even spread false information to cover their tracks, Mike's father was right when he said, "People just don't care anymore about responsibility and duty." I would add, that some Virginia Tech officials and state politicians pursued and promoted out-and-out lies with an unusually high degree of callousness; they intentionally investigated the Tech massacre in a way to prevent any repercussions on the school or its employees. They suffered from collective memory loss, and when speaking apparently could not tell the truth without lying.

CHAPTER IX

DENIAL AND DECEPTION

"Everyone sees what you seem to be, few know
what you really are; and those few do not dare
take a stand against the general opinion."
~Niccolo Machiavelli, Italian historian, politician, diplomat

Mistakes in judgment often are understandable and become deeply felt regrets because they were honest and made in the heat of the moment. In the case of Virginia Tech and its actions before, during, and after Cho's rampage, however, it is difficult to describe the school's mistakes, or its actions and inactions, as "honest." In the immediate aftermath of the April 16, 2007 carnage, Charles Steger's Virginia Tech was in shock, of that there can be no doubt—we all were. It is understandable that the Virginia Tech community could not accept that anything the school administration had done—or not done—played a role in enabling Cho to murder to so many.

In the first hour or so following the shootings, members of the school administration may have genuinely felt no guilt in setting the stage for Cho's slaughter. Everyone wanted to deny the harsh reality of what had happened. That denial, however, appears to have quickly turned into a recognition of the horrible truth—the school administration *did* play a role in allowing the conditions to exist for Cho's murderous rage. Indeed, the White family remembers President Steger meeting with the families late on the morning of April 17th. The badly shaken school president could say nothing that would give them solace. They remember a contrite school president responded to a question from a father, whose daughter was among the victims. The father asked, "Who is in charge?" To which Steger responded, "I am." Then to a follow-up question, "Who is responsible for this?" Steger hesitatingly and reluctantly said, "I am;" an answer he would begin to deny and retreat from almost immediately.

School officials conducted periodic, informal meetings with the families, but they were void of substance, at times resembling pep talks. Michael Pohle remembers thinking, "No one is in control or has taken control, there is no organization, we are getting conflicting answers—the whole atmosphere is chaotic." At one point Frank Beamer, the head football coach and long-time close buddy of President Charles Steger, addressed the families. That meeting, if well intended, was nevertheless particularly inane, only adding insult to injury. The White family described the meetings as being more like pep rallies, than meetings designed to impart information.

As that reality set in on April 16, 2007, the Steger administration appears to have quickly turned from shock to a cold and calculating campaign to cover up any and all of the school's complicity.

The problem for the school was that a solid case existed for Virginia Tech's culpability on many levels. From ignoring warning signs that Cho was a danger to himself and others, to the school's failure to warn the campus on the morning of April 16, 2007 about the double homicide at West Ambler Johnston Hall—the evidence against the Steger administration was glaringly apparent. In fact, Tech's failure to heed the numerous warning signs about Cho had come home to roost with devastating consequences.

Within hours, Virginia Tech set out to make the public believe a series of absurdities, such as the idea that no one in the school administration was aware of Cho's violent tendencies, and that it was reasonable to believe a murderer on the loose would not stay on campus. Tech needed a story that on the surface appeared reasonable. The school would count on the fact that few, if any, would examine its specious argument.

Virginia Tech began to repeat meaningless phrases that it hoped would turn attention away from the Steger administration by focusing on loyalty to the school and playing on people's emotions. The rallying cry became "We are Virginia Tech," then, "The Hokie Nation," and in an effort to put that dark day behind them, "Virginia Tech, Inventing the Future." The slogans of deception were quickly in place; the propaganda took on the tone and nature of a football rally—something Virginia Tech knows a great deal about.

Crisis Management

Initially, the school turned to the crisis management company, Firestorm Solutions, LLC. According to school records, Firestorm helped monitor and answer press questions, as well as monitor the call center. But

Firestorm's activities were much more extensive. School records show that Firestorm "assisted with communication messaging strategy and media relations, (as well as) ongoing strategy development and implementation." Firestorm did such things as monitor the media "for pertinent information regarding prime issues at hand." The company helped prepare school personnel for news conferences and to develop a crisis management strategy.

Firestorm also drafted a document called "Forward to the Future," which might have been the catalyst for the University's slogan "Invent the Future." In other words, Firestorm was central to the initial stages of building a strategy to deal with the crisis.

In an August 16, 2007 memorandum from Kay Heidbreder, the university counsel, to James Dunlap, the university's associate director of purchasing, Heidreder requested that the university pay Firestorm $150,000 for ten days of work. The school employed Firestorm April 19-29, 2007, because "Virginia Tech was inundated with press requests immediately following the events [the April 16 shootings]. Virginia Tech did not have the resources to meet information needs." Heidbreder also asserted that "because of the emergent circumstances, there was no time to bid for necessary assistance nor was any other competitive method practicable. Once the media crisis abated, University Relations terminated its relationship with Firestorm."

Three days earlier, on August 13, 2007, Larry Hincker (Associate Vice President, University Relations) sent a memo to Ellen Douglas, the university's Assistant Director Risk Management, explaining the bill. According to Hincker, "It was our understanding that this would be a combination pro-bono and for-pay services. The pace of the recovery and response was incredibly hectic and while the university legal counsel attempted to negotiate a contract, it was never signed by the time we dismissed the firm on April 29."

Hincker then wrote, "As you can see from the email note from Kim O'Rouke to Larry Hincker and Kay Heidbreder of Tuesday, August 7, President Steger has approved to pay this bill from state funds."

Issuing a no-bid contract in the wake of Cho's rampage is understandable; not having the contract signed is indefensible. For the university's counsel and legal staff to take the word of a board member that Firestorm's service would in part be pro bono, goes beyond naïve. Nothing is legally binding unless it is in a signed contract. The university's willingness to accept the word of a board member borders on incompetence, particularly when you consider that such a legal agreement would have been pretty much a boiler plate contract that the university or Firestorm should have had on hand. The university was initially hit with a bill for nearly $193,000. The bill ended up being negotiated down to

$150,000 and, as noted above, President Steger personally authorized its payment out of state funds.

Let's take a look at how this money was spent. An itemized expense account for Firestorm amounting to $10,649.41 includes $438.80 for a cancelled air ticket, another $125.55 for a cancelled hotel reservation, and $374.80 for yet another cancelled air ticket. Now, let's look at the hourly rates paid to Firestorm team members. The "principal" team member worked 115 hours at $450 an hour for a total of $51,750. The "preaction architect" (whatever that is), worked 107.5 hours at $150 an hour for a total of $16,125. A "research assistant" worked 7.5 hours at $100 an hour for $750, and finally, an "executive assistant" worked 6 hours at $75 an hour for a total of $300. The grand total was $68,925, discounted by 20 percent for a final bill of $55,140.

Firestorm employed the law firm of Blank Rome, LLP for not only advice on legal matters such as sovereign immunity, but to draft and help coordinate media strategy, as well as give advice on a potential press Web site. Part of Firestorm's fee went to pay the law firm $36,874.50. Blank Rome worked five days, from April 23 to 28.

Firestorm also brought in Dr. Ralph Diner, a psychologist with a background in Behavioral Medicine, including treatment of grief and trauma. He was employed from April 26 to May 7. His last four days were done free of charge. For six days of work, however, he was paid $12,000. Diner's invoice is in many respects the worst indictment of the school's poor treatment of the families. Diner is a nationally recognize grief counselor, yet his invoice indicates he met with only *two* mothers of the victims.

His invoice lists counseling several staff members, meetings with department heads, a tour of the campus, "discussed stress and press with the police and security," and went to the bookstore where he counseled with staff regarding their families' reactions to the events. His invoice contains a cryptic entry stating that he "met with Larry (Hincker) and was informed about the HR results and agreed to discontinue my involvement."

The documents detailing Diner's responsibilities at Virginia Tech show that his expertise was not used to counsel victims or their families, except in two cases. The official documents clearly demonstrate Diner's expertise was used for the benefit of the school, its staff, and its faculty.

Dr. Diner declined to be interviewed for this book, and Firestorm never responded to a certified letter I sent requesting an interview.

If you remember, Heidbreder wrote, "Once the media crisis abated, University Relations terminated its relationship with Firestorm." In fact, the media crisis was not over by April 29, 2007 when Firestorm was let go. Cho's rampage was still a major story and the media was still asking pointed questions about Virginia Tech's actions before, during, and after April 16th.

The crisis was becoming more serious because of the nature of the questions being asked about Tech's actions. In that sense the crisis was growing—not abating.

Firestorm's ties to Virginia Tech, then, lasted a scant 10 days. The shootings had struck a deep and responsive chord everywhere in the United States—and abroad. People wanted answers and explanations. The school was under a microscope and something needed to be done to explain Tech's embarrassing actions and inactions. Apparently Firestorm was not big enough to handle the enormity of negative publicity.

Virginia Tech needed a company with a history of handling, managing, and manipulating evidence; a firm that could twist the crisis to Virginia Tech's benefit or at least minimize the widespread and growing criticism of the Steger administration.

The trick would be to come up with a public line that would make the school's administration a victim, a line that was plausible and played to the emotions of the school's alumni and financial contributors. For that, Tech would need experts to help metastasize the deceit.

The school turned to one of this country's largest and most successful public relations firms, Bursen-Marsteller. On May 29, 2007, less than six weeks after the shootings, and one month after terminating Firestorm, Tech signed a contract with Burson-Marsteller to handle publicity about the shooting rampage.

Burson-Marsteller received $663,006.48 for developing a spin on the tragedy. That spin was, and still is, designed to minimize damage to the school and protect school officials from lawsuits. A comparison of the nearly $700,000.00 paid to a public relations firm with the $100,000 given to each of the dead victims' families gives you an idea of the extent to which Virginia Tech was running scared and was willing to buy its way out of a serious dilemma. Keep in mind that Virginia Tech has a university public relations office staffed by highly competent officials—as well as courses in public relations taught by outstanding faculty members—yet the school paid a princely sum to a public relations firm to help ensure that the truth about the shooting would be obscured in a frenzy of emotionalism.

Buying Burson-Marsteller's services only added insult to injury for the families. The math is lousy; the math says it all. The school's judgment and priorities were badly misplaced. The nearly $700,000 would have been better spent had it been given to the grieving families to help in the recovery process. Or, that money could have been spent on school security as a tribute to the victims.

For those who believe the dead victims' families $100,000 compensation was inappropriate, how much worse is it that Firestorm was paid $150,000 and Bursen-Marsteller received nearly $700,000 to do a job that could have been done internally if only the administration had been focused on an honest accounting of events rather than an elaborate spin-doctoring of the evidence.

Virginia Tech chose well. Burson-Marsteller came to prominence in the 1990s for organizing a campaign focused on smokers' rights in support of Philip Morris and the tobacco industry. (A tie to some of the most powerful influence peddlers in Virginia may have helped the firm land the contract.) Later, Burson-Marsteller played spin-doctor for Dow-Corning's campaign on behalf of silicone breast implants. Some silicone implants developed leaks once implanted in women's bodies, causing serious health problems. Dow-Corning hired Bursen-Marsteller to help minimize the negative publicity. Can there be any other conclusion that Burson-Marsteller was engaged by Virginia Tech to continue working the magic of misdirection and cover-up?

The school also moved quickly to protect its president and police chief. Within three days of the shootings, Virginia Tech created a Web site (www.wesupportvt.com) in support of President Charles Steger and Chief Wendell Flinchum. It took Virginia Tech's Office of Recovery and Support four months to get the Web site (www.recoveryvt.com) for the victims' families up and running.

On March 18, 2009, an OpEd article I wrote appeared in the *Richmond Times-Dispatch*. The article called for Virginia Tech President Charles Steger to step down and for Governor Kaine to reopen the investigation into the Tech shootings. A few days later, I received a well-written, thoughtful response from a lawyer in New York. He wrote, "While there are many bright, highly competent and well-intentioned people working in higher education, there is also a high level of mediocrity, incompetence and self-interest. In my opinion the latter traits have been displayed in this situation at Virginia Tech. And, such traits have been excused and ratified by the Governor's immediate political actions in this instance."

The lawyer's words strike at the heart of what appears to be under-the-table actions by a school administration whose main goal seems to have been to avoid making tough decisions regarding a deeply troubled student. Look at Penn State. There were no deaths at State College, but young boys' lives have been scarred forever; they have been psychologically and physically damaged. And how did Penn State's leadership respond? The school thought of the institution first and protecting itself. The following is a direct quote from the findings of the Louis Freeh report investigating Penn State sexual abuse scandal:

"Our most saddening and sobering finding is the total disregard for the safety and welfare of Sandusky's child victims by the most senior leaders at Penn State. The most powerful men at Penn State failed to take any steps for 14 years to protect the children who Sandusky victimized. Messrs. Spanier, Schultz, Paterno and Curley never

demonstrated, through actions or words, any concern for the safety and well-being of Sandusky's victims until after Sandusky's arrest."

It appears that Penn State responded with a wink and a nod, an incomprehensible willingness to turn a blind eye to child abuse. Both schools—Penn State and Virginia Tech—put the reputations of their respective institutions ahead of taking action. Neither school took the correct course of action when confronted with crimes—Virginia Tech at the double homicide in West Ambler Johnston Hall, and Penn State when confronted with eye-witness accounts of child abuse.

"Protect the school and its reputation" appears to have been the mantra of these administrations bent on shielding their actions from review and recriminations. Look at the Appalachian School of Law, Virginia Tech, and now Penn State. In all three cases, the inaction of school officials struck at the heart of common sense and human decency. In all three instances, at all three schools, the words "mediocre" and "incompetent" leadership describe the actions of the schools' administrations.

My family is part of the Hokie Nation. A member of our family is a graduate of Virginia Tech. We are so proud of the outstanding education he received at Virginia Tech. However, that pride does not preclude the shame we feel over the school's abysmal leadership—specifically, the school's overriding intent to protect and enhance the Virginia Tech image at all costs, including at the expense of the shooting victims' families.

The Emergency Response Plan

Indeed, the closer I look at Tech's actions, the more disheartened I become. The more I examine the words and actions of Virginia Tech officials regarding the April 16, 2007 shooting, the more I realize that school officials will say just about anything to conceal the truth. The school's willingness to avoid addressing the facts has run amok. For example, Virginia Tech has never adequately explained the inconsistency in the rapid warning of the campus in the Morva case some eight months before Cho's rampage, and its inaction on April 16th.

A closer examination of the earlier incident raises some disturbing questions. Following the Morva incident, a review of the university's Emergency Response Plan (ERP) recommended adding a section dealing with armed and dangerous individuals on campus to the ERP. Virginia Tech spokesperson, Larry Hincker, however, is quoted in the May 23, 2007 edition of the *Roanoke Times* as saying, "After we went back and looked at that (the plan), we felt that was not a correct assessment of our emergency plan…" Hincker then asserted that the emergency plan did contain a plan for armed intruders on campus.

I have read the Emergency Response Plan, and I find *no* reference to armed intruders. The recommendations following the Morva incident, therefore, were correct and Hincker was wrong. Guidance on dealing with armed and dangerous individuals should have been added to the report—and the university had been alerted to that need. The obvious question is, had such a section been added, would Tech have been better prepared to deal with Cho?

The ERP indicates that Cho's initial double homicide met the Level III incident criteria. This fact raises another question, why didn't the school follow more closely the guidelines that did exist? A Level III incident is defined as: "An incident occurring at the university that adversely impacts or threatens life, health or property at the university on a large scale. Control of the incident will require specialists in addition to university and outside agency personnel. Long-term implications may result."

Under the criteria for a Level III incident, the university should have taken immediate action after discovering the homicides at West Ambler Johnston dormitory. Look at the first criterion for a Level III incident—it was met. That criterion reads: "Serious hazard or severe threat to life, health, and property." The fifth criterion was also met. It reads: "Duration of event is unpredictable."

Even if you look at a Level II incident, as defined by the Virginia Tech Emergency Response Plan, clearly the school should have warned immediately. The first sentence of the definition of a Level II reads: "An unplanned event of unpredictable duration that may adversely impact or threaten life, health or property on a large scale at one or more locations within the university." Those words call for immediate action.

Another of Hincker's justifications for the school's inaction is contained in the explanation of why the Virginia Tech administration delayed in issuing a campus-wide warning. The reason for the school's timidity, the story goes, was the so-called panic that occurred when a warning was issued during the Morva incident eight months earlier. The panic—which was not really a panic, but the circulation of unfounded, alarming rumors—centered on false stories that Morva had taken a hostage in Tech's Squires Student Center. Police did surround the Student Center, and students leaving the facility did find officers with drawn weapons, but to call what took place in front of the Student Center a panic is a gross exaggeration and attempt to conceal what really happened.

Perhaps the most blatantly self-serving explanation of the school's inaction comes from Virginia Tech President Charles Steger himself. He is quoted as saying that the "panic" at the time of the Morva incident created a dangerous situation that could have cost hundreds of lives. This comment is not based on fact; it is another attempt to whitewash the school's inaction on the morning of April 16, 2007.

It is true that many accounts report that the lockdown during the Morva case was less than effective. However, this only serves to highlight the fact that Virginia Tech had experienced a less than perfect outcome for its lockdown procedures months prior to Cho's rampage, and their response to the problems that Morva's case had highlighted was not to improve the lockdown system, but simply not to use it at all. It begs the question: If you lock your front door and then your house gets broken into, do you get a better lock? Or do you simply leave your door hanging open?

Saying the campus is too big is simply another bogus reason Virginia Tech gives for its failure to lock down on the morning of April 16, 2007. One of the critical security functions for all universities and colleges is the ability to lock a campus down. Virginia Tech says it is too big to do that. But take a look at the State University (SUNY), Oneonta, New York. SUNY Oneonta has the ability to lock down every building on campus (with the exception of the gym) with four strokes on the computer keyboard. The fact is that school lockdowns on large campuses can be done. While SUNY is not as large as Virginia Tech, it is nevertheless a large school with a 250-acre campus, 5,808 full- and part-time students and 15 residence halls.

My evaluation of the Emergency Response plan and its implementation on April 16, 2007 does not stand alone. Others have identified many of the same flaws and questions I have. Vincent Bove, in his book, *Listen to Their Cries*, makes the following points on page 80:

> "How is it conceivable that two people are killed on a college campus during the week of the anniversary of Columbine and the killer is at large and lockdown is not immediately called for? Even if it were determined that the first two killings could not have been prevented because of the complexities and confusion surrounding mental health and privacy issues, it is inexcusable that nothing was done to prevent the 30 killings and multiple injuries that occurred two hours later."

Bove goes on to call for a full accounting of the decision making process from the Virginia Tech administration, and calls the university leadership to task for focusing more on the school's image and damage control than on mitigating the suffering of victims and their families.

Let's take a moment and look at the school's prompt reaction to the campus shooting on December 8, 2011, when Ross Truett Ashley murdered Virginia Tech police officer Deriek Crouse. The campus was immediately warned and the school was locked down. Ironically, its actions on December 8, 2011 undercut and show the fallacy of its defense for

Tech's more than two-hour delay in reacting to shootings at West Ambler Johnston Hall.

Granted, by 2011 the warning system at Tech was much improved, but even allowing for these improvements, the Steger administration's delay in 2007 remains inexcusable. We can all be thankful that no one has to make excuses for Virginia Tech's response in 2011.

Funding Threats

In the following examples we shall see that when the words, the slogans, and the appeals to emotions are not working, the school attempted censorship through control of funding. This transparent willingness to use any and all available means to silence critics is indicative of just how far some at Virginia Tech were willing to go to silence anyone disagreeing with their version of what happened on April 16, 2007.

The Collegiate Times, Virginia Tech's student-led campus newspaper, is operated by an independent firm—Educational Media Company of Virginia Tech, Inc. (EMCVT). The newspaper has engaged in investigative journalism in trying to get at the truth regarding the April 16th murders. In the process, the paper clearly alienated high-level school officials.

The paper has been a highly visible, on-campus forum for discussing the school's sluggish response to warning signs that Cho was dangerous and the school's lack of warning following the West Ambler Johnston Hall murders.

In a February 8, 2010 letter to EMCVT, Michelle McLeese, chair of Virginia Tech's Commission on Student Affairs (CSA), threatened to cut all funding to EMCVT because of the paper's willingness to print anonymous comments on its Web site. The paper and its Web site have contained some of most stinging criticisms of the school's actions on April 16, 2007. Some comments on the blog apparently offended members of the staff and faculty. McLeese said that publishing the anonymous comments violates Tech's "Principles of Community."

As you can see in the CSA's letter, reprinted in its entirety below, McLeese laid out plans to cut university funding to the paper, and to consider a ban on student organizations using university funds to buy advertising in the paper, school yearbook, and other publications owned by EMCVT.

<u>Letter to Educational Media Company of Virginia Tech</u>

VIRGINIA POLYTECHNIC INSTITUTE
AND STATE UNIVERSITY
Invent the Future

Commission on Student Affairs
Michelle McLeese, Chair
Blacksburg, Virginia 24060
mmcleese@vt.edu 540 250-2303
Educational Media Company at Virginia Tech, Inc.
General Manager, Kelly Wolff
362 Squires Student Center
Blacksburg, VA 24061
February 8, 2010

Dear Ms. Wolff:

I am writing regarding a decision just enacted upon by the Commission on Student Affairs at its February 4, 2010 meeting. Last semester, Fall 2009, the Commission became aware of discontent among students, faculty, staff, administrators and others regarding the online commenting system through the Collegiate Times (CT). The consensus of the Commission has been that the commenting system is irresponsible and inappropriate because it lacks accountability resulting in, among other things, countering the Principles of Community. Therefore, members of the Commission, along with a few administrators and faculty at Virginia Tech, participated in dialogue with key members of the CT staff including Editor-in-Chief, Sara Mitchell, Managing Editor of Editorials, Peter Velz, Opinions Editor, Debra Houchins, and Public Editor, Justin Graves. It is not possible for me to describe at length or in detail all the concerns of the Commission and those involved, although there is certainly room for continued dialogue regarding this issue. All parties had some constructive comments and dialogue and there seemed to be promise of collaboration to help move in the direction of fixing a problem recognized by many on both sides.

However, this issue continues to be a problem according to the Commission on Student Affairs because the sentiment is that nothing further than discussion or talking about these problems has been accomplished. Meanwhile, individuals and groups are continuing to be victimized verbally by individuals enabled by the commenting system.

The Commission has now decided to take action through the governance system. Although it is true EMCVT is not directly affiliated with the University for legal reasons, it still retains some benefits from the cooperation of the University. One such benefit is some financial assistance received annually from VT; this contract is currently up for renewal. The Commission has enacted a verbal resolution to request Dr. Sims' office not renew said financial contract with EMCVT until the Commission has resolved its discontent with the CT and its online commenting system effective immediately. In addition, the Commission discussed (and will decide at its February 18, 2010 meeting); the option of passing a verbal resolution that would immediately enact a policy with the Budget Boards at Virginia Tech to disqualify any funding requested to pay for advertising through the CT by student organizations. As a result, the Commission respectfully requests a meeting to attempt to reach mutual solutions or agreements to these concerns.

I thank you in advance for your time and attention. Should you have any questions or concerns please do not hesitate to contact me directly.

Sincerely,
Michelle McLeese
Chair, Commission on Student Affairs
CC Sara Mitchell, Editor-in-Chief of Collegiate Times
CC Ed Spencer, VP for Student Affairs
CC Guy Sims, Assistant VP for Student Affairs
CC Monica Hunter, Interim Director of Student Activities

Interestingly, no references were made to any Web site comments. Such specificity might have given their case some merit, but I doubt it. Indeed, the lack of specificity only deepens the impression that the school had other motives. Furthermore, if anonymous comments are threatening or are in violation of state or federal laws, the school need only go to a judge and obtain a court order allowing authorities to have the Internet server identify the origin of the posting. It is a very simple procedure. I would argue the last thing Virginia Tech wants to do is silence such comments; they can be an excellent way of identifying and stopping individuals who might attempt to copy the horrific events of April 16, 2007.

The vast majority of blogs and Web sites allow anonymous comments. Whether or not you agree with this anonymity, it is standard procedure protected by the Bill of Rights. Some of these anonymous comments may step over the bounds of propriety, but as long as no laws are broken, they are protected. Universities, of all places, should be champions of free speech. The free flow of ideas is the life-blood of institutions of higher learning. Virginia Tech itself confirms the right to free speech in its "Principles" that it now says are being violated:

"Virginia Tech's "Principles of Community"

The "Virginia Tech Principles of Community" were affirmed by the board of visitors March 14, 2005, and signed by eight university organizations.

Virginia Tech is a public land-grant university, committed to teaching and learning, research, and outreach to the Commonwealth of Virginia, the nation, and the world community. Learning from the experiences that shape Virginia Tech as an institution, we acknowledge those aspects of our legacy that reflected bias and exclusion. Therefore, we adopt and practice the following principles as fundamental to our on-going efforts to increase access and inclusion and to create a community that nurtures learning and growth for all of its members:

- We affirm the inherent dignity and value of every person and strive to maintain a climate for work and learning based on mutual respect and understanding.
- **We affirm the right of each person to express thoughts and opinions freely. We encourage open expression within a climate of civility, sensitivity, and mutual respect.**
- We affirm the value of human diversity because it enriches our lives and the University. We acknowledge and respect our differences while affirming our common humanity.
- We reject all forms of prejudice and discrimination, including those based on age, color, disability, gender, national origin, political affiliation, race, religion, sexual orientation, and veteran status. We take

individual and collective responsibility for helping to eliminate bias and discrimination and for increasing our own understanding of these issues through education, training, and interaction with others.

- We pledge our collective commitment to these principles in the spirit of the Virginia Tech motto of Ut Prosim [That I May Serve].

Ben J. Davenport Jr., Rector, Board of Visitors
Charles W. Steger, President
W. Samuel Easterling, President, Faculty Senate
Sue Ellen Crocker, President, Staff Senate
Sumeet Bagai, President, Student Government Association
Myrna Callison and Yvette Quintela, Co-Vice Presidents, Graduate Student Assembly
Kimball "Jay" Reynolds, President, Virginia Tech Alumni Association
Ray Plaza, Chair, Commission on Equal Opportunity and Diversity
Last updated: March 2005

If the university was upset with an anonymous comment, why not write a rebuttal?

The action of the Commission on Student Affairs prompted a storm of protests and the school quickly backed down. University spokesperson, Larry Hincker, subsequently told the *Roanoke Times* that the school does not support ending the contract with *The Collegiate Times* or its parent company, and is not contemplating a ban on advertising in the newspaper. Hincker further stated, "This is a student issue. These are students raising the issue with their fellow students, not an administrative issue."

Given the tight ship that school President Charles Steger runs, it is hard to believe that the Commission on Student Affairs would have issued a warning to ECMVT and *The Collegiate Times* without at least tacit approval from the highest level of the school administration.

The letter of response from the Education Media Company of Virginia Tech to the Commission on Student Affairs calls the attempt to cut off funds punishment for some of the paper's editorial decisions. The letter cites incorrect assertions made by McLeese such as the claim that the agreement with the Educational Media Company at Virginia Tech was up for renewal—it was not. Furthermore, the *Collegiate Times* received zero funding under the agreement. Take a look at EMCVT's response in its entirety:

February 11, 2010
Commission on Student Affairs
c/o Division of Student Affairs
112 Burruss (0250)
Blacksburg, VA 24061

Members of CSA:

Regarding the February 8, 2010 letter from Michelle
McLeese, Chair of the Commission on Student Affairs
(CSA), to Educational Media Company at Virginia Tech,
Inc. (EMCVT) regarding online comments posted by
members of the Virginia Tech community and others
at collegiatetimes.com, EMCVT respectfully submits the
following responses:

1) We have advised the *Collegiate Times* staff to
discontinue discussions with CSA members,
individually and collectively, on the topic of online
comments. We sincerely welcomed the several
concerned and impassioned University staff members
and students who engaged *Collegiate Times* editors in a
meaningful dialogue about the pros and cons of
anonymity in online comments over two academic
years and two editors-in-chief. A significant
conversation with readers such as that, as well as the
accompanying decision-making process for student
editors, plays a valuable role in student media
pedagogy. Both editors-in-chief, after considering
many different points of view, decided to maintain
anonymous commenting, just as a wealth of
newspapers across the country have done. In addition
to listening to different points of view, the editors also
surveyed practices at professional and college news
media, learned more about media law and debated the
relationships among free speech, anonymity and
democracy. It was an outstanding learning experience,
one that advisers to student journalists appreciate.

But this is no longer a dialogue; it is coercion. This is
made plain by the February 8 letter, a copy of which is
enclosed.

As attempted punishment for content decisions made by the editors of the student newspaper, CSA has threatened to harm the financial and institutional support resources for the diverse co-curricular student media activities that hundreds of students choose to join each year.

All further communication on this topic will be conducted in writing with EMCVT.

2) It would be helpful for CSA members to have a basic understanding of EMCVT's Relationship Agreement with the University to provide student media activity services in lieu of the Department of Student Activities doing so. This is especially true since the Relationship Agreement is a legally binding document between EMCVT, and the University, of which CSA is a part.

Until the University formed EMCVT in 1997, the student media groups were advised by UUSA staff and governed under the umbrella of the Student Media Board of Virginia Tech. The *Collegiate Times* is only one of seven registered student organizations (RSOs) advised under the umbrella of the Student Media Board's successor, EMCVT. The others are the *Bugle* Yearbook, College Media Solutions, *Silhouette* literary and art magazine, Student Publications Photo Staff, VTTV Channel 33 and WUVT 90.7 FM. Among other things, the Relationship Agreement states the University's historical relationship and rationale for affiliation with the student media organizations, establishes their RSO status, defines their editorial independence and provides the same support for student media activities, advising an administration as existed on average during the years 1993-94 through 1996-97.

To discontinue the Relationship Agreement with EMCVT would be to take apart the institutional structure of all of these student media organizations. It would be like shutting down Cranwell International Center and removing resources from the Council of

International Student Organizations as well as all of its member organizations because of a disagreement with the Indian Student Association.

Certainly, under these circumstances, it would garner significant national attention for Virginia Tech to dismantle all of student media at the University in an attempt to control content at the student newspaper.

3) Your letter referenced EMCVT's Relationship Agreement with the University by saying that "this contract is currently up for renewal." That is wrong. The Agreement paragraph requires 24-month notice to rescind or to begin renegotiations of it, and EMCVT has neither given nor received such notice.

4) The *Collegiate Times* receives zero dollars in funding under the Relationship Agreement. The *Collegiate Times* instead has subsidized operations, advising staff, administrative support and capital equipment for the student organizations whose revenue does not fully support their operations. Should CSA's proposed actions be implemented, EMCVT, while pursuing aggressive legal action to defend the free speech rights of students, would also be forced to consider each organization's ability to survive on its own. It is likely that such actions would harm or distinctly limit the co-curricular activities available at WUVT, *Silhouette*, VTTV and the *Bugle*, but not at the *Collegiate Times*.

5) The Relationship Agreement (Paragraph 6) states "Except through its seats on the governing board of EMCVT or to the extent permitted by the First Amendment to the United States Constitution, Virginia Tech will not seek to assert editorial control over EMCVT publications."

It is unfortunate and surprising that the members of CSA apparently have not been advised that a resolution "to request Dr. Sims' office not renew said financial contract with EMCVT until the Commission has resolved its discontent with the CT and its online commenting system effective immediately" is a clear violation of the

University's binding legal agreement not to assert control over editorial content, as is the pending resolution also referenced in the February 8 letter to advise Budget Board to disallow any student organization funding for *Collegiate Times* advertising.

The Association of College Unions International (ACUI) College Union Standards and Guidelines state:

"College Union (CU) staff members must be knowledgeable about and responsive to laws and regulations that relate to their respective responsibilities and that may pose legal obligations, limitations, or ramifications for the institution as a whole. As appropriate, staff members must inform users of programs and services, as well as officials, of legal obligations and limitations including constitutional, statutory, regulatory, and case law; mandatory laws and orders emanating from federal, state/provincial, and local governments; and the institution's policies."

Regrettably, that appears to us not to have happened in this situation. From the minutes of CSA's February 4 meeting: "Dr. Spencer noted that this can be taken all the way to the University Governance system to withdraw their support of the media association."

Both courses of action proposed by CSA are also very clear violations of established First Amendment case law. They consist of a governmental body such as CSA or Budget Board attempting to restrict funding, legal advertising or other resources as punishment for student media content with which it disagrees.

If the professional members of CSA have not brought this relevant legal information to your attention, it would be advisable to consult University Counsel about CSA's recent and planned resolutions regarding content published by the *Collegiate Times*. Kay Heidbreder sat on the University's Media Incorporation Task Force in 1996-97 and is familiar with the issues and the Relationship Agreement. We would also suggest the Student Press Law Center (splc.org) as a resource to bring CSA members up to speed on the legal ramifications of censorship by a governmental entity. Here is an excerpt from the SPLC's Web site:

"Student editors have the right to make all decisions related to the editorial and advertising content of student media. Courts have been consistent in ruling that at the public colleges and universities, school officials, including student government officers, may not exercise the power of a private publisher over student publications simply because they provide financial support. The fact that public universities are considered an arm of the state distinguishes them from a private publisher. Bazaar v. Fortune, 476 F.2d 570, aff'd en banc with modification, 489 F.2d 225(5th Cir. 1973)(per curiam, cert. denied, 416 U.S. 995(1974).

"As a result of these cases, it is now clear that:

"School officials cannot:

"(1) Censor or confiscate a publication, withdraw or reduce its funding, withhold student activities fees, prohibit lawful advertising, fire an editor or adviser, "stack" a student media board, discipline staff members or take any other action that is motivated by an attempt to control, manipulate or punish past or future content. Joyner v. Whiting; Schiff v. Williams, 477 F.2d 456(4th Cir. 1973); Leuth v. St. Clair County Comm. College, 732 F.Supp. 1410(E.D.Mich.1990); Kincaid v. Gibson, 236 F.3d 342 (6th Cir. 2001)(en banc)."

6) The *Collegiate Times* is a news organization and a means by which citizens may conduct a public dialogue on issues of importance to students and other constituents. We must clarify for CSA that the *Collegiate Times* has no role to play in the University's attempts, no matter how well-intentioned, to enforce speech codes that may be contained within the Principles of Community. In fact, upon reviewing CSA's letter, the Executive Director of the Student Press Law Center noted that speech codes have been struck down on campuses across the country, most recently at Temple University. He said, "the university is exposing the Principles to risk of legal challenge if it pursues this course of action, and one wonders

whether anonymous comments on news stories are really so important as to take that risk."

"It is axiomatic that the government may not regulate speech based on its substantive content or the message it conveys. . . . Discrimination against speech because of its message is presumed to be unconstitutional. . . . When the government targets not subject matter, but particular views taken by speakers on a subject, the violation of the First Amendment is all the more blatant.". Rosenberger v. Rector and Visitors of University of Virginia, 515 U.S. 819 (1995)

The letter threatening to punish EMCVT for apparently failing to take the "right" stance with respect to Principles of Community – which are not a part of the Relationship Agreement – is perhaps the clearest case of threatened viewpoint discrimination imaginable.

7) EMCVT demands that CSA rescind the "verbal resolution" referenced in the February 8 letter and cease all attempts to assert control over the editorial content decisions of the student editors of the *Collegiate Times*. Should CSA continue to pursue this violation of students' First Amendment rights, EMCVT will commence appropriate legal action against CSA and its individual members.

Further communication on the topic of online comments at the *Collegiate Times* or EMCVT's Relationship Agreement with the University may be addressed to EMCVT at 362 Squires Student Center (0546), Blacksburg, VA 24061.

Sincerely,
Kelly Wolff, General Manager
enclosures: CSA's February 8 letter; CSA meeting minutes of February 4, 2010, November 5 & 19, 2009
cc: Kay Heidbreder, University Counsel
Larry Hincker, University Relations
Ed Spencer, DSA
Guy Sims, UUSA
Monica Hunter, UUSA
Gary Long, Faculty Senate
Tom Tucker, Staff Senate
Bob Denton, Department of Communication

Wat Hopkins, Department of Communication
Frank LoMonte, Student Press Law Center
Tonia Moxley, *Roanoke Times*
Karin Kapsidelis, *Richmond Times Dispatch*
Chronicle of Higher Education
Ginger Stanley, Virginia Press Association
Gene Policinski, First Amendment Center
Kent Willis, ACLU of Virginia
Cary Nelson, American Association of University Professors
Greg Lukianoff, Foundation for Individual Rights in Education
Robert M. O'Neil, Thomas Jefferson Center for the Protection of Free Expression
Joan Bertin, National Coalition Against Censorship
Donald Luse, Association of College Unions International
Sara Mitchell, *Collegiate Times*
David Grant, 2008-09 *Collegiate Times* editor-in-chief
Lynn Nystrom, College of Engineering
Rob Perry, President, Board of Directors, Educational Media Company at Virginia Tech, Inc.
Board of Directors, Educational Media Company at Virginia Tech, Inc.

* * *

The willingness of the Virginia Tech administration to engage in this campaign of denial and deception may in part stem from recognition that the selection of its president was deeply flawed. And, because of the flawed selection process, a president ill equipped to handle a crisis headed Tech in the spring of 2007.

The overriding criterion for the selection of a university president appears to be the ability to raise money. If you read the official biography of Dr. Charles Steger that was published when he was named Virginia Tech's 15th president, you are struck by the emphasis on his ability to raise money. The total number of words in the biography is 969, of that, 184 tout his fundraising abilities—that is nearly one-quarter of the biography. Look at the words in Steger's official biography:

"In Dr. Steger's previous position as Vice President for Development and University Relations, he directed the university's successful (fund raising) campaign, which raised $337.4 million, exceeding the $250 million goal by 35 percent. It was the most successful fundraising effort in the university's history. Over 71,000 donors and 500 volunteers participated in this six-year nationwide effort led by Dr. Steger."

"In addition, he [Steger] currently serves as president of the Endowment Foundation for the Western Virginia Foundation for the Arts and Sciences (known as Center in the Square) in Roanoke. Dr. Steger also is director on the Boswil Foundation in Zyrich [sic] Switzerland. He received Outstanding Fund Raising Executive Award given by the First Virginia Chapter of the National Society of Fund Raising Executives in 1999 at its national Philanthropy Day Awards Dinner."

Virginia Tech, on the eve of the shooting, was preparing for the school's largest on-campus fundraiser in history. The nagging question is, did Steger "want" the first shootings at West Ambler Johnston residence hall to be the outcome of some sort of lovers' quarrel because the publicity would be easier to handle than a shooting rampage? Did Steger hope against hope that the first two murders were the product of a love triangle? The publicity associated with such a triangle would not distract from the upcoming fundraiser.

Or, did Steger want the shootings to be a failed robbery attempt or a drug deal gone bad? Did Steger and others in his administration emphasize money and the fundraiser over human lives and good judgment? The circumstantial evidence makes it appear that way.

Violence Prevention: Tech's Summit Versus the Student Symposium

Virginia Tech's denial and deception campaign appears to have moved into a new phase in mid-2010. Censorship and manipulation had not worked; a full-scale media propaganda campaign had been only partially successful. Now, the school appeared intent on wiping out as many of the reminders of the tragedy as possible. Tech's new tactic became clear to me in the spring of 2010 when I received an invitation from Professor Jerzy Nowak at Virginia Tech to participate in "Cultivating Peace: A Student Research Symposium on Violence Prevention" to be held from November 12-14, 2010. I checked with Michael Pohle and he was not going to attend, but because I was asked to moderate a session of the symposium, I accepted.

Professor Nowak's wife, Jocelyne Couture-Nowak, was the French professor murdered by Cho. As a tribute to her and to all those who were killed and injured, Nowak set up the "Virginia Tech Center for Peace Studies and Violence Prevention" (CPSVP) in the rooms of Norris Hall where 30 people had been butchered. In conjunction with the CPSVP and its affiliated "Students for Non-Violence" club, a student symposium on violence prevention was organized.

In June of 2010, I received an invitation from Mark G. McNamee, Senior Vice President and Provost, inviting me to take part in an "International Summit in Transdisciplinary Approaches to Violence Prevention" to take place on 12-13 November, 2010. My first impression was that the student symposium had been expanded, and I immediately accepted. The opening paragraph from McNamee reinforced my impression that the summit was intended to honor those who were killed or wounded at Tech:

> "On April 16, 2007, a terrible tragedy happened at Virginia Tech. The violent actions of one individual took the lives of 32 members of our community. In the subsequent three years, members of our community, as well as other communities around the world continue to struggle with the pain and loss caused by individuals determined to unleash violence upon innocent people. It is within this context that Virginia Tech is convening leading researchers and noted practitioners in the field of violence prevention to share research, engage in dialogue, and advance best and promising practices that take holistic and systems approach to the critical issued related to violence. …"

The more I thought about it, however, the more I was bothered by the two gatherings being held simultaneously. When I looked closely at the dates for the summit and for the student symposium, I noted they did not exactly coincide. In August, I queried the student symposium and found out that my suspicions were correct—the international conference had been organized *after* the student symposium. It appeared that the school was trying to sideline the students. This fact became even more apparent when I got to Blacksburg and found out that members of the press covering the international gathering weren't even aware of the student symposium. There were also widespread and disturbing rumors that the university had pulled funds from the CPSVP, making the organizers scramble to find financial backing.

The international summit and student symposium began on the evening of November 12th with a joint welcoming session. School President Charles Steger gave the opening address. This was my first exposure to Steger and I am not sure what I expected, but by any standard, I was taken aback by the undistinguished man who stood before us. I didn't find him particularly imposing, and his speech was bland. I was also bothered by the lack of eye contact with audience. There was no emotion in his voice and he never mentioned the tragedy at Tech.

I suddenly felt as if I had stepped back in time to when I was a political analyst at the CIA covering the communist world. I was once again watching an uninspiring leader drone on and on to a tightly controlled and manipulated conclave, and to an audience that responded with perfunctory applause.

I had hoped I would see and hear a university president who would dedicate the conclave to the victims of Cho's rage—those murdered and those wounded, both physically and emotionally. But April 16, 2007 was never mentioned. Indeed, no one speaking that evening ever mentioned the shootings. It was as if several hundred people had gathered in Blacksburg to discuss violence prevention in the abstract. It was as if the school had lured us to Blacksburg by invoking the memory of the tragedy, and then tried to ignore that it ever happened. The words "bait and switch" came to my mind.

Something else was curious. Participants in the student symposium were invited to attend the opening ceremony, but the reception following that ceremony was limited to "badge holding participants only." That meant the students and those attending only the student symposium were not invited to the reception. I thought that rather odd, considering the fact that the student symposium had been the catalyst for both gatherings. To this day I am not sure whether the students were excluded because of academic arrogance, or because the school was intent on keeping student participants as far away from the international conference as possible.

I also found it odd that the International Conference on Violence Prevention was held on the main floor of the Skelton Conference Center and the student symposium was in the basement. There were no signs directing people to the student symposium; those wanting to hear the students were left on their own to work through the maze of the conference center and find their way down to where the students had gathered.

I also thought it strange that there was no mention of the Center for Peace Studies and Violence Prevention Professor Nowak had established using the remodeled rooms in Norris Hall where Cho's rampage took place. When I accepted the invitations to both the International Conference and the Student Symposium, I assumed that the university would offer all participants the chance to see the CPSVP. Once again my expectations were not met. There was no mention of it during the opening ceremony, nor were participants encouraged to see Professor Nowak's center first hand.

More recently, my suspicions that the university wanted to downplay the shootings (or pretend they never happened), were confirmed when I found out that the Center had been downgraded from a "University Center," to an adjunct of the Sociology Department.

On Saturday, November 13, 2010, I moderated the first segment after lunch. It was entitled "Violence Prevention and Conflict Resolution." Again, throughout the morning sessions no one mentioned the April 16, 2007 shootings. The silence was deafening.

I was not the only one to find the absence of any reference to Cho's shootings disquieting. At lunch, I met a group of students and their professor from an East Coast university. When I noted the rather eerie lack of reference to the worst school shooting in this nation's history (and the reason why most of us came to Virginia Tech for the conference and symposium), they immediately agreed saying they too were puzzled. It was as if that terrible day had never happened, as if the school wanted to deny that a gunman had slaughtered 32 people and wounded at least 17 others.

After talking to the professor and students, I decided this silence would end.

That afternoon I opened my segment of the student symposium with the following: "Thank you Professor Nowak for sponsoring this symposium. I must begin by saying I am somewhat concerned that we are sitting on the campus where the most horrific mass murder took place in the history of this country—we are attending an international conference and a symposium on violence prevention, and there has been no mention of that tragedy. I find this fact troubling. So, as a tribute to the memory of those 32 innocent victims of April 16, 2007 slaughter, I would like to dedicate this session to their memory. Indeed, Professor Nowak's establishment of the Center for Peace Studies and Violence Prevention is an outstanding and fitting way to honor the memory of those 32 innocent individuals."

"It is an honor for me to sit on this panel—I believe that it is absolutely critical to bring in the minds and ideas of young people such as those seated next to me, if we are ever to make progress in preventing the all too frequent slaughter that occurs on our nation's campuses."

"When Professor Nowak asked me to participate, I asked, "What do you want me to say?" He said, "Perhaps something about yourself and your background. This symposium is not about me; it is not about anyone in attendance or the people on the panel, it is about finding solutions to prevent violence. ... "

"What I want you know is that my journey in this quest to find answers to campus violence began on January 16, 2002, when the mother of my oldest grandchild was gunned down on the campus of the Appalachian School of Law at Grundy, Virginia—less than 200 miles from where we sit."

"The parallels between that shooting and the shootings here at Virginia Tech are frightening. Parallels in the profiles of the killers, parallels in the failure of people in positions of authority to heed the warning signs, parallels in the poor responses at the time of the shooting (in both cases costing lives), and parallels in the lack of candor in raising questions as to what went wrong, failure to indentify individuals who failed in their responsibilities (and to hold them accountable), failure of law enforcement officials, and the willingness of politicians on both sides of the aisle to gloss over harsh realities and in so doing, to create a cover up."

My remarks drew thunderous applause. Clearly, I was not the only one puzzled by the silence.

Appalachian School of Law, Columbine, Virginia Tech

Within hours of Cho's slaughter I could see the disturbing similarities between the law school and Tech shootings. Within days those similarities became frightening parallels. I was so troubled that I wrote an article for our local newspaper:

The Rappahannock Record April 26, 2007

"Virginia Tech: Let the Cover-Up Begin"

The sad truth is that the terrible loss of life at Virginia Tech could have been prevented if state and school officials in Blacksburg would have learned the lessons from the shootings at the Appalachian School of Law on January 16, 2002. The parallels between the two tragedies are staggering.

Angela Dales, the mother of our granddaughter, was the student killed at the law school. In the five years since that tragedy we have repeatedly sought answers. But we have been met with disingenuous expressions of sympathy followed by outright refusal to answer our questions. The same will happen to the families of those lost at Virginia Tech.

Students, staff, and faculty warned law school officials that the murderer, Peter Odighizuwa, was a threat and they feared for their safety. The same is true at Virginia Tech—there were warnings about Seung Hui Cho.

Five years ago, no alarm was sounded on the second floor of the law school building after the initial shootings—an alarm that might have saved Angela Dales' life and prevented the wounding of three other students. At Virginia Tech, over two hours lapsed between the first shootings and the second. And, no alarms were sounded!

Court documents indicate that several weeks before the law school shooting, female staff and faculty members—citing Odighizuwa—expressed concern for their safety. The President of the Appalachian

School is said to have responded, "Oh you women and your hormones, nothing will happen." The President of Virginia Tech knew of the first shooting and did nothing to immediately close or alert the campus. Both men should be fired.

Both Peter Odighizuwa and Seung Hui Cho had harassed fellow students and the schools knew about it.

Both Peter Odighizuwa and Seung Hui Cho had been referred to mental facilities or were seeking psychiatric care, and the schools knew about it.

The office of former Virginia Attorney General Jerry Kilgore refused to help us get access to the investigation report of a threatening e-mail Angela Dales received prior to the shooting. The same will happen to Virginia Tech families when they turn to state officials for help.

The Virginia Tech families will learn the bitter truth that in dealing with these tragedies, all elected officials want to do is plant a tree, put up a plaque, or adopt a bill commemorating the shooting. None of them, Republican or Democrat, have the will or backbone to really investigate the causes of the tragedy and propose laws, or enact regulations, that will begin to deal with the prevention of these atrocities.

Since the horrible events on April 16th the phrase, "Let the healing begin" has been repeated over and over again. What would be closer to reality is, "Let the cover up begin."

The sad truth is that when put to the test, numerous elected officials and far too many members of the legal and law enforcement professions show that our beliefs and values mean little or nothing to them. Values such as honesty, courage, integrity—and justice— frequently disappear in a fog of deceit, treachery, and bureaucratic incompetence.

In our case, when the words of law enforcement as well as law school and elected officials took on a pejorative, even a disparaging tone—our pain deepened. When we turned to these individuals to find answers, to find "justice"—we found intellectual fraud and deceit. The same will likely happen to the families who lost loved ones at Virginia Tech.

What could be done to prevent another tragedy like the one at Virginia Tech? A great deal! First, the Virginia legislature should adopt a law stating that if a faculty or staff member identifies a student as mentally unbalanced and potentially violent, the student must be referred to mental health authorities for evaluation. At the same time an alert should be issued to all gun stores banning the sale of weapons and ammunition to that individual. Any person selling a gun to someone for whom a warning has been issued should serve a mandatory, long jail sentence.

Second—and by law—all educational facilities in Virginia, both public and private, should have in place a mandatory emergency plan. All students and faculty should be aware of the plan, and that plan should be periodically rehearsed as are fire drills.

Third, in the event of any shooting on school grounds, the school should immediately be closed. Police should be called and posted around the facility until it is clear that the shooter has been captured— not just a suspect as was the case at Virginia Tech.

At the time I wrote the article, I did not realize how accurate my words were, nor did I realize how they reflected the denials, deceptions, and lies that had taken place at Columbine. I was writing based on my personal experiences with the Appalachian School of Law and state officials. In fact, as I did research for this book, the parallels between the shootings at Columbine, the Appalachian School of Law, and Virginia Tech became glaringly apparent.

The first deceit that all three school shootings share is the assertion that no one saw the threat or had any hint that the killers were violent and possibly mentally unstable. Let's look at some of the facts:

Columbine—According to David Cullen's examination of that tragedy in his book *Columbine*, the police had very clear and specific evidence that Eric Harris was a threat and was planning violence. In his chapter entitled, "Telling Us Why," he examines the repeated complaints made by Judy and Randy Brown that Harris had threatened their children's safety. "Thirteen months before the massacre, Sheriff's Investigators John Hicks and Mike Guerra had investigated one of the Brown's [sic] complaints. They'd discovered substantial evidence that Eric was building pipe bombs. Guerra had considered it serious enough to draft an affidavit for a search warrant against the Harris home. For some reason the warrant was never taken before a judge. Guerra's affidavit was convincing. It spelled out all the key components: motive, means, and opportunity."

"A few days after the massacre, about a dozen local officials slipped away from the Feds and gathered clandestinely in an innocuous office in the county Open Space Department building. The purpose was to discuss the affidavit for a search warrant. How bad was it? What would they tell the public?"

"Guerra was driven to the meeting, and told never to discuss it outside the group. He complied."

"The meeting was kept secret, too. That held for five years. March 22, 2004, Guerra would finally confess it happened, to investigators from the Colorado attorney general. He described it as 'one of those cover-your-ass meetings.'"

"District Attorney Dave Thomas attended the meeting. He told the group he found no probable cause for the investigators to have executed the draft warrant—a finding ridiculed once it was released. He was formally contradicted by the Colorado attorney general in 2004."

"At a notorious press conference ten days after the murders, Jeffco [Jefferson County] officials suppressed the affidavit and boldly lied about what they had known. They said they could not find Eric's Web pages, they found no evidence of pipe bombs matching Eric's descriptions, and had no record of the Browns meeting with Hicks. Guerra's affidavit plainly contradicted all three claims. Officials had just spent days reviewing it. They would repeat the lies for years."

"Several days after the meeting, Investigator Guerra's file on his investigation of Eric disappeared for the first time."

According to Cullen, a grand jury report released on September 16, 2004, found that the Guerra file should have been stored in three separate locations, both physical and electronic. All three were destroyed, it concluded—apparently during the summer of 1999. The Grand Jury described that destruction as "troubling."

Appalachian School of Law—In the case of the law school, there is ample evidence that the Appalachian School of Law knew that the shooter, Peter Odighizuwa, was a threat. For example, his outbursts on campus—including throwing chairs and cursing people—were so well known and documented that he was barred from going into the Student Services office unless he was escorted by the president of the Student Bar Association or the dean, but he ignored those orders and went into the office, harassing its employees. His outbursts were so frequent and so widely discussed that he was nicknamed "the shooter," a title that was sadly prophetic.

Odighizuwa's penchant for violence was known even in Richmond. The morning after the shooting, Virginia Governor Mark Warner's spokesperson admitted to news media that Odighizuwa had a history of mental instability that school officials knew about. The governor was a member of the Board of Trustees of the Law School at the time of the shooting.

The most damning evidence that officials of the law school had prior knowledge of the threat Odighizuwa posed can be found in court documents filed in Wise County, Virginia. According to those documents, which were filed as part of a lawsuit against the school, three female staff members, just weeks before the killings, complained to school officials about Odighizuwa, expressing fear for their safety as well as the safety of others in the school. The complaint was made in a school meeting. The school's top three officials—President Lucius Ellsworth, Dean L. Anthony Sutin and Associate Dean Paul Lund—were said to be in attendance at the meeting. The documents assert that Ellsworth responded to the complaint by saying, "You women and your hormones and your intuition ... there is nothing for you to be afraid of ... it will be ok." Within a month, Odighizuwa gunned down Dean Anthony Sutin, Professor Blackwell, and student, Angela Dales. He wounded three female students. Incredibly the school maintains that it had no indication or warning that Odighizuwa was potentially violent.

Virginia Tech—At Blacksburg too, the warning signs were readily apparent and ignored. Professor Lucinda Roy documents her as well as others' attempts and to get Cho psychological help. In Chapter Two of, _"No Right to Remain Silent,"_ she writes the following:

"... As soon as I read the poem that Seung Hui Cho had written earlier for Nikki Giovanni's class, I realized why she had asked me to look at it. The tone was angry and accusatory, and it appeared to be directed at Nikki and her students."

"I followed a series of protocols I had developed during my time as chair. I consulted with trusted colleagues in the department—in this case Professor Fred D'Aguiar, who was serving with me as director of Creative Writing, and Cheryl Ruggiero, an instructor who had served as assistant chair in the Department of English. (Normally I would also have consulted Professor Nancy Metz, associate chair of English, but she was on research leave in the fall of 2002.) Fred, Cheryl, and I agreed that Nikki had been absolutely right to be concerned. Seung (the name he wished to go by) had read the poem aloud in class, and although his piece could perhaps be viewed as immature venting it could also be interpreted in a more threatening way. ..."

"On October 18, 2005, I alerted units that dealt with troubled students at Virginia Tech that we had a serious problem. It was the first in a series of e-mails I sent and phone calls I made about Seung. In one of the e-mail notes I characterized what had occurred in this way:

In the poem he castigates all of the class, accusing them of genocide and cannibalism because they joked about eating snake and other animals. He says he is disgusted with them, and tells them they will all 'burn in hell.' He read the poem with dark glasses on ... His name is Seung Hui Cho and I had him in my lecture class last year. The students in Nikki's class have asked for assistance because they are intimidated by him ... Nikki no longer feels comfortable teaching the student, and students have also requested relief. As I understand it ... I can remove Seung from Nikki's class as long as I offer him a viable alternative. I will be suggesting that he take an Independent Study in lieu of the class, and that he work with either me or Fred D'Aguiar. Nikki, who is never rattled by anything, is genuinely concerned about this student's behavior."

Then on page 32 Roy asserts, "I alerted several units [about Cho] at once: the division of Student Affairs, the Cook Counseling Center (CCC), the College of Liberal Arts and Human Services (CLAHS), and the Virginia Tech Police Department (VTPD)."

*　　*　　*

Now let's look at another, and very disturbing similarity between the three shootings, the failure of people in positions of authority to cooperate with the families of the victims or, in the case of Columbine and Tech, the governors' investigative panels.

Columbine—The Report of Governor Bill Owens' Columbine Review Commission, notes that " ...it [the Commission] was denied the privilege of interviewing [Jefferson County Sheriff John] Stone and his deputies, even though Sheriff Stone had agreed to appear before the Commission on three occasions." In discussing the commission's duties, the report also asserts, "With the notable exception of the conduct of Sheriff John Stone and a very few others, which foreclosed the Commission from completing its investigation in depth of the law enforcement response at Columbine High School, law enforcement and response agencies were quite helpful in providing most of the information Sheriff Stone had refused to produce for the Commission." (Page IX of the Executive Summary.)

Perhaps one of the reasons for Sheriff Stone's lack of cooperation can be found on page 213 of Dave Cullen's book. "Every few days, Jeffco spokesmen corrected another misstatement by the Sheriff. Several corrections were extreme: arrests were *not* imminent, deputies had not blocked the killers from escaping from the school, and Stone's [previous] descriptions of the cafeteria videos had been pure conjecture—the tapes had not been analyzed yet. ... He [Sheriff Stone] was quickly becoming a laughingstock, yet he was the ultimate ranking authority in the case."

Appalachian School of Law—There was no formal investigation by the state of Virginia of the shooting in Grundy. But here too, members of the police refused to cooperate—this time with the student victim's family.

More than a year before she was killed, Angela Dales had received the following anonymous email:

> *You f...king cocksucker, If you ever try to send me another virus again, I will track you down, cut your nipples off, and stick jumper cables in you and connect them to my truck. I'm not bullshittin. Maybe the sheriff will find you hanging from a tree in Longbottom.*

At the time, Dales had worked for the law school and apparently an email she sent to students contained a virus. When Dales' family met with police and asked to see a copy of the police investigation of the incident, they were refused access to the document. The police assured the Dales family that, while they did not know who sent the email, it was not related to the mass shootings that occurred on January 16, 2002.

As I mentioned previously, the problem is that if you don't know who sent the email, how can you say for sure it was not Peter Odighizuwa? The Commonwealth's Attorney put the family in touch with the investigating officer who promised to retrieve the report, look at it, phone a family member and answer any questions the family had. This has simply never happened.

So what are they hiding? If the email was not pertinent to the case, why not share the evidence to that effect with the family? The real problem is that the investigating officers had 60 days to get a court order and go to the Internet provider and find out who sent the message. They apparently brushed the whole incident aside and never got the court order.

Virginia Tech—Once again, the police refused to cooperate and provide critical evidence to an investigative body, this time to Governor Kaine's Review Panel. The refusal came in the form of the Virginia State Police, the ATF, and the gun dealers who declined to provide the panel with copies of the applications Seung Hui Cho completed when he bought the weapons. The Virginia State Police did describe the contents of Cho's gun purchase applications to members of the Governor's panel and their staff, but without the actual document in hand, there is no way to tell if the description was accurate or if pertinent information was left out.

*   *   *

A comparison of the shootings at Columbine, the Appalachian School of Law, and Virginia Tech shows disquieting common traits: repeated failures to heed warning signs, poor and incompetent decisions on the days of the shootings, and a willingness to deny facts, deceive, and in some cases, engage in out-and-out lies.

Unfortunately, what we learn from the Virginia Tech tragedy, and the other two school shootings discussed in this chapter, is that authorities will investigate only if they can do so with minimal or no repercussions to any person or institution. We learn that people will engage in specious arguments to cover up wrongdoings.

Part of the healing process after any disaster is learning from it so that even if we cannot prevent all future occurrences we can at least mitigate the damage. The problem in healing from school shootings is that there is no precise algorithm we can learn to help solve the problem. But there are patterns and indicators we can learn from that could go a long way toward identifying potential killers and preventing these campus massacres. However, the confluence of deceit, denial of facts, and incompetence on the part of some influential politicians, law enforcement officials, and school administrators prevent us from learning. When people engage in well orchestrated and cunning campaigns of denial and deception, there is no way we can ever comfort the grieving parents by saying that we will learn from your child's death and we can help prevent other killings from learning. When people engage in well orchestrated and cunning campaigns of denial and deception, there is no way we can ever comfort the grieving parents by saying that we will learn from your child's death and we can help prevent other killings.

CHAPTER X

THE HOKIE SPIRIT MEMORIAL FUND (HSMF)
(THE UNSAVORY SIDE)

"For the love of money is the root of all kinds of evil"
~The Bible (King's James Version) 1 Timothy 6:10

2007 (April 16) (7:15-9:51 a.m.) Seung Hui Cho kills 32 students and professors and wounds at least 17 others.

2007 (April 16) (afternoon) Virginia Tech school officials discuss cancelling the Capital Campaign public phase kick-off. This event was called "Ut Prosim weekend". This was a private discussion.

2007 (April 16-18) Virginia Tech creates the Hokie Spirit Memorial Fund (HSMF)

2007 (April 24) School officials hold a private meeting and announce the rescheduling of the Capital Campaign celebration for October 20, 2007. This was the same day Teresa and Mike Pohle buried their oldest son.

2007 (July 15) Virginia Tech distributes the HSMF disbursement protocol draft to the families for review 2007 (August 15) The final protocol is issued to the families.

2007 (September 15) The final deadline for individual families to

> submit their notarized protocol to the school in order to participate in the Hokie Spirit Memorial Fund disbursement.
>
> 2007 (October 20)   The celebration party to open the "Public Phase" of Virginia Tech's $1 billion Capital Campaign takes place. Many, if not all, of the families are still unaware of this fact, and do not learn about the "party" until the following day.

I have already documented a string of glaring omissions on the part of school officials, law enforcement personnel, and politicians. Omissions such as knowing about, but not telling, the Governor's Review Panel of critical errors in the timeline of events on April 16, 2007, and keeping that deception alive until it was explored more in depth during a jury trial five years later.

It is unfortunate that when it comes to examining the tragedy at Virginia Tech that one of the least discussed elements of the story involves money, and efforts made by school officials to keep the lid on that subject except for the message they wanted the public to hear. Money and greed are essential elements of what we must deal with, and they are a major consideration behind colleges refusing to disclose negative information.

The American people deserve to learn about the lengths some schools will go to so as to grow and protect their endowment funds, and that some will use any opportunity to improve their bottom lines. In the case of Virginia Tech, the terrible loss of life was also a fundraising boon. People may be shocked to learn the actual amount of dollars that rolled into Virginia Tech following April 16th, which was far greater than any amount mentioned by administrators during their press conferences. This financial windfall came even before Virginia Tech received a $900,000 grant from the federal government following the shootings.

In light of the more recent sexual abuse scandal at Penn State, and information concerning potential abuse cases at institutions such as Rutgers and Syracuse University, serious questions are being raised about schools' priorities in protecting their image and their money flow, and in their willingness to keep these horrible events secret, regardless of moral imperatives and the law. In the case of Virginia Tech, you have a real-life example of just how protective one school was and how it took full advantage.

I'm sure you know that college fundraising efforts never stop. There are departments within large institutions, such as Virginia Tech, whose sole mission is to fundraise. The resulting endowments are rarely used to help offset continual increases in tuitions at U.S. institutions, yet people are losing their jobs, incomes are falling, and hard-working families are finding it more and more difficult to send their children to college without falling further into debt. Although Tech proudly proclaimed it had achieved its $1 billion dollar campaign target in the few years following the massacre, tuition also continues to be raised like clockwork.

The Hokie Spirit Memorial Fund

In the days immediately following the shootings of April 16, 2007 there was a tremendous outpouring of kindness and caring for the victims and their families. In the New Jersey town where the Pohles lived, neighbors and businesses essentially wrapped their arms around the Pohle family and watched over them. Food was sent by the local supermarket and restaurants; their daily chores were done; people came to talk and make sure they were ok; their parish priest spent hours with them. The town did anything the Pohles asked and, no doubt, the same thing was happening for all the other families directly affected.

Not long after the massacre we learned that the Virginia Tech Foundation, a separate financial entity from Virginia Tech, had established a fund to hold the donations that began to pour into the school after the tragedy. That fund was called the Hokie Spirit Memorial Fund (HSMF)— the community of Virginia Tech, from its football team to its staff, faculty, students, and graduates, is known as "the Hokies."

The families were in no shape to understand what was happening because they were still in shock; they were, nevertheless, extremely touched by the thoughtfulness and generosity of so many.

As the days after the shootings began turning into weeks, in early June of 2007, the families learned that the school had decided that of the $7 million reportedly donated to date, $3.2 million dollars would be converted into thirty-two $100,000 scholarships in memory of each person killed. (The thirty-two $100,000 scholarships were separate from the $100,000 in settlement money the families of those killed received.) There were no collaborative discussions between the Virginia Tech Foundation, school administrators, and the families relative to that decision. The families put the best interpretation on that fact, reasoning they were not consulted out of respect for the tremendous pain and horror in their lives and the fact they were focused on trying to heal. That sort of reasoning was completely understandable and appreciated because it allowed time for more important family matters to be attended to.

But, as the news of Virginia Tech's decision to create these scholarships spread through the families, a number of them began to raise questions and objections about the one-sided decision-making that was going on. Ultimately, the school, hearing the families' concerns, moved away from its scholarship idea.

The next major announcement concerning the Hokie Fund came through the media, not the school. In early July, less than two months after the shootings, the media reported that Mr. Kenneth Feinberg had agreed to work pro bono for the Virginia Tech administration relative to how the HSMF funds would be disbursed after the fund was closed, which the school had determined would be August 1st. Although the involvement of Mr. Feinberg meant little to the families at the time, a number of the them wondered why the administration was in such a great hurry to close the HSMF so quickly, and many of the families wondered why the fund cut off was treated the way it was—with a short deadline. At the time, the families suspected nothing nefarious, but the only "answer" they heard, once again coming through newspapers as opposed to any direct communication with them, had to do with the administration wanting to disburse the funds to the families as quickly as possible. That explanation appeared to be a very kind and thoughtful gesture on the school's part; however, there was never a reason given as far as to why donations would no longer be accepted for the families. After August 1st, the school decided that additional donations received by the school would be deposited in Virginia Tech's Hokie Scholarship Fund. As was the case all along, this was another decision made solely by Virginia Tech. The families were too distraught to question what was taking place and the timing behind Tech's actions did not make any sense to them until later in the fall of 2007. After receiving criticism for their handling of the HSMF, school officials ultimately decided that the official close date for HSMF donations would be delayed until August 15, 2007.

During this same time, the families were informed that Feinberg, working under the direction of the school administration, was developing a formal protocol to be sent to "eligible" families detailing the conditions under which each claimant could apply for a disbursement from donations placed into the HSMF. The first draft of that document was delivered to families for review in mid-July. Additionally, a series of meetings with the families was conducted by Mr. Feinberg; however, the families felt their "input" had little impact and that the end result had already been determined. This was confirmed for the families when they read Feinberg's own words he had published in the August 27, 2007 edition of the *Virginia Law Review* where he wrote about the HSMF disbursement process: "*It is obvious, however, with fixed amounts being predetermined and no discretion being afforded the Fund Administrator in the calculation of individual awards, that requested hearings will not include any discussion of adjusting compensation…".* The disbursements and the amounts were fixed by Virginia Tech alone. In other words, these meetings were a meaningless exercise under the guise of open communication with the families and Mr. Feinberg's hands were tied.

The following month, on August 15, 2007, just four months following the shootings, Feinberg distributed his "Final Protocol," which documented the conditions under which impacted families had to comply in order to apply for disbursement of funds that were contained in the HSMF. That protocol was required to be notarized and returned no later than September 15, 2007 in order to participate in the program. At that time the total amount of donations in the HSMF, publicly reported by school officials, were reported to be just under $8.5 million, and would be disbursed during the month of October to approximately 80 individuals/families.

Over the course of the summer while this was going on there was also plenty being written about the HSMF in the papers, and reported in the news. By now, the families began to suspect what was happening—the school had grabbed control of the money and was determined to get the families out of the picture as quickly as possible. Virginia Tech would use the tragedy to profit the best it could. The families had next to no input on decisions regarding how the funds would be distributed, and the school would get free reign over the enormous amount of money flooding in within a scant few months following the mass killings. The families felt horrible. The money was not the issue—the issue was the school's seizing this pot of gold and profiting from the death of its faculty and students.

By mid-summer, the press was extensively reporting the generosity of individuals and corporations, and the huge amounts of money flowing into the school. It was about this time that the families began to get anonymous and public criticism because of the money involved. The families were accused of seeking to profit from the death, or wounding, of their loved ones. The callous individuals hurtling these barbs only saw the millions coming into the HSMF, while the school administration was fully engaged with its public relations firm. The goal was to drive Tech's communications efforts toward publicly speaking out about its concerns for the families, even though the school had pressing financial needs as well. I will examine the attacks on family members in Chapter XII, "The Families Need to Move On."

The money side of the Virginia Tech story, however, is not limited to what has been described up to this point. Concerns for fundraising appeared to remain a high priority based on other actions quietly being taken in the immediate aftermath of the tragedy.

At the time of the shootings, most families were unaware that Virginia Tech had previously scheduled the single largest fundraising event in the school's history to formally announce the public phase of its $1 billion

Capital Campaign. That gala was originally scheduled for the last weekend of April 2007, less than two weeks after the massacre. Appropriately the event was canceled; however, what neither the families nor most others knew was that on the afternoon of April 16th, even before all of the dead bodies had been removed from Norris Hall, efforts had begun within the administration to resurrect the Capital Campaign initiative. In an email sent from then Chairman of the "silent" phase of Virginia Tech's Capital Campaign, Gene Fife, to Elizabeth Flanagan, Vice President of Alumni Affairs, Mr. Fife proposed that the "gala/party" was inappropriate in wake of the tragedy. He went on to propose an idea where they could *"have a large but low key working dinner during which we review the facts of today, what we have and will be doing with the situation and to solicit support both financially and morally."* He then concluded with, *"The only alternative I see is to cancel the planned events and reschedule it at another time—probably next fall."* The fundraising effort was so important to the Virginia Tech administration that it could not wait; school personnel, who could have been used to deal with other, immediate aspects of the tragedy, were siphoned off. Through the extraordinary efforts of the Virginia Tech staff the entire event for over 700 attendees was quietly rescheduled by April 24th, only eight days following the worst school shooting in American history. The efficiency and thoroughness in rescheduling the fundraiser was in stark contrast to many aspects of the school's dealing with the families and the survivors.

A group of senior administrators were informed of the results of this rescheduling effort during a private meeting held on April 24th, when they were informed that the new date for the event had been set for October 20, 2007. Coincidently, April 24th was also the exact same day Teresa and Mike Pohle buried their son, Mike Jr.

Neither the families nor general public had any idea of this new plan. In addition, they had no idea of the relationship between the September deadline for formal submission of the Hokie Spirit Memorial Fund disbursement protocol and the largest fundraising gala in Virginia Tech's history to be held one month later. Virginia Tech stuck to that schedule, yet kept it very quiet. On October 20, 2007 their event proceeded as planned.

In putting together a simple chronology of events you come up with a disturbing question: Did the school develop and stick to a cold and calculating plan to keep the families in the dark and reap huge amounts of money based on a horrific tragedy? Remember, even while the families were struggling, they were being pressed to complete a process dictated completely by the school, and without transparency. I call your attention to the timeline at the beginning of the chapter.

Given the above, the timing of the school's dealings with families relative to the Hokie Spirit Memorial Fund and the timing of their Capital Campaign party attended by over 700 donors appears to be far more than mere coincidence. In other words, Virginia Tech's fundraising plans secretly were set in stone only eight days following the shootings, and remained the school's secret. This also suggests that the clear objective was to ensure that any funds intended to support the families had to be identified by Virginia Tech before the rescheduled kick-off for the public phase of their $1 billion Capital Campaign event. The whole thing was laid out like clockwork!

On October 21, 2007 an article appeared in the *Roanoke Times* discussing the fundraising gala held the previous night. Mr. Gene Fife, Chairman of the "private phase" of Virginia Tech's Capital Campaign, was quoted in that article with a statement that tore through the heart of the families. His statement was: *"You can't wash it away and pretend it didn't exist or happen; on the other hand, you can't just wallow in it forever."*

On October 30, 2007, nine days following that major fundraising event, President Steger released a statement to the media discussing the Hokie Spirit Memorial Fund and the families. In his statement, Steger said that it would have required the "wisdom of Solomon" to determine the best use of the funds donated to Virginia Tech. He added that even though the school had tremendous needs, they (the administration) decided to disperse the "bulk of the funds" to the families. All along, school statements appeared to be a calculated effort designed to convey the impression that Virginia Tech was focusing on the needs of the families first. In fact, as I have pointed out, the families were never brought into the equation. They were never consulted and were given a take-it-or-leave-it deadline to participate in the fund.

In his comments President Steger stated, "The University never actively solicited monies." Steger chose his words carefully; they were clever and danced around the truth. He immediately raised the families' suspicions. Their suspicions were fed by a rumor that major donors were quietly being given guidance on the timing of their donations. Specifically, the rumor was that major donations should be delayed until after the families had received their money. That way the donations would go directly to the Capital Campaign and would not be considered part of the Hokie Spirit Memorial Fund.

By reviewing the Capital Campaign financial results in the months following April 16th there appears to be an interesting pattern consistent with and supporting that rumor. The table below shows the gains in the value of Virginia Tech's endowment fund by month from May to December of 2007. For reference, the fiscal calendar for both Virginia Tech and the Virginia Tech Foundation ends June 30 of each year. With that as background, note the monthly increases for May and June following the shootings, then for the next three months where they drop considerably, followed by the dramatically upward movement starting in October of 2007, when their Campaign fundraiser was held.

Virginia Tech Capital Campaign
Monthly Increase in Value

Month & Year	Capital Campaign Total (Millions)	Monthly Increase (Millions)
May 2007	$501,849,743	+ $ 15.7
June 2007	$524,731,181	+ $ 23.0
July 2007	$533,258,936	+ $ 8.5
August 2007	$541,988,603	+ $ 8.7
September 2007	$551,477,067	+ $ 9.5
October 2007	$590,079,731	+ $ 38.6
November 2007	$601,766,987	+ $ 11.7
December 2007	$633,537,102	+ $ 31.8

Now that I have discussed Virginia Tech's Capital Campaign fundraising effort, the seedy side of this story continues. I will now return to the Hokie Spirit Memorial Fund and how Virginia Tech appears to have profited quite handsomely in another area. The question that leads into this segment is, does $8.5 million truly represent the "bulk" of the funds that were received at Virginia Tech in the aftermath of the tragedy? The answer is, unfortunately, not by a long shot. To better set the scene, it is important to note that the Virginia Tech Foundation and Virginia Tech are two completely separate organizations from a financial perspective (although both are obviously very connected).

What follows are two tables. The first shows the changes in financial performance of the VT Foundation over four consecutive years, including the fiscal year that ended June 30, 2007. Again, the VT Foundation was the sole entity that established the Hokie Spirit Memorial Fund for donations to be held following the shootings. When you look at the table, note the rather large increase for the fiscal year that included April 16, 2007. From this, presumably, came the $8.5 million that was disbursed to the families.

Virginia Tech Foundation

Financial Year	Increase in Net Assets (Millions)	Increase/Decrease from Prior Year (Millions)	Percentage Change
7/1/2003-6/30/04	+ $ 56.9	N/A	N/A
7/1/2004-6/30/05	+ $ 57.6	+ $ 0.7	+ 1.23%
7/1/2005-6/30/06	+ $ 80.9	+ $ 23.3	+ 40.45%
7/1/2006-6/30/07	**+ $ 132.0**	**+ $ 51.1**	**+ 63.16%**

Outside of the Virginia Tech Foundation, however, what shocked many families was the sudden and sharp improvement in the financial situation of Virginia Tech, a separate financial entity. In the table below, which contains information from Virginia Tech's own financial reports, you will see an amazing change in the school's asset amounts for the time period that includes the April 16th murders as compared to the three previous years. Clearly this money was coming in as part of the outpouring of sympathy in the wake of the shootings. This sudden increase raises all sorts of questions about the school's ethical behavior in handling its newfound wealth. How is it that donations pouring into the school and were "allegedly" going to the Hokie Spirit Memorial Fund or other funds established, and controlled, by the Virginia Tech Foundation found their way to the school itself? Was the temptation just too great? Was someone diddling with the books to enrich the school? The percentage change from previous years is truly astounding. The question is where did that huge gain come from? I submit that answer is simple: From the blood of innocents who were killed or wounded.

Virginia Tech University

Financial Year	Increase in Net Assets (Millions)	Increase/Decrease from Prior Year (Millions)	Percentage Change
7/1/2003-6/30/04	+ $ 61.2	+ $ 4.0	+ 6.99%
7/1/2004-6/30/05	+ $ 58.8	- $ 2.4	- 3.92%
7/1/2005-6/30/06	+ $ 39.4	- $ 19.4	- 32.99%
7/1/2006-6/30/07	**+ $ 148.9**	**+ $ 109.5**	**+ 377.91%**

From the tables above, there can be no arguing that there is a huge difference between the $8.5 million figure that was publicly announced by the President of Virginia Tech in October of 2007 as representing the "bulk" of the funds that were being disbursed to the families and the staggering $160 million net increase above the three-year norm for the fiscal year ending June 30, 2007. Again, we have to ask, "How is it that Virginia Tech, a separate financial entity from the Virginia Tech Foundation, realized such a tremendous windfall?

The final question concerns the Hokie Spirit Scholarship Fund. Remember, Virginia Tech did state that once the HSMF was closed, any additional donations would be kept by the school and placed into the Hokie Spirit Scholarship Fund. That is a fitting tribute to those who died and were wounded on April 16th. But, what really happened to those donations?

In an email sent in 2010 to one of the families whose son had been killed on April 16th, a school official discussed scholarships indicating that as of late 2010, the Hokie Spirit Memorial Scholarship Fund was endowed at about $1 Million dollars. He stated that no scholarships were awarded from 2007 to 2009. In 2010, however, he said that just over $95,000 was awarded to 35 students (an average of just under $3,000 per student). For 2011, and beyond, he expected that a total of around $48,000 would be awarded based on the endowment earning about $12,000 per quarter. Is Virginia Tech really telling us that only $1 million went to the Hokie Spirit Scholarship Fund at a time when the school and the Foundation were flooded with donations? This just does not make sense. There was never any transparency in the handling of these huge sums of money and the school made no effort to clarify its handling of its new wealth.

So, the bottom line is that we have a school that was never transparent, never involved the families, kept information private, and cashed in big time on the blood of those killed and wounded on that terrible April day. It is now obvious that the school realized a net gain of well over $160 million, which is far greater than has ever been disclosed. Virginia Tech controlled every facet of the donations being sent to the school. Subsequently, I argue that an amount of just over $8 million spread out across 80 families does not represent anything close to the "bulk" of what was donated out of the extreme kindness, generosity, and compassion of so many people throughout the United States and the world.

For the families, the lies and half-truths are appalling. The healing process has been hindered by the school's duplicity and greed. The families would have liked a say in how the money was distributed; many of them would have liked the bulk of the money to go to scholarships in the names of their loved ones, or charities of their choosing. That would have been a fitting tribute; that would have helped them. The families are not after any money; you could not give them $160 million for the life of any of their children, but to take the money that has come as a tribute to the dead and wounded, and to ride roughshod over them defies description.

Senior Virginia Tech officials appear to have been involved in the solicitation of donations by providing guidance relative to when donors should send in their funds so as not to have an impact on their Capital Campaign interests. Additionally, senior Virginia Tech officials used an arbitrary decision-making process to determine what donations were intended for the Hokie Spirit Memorial Fund and what were not. In other words, Virginia Tech controlled and manipulated everything, and may have even diverted money from the Virginia Tech Foundation to Virginia Tech (the school) so they could hide such a tremendous gain from casual investigation.

CHAPTER XI

THE LAWSUIT AND TRIAL

*"Safety and security don't just happen, they are the result
of collective consensus and public investment. We owe our
children, the most vulnerable citizens in our society, a life
free of violence and fear."*
~Nelson Mandela, former president of South Africa

It was not about money; it was never about money.

If you were to ask the parents of Erin Nicole Peterson or Julia Kathleen Pryde whether $8 million is a fair price for the lives of their children, they would throw the offer in your face. If you were to ask them if $80 million is a fair price for the lives of their daughters, they would say there is no amount of money that is worth a child's life—period. There is nothing that can compensate parents for the agonizing silence when they enter their dead child's bedroom; there is nothing that will ever make the pain completely go away.

For the plaintiffs, the whole purpose of the lawsuit was to find out the truth that had not been revealed by the Governor's report that was supposed to have given them a complete picture of how their daughters were killed in the largest school massacre in modern U.S. history.

And it was not just about two families. Pryde and Peterson may have been the names on the suit, but they were not the only ones driven to find the truth. All the families of the victims were in the courtroom in spirit. Andy Goddard, father of Colin Goddard, who was seriously injured in the shooting, came every day to listen to the proceedings and take notes. Andy sent his notes each evening to families of the killed or wounded who were not able to attend the trial.

When the Pryde and Peterson families filed their lawsuit, many of us wondered if they could get a fair trial or if the cards were stacked against them. Stop to think of what they were doing: they were suing Virginia's largest state university, a school that is the most powerful economic engine in southwest Virginia. The school has a powerful lobby in Richmond, and one member of the school administration, David Nutter, actually served in the Virginia House of Delegates at the time. As I have already noted, Nutter did not back legislation meant to strengthen school safety. Furthermore, the trial was to be heard by a Virginia judge appointed by the Virginia legislature. The potential for conflict of interest and the possibilities for undue influence and miscarriage of justice were alarming.

Not only did the school have powerful support in Richmond, but Tech was probably counting on swinging public opinion in its favor with the fact that 30 of the 32 dead victims' families had settled with the state. The strategy apparently relied on the assumption that no one would learn what had motivated the other 30 families to sign, and that the factual flaws in the Governor's report would never be discovered. Tech was gambling that there would be no need to formally acknowledge the errors, if discovered, until the two-year statute of limitations for filing legal claims or challenging the legitimacy of any settlement had expired.

The state of Virginia appeared willing to do anything to keep Virginia Tech from being sued. Michael Pohle remembers the families of the deceased being told, through their own attorneys, that the state would withhold payment for medical care for the wounded survivors if the families of those killed did not settle. Given the emotional roller coaster the families were on and their inability to think clearly as they came to grips with their loss, they were easy prey.

Indeed, as soon as the terms of the settlement offer were known, the families began speculating among themselves that the wounded were being held hostage to get them to sign. Once the family meetings were held in October, 2008 with Virginia Tech Police Chief Wendell Flinchum and law enforcement officials (following the settlement), some family members, including Michael Pohle, publicly challenged the settlement, arguing they had been lied to and the state had used the wounded as pawns to force families to settle.

The fact that the families' attorneys carried this message raises serious questions. Yes, on the one hand it would be appropriate for them to convey such information to their clients, but it is odd that the some of the families do not remember their attorneys going into detail about what other options were available other than accepting the settlement terms. Some families had the feeling they were being rushed into a settlement.

The state played the same game with the families of the wounded. Andy Goddard recalls being told the families of the deceased would get nothing if they, the families of the wounded, did not settle.

Pryde/Peterson v. Commonwealth of Virginia

Despite all the maneuvering and not so subtle pressures brought to bear on the Pryde and Peterson families, they filed a lawsuit in the Fairfax County Circuit Court in northern Virginia on April 16, 2009. At the time, the Pryde and Peterson families issued a statement explaining their actions and why they did not go along with the other victims' families in reaching an out-of-court settlement. The two families said they declined to go along with the earlier settlement because they did not have all the facts on the handling of the shooting. The press quoted the two families as saying, "We believe that our suit is necessary to reveal truths that ultimately will benefit all those who have shared in this tragic loss." The following is the statement issued by the two families:

"We raised our daughters with a sense of integrity, a desire to seek the truth and a belief in keeping their word. Virginia Tech did not keep its word to us. We have filed this lawsuit in the hope that we will receive accountability for the tragic events of April 16, 2007."

"The faculty and students of Virginia Tech have been extremely supportive of the families during this difficult time. Erin and Julia loved Virginia Tech and they felt at home there and were receiving a wonderful education. But, on April 16, 2007 the administrators who ran the university let our daughters down in ways we are just now learning."

"Sadly, the Report of the (Virginia Tech) Review Panel to the Governor, issued in August 2007, contained important inaccuracies, despite the panel's best efforts to get to the truth. University officials, it now appears, may have been less than candid and forthright in their responses to the questions put to them by the panel."

The court proceedings began on Monday March 5, 2012 with the jury selection process. Andy Goddard sat and listened to the opening day remarks as Judge William Alexander introduced the plaintiffs and their lawyers as well as the lawyers for the Commonwealth of Virginia. Judge Alexander explained that this was a civil trial and as such, had a lower standard of proof than a criminal trial. In a civil trial, the plaintiffs have to prove there is a preponderance of evidence that Virginia Tech, acting as an agent for the Commonwealth of Virginia, was negligent in failing to warn students of danger on the campus. The judge noted that many of the prospective jurors had ties to Virginia Tech, but that would not disqualify them as long as the relationship had not made it impossible for them to be impartial. Judge Alexander also cautioned that once the jury was selected, the jurors must listen to the evidence, instructions on the law from the judge as well as all the arguments, and only then decide. Their decision must be made on what they had heard during the trial.

By noon of the second day the jury was selected and seated. Judge Alexander then advised the jury that they must:

- Decide if the Commonwealth of Virginia was negligent not to warn Ms. Pryde and Ms. Peterson of danger on campus.
- Determine if this negligence was the proximate cause of Ms. Pryde and Ms. Peterson's deaths, and if so what compensatory damages should be awarded.
- Bear in mind that the standard of proof is a preponderance of evidence.

The prosecution then began its case. Andy Goddard knew the chronology of events by heart; he could repeat them in his sleep. As he listened, he already knew when Ryan Clark and Emily Hilscher were murdered, between 7:05 and 7:12 a.m. He also knew that between 7:21 and 7:24 a.m. the police were on the scene and found bloody footprints leading away from the crime scene as well as a bloody thumb print on a door at the end of the footprint trail.

Goddard continued to listen to the already well-known facts: by 7:50 a.m. the police knew they were looking for a 9mm automatic weapon because of the shell casings found near the bodies. It was readily apparent that the crime was not a murder-suicide because the police found no weapon at the crime scene.

According to Chief Flinchum's testimony, he arrived at the crime scene between 7:44 a.m. and 7:49 a.m. He was, then, aware of the above information. The chief admitted on the stand that he had the authority to issue a warning; he also indicated that he never raised the subject of warning the campus in his talks with President Steger. By 8:15 a.m., an hour after the shootings, the students, staff, and faculty had not been alerted to the murders. No one other than a few police officers and school administrators knew that a gunman could be present on the campus. Chief Flinchum's failure to warn students because he perceived no threat and he believed the gunman had left the campus does not jibe with the fact that his officers were looking for a gunman on campus, and two fully armed and equipped swat teams were being mustered to assist in an arrest. Some believe that Flinchum's failure to press for a campus-wide warning and lockdown are tantamount to gross negligence.

Flinchum's denial that a campus-wide warning was discussed on the morning of April 16, 2007 stands at odds with official notes from Policy Group's meeting that fateful morning. The discrepancy can be found in a document from the Virginia Attorney's office, "Designation of Expert Witnesses by Defendants Commonwealth of Virginia Charles W. Steger and James A Hyatt," and signed by Peter R. Messitt, Senior Assistant Attorney General and dated July 28, 2011.

One of the state's expert witnesses, Steven J. Healy, a managing partner with the professional services firm, Margolis, Healy and Associates, interviewed two people, Lisa Wilkes and Kim O'Rourke, senior administrators and participants in the senior administrative group that convened in President Steger's conference room in Burruss Hall. In her notes, Ms. Wilkes wrote, "a lockdown is not necessary," relaying her understanding that there was no imminent threat to the campus community. Ms. O'Rourke, in her notes wrote that "police don't believe a lockdown is necessary at this time."

According to the state's own expert, Steven J. Healy, "the senior administration reached their opinions about the absence of danger to the rest of the campus community through their on-going communications between Chief Flinchum, the on-scene commander at WAJ, and Zenobia Hikes, Vice President for Student Affairs, who was at Burruss Hall with the senior administrative group, and Edward Spencer, Associate Vice President for Student Affairs, who was at WAJ at the command post since 7:45 am."

To date, no one has explained the discrepancy between Flinchum's sworn testimony that a lockdown was not discussed and the official notes from the meeting in Burruss Hall stating the exact opposite.

As I read Andy's courtroom notes I could only think that Flinchum's actions do not comport with his testimony. The police chief not only violated the basic tenants of crime analysis, he violated common sense. The idea literally takes one's breath away. How could a man in such a position be so inept when faced with a murder scene?

Andy religiously sat in the courtroom throughout the trial. He listened in amazement to school officials' robotic, sterile attempts to defend and explain away their limp response to the early morning murder scene.

As he took notes, time and time again Andy found himself writing, "I don't know the details," "I don't remember," "It depends on what you mean by immediately," and "I have no recollection." When he was finished listening to Chief Flinchum's testimony, followed then by a number of university officials including the Associate Vice President of University Relations Lawrence Hincker and President Charles Steger, he could not help but wonder if some sort of collective dementia had hit the school hierarchy.

Andy concentrated on what little substance the defense witnesses said, and took copious notes. But it was only in the evening, when he went over what he had written, that he realized the fine degree to which the school's defenders had been coached. Their answers read as if they had been reciting from a script. In fact, the answers often did not match the questions. The whole scene struck him as an incredibly well-rehearsed theatrical charade.

When asked hard-hitting questions by the plaintiff's attorney, defense witnesses were repeatedly at a loss for details and specifics, while others said it was all a blur. For example, Hincker admitted that the erroneous timeline President Steger used at his 7:40 p.m. press conference the evening of the 16th was typed on his computer, but he didn't know who had typed it, nor who had sent it to his personal computer where it could be printed and distributed to the press. Hincker was at loss to say who else might have written it or who would have had access to the computer. In sum, he denied all knowledge of the erroneous timeline yet, somehow, it was mysteriously provided to President Steger and was the "factual" chronology of events presented on national television. Remember, this press conference occurred almost 12 hours following the shooting, which was more than a sufficient amount of time for Virginia Tech officials to confirm the facts they were about to share with the entire world. Unfortunately, that also allowed time to modify "facts" as well. Among a number of issues contained in the false timeline presented during Steger's press conference was the critical error associated with Karl Thornhill and the time he was actually identified as a person of interest—the false timeline put it at 7:30 a.m.; in fact, the correct time was not before 8:30 a.m., more than an hour after the dorm shootings had occurred.

Hincker, Flinchum, and others knew about those errors and did next to nothing to correct the record for either the public or investigators. This meant that the Governor's Review Panel worked from flawed information—and school officials were aware of those flaws. It appears that school officials knowingly allowed the incorrect timeline to stand because it gave the school a fig leaf to cover the fact that no warning had been issued. The email issued at 9:50 a.m., as 30 people were being murdered, said there was a gunman loose on campus—that had been true since 7:15 a.m.

The fabricated timeline was the school's weak excuse for not warning the campus. As flimsy as the alibi as was, Tech could argue that if the first two shootings were a domestic incident and that the police had a person of interest, there was less urgency to warn. Whoever typed the phony timeline knew that line of argument—Hincker undoubtedly knew that argument even if he wasn't the typist.

Hincker evaded all questions about this crucial fact. The erroneous timeline was in the initial version of the Governor's Review Panel Report and was only corrected at the last minute in the final version. By then it was too late; the school's tactics appeared to be working. The vast majority of the families had settled and most of the general public had bought the lie about the sequence of events. When the initial report was released with the incorrect timeline, Hincker did not contact the panel to call the error to their attention.

It is truly remarkable that Hincker, who participated in preparing information going to the panel, said nothing about the timeline's errors. When asked on the witness stand if he contacted the panel chairman, Col. Gerald Massengill, about the problems, Hincker said, "no." Hincker also testified that it was "not his place" to call Massengill when the first report was issued even though he knew it was wrong. The errors then, were known, and Hincker, who knew that fact, admitted on the witness stand that he said nothing.

Andy Goddard, however, could not forget; he could not hedge. For him there was no blur. For Andy Goddard, the events of April 16, 2007 were clear and vivid. The memory of that day still follows him.

On the morning of the massacre there was one group of individuals who controlled the decisions surrounding sending communications to the campus, and given their respective roles in the university hierarchy would need to know details about what was going on, and when. That group, called "The Policy Group," was chaired by President Steger. Among the ten members in attendance that morning were Larry Hincker (Associate Vice President for University Relations), Ralph Byers (Director of Government Relations), Kim O'Rourke (Chief of Staff to President Steger), and Kay Heidbreder (University Counsel). Each was called to testify during the trial.

Although the source of the false timeline was never established during the trial, given the "selective amnesia" that seemed to afflict university officials who were placed under oath, I offer the following possible scenario.

As the events of April 16th unfolded, the Policy Group would need to know the details of the events that occurred in order to communicate with the families, government officials and the media. Additionally, they must have realized they could be faced with legal claims against the university. So, it makes sense that the school wanted close control of all communications. I propose that to meet both the demand for information from the public and the need to provide protection from exposure to legal actions, there appears to have been only one person who had both firsthand knowledge of all the information being provided to the Policy Group, as well as the expertise to determine what areas might expose Virginia Tech and the state to legal action if the truth about the timeline and actions taken by officials became known. That person, of course, would be University Counsel Kay Heidbreder. It would make sense for someone in her position to compose, or at least review, any communications going out to the public. In this scenario, she may well have been involved in the promulgation of the flawed timeline.

It is also important to note that Heidbreder was part of the defense team at the trial even though she was part of the Policy Group on April 16, 2007—a very clear conflict of interest. It is hard to believe that Ms. Heidbreder, a lawyer, or the defense team, would miss that point.

Did she type the timeline on Hincker's laptop, sign off on it after he'd typed it, or did she in fact have anything to do with it? We will never know, since no member of the Policy Group can recall any information about who wrote the timeline.

For Andy Goddard, there was no forgetting the events of April 16, 2007.

*　　*　　*

Throughout the trial Andy's thoughts were never far from his son. Sitting in the courtroom day in and day out, he continually thought, "How lucky I am, I have my son." Thoughts of his son's birth in Kenya and childhood in Bangladesh and Indonesia flooded back, particularly the concern that relatives had for Colin and the whole family's safety. He remembered how family and relations worried and could not wait for his family to return to the safety of the United States.

As Andy listened to the defense witnesses run from the truth, he remembered April 16th vividly. He remembered wondering how Colin's younger sister, Emma, would handle the news her brother had been shot and seriously wounded.

Emma is seven years younger than Colin and when they adopted her in Indonesia, Colin took to his new sister immediately. He helped feed and care for her from the time she was just a few days old. The bond between the two was solid in the very best sense of a brother-sister relationship. Emma idealized her older brother. Indeed, even after the shooting she would consider no other school than Virginia Tech because her brother had gone there.

Goddard also remembered sitting by his son's bedside watching Colin bleed profusely from his open wounds. The doctors had not sewn his son's wounds shut; they wanted him to bleed to help clear the debris. Andy remembered watching the nurses take away the bloody sheets as Colin bled; he remembered the tubes and the IVs giving his son life-saving liquids to help replace the fluids he was losing. Unlike Larry Hincker, Andy had no problem remembering every last detail. He remembered being told that his son's femur had been shattered and that he would have a titanium rod in his leg. He remembered wondering if Colin would be able to walk without using a cane, or whether he would be able to play sports.

Andy could not forget reporters trying to sneak into the hospital to get photos of his son and other victims. He was especially repulsed by a female reporter who tried to sneak a camera into the hospital by saying she was carrying a pump to help breast feed her child. The bag she was carrying contained a camera. Another reporter tried to sneak in dressed as an emergency room nurse.

But even with all these details from that horrific day in 2007, there were some things Andy had no way of knowing. He had questions he could not answer. So he sat in the courtroom listening to testimony from officials and taking notes to answer the biggest most pressing question: Why? Why had officials failed to act to protect his son and the other students? And why had they allowed errors in the follow-up investigation to stand?

*　　*　　*

On Wednesday the trial testimony became argumentative. Andy zeroed in on the contentious exchange between the plaintiff's attorney, Bob Hall, and two Virginia Tech employees—Ralph Byers, Tech Government Relations Director, and Kim O'Rouke, Chief of Staff to University President Charles Steger. To Andy, Byers' hostility appeared defensive, as if he might be pushed into areas he did not want to discuss. Byers was clearly agitated; it was as if he thought that he might be forced to deviate from his rehearsed remarks and inadvertently say something that would reflect negatively on the school and its president.

Two emails were brought up that made Byers particularly uncomfortable and defensive. These emails were sent very early in the process, long before the Policy Group had had a chance to discuss much. The first was sent to Laura Fornash, who worked as the university's General Assembly lobbyist in Richmond and later became Virginia's Secretary of Education under Governor McDonnell. Byers directed Fornash to email the Governor's office that Virginia Tech police had "one (student) dead and one (student) injured and a gunman on the loose." He further directed Fornash to convey that the information should not be released to anyone outside the Governor's office.

Byers feebly tried to back away from the phrase "gunman on the loose" because it deals a mortal blow to the school's defense for not warning the campus. While other defense witnesses had problems remembering the actions of school officials, Byers had no problem in saying that no one on the Policy Group—convened to handle the crisis and with the authority to urge President Steger to issue a warning—used the phrase, "gunman on the loose." Those words were, Byers contended, were shorthand for "the perpetrator has not been apprehended yet."

A question that was not raised in the courtroom, but that needs to be answered, is why Byers went through a lobbyist and did not directly contact the governor's office? Bad judgment again seems to have reared its ugly head. Byers had used Fornash in the past as a front person giving Fornash message control, and that appears to be the motivation in this case. Common sense, however, given the gravity of the crime, would seem to dictate contacting the governor directly and then the lobbyist.

The second email Byers sent was to his administrative assistant to lock the door to her office, where she sat alone while the Policy Group met nearby in Steger's boardroom. This time, Byers explained his actions by saying he wanted to protect his assistant from inquiries about the shootings once word got out. Pressed by Hall, he did admit that he was being cautious.

Byers emphasized the importance that members of the Policy Group placed on student safety. But his answer to Hall's question of how do you keep the students safe by keeping them ignorant about a possible threat, he could only give a limp response: "You do what we were doing. You try to do the best you can with information you have at the time."

Andy Goddard could only shake his head in disbelief as he listened to Byers. Goddard remembered watching his son struggle to recover from his four gunshot wounds, he remembered the blood-soaked sheets, he remembered wanting to help his son but not knowing how—that was a battle Colin had fought on his own, and continued to fight through his recovery. Andy Goddard had felt so helpless and so vulnerable. He put his head in his hands and thought, "If this is the best you school officials could have done with the information you had at the time, you should never hold any position of responsibility."

*   *   *

Hour after hour, the testimony went over the facts of the case. At 8:16 a.m., Emily Hilscher's roommate, Heather Haugh, returned to the dormitory and was questioned. It was during this questioning that the name of Emily's boyfriend, Karl Thornhill, was raised. Thornhill had dropped Hilscher off that morning and proceeded to Radford University where he had an 8:00 a.m. class.

Haugh went on a police computer and opened her Facebook page to show the police pictures of Thornhill, including a photo Emily took of Thornhill at a shooting range. The photo shows Thornhill holding what appears to be a .22 rifle. Based on that information the police made Thornhill a "person of interest" and began to search for him on campus, but still did not warn the campus of their suspicions or the fact that a killer was on the loose.

Andy Goddard and the jury listened to the defense's flimsy line of reasoning—Thornhill is Hilscher's boyfriend and he goes to shooting ranges, so he must have shot her—to justify the police officer's decision to classify the double homicide as a "domestic incident." The defense also said that because the victims were male and female, that appeared to make the murders some sort of domestic-related incident. But there was absolutely no evidence to support this contention. President Steger testified that he was told by Chief Flinchum at 8:11 a.m. that the deaths were a domestic incident. Andy could only wonder if classifying a murder as a domestic incident makes the person firing the gun less dangerous.

If you factor in the following, absolutely nothing makes sense about the assumptions the police were making and the actions they took in the first hour after the shootings. First, if Karl Thornhill was the killer, why did he drop Emily Hilscher off at her dorm and then some time shortly thereafter return to her room and kill her? Why bring her back to the dorm to kill her and risk the chance of witnesses?

Second, why kill Ryan Clark? It was well known that Ryan, the other victim, had no romantic interest in Emily Hilscher—this would have ruled out a love triangle. Furthermore, to say that Thornhill was a suspect because he went to shooting ranges was ludicrous. Guns and shooting ranges are a way of life in rural Virginia.

I agree with Andy Goddard: The testimony of President Charles Steger, Virginia Tech Police Chief Flinchum, and Virginia Tech Associate Vice President for Public Relations Larry Hincker, can only be described in one word, "bewildering." For example, on the witness stand President Steger admitted that the killer could have been on campus—even hiding in West Ambler Johnston Hall. But when he was informed of the murders, it never occurred to him to issue a warning. Steger's own words before the jury appeared to indict him; he admitted that no one knew where the gunman was, and he had no thought of warning.

Even more disturbing, Flinchum testified that if the two dead students were "targeted" then the shooter would not be dangerous. How and why could Flinchum make this assertion? He tried to explain that he thought the shootings in room 4040 were an isolated incident, and thus they were targeted murders. There are two problems with this argument. First, room 4040 is not really isolated. It is on the middle floor of a seven-story building, near the elevators and half way along that wing of West Ambler Johnston Hall. Hardly isolated and the police knew that fact—they had to use the elevators and pass other rooms to get to 4040. The second problem is that Flinchum gave no evidence in his testimony as to how and why "targeted" murders mean the killers are not dangerous to others. Flinchum's assertion left Andy thunderstruck.

When Chief Flinchum was questioned about the timeline and asked if he knew the timeline used by President Steger was wrong, he said he didn't recall. Flinchum acknowledged that he prepared a timeline for the panel and agreed that there were differences with the one used by Steger. Here,

Flinchum—just as Hincker—suffered from faulty memory. He could not recall ever correcting Steger. When Flinchum was pressed on the stand as to why he did not tell the panel about the timeline errors, he said he assumed they knew—the errors were common knowledge. But if the errors were commonly known, why weren't they corrected? By this point in time, Andy Goddard was getting a headache from the verbal twists and turns of school officials.

Flinchum asserted that when the first version of the Governor's report came out he knew of the errors and called them to the attention of Kay Heidbreder, general counsel and Special Assistant to the Attorney General assigned to Virginia Tech. He did not call the errors to the attention of the panel chair, Massengill. The unanswered question is what did Heidbreder do with the information? If the state paid TriData over $700,000 to write and correct the report, didn't Heidbreder have an immediate responsibility to report the errors in the report? If she did not, was she negligent? Again, Goddard thought, "How could this woman be working for the defense given the role she played at the university?"

The school's defense attorneys could not explain away the nearly two and one-half hour gap following the double homicide at West Ambler Johnston Hall and the school's decision to alert the campus to the shooting. The jury saw through the defense's lame attempts to justify the Steger administration's inaction.

Indeed, even for the casual observer it is next to impossible to explain why the school did not warn the university community that two people had been murdered and that their killer was on the loose. How could the school not see a threat? No one could predict the massacre at Norris Hall. But how could anyone who was aware of the two murders on campus, with no known motive, and the perpetrator's identity and whereabouts unknown, make the assumption that no potential threat existed? What did the Steger administration and the Virginia Tech police expect the killer to do—just lay down his weapon and surrender after murdering two people? The warning came over two hours after the double homicide and just minutes before Seung Hui Cho slaughtered 30 people in Norris Hall. The defense attorneys' justification for the time lag fell on deaf ears.

The Verdict: Tech Is Accountable

To those reading this book who say Steger and school officials shouldn't be held accountable for their inaction, I would remind you that schools advertise they offer a safe and secure environment for learning, and that the courts have ruled that schools have a "special relationship with students" and do have a responsibility for safety. We can only ask you how can anyone justify not issuing a warning on April 16, 2007, when there were bloody footprints leading away from a double homicide in the middle of the campus? Furthermore, earlier the school had:

- Issued a campus-wide warning when a convict, William Morva, escaped from a Blacksburg jail and killed two people and there was no evidence Morva was on campus.
- Issued a campus-wide warning about measles.
- Issued a campus-wide warning about mold in the library. (Is it believable that the presence of mold spores reaches the threshold for a campus-wide alert, yet a double homicide does not?)
- Issued a campus-wide warning about mumps.
- Issued a campus-wide warning about a bomb threat even though the school knew it was probably false. The warning was issued several times, on several different days.

The Peterson and Pryde families must have been devastated as they listened to Steger, Hincker, and Flinchum parse words; twist and turn the events of April 16, 2007; admit to errors and testify that they saw no need to warn their students. No wonder Erin Peterson's father broke down sobbing in the courtroom. University authorities thought to warn the trash collectors and stop garbage collection; they thought to stop bank pick-ups and deliveries; the school of veterinary medicine locked its doors; the Blacksburg schools locked down—but Steger, Hincker, and Flinchum didn't think to issue a warning that might have saved Erin's life.

At the heart of the Pryde and Peterson lawsuit was the contention that if university officials had warned the campus promptly following the earlier shootings, the young women would have taken precautions, altering their schedules. The lawyers for the Pryde and Peterson families pointed out that the school found time to contact the governor to report one student dead, another injured, and a gunman on the loose, but couldn't find the time to alert the campus.

"Our daughters and the other students and faculty were entitled to that information, too, and would be alive today if that information had been shared," the parents' lawyer, Bob Hall, said in a statement on behalf of the Prydes and Petersons. "All we've been looking for is accountability."

On Wednesday, March 14, 2012, the jury agreed with Hall and held Tech accountable. Hall welcomed the jury's decision and its award of $4 million to each family, an amount that was later reduced to $100,000 each—the cap in civil cases against the Commonwealth of Virginia.

The money means nothing to the two families. Celeste Peterson told the court that she has kept her daughter's things in a closet. Sometimes she goes in there and sits on the floor so she can touch the things that Erin once touched.

Celeste Peterson said her daughter made her want to be a better person. Erin once asked her parents why she couldn't help everyone who needed help. Once again a decent, loving human being has been sacrificed on the altar of incompetence. In her memory, the Petersons have set up a nonprofit fund to give college scholarships to high school students—most of the students who have received the scholarships have gone to Virginia Tech.

Every day Karen Pryde remembers her thoughtful, caring, and loving daughter. She remembers how supportive Julia was of her friends and her involvement in numerous projects to support children's and environmental causes. She remembers how much Julia loved Virginia Tech and how thrilled she was with the Biological Systems Engineering (BSE) department. Julia was concerned about the world around her and wanted to do something about bringing clean water to everyone. She had gone to South America on a school project for clean water and the trip made her even more determined to make a difference. Each year since her death, Julia K. Pryde memorial scholarships have been awarded to Virginia Tech graduate students in the BSE department for work projects abroad with an emphasis on water purity projects abroad in underdeveloped countries.

Karen Pryde often thinks about her wonderful daughter who was focused and independent from her earliest childhood. As a toddler Julia refused to take those first tentative single steps when it was time to learn to walk. She simply started out running.

Karen Pryde remembers Julia's determination. When her brother Keith was four years old, he was enrolled in swimming lessons at the local swim club. Julia wanted to join but because she was three did not meet the minimum age requirement. She threw a fit and within a couple of years showed them—Julia won her first swim race at age five by half the length of the pool and was named MVP for her age group four times.

Julia could be withdrawn, but not when it came to sports. She was athletic and coordinated and excelled in whatever sport she took on, but her mother remembers that what you could not forget about her was how she encouraged and cheered her teammates on—she was a team player in the truest and best sense of the words. Hers was the whistle, the yell—the words of encouragement you could hear above the rest. She played center forward and goalie in soccer; pitcher, infielder, and catcher in softball and was often the anchor for the swim club, the Y, and her high school swim teams. After her murder, her friends and classmates told Karen and Harry Pryde how much Julia had meant to them; how much her words of encouragement had pushed them to do their best.

Julia's determination was not limited to sports, it extended into her academic life. She was bright and demanded excellence of herself and others. In junior high Julia had a math teacher who was past her prime and not really up to dealing with the challenges of her very bright class. Julia complained, but her parents did not see there was anything that could be done—you just suffer through the teacher you have. Wrong. Julia went to her advisor and stated her case on behalf of the whole class. Her advisor could do nothing. Undeterred, Julia marched into the principal's office and told him what was happening. The teacher ended up retiring early. Julia's mom and dad were a little awed by what their precocious daughter had done and that she had shown the courage of her convictions at such a young age—and took action.

When time came for Julia to go to college, she knew what she wanted and her school was in Blacksburg, Virginia. Julia would apply for early admission to Virginia Tech's College of Engineering, and that was it, end of discussion.

Julia started as a computer science major but during her freshman year she was required to take a course that exposed her to all sorts of engineering possibilities. She discovered what was to become her major and her passion—Biological Systems Engineering.

As Julia's first year at Tech drew to a close, she looked for ways to help pay for college and enhance her love of the environment and the outdoors. She found it in a scholarship program with the Student Conservation Association and headed out to Idaho to learn to be a wildland firefighter. That first year she returned to live in south Jersey, building nature trails while waiting impatiently to be called upon to help fight fires. Her chance did not come until the next year. After more training she was sent to an American Indian reservation in North Dakota to record dwellings as part of emergency planning when she got the call to report to Arizona to help with a very large fire there. She and her teammates were thrilled; her parents, less so. Karen Pryde was not happy with her daughter being in harm's way. But today, every time Karen Pryde sees a report of a wild fire burning out of control, she wishes her daughter were there pursuing her dreams and her goal in life.

At a memorial service held at Julia's high school, a school friend reminded Karen Pryde of one of Julia's special acts of kindness. She had gone to New York City with friends and a homeless man came up to her and asked for money. She responded by saying, "Sorry, I don't have any." The man then asked for a cigarette. Again Julia responded, "I don't smoke." At that, the man turned and walked away. Julia went after him and tapped him on the shoulder; when he turned around she put her arms around him and said, "I can give you a hug." The homeless man was overcome and responded, "That is just what I needed."

Karen Pryde remembers vividly her daughter telling her the story of the homeless man. She also remembers cautioning her that she should not have done that. Julia just chuckled and shook her head and gave her mom one of those "you don't understand, mom" looks. Every time Karen Pryde tells the story she just wishes that Cho had met Julia and experienced her compassion and concern for her fellow human beings—especially those less fortunate than her. Perhaps none of this would have happened.

* * *

In a written statement following the decision, Virginia Tech officials expressed disappointment, calling the shootings "an unprecedented act of violence that no one could have foreseen." The state attorney general's office issued a similar statement, saying, in part: "Only with hindsight can one conclude that Cho's unprecedented acts were foreseeable."

The university's president, Charles W. Steger, wrote a letter to faculty and staff. "We stand by our long-held position that the administration and law enforcement at Virginia Tech did their absolute best with the information available," he said, echoing the university's defense in state and federal investigations. He suggested that Virginia Tech would appeal the verdict. Both the statement and the letter are simply not true. If a faculty member threatens to resign because she is afraid for her safety as well as the safety of her students, how can school officials say they saw no potential for violence? Such an assertion is glossing over blatant malfeasance by those bent on deceit and covering up the abysmal, mediocre leadership Virginia Tech officials demonstrated on April 16, 2007.

* * *

For decades the legal responsibilities and relationship of schools to faculty, staff, and students have gone through periods of change.

Before the 1960s, most courts in this country believed that universities and colleges acted in place of parents, *loco parentis*. In the 1960s and 1970s the courts decided that college students were no longer children, but *constitutional adults*. As a result, *loco parentis* was no longer the foundation upon which the relationship between institutions of higher learning and students rested. In the 1980s, the courts began to reject student injury claims. The legal system began to view universities and colleges as "bystanders" basing their logic on students' Constitutional rights and freedoms.

Courts in this period argued that institutions of higher learning had no duty for student safety; students had a duty to protect themselves. "Duty" became the underlying principle in law related to the student-university relationship. The net result was that legal precedents became confusing and contradictory.

From the late 1980s on, however, universities began moving away from the "bystander" concept. More and more the courts ruled that universities and colleges do have a duty regarding the safety of students. Robert D. Bickel and Peter F. Lake argue in their book, *"The Rights and Responsibilities of the Modern University,"* that the term *facilitator* is "the appropriate legal and cultural balance between university authority/control and student freedom."

The jury decision in March 2012, against Virginia Tech, was a critical step forward in defining this facilitator role and confirming that failure to warn students of an imminent threat is gross negligence and a violation of the duties owed by universities and colleges to students, staff and faculty.

The Pryde and Peterson families wanted what all of us who have lost family members to needless gun violence want: they wanted justice, they wanted answers, and they wanted to expose the negligence and incompetence for which they had paid such a high price. They also wanted to make sure that lessons were learned from Virginia Tech, and that actions would be taken to prevent other parents from suffering as they had suffered.

When you read the transcript of the trial, you fully understand why it took a jury of seven men and women in Montgomery County Virginia less than four hours to find Virginia Tech guilty of contributing to the deaths of Erin Peterson and Julia Pryde: and by implication, guilty of contributing to the deaths of thirty other students and faculty members as well as being complicit in the wounding of at least seventeen others.

Of course, for every step forward, there is pushback, especially from those who have political and financial concerns in the outcome of the lawsuit.

Politics Corrupts the Court

For a short period of time the jury's decision holding Tech accountable appeared to be important far beyond giving the two families some sense of justice. First, the verdict sent a strong message to colleges and universities that they do have a special relationship with students, faculty, and staff, and the relationship involves safety.

Second, the level of accountability had been raised. Institutions of higher learning would now be expected to do something about specific manifestations of mental illness and threats of violence from students or employees and if they did not take preventive measures, they would be held responsible for the violence that might result. If nothing else, the Pryde and Peterson families, for a few short months, could take some solace in the fact that colleges and universities would now be under a microscope when it comes to campus safety.

On October 31, 2013, however, the Virginia Supreme Court issued a decision reversing the Montgomery County Circuit Court jury trial verdict that found Virginia Tech negligent for not warning the campus on the morning of April 16, 2007. The decision appears to be politically motivated and is a skillful manipulation of facts, evidence, and language. Most troubling of all is the fact that the Court gave Tech a pass in a decision that is badly flawed and leaves the parents of students on the campuses of Virginia's schools with next to no legal recourse if their son or daughter is wounded or killed as a result of incompetence on the part of people in positions of authority.

Judge Cleo E. Powell wrote the decision. Judge Powell is considered to be one of the more conservative judges on the Virginia Supreme Court. Her poorly written narrative is especially troubling because she claims the court bases its decision on facts, yet she has some facts wrong and ignores others. In the opening paragraph she writes:

> *"In this case, we hold even if there was a special relationship between the Commonwealth and students of Virginia Tech, under the facts of this case, there was no duty for the Commonwealth to warn students about the potential for criminal acts by third parties."*

This sentence is a cynical and insidious in the way it plays with English syntax. The above sentence is intentionally vague. Under the rules of standard English, for conditional sentences you are to use "was" if what you are saying is factually correct; you are to use "were" if what you are saying is not factually correct. When I say, "If I were the King of England, I would give everyone a Bentley" I use "were" because I am not the King of England. In the Virginia Tech case, Judge Powell, by using "was" is admitting that a special relationship did and does exist between Virginia Tech and its students. Judge Powell should have used a straightforward, declarative, active voice sentence if she wanted her meaning to be clear, but apparently she needed to leave herself some wiggle room.

One of the arguments the state has made in the past is that a special relationship did not exist. Clearly, Judge Powell wanted to play a game with the readers and decided to admit that fact, but used a sentence structure that obscured this critical point. In fact, Judge Powell, in her attempt to obscure, may have set a legal precedent that Virginia Tech (and by implication all educational institutions in the state) has a special relationship with its students. Instead of playing grammar games, Judge Powell should have, at minimum, had the moral courage to be candid in asserting that a special relationship does exist, and then argue why the Virginia Tech massacre is an exception.

*   *   *

In the section of the ruling entitled "Facts and Proceedings," the second paragraph, first and second sentences read:

> *"During the investigation, police came to believe that they were investigating a domestic homicide because there were no signs of forced entry or robbery. They believed that a "targeted shooting" had occurred…"*

1. The fact is that the police did not do their duty. This was not a love triangle or "domestic homicide." One simple question about the relationship between the two victims to any student whose room was near the crime scene would have debunked the love triangle or "domestic homicide" theory.
2. The fact is that there were bloody footprints leading away from the crime scene, and a bloody thumbprint on a door leading to the stairway, in a building in the middle of the campus.
3. The fact is there was no evidence that the killer had left the campus.
4. The fact is that Virginia Tech set its own precedent for warning a few months earlier when a killer, William Morva, was on the loose in Blacksburg. There was no evidence he was on the campus and yet the school locked down and warned the staff, faculty, and students.
5. The fact is that portions of the school took the initiative and complied with Virginia Tech's rules and locked down and warned. Those parts of Virginia Tech were complying with the school's own rules and the Clery Act; President Steger and Police Chief Wendell Flinchum were not.
6. The fact is that the school had warned the campus before on numerous occasions for such things as *mold* and *the flu*, <u>why not for murder?</u>
7. The fact is that Judge Powell and the Supreme Court accepted the explanation that the West Ambler Johnston Hall murders was an "… isolated incident and posed no danger to others …" without asking what made the police think that someone who has murdered one student and wounded another is not a threat to others?

8. The fact is that there is evidence that Virginia Tech Police Chief Wendell Flinchum may not have been telling the truth on the witness stand (during the Pryde and Peterson trial) about discussions which occurred on whether or not to warn and lock down the campus following the double homicide at West Ambler Johnston Hall.

9. The fact is that Judge Powell was *wrong* when she said on page two of her opinion that "…the Blacksburg Police Department led the investigation." The 7:51 a.m. entry in the Governor's Review Panel Report states, "Chief Flinchum contacts the Blacksburg Police Department (BPD) and requests a BPD evidence technician and BPD detective to assist with the investigation." The report repeatedly has Chief Flinchum calling the shots and asking the BPD for officers and assistance.

The error raised in point #9 above is so disturbing that I decided to get to the bottom of it and wrote Blacksburg Chief of Police Kim Crannis asking the following:

> "A question has arisen that you could help answer: The Governor's Review Panel Report states that Virginia Tech Police Chief Wendell Flinchum was in charge of the investigation after the double homicide at West Ambler Johnston Hall.
>
> "The decision written and made public by Virginia Supreme Court Justice Cleo E. Powell flatly states that you were in charge.
>
> "Could you help me clarify the command? Did you assume control of the investigation from Chief Flinchum? If so, when? Did the change of incident command follow FEMA guidelines?"

Within days I received a letter from Chief Crannis in which she said the following:

> "On that date, the Blacksburg Police Department responded to the request for assistance from the Virginia Tech Police Department, pursuant to a Mutual Aid Agreement between the Town and Virginia Tech. That agreement provided that 'all law enforcement personnel responding to an emergency request as described in his agreement will report to an(d) take direction from the Chief of Police of the requesting agency.'"

In order to double check that Justice Powell was wrong, I then filed a Freedom of Information request with Steve Capaldo, Associate University Legal Counsel, Virginia Tech, asking for a copy of the agreement between the school and the town of Blacksburg. Here is what that agreement says in paragraph two on page two:

> "2. *All law enforcement personnel responding to an emergency request as described in this agreement will report to and take direction from the Chief of Police of the requesting agency or his/her designee. ...*"

Chief Flinchum was in charge—Justice Powell was just plain wrong. This mistake is so serious that it raises questions about the validity of the other assertions in her decisions. Indeed, Justice Powell and the rest of the court appear to have bent over backwards to view the evidence in a light most favorable the State and Virginia Tech. Furthermore, the Virginia Supreme Court's error on this point is particularly troubling because it gives credence to speculation that the Court's decision was politically motivated. In other words, the Court apparently was determined to overturn the jury verdict of the Montgomery Circuit Court regardless of the facts and evidence.

On the witness stand Chief Flinchum admitted that he had the authority to issue a warning but indicated he never raised the subject with the school's senior administrative group (called into session to discuss the murders). Flinchum's denial that a warning or lockdown was discussed that morning stands at odds with the deposition taken from two notetakers at the meeting, Kim O'Rourke and Lisa Wilkes. Ms. O'Rourke's notes are especially damning. She wrote, "... police (read Chief Flinchum because he was the one communicating with the administrative group) don't believe a lockdown is necessary at this time."

The Supreme Court also did not consider the fact that a lockdown would have saved lives. Two students were allowed to leave West Ambler Johnston Hall and go their French class in Norris hall where they were slaughtered. A lockdown, then, would have saved a minimum of two lives; there is no disputing that fact. Judge Powell ignored it or was just plain ignorant of that detail.

* * *

In the "Facts and Proceedings" the Judge ends with the sentence *"Police also learned that the female's boyfriend was a gun enthusiast."* Judge Powell makes no further comment. I would ask Judge Powell to consider that probably more than half of the male students on the Virginia Tech campus are gun enthusiasts. So what is the point, judge? If being a gun enthusiast was enough cause to place a person suspicion, then definitely the campus should have been locked down and warned, and all those young men rounded up and questioned.

*   *   *

Paragraph six consists of two puzzling sentences. *"Police subsequently executed a search warrant of the home of the boyfriend of the female victim found in West Ambler Johnston Hall. They found nothing."* The reader is not told that the search of the boyfriend's townhouse took place some *six hours* after Cho was dead. No one has ever explained that fact. The police already knew who the killer was and that the killer was dead. Furthermore, the police violated the law by entering the house without showing the Thornhills the search warrant. What is the point of this paragraph within Judge Powell's written decision? Reference to the search of Thornhill's townhouse is not logical, makes no sense and draws attention to the police violating the law. It is actually counter-productive unless by leaving out the timing of the search, Judge Powell was trying to play up the idea that the police were conducting an intensive investigation, when in fact they were harassing a grieving young man and his family.

*   *   *

Paragraph seven of the ruling ends with this: *"… the shootings appeared targeted, likely domestic in nature, and that the shooter had likely left the campus."* These words are particularly repugnant. Judge Powell combines the false assertion of a domestic crime, with the incorrect use of "targeted" killing, and ends with the indefensible assertion that *"the shooter had likely left the campus."*

As pointed out earlier, there is no way this could have been a domestic crime. Now, Judge Powell accepts the incorrect use of "targeted" killing. In fact, "targeted killing" is a concept used by experts and defined as "people far from any battlefield who are determined to be enemies of the state and are killed without charge or trial." For a Virginia Supreme Court justice not to know the definition of "targeted killings" is troubling.

*   *   *

Judge Powell twists her logic into a pretzel in order to accept the explanation of Ralph Byers, Virginia Tech's Executive Director for Government Relations for backing away from the 8:45 a.m. assertion in an email to the Governor's office: "gunman on the loose…." Judge Powell never explains why the school administration was correct in warning the Governor's office some 150 miles away, and not warning the campus. The excuse that the school wanted to notify the next of kin before releasing information to the public is specious. You can withhold the names of those killed and still warn the campus.

*   *   *

Judge Powell's handling of the doctrine of foreseeability is proof that her conservative ideology dictated the decision, not logic and law. Powell and the rest of the state Supreme Court were apparently unwilling to consider other courts' definitions of "foreseeability" and ignored the definition of "foreseeability" as spelled out in *Turpin v. Granieri* 985 P. 2d 669 (Id. 1999) in which the court wrote:

> *"Foreseeability is a flexible concept which varies with the circumstances of each case. Where the degree of result or harm is great, but preventing it not difficult, a relative low degree of foreseeability is required... Thus foreseeability is not to be measured by just what is more probable than not, but also includes whatever result is likely enough in the setting of modern life that a reasonable prudent person would take such into account in guiding reasonable conduct... We only engage in balancing of the harm in those rare situations when we are called upon to extend a duty beyond the scope previously imposed or when a duty has not been previously recognized."*

The New York Supreme Court has ruled that the fact that a defendant could not anticipate the precise manner of an accident or incident, or the exact extent of injuries does not preclude liability as a matter of law where the general risk and character of injuries are foreseeable. The New York court hit the nail on the head. In dealing with an unstable person such as Cho, or any murderer, the exact nature of the violent behavior or when or how it will occur cannot be predicted. But that he or she will be violent is predictable and preventive measures, including warnings and lockdowns, can be taken.

Virginia Tech official Ralph Byers used the words "killer on the loose." More violence, then, was foreseeable. The exact time and place of that violence may not have been predictable, but it most definitely was foreseeable and therefore there was a duty to warn.

*   *   *

In the Analysis section, Judge Powell lays out the Commonwealth's argument for dismissing the case. She writes on page eleven: *"... we have imposed a duty to warn of a third party criminal acts [sic] only where there was 'an imminent probability of injury' from a third party act."* What greater indication of imminent violence does the Virginia Supreme Court need than Ralph Byers words at 8:45 a.m. that there was a killer on the loose?

*　　*　　*

On page 15, the final page of the decision, Judge Powell writes *"Most importantly based on information available at that time, the defendants believed that the shooter had fled the area and posed no danger to others."* This sentence is one of the most disturbing and bogus in the report.

1. There was absolutely no evidence that the killer had left the campus.
2. There was absolutely no evidence the double homicide was the result of a lovers' triangle.
3. There was absolutely no evidence the killer was not a threat to others on the Virginia Tech campus.

*　　*　　*

Judge Powell also writes, *"Based on the limited information available to the Commonwealth prior to the shootings in Norris Hall, it cannot be said that it was or reasonably foreseeable that students in Norris Hall would fall victim to criminal harm. Thus, as a matter of law, the Commonwealth did not have a duty to protect students against third party criminal acts."*

If you buy the incorrect definition of words, concepts and facts that Judge Powell lays out then the above is correct. But, unfortunately her words run counter to facts, evidence, and the truth.

*　　*　　*

The conclusion of the decision reads: *"Assuming without deciding that a special relationship existed between the Commonwealth and Virginia Tech students, based on the specific facts of this case, as a matter of law, no duty to warn students of harm by a third party criminal arose. Thus, we will reverse the trial court's judgment holding that a duty arose and enter final judgment in favor of the Commonwealth.*

Reversed and Final Judgment

In the conclusion of the decision, Judge Powell wrote: "Assuming without deciding that a special relationship existed between the Commonwealth and Virginia Tech students, based on the specific facts of this case, as a matter of law, no duty to warn students of harm by a third party arose."

But in fact, as I have already shown through her use of English, Judge Powell *did admit* that a special relationship exists between Tech and its students and therefore there was a duty to warn. The opening sentence of the conclusion is wrong, just as she and the court are wrong on some of the facts of the case. There is no doubt—Virginia Tech had a duty to warn the staff, faculty, and students on the morning of April 16th.

The Virginia Supreme Court's judgment is the latest in a long series of decisions refusing to recognize the responsibility of a business proprietor, in this case Virginia Tech, to protect "its invitees from unreasonable risk of physical harm." If that is the case, then you have to ask if schools do not have a responsibility to warn then why do they advertise themselves as a safe learning environment, why do they have police forces, why do they have elaborate and expensive warning systems, why do they warn and close down when a murderer is close by or there is mold on the campus?

The state's defense is so weak and so full of holes that Judge Powell had to play with or ignore evidence and accept the state's argument without question, and most troubling she showed no intellectual curiosity when there was evidence that a key witness in the trial may have perjured himself. The most plausible explanation for the court's miscarriage of justice is that the decision is politically motivated; a decision designed to protect members of the Virginia Tech administration from liability.

*   *   *

Just as this book was going to print the Virginia Supreme Court, on January 21, 2014, refused to reconsider its decision to dismiss the wrongful-death verdict against Virginia Tech.

I know it is very fashionable in some circles to talk about the liberal courts and the liberal media. But the Virginia Supreme Court's decision, which examined some evidence in the most favorable way to the state and school and ignored other, smacks of far right-wing conservative political bias that no one is ever responsible for someone else's actions. How else do you explain a critical error such as the court's not knowing who was in charge of the investigation, despite the sworn testimony the Justices had in front of them? Did the justices not read the documents? Did someone intentionally not tell the truth to make sure Virginia Tech Police Chief Wendell Flinchum could never be held accountable? How could an error of this magnitude make it into a unanimous Virginia Supreme Court decision and the court not correct it?

There are lawyers in my classes at the FBI and CIA. I would fail them for an error of this monumental proportion. I have nearly 50 years of experience in intelligence and crime analysis and I always believed that while judges have liberal and conservative bias, they would nevertheless be fair, would be factually correct, and would not ignore facts and evidence to the detriment of one side or the other. Clearly, I have been wrong.

CHAPTER XII

THE FAMILIES NEED TO MOVE ON

"Thinking is hard work, which is why you don't see a lot of people doing it."
~Sue Grafton, American author

Those who say it is time for the Virginia Tech families "to move on" are often blinded by the total settlement figure. All they see is the money. Many do not understand that the pain from the loss of a child or spouse cannot be mitigated by any amount of money, nor will time completely heal the wound. They don't stop to think that the lawyers for the families got $1 million and each family of a deceased loved one received $100,000. That is not a fortune—it is an insult. They don't stop to think that $100,000, $1 million, or a $100 million cannot replace their child or family member. Ask any parent or spouse who lost someone on April 16, 2007 and he or she will say keep your money and give me my loved one back.

The Virginia Tech Settlement Agreement and Release

1. Direct payments to victims' and personal representatives of victims' estates $3,850,000   (The $100,000 for the families came from this pot of money.)
2. Charitable Purposes Fund $1,750,000
3. Hardship Fund $1,900,000
4. Attorneys' fees $1,500,000 (approximate)

These well-meaning people who talk about "moving on" often speak without thinking; their attempts at kindness can, in fact, be very cruel. They do not realize that the first thing to know about a tragedy—particularly the sudden loss of a child or spouse—is that you will never really get over it; you learn to live with it, you learn to cope, but it is always there. These people don't stop to think about what they are saying; they have no idea of the negative impact their words can have. Furthermore, everyone attempts to recover from such tragedies in his or her own way, in his or her own time—there is no standard or set time to "move on."

There is, furthermore, no one formula for the recovery process. Some simply remember and are thankful for having the time they had with their lost loved one; some say this was all God's purpose and we will trust in him; others devote themselves to preventing future campus shootings; and some simply remember and cry. All are valid forms of recovery and no one has the right to judge or tell any parent or spouse how or when she or he should begin to put her or his life back together.

When you listen to the families talk about the child they lost or the spouse who was gunned down, you hear stories of amazing, wonderful human beings; you begin to realize the full magnitude of what was lost that day—it becomes overpowering; the loss is suffocating.

My work on this book has made me realize how remarkable the families of the Virginia Tech tragedy are. They are an inspiration. The pain is there, it will never go completely away, but they are moving ahead with their lives in a variety of ways. I have come to admire the Tech families I interviewed for this book; they represent, in so many ways, the finest qualities of human character and nature. Each family is strong in its own unique way.

My admiration for the Virginia Tech families becomes even greater when I reflect on the fact that there is some pain that time will never fully heal, especially when victims' families are lied to. The people who say it is time to move on do not realize that if a parent or family member dares to raise questions or ask for explanations he or she may encounter vicious criticism, and even threats for personal safety. Indeed, there is a small, but at times highly vocal group of people who are incredibly cruel and callous. They belittle the families of school shooting victims in their attempt to find answers and to hold people accountable; they call these families moneygrubbers and greedy. The people who call on the families to "move on" do not want to hear about the sarcasm, threats, and verbal abuse some victims' families have encountered. But they need to. They need to understand the harsh reality of what really happens.

The Compensation Debate

Why are the families due financial compensation for their loss? It is simple. Schools advertise that they provide a safe and secure learning environment. They spend millions on security systems; there are federal laws governing requirements to warn faculty, staff, and students of threats, and schools accept money from families to educate their children in a protected environment. The exchange of money creates a contract. When school, medical, and police officials break that contract because of incompetence or stupidity, and it results in injury or death, families are owed compensation.

Furthermore, the loss of a child or spouse causes untold emotional hardship, which may result in thousands of dollars in medical costs. The psychological trauma of a lost child can immobilize a parent, making it next to impossible for the parent to hold down a job for years.

Following the state of Virginia's settlement with 30 of the Virginia Tech victims' families, a number of people wrote letters to the editor and blogs criticizing this use of taxpayer money. Some incredibly unkind individuals accused the Tech families of greed, of trying to make money off the tragedy. This accusation is simply not true. Specialists in grief counseling will tell you that rarely do victims of such horrors as the Virginia Tech massacre ask, "How much can I get out of this?" "Who can I sue?" Certainly, the Virginia Tech families didn't. Litigation is usually the last resort and comes when victims' families realize they are not being told the truth. Again, grief counselors will tell you that it is far more likely that the survivors and families of survivors and victims will be more concerned about the wellbeing of others than about themselves. Civil litigation did not occur in the Virginia Tech case until it was readily apparent the families were at a disadvantage in access to reports and documents, and that people were not telling the truth. The families didn't want money; they wanted what they needed the most and did not get—accuracy and accountability.

These same individuals frequently argue that no one can be held responsible for anyone else's actions and that therefore the financial settlement was not justified. This assertion is not only contrary to a whole body of legal opinion, but shows a lack of knowledge, understanding, empathy, and conscience. Furthermore, to deny a family a miserly $100,000 compensation for the loss of a child is disgraceful.

Don't forget:

Less than six weeks after the shootings Virginia Tech signed an agreement with one of the nation's largest public relations firms,

Burson-Marsteller, to spin the story of the tragedy in such a way as to do minimal damage to Virginia Tech and its administration. In other words, the school paid $663,000.00 to a public relations firm, when Virginia Tech had its own office that dealt with public relations.

And for those of you worried about wasting tax payers' money, remember that Tech has some of the best minds in the country, yet it spent nearly $700,000 on outside public relations talent.

From my 48-years of work with law enforcement and intelligence officers, I can assure you there were people far more qualified than TriData employees to write the report on the shooting massacre at Virginia Tech. And, they would probably have volunteered to do the work.

This cavalier spending of over a million dollars by the state and by Virginia Tech University in an effort to manipulate opinion following the nation's worst school shooting was the waste of taxpayers' money, not the $100,000 the families received for the murder of their children and spouses.

So all of this begs the question: why are people ignoring the actions of the school and the state of Virginia? Why are they focused on pushing the families past a tragedy that can only be endured, never forgotten? In fact, when these well-meaning people say it is time for the Virginia Tech families to move on, they are really saying, *we* need to move on; *we* don't want to think about that tragedy or any school shooting. *We* don't want to think this could happen to *us*.

Unfortunately, when you have lost a loved one so suddenly and so tragically, not thinking about that loss simply isn't an option. The Virginia Tech families will never stop thinking about the events of April 16, 2007— it will be with them every day of their lives.

Threats and Diatribes

Not too long after I began working on this book, I asked Michael Pohle if he or his family had run into any hostility, verbal abuse, or threats because of the financial settlement the state of Virginia reached with the families. His answer was "yes," and I found out from talking with other families that the Pohles were not alone.

Michael Pohle said there had been sarcastic remarks about all the money they had received, including snide comments about the Pohle family being rich. As if any amount of money was worth the life of Michael Pohle, Jr. What the Pohles and many of the Tech families encountered is an inexplicable and totally repulsive phenomenon—envy over financial compensation for the murder of a child, coupled with an irrational hatred of victims who dare to question or speak out.

I then proceeded to tell Pohle what had happened to me. On the second anniversary of the law school shooting in Grundy, I wrote an OpEd that appeared in several newspapers, including one in southwestern Virginia. My wife had gone to upstate New York to visit her brother and I was home alone when I received a phone call from a man who had read the article. He warned me that what I had written had made "officials in Grundy and the law school look bad." He said I could be on a "hit list," and warned me to be "careful when I visited family in that part of the state." He cautioned me to "stop at every stop sign, obey every traffic law." He also warned that if a law enforcement officer wants to get you, he or she will. "A favorite trick," he said, "is to stop someone and plant contraband or drugs in the individual's car." In an ominous tone he asserted, "People have a way of going to jail in Grundy and not coming out alive."

A few weeks later, I was teaching at the CIA. My biography carries a reference to the book I wrote on the Appalachian School of Law murders. After the class, one of the CIA managers came up to me, saying he was born and raised just outside Grundy. He wanted to know more. When I told him about the book's contents he warned me to be careful. "People down there have a way of doing things. There are deep abandoned mine shafts where bodies can disappear."

He then relayed a story about what happened when he was growing up. A couple of police officers were having sex with underage high school girls and got them pregnant. A doctor treated the girls and subsequently reported the pregnancies to the authorities. A few months later, the doctor was found shot to death in his car. The vehicle had over thirty bullet holes in it. The cover story was that he refused to stop for a traffic violation. The subsequent investigation came to naught, and the officers were not held accountable. "So," he said, "be careful and look over your shoulder at every turn when you are in the Grundy area." He too warned me and indicated that there was risk for me in trying to hold people accountable.

Grundy is less than 130 miles from Blacksburg and some of my work colleagues have expressed concern for my safety because of my work to get at the truth about April 16, 2007—and to hold people accountable. A close friend of mine cautioned me (half joking and half serious) not to make dinner reservations in Blacksburg and to get a remote starter for my car.

More recently, when I told someone here in Kilmarnock, Virginia that I was working on a book that is an exposé of the Virginia Tech shooting, she asked me, "Have you received any threats?"

What strikes me now is the attitude of fear and the idea of a cover up were so pervasive that warnings came to me from multiple sources. The Virginia Tech families have experienced the same atmosphere of distrust and aggression and on such a large scale that it has had a lasting impact on many of them.

* * *

An especially disturbing is story is the one I was told by one family who lost a child at Tech. I am not identifying the family by name out of respect and concern for their safety.

As part of their healing process, as part of their moving on, they decided to speak out publicly about the need to keep guns out of the hands of individuals who are dangerously mentally ill. They were quoted in the local papers and spoke openly about their feelings on television interviews.

Shortly after a television appearance, the husband was working on his wife's car and found intentional sabotage. Earplugs with a rope cord were wrapped around the brake line and tied to the end of the tie rod. The saboteur hoped the brake line would rupture causing the brakes to immediately fail. Then a few weeks later the husband was working on the car again and found that the passenger-side tires had razor-like slits as if someone had taken a box cutter on the sidewall. The wife's car had been parked in an open parking lot where she works. When the family went to the wife's employer's security office, they found that the parking lot security cameras had malfunctioned, so the criminal was never identified.

The intimidation worked. The family had already paid a heavy price because of Virginia Tech's incompetence and stupidity—they could not risk another family member being killed by a mentally ill person. The family stopped speaking in public on gun control.

* * *

The rabid second amendment advocates have also taken a turn at belittling and ridiculing any member of the Tech victims' families who disagrees with them on keeping weapons out of the hands of those who are a danger to others.

Colin Goddard, and his work for the Brady Campaign, has received some harsh, off-the-wall criticism. One gun rights advocacy blog has been especially vicious. The author labels Goddard a medieval alchemist, turning the tragedy into "gold." In other words, he is accusing Colin of profiting from the sufferings of others.

The blog, instead of examining the constitutional arguments of the second amendment, engages in immature name-calling. For example, the blogger writes, "… Goddard has managed to transmute the lead of four bullets shot into his body at Virginia Tech, into the gold of a paid position on the Brady Campaign's … staff." Such words are indicative of an individual who relies on emotion rather than thought. In fact, the blog's author is telling much more about himself than those he criticizes. I would argue that to engage in such immature rhetoric against the victims of violent crimes is the sign of a disturbed individual. The blog's argument that Colin Goddard is becoming rich because he works for the Brady Campaign is nonsense.

If Colin Goddard wanted to make money off that tragedy he would work for the National Rifle Association (NRA). The NRA has money to burn and uses its wealth, power, and influence to buy one politician after another. The NRA is rolling in cash, and has not hesitated to exploit school shootings for its own purposes by calling for more people to own guns.

The author of the blog, who is wheelchair-bound due to an automobile accident, is doing his own exploiting. He uses his personal tragedy to gain sympathy by posting that fact on his blog. Readers of the blog do not need to know whether the blogger can walk or not—that is immaterial to the right to own a gun. We are all sorry about the young man's tragedy and would do anything we could to give him back the ability to walk, but to exploit his condition to gain sympathy is disappointing. Furthermore, all the rights granted U.S. citizens in the Constitution have some limitations. The right to freedom of speech does not extend to libel, slander or profanity. The right to own a gun should not be extended to those who are a danger to themselves or others.

It is troubling that someone would stir a cauldron of medieval hatred, paranoia, and self-pity in order to defame a young man who is walking around with bullets in him, bullets that could move at any time and cause potentially serious damage.

She Was Our Sunshine

For the family of Emily Hilscher the loss has been catastrophic. Life without Emily has at times been nearly unbearable—the family is still a long way from recovery.

Before April 16, 2007, life for the Hilscher's with their two daughters, Erica and Emily, was a cavalcade of activity and exuberance. Every evening the dinner table was theater. The two girls would re-enact funny commercials, or a scene from a movie, or events from the day at school. Bits of costumes were often involved.

Emily loved people and wanted everyone to be as happy as she was. She had a deep affection for animals, especially horses. Emily embodied life itself: she was vibrant, enthusiastic, and called herself "the pixie" because she weighed only about 115 lbs. According to Beth, Emily's mother, "She was our sunshine."

At five, "the pixie" announced she wanted to learn to ride horses and began taking lessons. She had two instructors and a broken arm by the time she was ten. After that she began riding with a man who would become her incredible friend, mentor, and trainer, Moody Aylor. Moody, an older man who is a strong disciplinarian, held Emily's nose to the grindstone. When she would fall off a horse, he would not ask how she was, he would ask, "What did you do wrong?" The two would get into spirited arguments, but the bond between them was deep and strong. Emily adored Moody. She loved him as if he were a second father.

Like a father, Moody Aylor was proud when his star pupil, Emily, got on the equestrian team at Virginia Tech. One can imagine his anticipation of watching Emily become a national or even international competitor. Moody Aylor has been overwhelmed by her loss. Like a father, he will never forget.

On April 16, 2007, Beth and Eric Hilscher were up early that day as usual. They ran and owned a business designing and building radiology clinics around the country, from their home in Rappahannock County, Virginia—approximately 200 miles from Blacksburg and a little over 150 miles from Roanoke.

Every morning Beth exchanged instant messages with Emily, who would start her daily message to her mother the same way, "Good morning, mamacita!" The morning of April 16, 2007, however, there was no message from Emily. Beth thought it was odd, but didn't suspect anything was wrong in the absence of her daughter's email.

According to Beth, "The only way we knew Emily was shot was because her boyfriend, Karl Thornhill, contacted his mother to reach us after he had been contacted by his best friend, Ben. Ben had been contacted by his girlfriend, Heather Haugh, who was also Emily's roommate and told him that she arrived at the dorm that morning to find chaos and was questioned by police about Karl. Haugh arrived at the dorm between 7:30 a.m. and 8:00 a.m. Karl reached us after 8:00 a.m. and was driving from Radford to find Emily."

Sometime around 8:00 a.m., Beth received a phone call from Birgitt Thornhill, Karl's mother. Birgitt said something may have happened to Emily; she may have been shot, and they needed to call Karl to find out what was going on. Beth was stunned and screamed for her husband—how could this be? Birgitt said Karl was on his way to Tech to find Emily and find out what had happened.

Eric Hilscher got Karl on the phone. The young man put on a show of control and assured them he would find Emily and take care of her. While the Hilschers were frantically trying to find out about their daughter, on the other side of Rappahannock County, their good friend and FedEx driver, Gary Ford, was busy with deliveries. He got a call from another driver saying he was missing a package and wanted to know if Ford had it. In the process the driver asked, "Have you heard about what is going down at Tech?"

Ford turned on the radio and began listening to the streaming story of the shootings at Virginia Tech. For reasons he cannot explain, Ford stopped his deliveries and drove across the county to the Hilscher's home. He had many other customers with children at Tech, but inexplicably he drove directly to the Hilschers' home.

Meanwhile, Emily's father called the Montgomery Regional Hospital in Blacksburg and asked if a female student had been brought in from Tech. The answer was, "Yes," but they did not know her identity and her wounds were so serious that she had been transported to a trauma hospital in Roanoke.

Only after the Hilschers made numerous calls were they able to locate Emily at the trauma hospital in Roanoke. Eric called the hospital and just after 10:00 a.m. they confirmed that a young woman had been brought in from Blacksburg. Eric was told she had passed. Only after Eric's begging did a hospital administrator go to look for her in the trauma unit. The administrator verified Emily's identity by her "pixie" tattoo on her right hip. (That was the only identification made until the Hilschers saw Emily the next morning after her autopsy.)

What is important to the Hilschers is, "Emily was shot; she was transported as a Jane Doe even though she was taken from her dorm room. No one called to tell us she had been shot. Repeat...no one. Not the Virginia Tech Police. Not the Virginia Tech administration. No one at the hospitals because they couldn't...she was a Jane Doe." The Hilschers want to know, "How could that be?"

Both Beth and Eric Hilscher would later find out that Emily had been transported to Montgomery Hospital where she was stabilized, but Montgomery Hospital could not do any more for her and they transported her to Carilion in Roanoke because that hospital has an advanced trauma unit. She could not be airlifted because the winds were too high.

Stunned and in disbelief, Eric Hilscher hung up the phone. His beautiful daughter, the wonderful young woman who was the embodiment of all that was good and sweet in life, was dead—it was beyond comprehension.

Just as the Hilschers got the message no parent ever wants to get, Gary Ford, the FedEx driver arrived. Once Ford confirmed his worst fears, he told the Hilscher's to pack; he would take care of everything. The Hilschers' older daughter, Erica, was a student at Longwood. Ford made arrangements to meet and pick Erica up at a rest stop on I-64, en route to Roanoke. Within a couple of hours of learning about Emily's death, Gary drove the

Hilschers and stayed with them for the next two days, getting them where they needed to go an making arrangements to get Emily home.

"We called our local police department in Rappahannock to see if they had been contacted by any authorities regarding Emily, but they had not. We informed our police department that we had learned of Emily's death and were heading for Roanoke. We did not get a call confirming Emily's death until approximately 3:00 p.m., and it was from our Rappahannock County police. We never got a call from anyone else. It is possible, that we might have been able to reach Emily before her passing if someone had called us. And why wouldn't someone call us? Do you just transport someone and forget about her? Not knowing that there was more violence to come that morning, why didn't Virginia Tech do more to help Emily?"

When they arrived at the trauma hospital in Roanoke, the Hilschers were told they could not see their daughter until the next day. She had already been transferred to the coroner's office.

After leaving the Roanoke hospital, Gary drove the Hilschers to Karl Thornhill's townhouse in Blacksburg. The Hilschers pulled up to Thornhill's townhouse just after the Blacksburg police SWAT team had left. The police had forced Karl Thornhill, his sister, and his mother to lie face down on the living room floor while they searched for possible evidence that Karl was involved in the mass shootings.

Apparently, the Blacksburg police still believed Karl had something to do with Emily's death. The Thornhills pleaded with the police to finish as quickly as they could as they knew the Hilschers would be arriving at any time, and that it would be upsetting for them to find the police there. Karl and his mother, Birgitt, said they were shocked that after the police left the house, they stood out in the parking lot and talked. They (the police) were even heard to be laughing about something. It was all surreal, as Karl was suffering from the death of his girlfriend and yet was treated badly for the second time that day.

The search had taken place in the late afternoon—almost seven hours after Thornhill had been determined not to be "a person of interest" in the killings. Just as in Chief Flinchum's incompetent handling of the crime scene at West Ambler Johnston Hall, the Blacksburg police's clumsy and abrasive handling of the Thornhills violated standard legal and police policy—the police did not show the Thornhills their search warrant until they had entered the house and the search was under way—technically breaking the law.

From Karl Thornhill's townhouse, Gary drove the Hilschers back to Roanoke. Some people can be incredibly kind. In a wonderful, thoughtful, and generous act of kindness, Wendy Blair, the owner of Rose Hill Bed and Breakfast in Roanoke had called the hospital in Roanoke and offered the Hilschers a place to stay away from the media. The Hilschers spent the night at Rose Hill. Blair kept their presence a secret in order to keep the media out. The next morning she made them breakfast and packed a bag of healthy snacks for them. This act of kindness will forever be with the Hilschers. After breakfast, the Hilschers drove to the hospital where Eric, Beth, and Erica spent time by themselves with Emily. Karl Thornhill arrived at the hospital shortly after the Hilschers. Later that morning, Karl too spent time alone with Emily, the young woman he loved so much.

The question that kept repeating in the Hilschers' minds was why the school or the police hadn't notified them their daughter had been shot? They might have gotten to the hospital and been with Emily before she died. They might have been able to comfort her in her last hours. In a meeting with Chief Flinchum several months later, Beth Hilscher posed the question, "Why didn't you notify us that Emily was shot?" The chief responded, "It is not the job of the police to notify the families, the hospitals usually take care of that."

Sometime in the early afternoon on Tuesday, the Hilschers made arrangements for an ambulance to carry their daughter's body home. Without signing any papers or meeting with anyone, the hospital loaded Emily into an ambulance that followed about 40 minutes behind the Hilschers as they began their tearful, painful, solemn three-hour trip home—the first steps into a long road of despair, anger, and depression.

To quote Beth Hilscher, "Once we learned of the circumstances surrounding the death of Emily and the 31 others, we were shocked to learn of Cho's path of behavior that lead to that day, and the involvement of the Virginia Tech Police Department with him. While there were many instances over the course of his attendance at Virginia Tech of unacceptable behavior, one situation stands out in particular. It is our understanding that the Virginia Tech police were called to investigate the wellbeing of Cho on December 13 after a suitemate notified them that Cho had sent him an alarming Instant Message. The police took Cho to the station for evaluation and it was determined that a counselor from the New River Valley Community Services Board should come and evaluate him. That counselor determined that Cho was an 'imminent danger to self or others'. Cho was transported to St. Albans Psychiatric Hospital for evaluation. To make a long story short, it was determined by a judge that Cho, while not being found to be a danger to self or others, was still to receive follow-up outpatient treatment."

When Beth Hilscher asked Chief Flinchum how Cho was able to return to campus after his commitment hearing without having to check in with anyone, his response was that the police department did not have any policy for follow up once a student leaves for a mental health evaluation. Beth Hilscher questioned whether they (the police) should have taken Cho's dorm key and had him report to them to retrieve it as a way of monitoring him, as they had felt strongly enough about his situation that they had called for the evaluation. She was again told that there was no process to follow up.

When the Hilschers learned that the Cook Counseling Center received a psychiatric summary from St. Albans, but no one there followed up either, they were stunned. According to Beth, "How interesting that Cho's records disappeared from the Cook Counseling Center. How interesting that when they were found, they were devoid of any information."

After Emily died, the Hilschers had a meeting with a Virginia Tech detective and an FBI agent. They came to the Hilschers' home. According to Beth Hilscher, "We asked that we be allowed to come and clean out Emily's dorm room on our own. It was not made clear at that time that her room was the actual location of the shootings. However, a couple of days later we were called and told we could come to Tech to collect Emily's belongings and that they had been packed up. We did drive down to get her things and found that her dorm room had been totally emptied and painted a sterile white. Her belongings were packed in several boxes and were in a storage room in the building. When we got home we found that many of Emily's belongings were missing. There was no accounting for them. Our complaints fell on deaf ears. Our liaison with Virginia Tech was a wonderful man named Kenny Webb. He was the interim chair in Emily's school and had taken on the assignment of caring for us. He worked hard to find answers for us about Emily's missing belongings and he too came up empty. We had been given a hand-written and very inadequate inventory, which did not exactly match the contents of the boxes, and there was no accounting for things that may have been destroyed. We were never given the names or contact info for the people who packed up Emily's room, in spite of our inquiries. The items were gone and that was that. Some of the missing items had been very dear to Emily."

"As time has passed, we have become more and more angry with the Virginia Tech administration. No one has ever called us. They never will. There has been a continuous denial of any wrongdoing on the part of the administration and the police. There are continuing offers for football tickets from Steger's office and flowers come every Christmas. The one thing we want the most, we will never get ... an apology. An admission that the university failed to respond to the many shouts for attention from Cho, failed to properly notify us of our daughter's plight, failed to protect students required to live on campus, and failed to notify students and staff of potential danger."

Over the months to come, the Hilschers looked for a way of recovering from their loss. They decided they had to get away and do something together that was challenging and yet provided time together to heal. They bought a 50' schooner in the fall of 2008, packed up and the three of them sailed to the Bahamas for six months. The trip provided some respite, but when they returned, everything was waiting for them— the memories, the horror of what had happened all came flooding back, along with the need to pick up the pieces and get back to work.

It was difficult, next to impossible to concentrate on work. Between the failing economy and the difficulty in concentrating, Eric and Beth watched their business shrink to nothing. It was a business they had built from scratch over eleven years. Beth sought counseling for three and one-half years, but Eric, a powerful man, relied on his wife and daughter to help him with his grief. They had built their home themselves and it was where they raised their two girls; now, the family home had become a sad, quiet place of memories, a place without hope. They sold their home and made a needed change by moving to Richmond. Their daughter Erica was there, working as a counselor serving the homeless, and they wanted to be closer to her.

The three are still trying to move on, and every day they try to put more of the pieces of their lives back together. There are good days and there are bad days. The Hilschers have had the pleasure of meeting and getting to know some wonderful professors, instructors and students at Virginia Tech. There were some outstanding people at Virginia Tech such as Kenny Webb, the Hilschers' mentor, and Teresa McDonald, Emily's equestrian coach. They continue to be friends today.

"The loss of Emily has been devastating to us, of course. We have struggled as a family to take care of each other. It has been very difficult, and continues to be, to focus our energy on work. We have left our home of 15 years to be near our daughter, Erica, and to see if a new place will help us to heal."

"We ask ourselves everyday why this tragedy had to happen. We have found that with time our grief does not go away, it merely changes. We are thankful for the many friends and family who continue to help and support us. We live in a way that would make Emily proud of us. We try to look forward and make good things happen, as Emily always did."

Through His Eyes

Suzanne Grimes thanks God every day that her son, Kevin survived. But the trauma of April 16, 2007 has left a wound that has yet to heal. She lives with the knowledge that Kevin's life over the last six plus years has been a struggle to return to some form of normalcy. The initial numerous doctors' appointments, months of physical therapy and the disruption of a life because of the physical and emotional scars of April 16th had a traumatic effect on her as she watched her son through it all. She held his hand through the pain and the nightmares, and yet at the same time was an emotional mess. As time passes, the memories of doctors' appointments have diminished, but a trigger can bring back reminders that are vivid. Images such as seeing Kevin's face being transformed when he sees someone who cannot walk—those images will forever be etched in her mind.

Her struggle to return to some sense of normalcy continues to this day. Grimes wakes up in the middle of the night in a panic: she is in the German class with her son that fateful day; other times she is in the back of the ambulance with Kevin as they rush to save his life. After Kevin returned to Virginia Tech and his graduate program in the fall of 2007, Suzanne thought her resentment would subside, but it did not. Every time the phone rings, she thinks Kevin has been shot, he has been hurt, or that someone has killed him. Even now, she fears that something will happen to Kevin, not that he is incapable of taking care for himself. She just worries. She has a nightmare that returns over and over again. There will be a phone call from the school administration that something has happened. She did not get such a call on April 16th, but she nevertheless worries that such a call will come in now—Kevin works for Virginia Tech.

A particularly traumatic time for Suzanne was the period of limbo on April 16th when she did not know if Kevin was alive or dead. Suzanne remembers the chaotic, panicked voices as she attempted to find Kevin; no one knew what was happening and no one could tell her if he was alive. No one called to say there was a shooting on campus. She now realizes why the school did not call; administrators did not have an emergency plan or if they had one, did not follow it. In her opinion, the school was too busy trying to figure out how to shield itself from bad publicity from the failure to warn following the shootings at West Ambler Johnston Hall.

The sounds of 4th of July fireworks send the nerves of her spine rattling; she jumps when she hears loud, unfamiliar sounds. In large crowds she looks at unfamiliar faces—she wonders, is he a killer? Will she try to murder me? When entering a restaurant she surveys those seated looking for any hint of threatening behavior; she often scopes out the number of entrances and exit points.

Grimes no longer looks at the photos, articles, and documents dealing with the Virginia Tech tragedy, because it brings back her feelings that the school hid and distorted the truth. That truth is that the school put protecting itself above her son's safety.

Suzanne Grimes rarely watches the news; the shooting at Northern Illinois University, Ft. Hood, or the mass killings in Aurora, Colorado, and Sandy Hook elementary school bring the horrors of Virginia Tech flooding back. She is acutely aware of the fact that she lives in a different world from those who have not been involved in a shooting tragedy. She realizes every day of her life how precious and how fragile life is. The realization is overpowering. She is so thankful to have Kevin, but she feels the pain of the parents who lost their children with a powerful intensity.

How does Suzanne Grimes move on? She began by taking nearly three years, from the fall of 2007 to January 2010, to investigate and try to get answers to how this could have happened. Many answers still elude her, but what has not escaped her investigation is the fact that the families were not told the truth. Over the course of her research, Grimes came to a number of key realizations—first and foremost, that the families were deceived.

Suzanne spent endless hours sitting in front of a computer looking at documents. At times she spent 12-16 hours a day doing her research. She vividly remembers going to Wal-Mart for copier ink or paper and then returning to try to put the jigsaw puzzle together. Suzanne takes solace in the knowledge that her research has benefited all the Tech families by helping to uncover the truth. Looking back, she sees the financial, physical, and emotional toll the shooting and subsequent cover up have had on her and her family—but it was worth it.

While going through shooting-related documents, including emails, in April 2008, Grimes realized that Tech orchestrated the first Governor's Review Panel Report. She realized after the settlement of June 2008 that the families were deceived: "We were led down a path of no legal return." It is so disheartening for Suzanne that the families of the deceased never got what they wanted—the truth. It is upsetting to her when she realizes how the families of the deceased and survivors were manipulated.

Grimes realized during the commemoration day, April 16, 2009, that former Governor Kaine would not and did not want to change anything in the panel report. "I realized that he had bigger avenues to pursue, such as his political career, and just wanted the tragedy to go away. I realized then, that we, the families, would never receive an apology from the school administration or that they would never admit that they did anything wrong." She understands now, that if the university had come forward and admitted its mistake in not notifying the campus after the double homicide, there might never have been a lawsuit.

For Suzanne Grimes, it is clear—that the school needs to admit its failure in not issuing a warning; she recognizes that the school's emergency plan was woefully inadequate.

More and more Grimes realized the families had been manipulated. They had been left out of pertinent decisions concerning the allocations of the funds raised in memory of Cho's victims. On top of that, there would never be an admission of responsibility or an apology from any of the parties in charge of the security of the campus or the investigation of the shooting.

Suzanne Grimes moved on by seeking the truth and exposing the lies. There are times when she starts thinking about how the school administration failed in their responsibility to protect the victims. She gets moody, upset, and angry. When that happens she goes for a run, swims laps or does something—anything—to take her mind off of the shooting.

Following one of the families' meetings, David Ford, Vice Provost for Academic Affairs, approached Suzanne to offer her an apology for what happened. He told her, "There is not a day that goes by that I don't think about that day." Her reply was cold, "Good, because my son has to live with his injuries; he still has a 9 mm bullet in him and he has emotional scars that will never be erased." She will always remember the expression on Ford's face. Her tone had been blunt. Indeed, it took her a long time to be able to talk to anyone in connection with the university without bitterness.

Suzanne also has moments, such as around Kevin's birthday, when she should be happy, but sinks into the depths of depression. She worries about what Kevin will be like when he is her age. What his physical and emotional health will be in the future. While walking on the beach during a recent family vacation, she told Kevin, "I wish that I could trade places with you that day, I wish that I could have been sitting in Norris Hall." Grimes says that if she could give Kevin anything she would give him that. "It is so unfair!"

Suzanne Grimes says that her relationship with Kevin has always been close, but now they have a unique, strong bond. For her, it is incredible that people in positions of responsibility at Virginia Tech have total amnesia on the witness stand and all they can say is, "I don't remember" or "I don't recall." Suzanne has no memory problems. She can remember every detail of that day and of the days thereafter.

As time has passed it has become apparent to her just how strong her son is, how he handled his own emotional healing through physical activity. Her son's strength has had a profound and positive impact on her ability to recover. It was Kevin's determination to not to let April 16th control him or to let it be the most important aspect of his life that gave her strength.

To this day, Suzanne Grimes has a clear vision of what Kevin went through in German class when Cho entered. She explained, "The difficulty is that a mother and son have a natural connection, but the magnitude of what he went through created a unique bond—sometimes we read each others thoughts." There are times she wishes she could erase it all, make the horrific nightmare disappear, but she cannot.

She knows that her life would be radically different had Kevin died that cold April day. "I pray each night, I thank God for him, for my children, grandchildren and for my husband John. I pray for the parents and families of the 32 people killed; I pray to try and give them some comfort." When these and other worries begin to close in on her, husband John and others listen and comfort her. Her focus has shifted from her preoccupation with April 16th to something she realized she had neglected—her family, her relationships with them and her own emotional healing. Even though she has distanced herself from the April 16th families, she thinks about them and wonders how they are doing, how they are healing.

Even though a move to Florida has helped Suzanne transform her life, her vivid memories of that horrific day were captured in the iconic photograph of her son begin carried out of Norris Hall like a sack of potatoes—a photograph that made the front pages around the world. Suzanne Grimes will move on only when the truth is told—when the truth is made public. She continues to pray that the complete truth will come out some day and people will be held accountable for their actions and inactions.

Our Beloved Ross

For Lynnette Alameddine, everyday she thinks of her precious son, Ross, and imagines what he would be doing now.

The night before Ross was murdered he talked with his mother on the phone for 40 minutes. It was a wonderful, caring and loving conversation between mother and son. Ross thanked her for allowing him to follow his dreams to go to Virginia Tech and to get into technology.

The next morning Lynnette's living hell would begin.

She remembers April 16, 2007 in vivid detail. It started with two phone calls: one from a friend in Florida, and one from a friend in New Hampshire. Both told Lynnette that there had been a shooting at Virginia Tech, and she should turn on the news. That was sometime after 8:00 a.m. and CNN was broadcasting that two students had been shot in a dorm. Lynnette thought it was horrible and was surprised that something like that would happen. Ross did not live in a dormitory and she told herself he was all right. But nearly two hours later when the news broke of multiple killings, deep down inside she knew Ross was in one of the soon- to -be fatal rooms. Somehow she knew he was in *that* building, Norris Hall.

Fighting back panic, Lynnette called her son, but there was no answer. She waited and Ross didn't call back. That was unusual. In August, at the time of the Morva incident, he had called to say that he was "ok" and that he knew she had seen something on the news by now, and didn't want her to worry. This time, there was no word, and the silence was as if someone had punched her in the gut.

Lynnette phoned the school and talked with a Tech staff member, who gave Lynnette a hotline number to call. The person at the hotline told her to call the local hospitals. Lynnette responded, "I am in Boston, how would I know about local hospitals?" With that, she was given the number of the Lewisgale Hospital-Montgomery. (There were five possible hospitals.) A staff person from the Emergency Room at Montgomery Hospital told her that no one by the name of Ross Alameddine had been brought in, and that she could call every hour if she wanted. Lynnette was also given the names and numbers of all four other area hospitals to call, as the hospital staff person told Lynnette that other victims were being transported to those hospitals as well.

By early afternoon, there was still no word. Sometime around 1:40 p.m. Lynnette talked to someone at the *Boston Herald* who told her incorrectly that there were no New England casualties. Lynnette began to hope against hope that no news was good news. Perhaps in the turmoil, Ross was unable to phone; perhaps he was helping in some way—surely that must be the reason for his silence.

But as the afternoon gave way to early evening, the flicker of hope she allowed herself to cling to, faded.

A friend told Lynnette to call Channel 7 in Boston. Lynnette was desperate and willing to do anything for information. Just sitting and not knowing was agonizing. She was told that the Channel 7 interview would be aired on CNN, as well as the local news stations, and she agreed—"I'll do anything to get information about my son, Ross. I am desperate. I want news of my son. I want to know if he is ok." The film crew went to Lynnette's house and filmed the painful interview.

Around 5:30 or 6:00 p.m. it was announced on CNN that the Virginia Tech police were interviewing the survivors. Lynnette called the campus police. Lynnette was curtly told, "Ma'am, we don't even know who's alive, let alone dead. If your child is dead, you will get a call from your local police."

Lynnette Alameddine waited.

Sometime around 10:45 p.m. she received a call from a Virginia Tech chaplain who said, "Ross is gone."

At 12:45 a.m. Lynnette's local and state police arrived. She met them at the door with tears streaming down her face, telling them, "I know why you are here."

Lynnette Alameddine wanted desperately to get to Blacksburg. Virginia Tech staff were trying to arrange for a flight, but were having difficulty. Senator Kennedy called to wish her condolences and wanted to know if there was anything he could do. She told him that she needed to get to Blacksburg, but Virginia Tech was having problems arranging a flight. Senator Kennedy said, "If they don't get you on a flight today, call us back and we will see that you get there." Senator Kerry also offered the same, when he called and spoke with Lynnette.

Lynnette called the school to get a place to stay. She was told that there was no room at the Virginia Tech Inn, but a family was willing to put her up. Lynnette said that was not acceptable. The school called back five minutes later to say there would be a room at the Inn after all.

When Lynnette arrived on the Tech campus, she talked with a Virginia Tech policeman and a State police officer. She kept asking how could this happen, why no warning? Despite the fact that the school had previously issued warnings and locked down—as I have cited earlier—she was told that the campus was too big to lock down. With this response, Lynnette became more angered. She told them that the Boston officials shut down the City of Boston just two months prior for suspicious objects (neon signs) that were placed near bridges and bus terminals. Lynnette also told them that the officials stopped the services of the buses, subways and trains, as they felt they were potential threats to the city. "This is a school. There was a murder and a gunman loose on campus. You locked down the school in August, why not now?"

Alameddine would later find out from one of Ross's friends, a young woman, had heard of the dormitory shooting and had stayed away from a different class that morning. Would Ross have done the same thing if he had heard that a shooting had happened? Beyond a doubt, Lynnette knows that her son would have remained in his apartment had he known of the shooting. The more Lynnette found out, the more upset she became.

At the time of this writing, it is almost six years since the shooting at Virginia Tech and life is still hard for Lynnette. She thinks of Ross every day and remembers him with tears in her eyes. He was mature and intelligent beyond his years; he was funny; he was wise; he made her laugh. Ross and Lynnette had a terrific relationship. She remembers how Ross loved to build computers. In fact, the night before he left for Tech, he finished building a computer for a friend.

Ross was always helpful and thoughtful of others. After every meal he would pat his mom on the back and say, "that was great." Lynnette misses those gentle pats Ross gave her and gets emotional when she thinks that she'll never have them again. Ross loved all types of music, especially jazz. Ross enjoyed singing and playing the piano. Every day Lynnette thanks God that a friend made a CD of him singing "Golden Slumbers" by the Beatles, at the Coffee House at his high school, Austin Preparatory School.

An especially poignant tribute to Ross came from two professors who made a DVD telling Lynnette how wonderful Ross was. The tribute was especially meaningful and heartfelt because the professors made the DVD despite specific instructions from Virginia Tech officials to staff and faculty not to contact or to talk to the families. The university's obsessive intent on controlling all communications between school personnel and the families sank to a new low when it insisted on limiting genuine expressions of sympathy.

Lynnette often remembers Ross's caring approach to others. In an ironic twist of fate, months after the shooting, she found out from one of her son's close friends, Bryan Griffith, that Ross sat next to Cho in an English class. The class was a horror literature/film course. Ross and Bryan sat in the back row; Cho sat to Ross's right. Everyone in the class recognized there was something strange about the young man who never uttered a word. Both Ross and Brian had tried to engage Cho, to help him, to help **a** painfully shy and quiet young man. Bryan would ask Ross a question about a movie, and he would respond, "I don't know." Ross would then turn to Cho and ask, "What do you think?" He never got a response. In the end, they gave up and just assumed that Cho was one of those "quiet smart kids."

Ross often spoke about his friend, Valerie Weeks, who worked as a driver for the Blacksburg Transit, the bus system that served Virginia Tech. He met her after going roller-blading and getting caught in a downpour. By chance, Ross got onto the bus, ringing wet. The two struck up a conversation. Ross would see her periodically and as their friendship grew, he learned that she had been enrolled at Virginia Tech, but dropped out. Also, Valerie worked in a Virginia Tech office. Ross insisted that she quit her job and return back to school. He repeatedly encouraged her to advance her education and truly make something of her life. The day after the shooting, Valerie left a note at the makeshift memorial. It stated that she was going to quit her job and was enrolling back in school.

Lynnette becomes agitated when she thinks back on the way Virginia Tech handled the 32 scholarships established in memory of the deceased. She vividly remembers that the school never asked for input from the victims' families. Lynnette wanted the scholarship honoring Ross to go to Austin Preparatory School, as it was the high school from which he graduated in 2005. It took a year to get Virginia Tech to agree to put it on the Virginia Tech website.

The school also never asked the families about what they wanted on the permanent memorial stones. Lynnette did not want Ross's middle name used, but the school engraved it without asking. Only after considerable effort did Tech agree to actually change it, and use Ross's middle initial, instead of his middle name. It was one bad decision after another. On the Virginia Tech "We Remember" website, there were color photographs of most of the victims—a couple of photos were black and white. Unilaterally and arbitrarily, the school changed them all to sepia tone—it made the victims look as if they had died a hundred years ago. It looked more like "We Forget" than "We Remember." It was a horrible thing to do, and only after an outcry from a number of families, did the school return the photos to the original display.

Lynnette suggested certified homicide bereavement counselors to be brought in for the families. It would have been for free, but that request was denied.

Time and time again, the school officials did not listen to the families and ignored their wishes. For example, Lynnette and another mother of a victim, suggested to the Office of Recovery and Support to have a day or session in which friends of the deceased could come together to remember them. Lynnette suggested having food, as part of a relaxed gathering of remembrance. They agreed but never followed through. Five of Ross's friends came for his designated time. But when the gathering took place, they were counseling sessions with everyone sitting around in a semi-circle. The participants were given Teddy Bears—the attendees felt insulted; they felt they were being talked down to. Lynnette was very upset by this, but then chalked it up to yet another insensitive Virginia Tech action.

After the massacre, the rooms in Norris Hall were renovated. Lynnette asked to see the classroom where Ross was killed and was assigned a Virginia Tech police officer to give her a tour. When he showed up, he was accompanied by a counselor. The officer pointed out bullet holes in the corridor and in the classroom.

Alameddine was dismayed at what she saw. She could not only still see the bullet holes in the walls, but also in the blackboard. Lynnette wanted the holes completely covered up. She felt that if she had spackle and paint, that she could have done it herself. Visibly shaken, Lynnette e-mailed the Recovery and Support at Virginia Tech, and was told that nothing more would be done to repair the walls, as it had cost one million dollars already to do the renovations. Lynnette found out later, that the "bullet holes" in the corridor were actually from coat hooks that were taken down; she had been given incorrect information.

Doing something poorly, as Tech did so many times in dealing with the families, is nearly as bad as doing nothing at all.

* * *

All of the families I talked to want the truth to be told, and nearly all want some sort of apology from Virginia Tech or President Steger—or both. Many of the Virginia Tech victims and families of the victims are looking for some sort of accountability; they want someone to take responsibility and be held accountable for what happened on April 16, 2007.

What makes life so difficult for so many of the families and victims to move on is the knowledge that they have been lied to. Many at Virginia Tech were truly wonderful and caring, but many were not. Certainly Tech President Charles Steger showed an aloof indifference and Virginia Tech Police Chief Wendell Flinchum an incredible lack of remorse.

Imagine: Your loved one is dead. You are told to move on, and you know you must. But though the agony ebbs and flows, it never goes away; moving on is agonizingly slow. Just when you think you have made some progress toward recovery, there is a sound, a smell, a sight, and everything comes flooding back; the unbearable, suffocating pain. It is April 16, 2007 again, the black cloud engulfs you, the air is sucked out of you, you gasp; if you are driving you pull to the curb, put your head on the steering wheel and cry. You think of what should have been and what might have been. You think of the child or spouse you desperately miss. You think and you sob. You remember everything that once was. You have a sudden urge to run as fast as you can, anywhere; you want to run away from it all. You remember your child's face, you remember your spouse's smile; the sweet memories become unbearable; life itself becomes unbearable. You remember the joy and the good times, and your head throbs. And people tell you to move on.

You remember that a few months after the shooting, a Virginia Tech official told an audience that the families should not be allowed to wallow in the tragedy. You remember that the state of Virginia gave you $100,000 compensation for your loss while Tech President Steger is paid an annual salary is $748,892. Steger's pay includes $479,842 in salary (including a $22,852 bonus), $245,000 from deferred compensation, and a $20,000 car allowance. This is the man who did not issue a warning that might have saved your loved one's life. And people tell you to move on.

You try to find some meaning in your loss; you speak out against gun violence in the hope of preventing others from going through what you have gone through, and your car is sabotaged. You work for the Brady Campaign to help keep guns out of the hands of those who are dangerously mentally ill and you are subjected to the wrath of right-wing bloggers. You ask for details of your loved one's death and you receive threats. And people tell you to move on.

You have to wonder if, when they say, "move on," what they really mean is "shut up."

In the final analysis, none of the families of those killed or wounded at Virginia Tech will ever be able to truly "move on" until the truth is told and people such as President Charles Steger and Virginia Tech Police Chief Wendell Flinchum are held accountable. Only then will they be able to find some peace and, perhaps some semblance of a normal life.

CHAPTER XIII

WHAT PARENTS AND FAMILIES CAN DO

*"Death is a billion-dollar business. They can't even
pass a law where it takes seven days to get a gun.
Why don't you have to go through the same screening
you do to get a driver's license. It's totally insane."*
~Jon Cusack, American actor, producer, screenwriter

After I wrote my first book on the shooting at the Appalachian School of Law, it was common for parents to thank me, but also to say the subject matter was so disturbing they could not read what I had written. They would usually then encourage me to keep working for campus safety. Most said they had children in university or about ready to enter; the subject was just too terrifying for them to even think about. But they are exactly the people who need to be the most concerned; they are the people with the most at stake—the safety and lives of their children.

No matter how painful the subject of school shootings and school safety is, all parents must think about it and think what they can do to protect their most valuable legacies, their daughters and sons. While we will never completely eliminate school shootings, a great deal can be done to dramatically reduce the number of these shootings and to make them a very rare occurrence. Parents can play a key role in this effort.

Awareness Is Key

First, parents and families have to understand the magnitude of the problem all of us face in trying to make our schools safer. Second, parents and families must be aware of the fact that the people in whom we put our trust, school administrators and politicians, may not have the safety of our loved ones as a primary goal. All too often a toxic mix of concerns for budgets, fundraising, and careers trump safety with tragic consequences. Third, parents and families must recognize that they play a vital role in ensuring school safety by demanding that people be held accountable for their actions or inactions. Fourth, and finally, parents and families must put political differences aside and recognize that improving campus safety is a bipartisan goal for all to pursue.

The problem of school safety is multi-faceted, but in the final analysis, it all boils down to the decisions made by people in positions of responsibility. Some steps toward improving school safety are relatively easy; others are not.

Let's look at an easy but critical first step that parents can take. It should be part of every family's regimen in preparing to send their daughters or sons to college: school selection. In choosing a school, parents should familiarize themselves with the prospective school's security procedures, policies, and emergency plans. The stark and sad truth is that when you send your son or daughter to a college or university, in many instances, you may be doing so at a terrible risk unless you have thoroughly investigated the school's security plans and procedures.

Parents should be armed with questions about the school's safety rules and procedures and should make it clear to school officials that they will not send their children to any school where safety is not the number one priority. Here are questions parents should ask:

Emergency Plans:

1. What type of security plans and procedures does the school have and does the school regularly review and update both its plans and procedures?
2. Does the school have a campus-wide warning system in place, such as sirens, text messaging, and cell phone warnings?
3. Has the school brought students into the dialog on what should be done in the case of an emergency?
4. Does the campus security or police have the authority to move immediately against anyone on campus who poses a threat to self or others?
5. How quickly can campus security lock down or secure all buildings on campus?

6. What is the relationship between campus security and the local and state police? How closely do they cooperate and do they have a coordinated emergency plan?

Weapons:

1. How does the school define weapons?
2. What is the school's policy on bringing guns, or any weapon, on campus?
3. What would happen to a student if he or she were found to have a weapon on campus?

Mental Health:

1. Does the school have a plan in place that identifies aberrant behavior, and what steps will the school take to remove potentially dangerous individuals from the campus? (Parents should get a copy of that plan.)
2. What is the school's policy if a student is caught sending harassing or threatening emails to someone?
3. Can a student, staff, or faculty member be directed to seek a psychological evaluation and treatment?
4. How quickly are parents notified if a student is causing a problem or disturbance—or appears to be exhibiting behavior that others consider threatening?

I would advise you, the parents, to listen carefully to answers you get and do not accept vague generalizations—pin school officials down. Demand facts and proof—it may save your child's life.

Accountability is a significant part of the problem. If school presidents and other officials have nothing to lose, if they will not be held accountable, what incentive is there to tighten campus security?

While parents may not want to think about school selection this way, they need to look at schools that have the most to lose financially in the event of negligence leading to injury or death. Parents therefore need to know what legal recourse they have if their child is killed or hurt by someone on school grounds. Virginia, for example, is one of the most difficult states to prove premises liability. Premises liability is the legal concept that a landowner is liable or responsible for injuries suffered by persons who are present on his or her premises. There must be negligence or some sort of wrongful act in order for the owner to be liable.

The Virginia Supreme Court is highly reluctant to recognize the responsibility of a business proprietor to protect "its invitees from unreasonable risk of physical harm." That fact was demonstrated in the Court's poorly reasoned and poorly written decision to nullify the Montgomery Circuit Court's decision that Tech was guilty of negligence. (See Chapter XI)

Plans That Work

As a baseline for good campus safety, parents should also familiarize themselves with the rules and practices of colleges and universities that have campus safety policies and procedures. The following are two such schools, one state, and the other private.

Several years ago, before I began working on this book, I spent some time discussing campus security with the Chief of University Police, State University of New York—Oneonta (SUNY—Oneonta). He is truly an impressive man in charge of an impressive security operation on a large college campus. If every school in this country had a security plan like the one at Oneonta, our school grounds would be far, far safer places.

The campus security at SUNY-Oneonta is a police department; therefore its officers carry weapons. The Regional Police Academy is tied to, and works with, the campus police department. The academy runs a wide variety of specialized law enforcement courses, trains new officers, and trains officers to be instructors.

The chief told me that the SUNY-Oneonta campus has had an emergency plan in place since 1994, but since the tragedy at Virginia Tech, the school has tightened and improved that plan. The chief began by telling me that it is against the law to bring a weapon of any kind on a school campus in the state of New York. That law covers both state and private schools. Every state university in New York is required to have an emergency plan in place, and the Oneonta and Binghamton campuses were the first to meet the state's new standard for security. Highlights of the SUNY—Oneonta plan include:

1. The ability to lock down every building on campus (with the exception of the gym) with four strokes on the computer keyboard.
2. Radio systems in all buildings for emergency use.
3. Blueprints of all campus buildings are on hand in the police headquarters in case of an emerge
4. A Behavioral Assessment Team that meets every week to discuss student problems and activities. The group is made up of the Chief, the Director of Counseling, the Director of Residence Life, the Associate Vice President for Judicial

Affairs, the Vice President of Student Development, and the Health Center Director.

5. The Chief of Police has the power to act immediately and to take whatever action he deems necessary if an individual is thought to be a danger to self or others.

6. A campus-wide siren for notification that there is an emergency on campus.

7. The ability to notify all students, staff, and faculty of an emergency through NY ALERT—a cell phone/email/text messaging system. All New York State University campuses will have this system in the near future.

8. A video and card access system for all campus buildings.

9. A sophisticated key system for all buildings. The keys cannot be duplicated.

10. The school gives its officers extensive training through a variety of courses including Active Shooter Course and Patrol Officers Course.

11. A full-time Emergency Management Coordinator.

12. The school is linked to major criminal databases in Albany.

13. The school regularly reviews its crime prevention security analysis for all campus buildings.

14. The University Police Department has an ambulance on hand, on campus.

15. It is a state law that university police departments on state-affiliated schools must have a Memorandum of Understanding with the state police on immediate emergency response responsibilities and actions. SUNY-Oneonta has such a memorandum and maintains close ties with the New York State Police and the city of Oneonta Police Department.

16. Students are given a full security briefing as part of their campus orientation.

17. Each staff and faculty member has at her or his desk a bright orange Crisis Management folder for immediate and easy reference. The folder contains phone numbers and contacts. The subjects covered are:

    a. Emergency Responses—Shelter in Place, Notification, and Building Evacuation.

    b. To Report an Emergency on Campus—Bomb Threat, Fire, Accident or Medical Emergency.

    c. Threat of Physical Harm from a Person or Persons— Threat by Email, Text Message, Phone, or Note— Threatening or Aggressive Behavior, and Policies and Procedures.

    d. Student Emergencies—Disturbed or Disturbing Emotional Behavior, Serious Illness or Injury, Threatening or Irrational Behavior, Crime in Progress or has been Committed, and Sexual Assault.

    e. Non-Emergency Student Problems—Disturbed or Disturbing Emotional Behavior, Illness or Injury, and Learning, Psychological, or Physical Disability.

In other words, if I wanted to know how SUNY-Oneonta would have dealt with a student like Cho, all I had to do was pick up one of these orange folders and run my fingers down the list. It raises the question, if such consistency in approach had existed at Virginia Tech could Cho's behavior have been headed off while it was still a non-emergency student problem? There's no way to know, but it is certain a consistently understood and applied policy towards troubling student behaviors makes it easier to prevent escalation of such problems to actual emergencies.

SUNY—Oneonta is not the only bright light. Smaller schools with smaller budgets are also working hard to improve campus safety. After visiting SUNY—Oneonta, I phoned Hartwick College, also in Oneonta, and asked to meet with the head of campus safety.

Hartwick College is a small, private liberal arts college with nearly 1,500 students. Just as in the case of SUNY—Oneonta, Hartwick College had security and emergency plans in place before the Virginia Tech tragedy.

Hartwick has a professional staff and always looks at ways to attract, hire, and keep professional security personnel. The campus security at Hartwick is not a police force so by law its officers may not carry weapons.

As already noted, it is against the law in New York for anyone to bring a weapon on campus and a recent incident was cited where someone spotted a shotgun in a car parked on campus. The Oneonta police were called. The car did not belong to anyone associated with the school, but to a town resident who parked it on school grounds after meeting a co-ed and returning with her to the school dorm. The individual was found, arrested and spent the night in jail—the law had been broken. According to the head of security, "We will not tolerate any weapons on campus." This is the attitude all parents should look for from campus security officials.

If a student is caught with a weapon, the Oneonta police department is called immediately and he or she is suspended. Usually the student voluntarily withdraws for the term.

At Hartwick, senior school officials meet once a week to discuss campus problems, specifically case reviews of individuals who are having academic, behavioral, or emotional problems. The school aggressively follows up on any individual who has been brought to its attention for having any of those problems.

The campus also has a hot line. Anyone can dial #3333 to report any individual on campus who is a cause for concern. It was indicated that if aberrant behavior is brought to the attention of security, they have the right to act immediately to ensure campus safety. They do not have to consult with any other school official before acting. Hartwick College has access to NY ALERT—the campus-wide cell phone, email, and text messaging system already in use at the nearby SUNY campus.

As an indication of just how serious Hartwick takes campus security, it was emphasized that "no weapon of any kind" does not simply refer to guns or knives, but includes slingshots or toy guns. None of these are allowed on campus. Here again is the no-nonsense attitude parents should look for.

*   *   *

The initial selection of a school based on its security policy is one of the best ways for parents to keep their children safe, but it can go only so far in reforming security for U.S. universities as a whole. Nor does the answer lie in simply improving technology. In the final analysis, the most expensive and sophisticated security system is only as good as the people in charge; the best psychological counseling is only as good as the individuals doing the counseling, and the best contingency or emergency plans are only as good as the people who implement them. Improving campus safety begins at the top. Therefore, correcting the current system under which school presidents and senior officials are selected is a critical part of the campus security equation.

Priority: Fundraising or Safety?

Somewhere along the way higher education in the United States lost its focus on students and scholarship, and we are paying a terrible price. We have to ask for a reexamination of how and why school presidents are selected. If faculty members are concerned about their safety and the safety of their students, yet school administrators ignore signs of abnormal violent behavior on the part of students or staff, then the atmosphere is counterproductive to learning and unequivocally counterproductive to safety.

A contributing factor to this deterioration in the quality of school leaders was the change to running state-funded colleges and universities more like businesses than institutions of learning—Virginia Tech being a primary example. With that change in attitude came school leaders with little or no background or concern with campus safety.

Professor Lucinda Roy points this out in her firsthand account of the tragedy at Virginia Tech, *No Right to Remain Silent*. She writes: "… Nowadays, some of those in leadership positions at universities have little experience working with students and almost no experience in the classroom. It has become more important to hire administrators who know how to raise money than it is to hire those who know much about students." She further asserts, "If you examine a typical state-funded university, you will find that many of its resources are dedicated to generating funds. As the public began to opt out of subsidizing public education in the past two decades, something had to fill the gap. A university that is focused on staying afloat cannot pay as much attention to students as it did in the past."

Sometime in the 1970s state governments throughout this country decided to reduce financial support for state colleges and universities. A professor at Virginia Tech told me that when he joined the faculty in the 1980s over 60 percent of the university's budget came from the state government. By 2011, he said, that figure was down to around 17 percent. He did not reveal his sources, but I have heard similar figures from others. The point is that state schools needed to raise money and turned to private sources of revenue. The net result has been that schools seek presidents who are more public relations experts than educators and few, if any, have had training in crisis management. Here again, Virginia Tech is a prime example of the serious consequences of this trend and the dangers in moving to the business model to run state schools. Under President Charles Steger's leadership, Tech had signed a legal document with the state's General Assembly allowing the university to act like a private institution and seek vast amounts of funds to offset the reduction of state funding. This move alone ensured that Steger would concentrate on fundraising above all else. This document is one of Steger's signature achievements.

Robert Bickel and Peter Lake, in their exhaustive and insightful look at risk and responsibility on college campuses, point out that the net result of this move toward funding of state universities is that most college presidents today are "glad-handers" and fund raisers—not educators.

Even worse, most college and university presidents are woefully lacking knowledge of safety and security matters. Indeed, Virginia Tech's President Charles Steger is a case in point. Read his biography or listen to his defenders—the repeated emphasis on how much money he has raised for the school drowns out all else.

In order to make our colleges and universities safer, we will have to spend hundreds of millions (if not billions) of dollars on such things as security training and equipment, and mental health programs. These expenditures cannot be tallied on a profit sheet—they are expenses on behalf of our nation's future; they are long-term investments we must make to preserve this nation's greatness. These expenses defy the business model and account sheets, but they can be—and are—crucial to saving lives.

To run state colleges and universities on a for-profit basis is not only counterproductive in the long run, but it has cheapened the quality of education. Look at it this way: if you pay for your daughter or son to go to college, under the business model some lawyers argue that you have paid money and established a contract, and your child is owed a degree. This is nonsense. In fact, all the money does is give a person *access* to facilities that offer the opportunity of getting an education. There is no guarantee that anyone, once enrolled, will meet the standards the school has set to grant a degree. The use of this business model has lowered standards.

At one point in my career I worked with a former senior member of an English Department at a major Washington DC area university. She designed and implemented a test that all graduating seniors from the school, no matter what their major, had to pass in order to get their degree. So many seniors were flunking that the alumni association and parents were up in arms and were threatening to cut off money. The school dropped the test.

I suspect that what happened to my friend has happened elsewhere. A few years ago I was asked to teach 140 intelligence officers in a major component of the U.S. Intelligence Community. At the end of the training I was asked by senior management to evaluate the quality of their officers. My evaluation was that approximately 43 percent of the people I trained were sub-standard in the use of basic English; an English sentence was an alien concept for many of them. The vast majority of these officers had a four-year college degree.

More recently, in 2013, I was working for a component of the Intelligence Community and when I was through, the consulting company who had hired me asked for an evaluation of the students I had worked with. I reported that one of the students was seriously lacking in his abilities to be an intelligence analyst. The company asked me to rewrite the evaluation because of the "tone" of what I had written. They wanted me to say everything was just fine. I did rewrite, but the reference to the deficiencies stayed in.

Whether it is our students, or our fighting men and women, their lives seem to be expendable as long as a profit is made. To say that this country is in a sorry state of affairs doesn't begin to describe the magnitude of the problem. Is it surprising then, to find that we are hiring glorified bankers and campaign managers to lead some of our greatest educational institutions?

*   *   *

It is clear that more than a decade after the shootings at Columbine and the killings at the Appalachian School of Law and more than six years after the massacre at Virginia Tech, far too many school officials, law enforcement personnel, and politicians remain mystified and perplexed over how to meet the threat of school violence.

Yes, measures have been taken to improve campus safety, but not nearly enough. Most of the measures involve security and warning systems. Little has been done to improve campus mental health facilities, or to bring staff, faculty, and students together and explaining their rights and duties and making them part of the solution to the problem.

Lobbying and Ineffective Controls

All the crocodile tears and all the hand wringing have not produced the analysis, the will, or the determination necessary to adopt truly effective measures to minimize the threat of school gun violence in schools. Part of the reason for this failing is the unwillingness of state and federal politicians to address the vexing issue of keeping guns out of the hands of individuals who are a threat to themselves and others.

This failure to make more meaningful progress in school safety is not for lack of trying or lack of ideas, it is more for a lack of willingness to tackle difficult questions such as keeping guns out of the hands of convicted felons, convicted domestic abusers, terrorists, and people who are dangerously mentally ill.

If there is no willingness, no courage on the part of people in positions of authority to act, then there can be no real progress toward reducing the number of school shootings. The highly charged and dreaded words "gun control" always interrupt a rational discourse and dialogue on the problem of school safety. Politicians are so afraid of the National Rifle Association (NRA) that many cower whenever the words "gun" or "guns" are raised.

Bumper stickers such as "guns don't kill, people do" or "locked and loaded" appear on cars and trucks in church parking lots everywhere in Virginia. Good Christians apparently don't see the oxymoron. When it comes to commandments such as "thou shalt not kill," they seem to share Cho's selective mutism and remain silent.

The NRA has so brainwashed the public that even to raise the subject of preventing school shootings brings responses such as, "Ok, but no one is going to take my gun away from me." No one ever said anyone was going to take guns out of the hands of decent, law-abiding citizens—but that is the Pavlovian response of many. I can talk rationally and calmly about a wide variety of topics with most everyone in the small Virginia town where I live, but bring up school shootings and the NRA's brainwashing kicks in.

Some estimate that the NRA is the second most powerful lobby in Washington DC. I would not be surprised that if on many domestic political issues the NRA *is* the most powerful lobby. One of its latest excursions into mind control and violation of the constitutional right of freedom of speech is to get states to adopt laws that make it illegal for doctors to ask patients if they have a gun at home. According to the May 13, 2011 edition of *USA Today*, three states are considering laws that would penalize doctors and other health care providers for asking patients or their parents whether they have a gun at home.

According to *USA Today*, "The National Rifle Association and other pro-gun interest groups argue that doctors violate patients' Second Amendment right to keep and bear arms by inquiring about gun ownership. Doctors say they ask only because of safety concerns. Prohibiting them from asking about guns violates the First Amendment, at least one constitutional law expert says."

What about the right of any doctor to ask any patient any question pertaining to the patient's wellbeing? If you are going to apply order of importance to the amendments, then it is not unreasonable to think that the most important consideration on the founding fathers' minds was freedom of speech. Freedom of speech is guaranteed in the First Amendment, but many, including the NRA, appear to believe there is only one amendment in the Bill of Rights that counts and is free of any qualifiers—the Second Amendment. And, following that logic the Second Amendment trumps all the other amendments.

What a shame if the power of the gun lobby, coupled with the cowardice of politicians, rewrites history and interprets the Constitution to the benefit of a paranoid minority. And what a tragedy if this minority then plays into the hands of killers who are looking for guns to carry out their own twisted fantasies of revenge.

*   *   *

Parents need to look closely, and learn, from the attempts to manipulate the events of the morning of April 16, 2007. For example, Virginia Tech President Charles Steger testified in the Pryde and Peterson trial that the email alerting the campus to the shootings was watered down and delayed until 0926 (just moments before Cho slaughtered 30 people in Norris Hall) at the request of Zenobia Hikes, former vice president of student affairs. Hikes died on October 27, 2008, and therefore, conveniently, cannot refute or deny Steger's assertion.

Steger testified that Hikes argued that a notice about one student killed and another critically wounded, without family notification, would cause unnecessary panic and heartbreak. Steger said he found her argument "reasonable" and he thought it would be "horrible" to hear about it (the death) on the radio. So, Steger went on, he waited for more information to make a useful (he did not explain "useful") notification. All I can say is that what he sent out only referred to a "shooting incident" and the email was certainly *not useful*. Furthermore, Hikes was very junior and to put the word "panic" in her mouth is, well to put it nicely, highly doubtful because preventing "panic" had been a major (but bogus) theme coming from high levels at Tech in relation to decisions made before and during the massacre.

Steger's words were so egregious that six Virginia Tech faculty members wrote a letter to the editor of the *Roanoke Times* questioning the veracity of the school president's testimony. The six pointed out that Hikes was too junior to make such a call. They also point out that, *"Emergency and safety protocols dictate that policy decisions of this magnitude are made by others in positions superior to hers [Hikes], so it is distressing to us that she is the only member of the Tech Policy Group to have been singled out."*

Following the killings on April 16, 2007, there were rumors that the Steger administration instituted draconian measures to keep faculty members silent as part of the school's aggressive campaign to manage the spin on the tragedy. It is therefore interesting to note that the six members who defended Hikes wrote the following in the first paragraph of their letter: *"In spite of the risks involved in speaking out, we felt a moral obligation to write on behalf of Dr. Hikes, who, due to her untimely death, is no longer able to speak out on her behalf."*

Notes taken by Kim O'Rourke, chief of staff to university President Charles Steger, for the Policy Group on the morning of the 16th of April, do not single out Hikes as the main catalyst for delaying notifying the campus or revising the message. Those notes were shown to the jury during the trial.

Before closing this chapter, I need to remind you, the reader, of the magnitude of the task parents face in trying to tackle the problem of school safety. By the latest tally, Virginia Tech has spent over $1 million on public relations agencies to deflect attention away from what some have described as the worst massacre on a college campus in modern history. Can families compete with that kind of money? Furthermore, the school seems to be protected by politicians on both sides of the aisle in Richmond. The difficulty in simply getting one's argument heard is almost overwhelming.

The legal system does not want to tackle the problem of gun violence. Indeed there is no consistent standard of responsibility for those in management positions when one compares various crimes. If you are a manager anywhere, you can be held accountable for sexual harassment in your office even if you did not know it was taking place because you *should* have known about it. If you say something that someone perceives as sexist, you are held accountable—you might even lose your job. However, when it comes to shootings on campuses, even if you ignore the warning signs, if you know the potential for violence exists, you are not held accountable when an individual known to be unstable erupts into full blown violence—the legal system looks the other way. Bluntly, if you tell an off-color joke, you could lose your job. If you ignore the warning signs for a potentially violent individual and people are injured or killed, no sweat—you will not be held accountable.

There are a number of areas where laws should be enacted immediately as first steps to reducing gun violence. For example:

- A law restricting the quantity of guns that can be sold at one time, such legislation would help prevent trafficking in arms.
- A law making background checks mandatory for all gun sales would close the gun show loophole and be a major step forward in keeping guns out of the hands of convicted felons.
- A law licensing all gun owners and registering all weapons; such a law would promote responsible gun ownership.
- A law restricting (and prohibiting) the sale of certain types of weapons and ammunition, such as automatic assault weapons and high capacity clips; this law would help keep such weapons out of the hands of the dangerously mentally ill.
- A law requiring safe storage of all weapons; this legislation would greatly reduce a child's access to guns and the all too frequent killing of children.
- A law indicting those who engage in straw purchases (an individual who legally buys a gun, but is buying the weapon for someone who is prohibited from gun purchases); such a law would help in shutting down corrupt gun dealers and controlling the secondary gun market.

In the final analysis, until people are held accountable for their actions or inactions when it comes to campus shootings, there is no real incentive to spend the money or select leaders who will help ensure campus safety. The answer then ultimately rests with parents demanding high safety standards at all colleges and universities and financial donors making their contributions contingent on schools putting safety first. Together, if we push hard enough, we can make our children safer than they have been in years past.

CHAPTER XIV

DOING NOTHING IS NOT THE ANSWER

"Violence is seldom predictable with any certainty; its precise timing and location are even less so. Thus when it comes to rare but catastrophic events such as campus rampages, preventing violence is more important than foreseeing it."
~Helen de Haven, associate professor, John Marshall Law School

The Chinese characters that make up the word "crisis" include one that may be translated as "opportunity." We are a nation in crisis—a gun violence crisis—and the opportunity to do something about it is now. If the murder of 20 beautiful elementary school children and their teachers, in Newtown, Connecticut is not enough to spur action to address the crisis, then what is? If the cold-blooded murder of two volunteer firemen in western New York by a man who did what he liked doing best, killing people, is not enough to take action, then what is?

From Columbine, to the Appalachian School of Law, to Virginia Tech, to Northern Illinois University, to a Sheikh temple in Wisconsin, to a Connecticut elementary school, the bodies pile up. On and on it goes, the unabated gun violence. The self-proclaimed greatest nation on the earth appears paralyzed in the face of this murderous rampage. The gun-related deaths are so frequent that they have become as American as apple pie. The United States has become the laughing stock of the world if for no other reason than it has appeared incapable or unwilling to take tough measures to prevent these slaughters.

Some naively argue the shootings are God's will. Others contend that we will never be able to stop these killings; we are not responsible for what others do. The National Rifle Association insists that the best way to stop a bad guy with a gun is a good guy with a gun. But in a fit of rage or drunken stupor, a good guy with a gun is just one pull of the trigger away from being a bad guy. More guns will probably lead to more carnage, not less. It is just common sense: if you don't have access to assault weapons and high capacity magazines, you cannot use them to kill people.

Others suggest that what is needed is armed guards or police at all of our schools. Maybe it is. But remember, there was an armed guard at Columbine; Ft. Hood is a military base with armed personnel everywhere; and Virginia Tech had armed police on the campus. The presence of armed personnel prevented none of those shootings.

Still others insist that guns don't kill; that banning assault weapons or high capacity magazines will not stop the killings. Well, as a matter fact, guns *do* kill, and banning assault weapons and high capacity magazines would greatly reduce the chances and probability of mass killings. If you buy the argument that guns don't kill, then why do we license other inanimate objects as well as their owners? Cars in the hands of people addicted to alcohol or drugs or dangerously mentally ill individuals kill, and we have taken steps to keep cars out of the hands of people in both categories. Guns kill in the hands of addicts and dangerously mentally ill people and we need to do the same; we need to keep these weapons out of their hands. Yet we do nothing, and doing nothing is no longer an option.

Another argument against banning weapons in any form is that it destroys our Second Amendment rights to bear arms. But all the rights granted us in the Constitution have limitations. For example, despite our First Amendment rights to freedom of speech, I cannot use profanity in this book nor can I use sexist or racist vocabulary.

Clearly the Second Amendment says no one has the right to take away our right to bear arms. I doubt, however, that the founding fathers would have supported the right of the dangerously mentally ill to own assault weapons whose main purpose is to kill human beings.

A ban on assault weapons, which are intended for use by the military and law enforcement, is not a ban on our individual rights. Such a ban is a step toward sanity in protecting average citizens and guaranteeing them the right to life and the pursuit of all the freedoms guaranteed us in the Constitution. I would argue that such a ban helps guarantee the rights of all citizens to life, liberty and the pursuit of happiness.

The public, then, is being duped when it comes to what is being done to keep our schools safe and prevent school shootings. The far right of our political spectrum has framed the argument solely in Second Amendment terms, wrapping themselves in a blanket of constitutional patriotism and labeling all those who question them as unpatriotic. The hysterical tone of these self-described patriots has reached such a crescendo that it drowns out any talk of protecting the Second Amendment *and* keeping guns out of the hands of those who are dangerously mentally ill. Furthermore, even a hint that incompetent school and police officials have played roles in these killings cannot be heard over the din. Holding people accountable for their actions or inactions that result in injury or death is brushed aside in the frenzied rhetoric.

The result is that two issues critical to improving school safety (keeping guns out of the hands of people who are dangerously mentally ill as well as holding people accountable for their actions or inactions that facilitate these murderous rampages) are not heard, much less discussed.

Thousands of dollars have been and are being spent on warning systems, period. A considerable amount of time and effort has been expended on drawing up security and safety regulations, but once these regulations are in place, it takes a human being to activate such a system. In other words, no matter how good an electronic system is, how well thought out safety rules are, it always boils down to the human factor—to those who have the authority to make decisions. And if there is one lesson to be learned from the Virginia Tech massacre, it is that people failed to do their duty—to warn. Those in authority who failed to warn have not been held liable.

Under Virginia Tech's Emergency Response Plan in effect on April 16, 2007, it was the Emergency Response Resources Group (a.k.a. ERRG in Tech's plan) that had the authority, and responsibility, for sending out a warning. President Steger was part of the Policy Group, which, per the plan, sat above the ERRG. Therefore, according to the plan, Steger had no responsibility to send out a warning. Chief Flinchum, however, had the authority to issue a warning based on the school's published Timely Warning procedure in compliance with the Clery Act to issue a warning, but he did not do so. Secretary Duncan cited the conflict between Virginia Tech's published timely warning procedure and internal procedure 5615, which was not well known. The Emergency Plan was under a different jurisdiction (see below). The school's leadership did not follow either its Emergency Plan or Timely Warning procedures as written—neither Steger nor Flinchum have been asked to answer for that.

At the Appalachian School of Law, President Lucius Ellsworth belittled faculty members' requests for campus security, chalking their concerns up to "women's hormones" and assuring them nothing would happen. Within weeks, three people were dead and three more seriously wounded. Ellsworth has never been called to task for his disregard of security.

The pattern is the same over and over again—dangerously mentally ill people getting their hands on guns, people in positions of authority turning their backs on warning signs, and innocent people being gunned down. As of this writing, no one appears ready to hold individuals accountable for their failure to act and to warn when faced with an imminent danger of violence—that is true for both Virginia Tech and the Appalachian School of Law. The pattern is there: poor decisions, inactions, and no accountability.

The publicity surrounding improved warning systems gives the public a false sense of security, gives the politicians and school officials the fig leaf they need to say they are doing something. But unless these expenditures on new warning and security systems are coupled with holding people accountable, nothing meaningful is being done, and doing nothing is not an option; the stakes are too high—they are the lives of our children and loved ones.

1999 (April 20)   **Columbine shootings**—*12 students, one teacher killed and 21 students wounded.*

2002 (January)   **Appalachian School of Law shootings**—*one student, one professor, and the dean are killed and three students are wounded.*

2007 (April 16)   **Virginia Tech shootings**—*32 students and faculty are killed and at least 17 others are wounded. State pledges to spend more on mental health care.*

2008 (February 14) Northern Illinois shootings—*four are killed and 21 others are wounded.*

FY 2009-FY 2011 Virginia spends $424.3 million on mental health in 2009. *Despite the pledges made after Virginia Tech, to increase spending on mental health, that figure drops to $385.5 million in FY 2011.* **Virginia ran $311 million surplus in its general fund in FY 2011, funded partly by cuts to spending on mental health.**

2010 (January 14) Virginia State Senator John Edwards

introduces a bill to amend and tighten school security. *The Virginia House of Delegates waters the bill down so that the state's college and university presidents do not have to understand the contents of their school's security plans.* Virginia Tech employee and member of the House of Delegates, David Nutter, refuses to vote for the bill in any form.

2011 (January)   Tucson shootings—*six are killed and 18 others are wounded including U.S. Representative Gabrielle Giffords. Speaker of the House John Boehner tells the media now is not the time to discuss ways to curb gun violence.*

2012 (April 16)   Members of the Brady Campaign meet with House Majority Leader (R-Va.) Eric Cantor on the fifth anniversary of the Virginia Tech shooting. Cantor tells those gathered he will not allow a vote on a bill calling for stronger background checks in order to buy a gun because it is sponsored by a Democrat. Senator David Vitter (R-La.) declines to meet with the Brady Campaign members, claiming he is too busy.

2012 (July 20)   Aurora movie theater shootings—*12 are killed and 58 others are wounded.*

2012 (August 5)   Sheikh Temple shootings in Oak Creek, Wisconsin—*six are killed and four are wounded.*

2012 (December 12) Clackaman Town Center Mall, Portland, Oregon, shootings—*two dead.*

2012 (December 14) Sandy Hook Elementary School, Newtown, Connecticut—*20 first graders and six teachers and school staff are murdered.*

Duplicity In Richmond

Most disturbing are the politicians who came to Virginia Tech following the massacre, cried in front of the families and media, and then worked to water down and undermine responsibility for campus safety at senior levels. These efforts were clearly intended to reduce the liability of school presidents and other top-level leaders.

One of the worst examples of this duplicity is then-Virginia State Delegate David Nutter. Nutter is both an employee of Virginia Tech and was an elected official from Blacksburg in the Virginia House of Delegates. Common sense would make you think Nutter would be in the forefront of efforts to prevent school shootings. But, Nutter has proven common sense wrong.

Immediately after the shootings, Nutter met with the families, wept, and offered his sympathies. But when it came to adopting measures to help strengthen school safety, Nutter balked.

The prime example of his chicanery came nearly three years after the massacre at Virginia Tech when the lower house of the Virginia legislature significantly weakened state Senator John Edwards' bill to amend and reenact the Code of Virginia relating to crisis and emergency management for public institutions of higher learning. Specifically, members of the lower house took exception to university presidents and other school officials having to certify they comprehend and understand the school's emergency plan—a plan that they play a role in creating. Here is the sentence as it cleared and passed the senate unanimously:

"In addition, the members of the threat assessment team, as defined …(by law)…, and the president and vice-president of each institution of higher education, or in the case of the Virginia Military Institute, the superintendent, shall annually certify in writing to the Department of Emergency Management, *comprehension and understanding* of the institution's crisis and emergency management plan."

Here is the sentence the lower house insisted on and appears in the final bill:

"In addition, the president and vice-president of each public institution of higher education, or in the case of the Virginia Military Institute, the superintendent, shall annually (i) review the institution's crisis and emergency management plan; (ii) certify in writing that the president and vice-president, or the superintendent, have reviewed the plan; and (iii) make recommendations to the institution for appropriate changes to the plan."

Stop to think what members of the Virginia legislature have done: they have said that presidents of the state's colleges and universities do not have to comprehend and understand a document that is critical to the security of our children.

While the State Senate passed the original bill unanimously, the House of Delegates objected. The two most ardent opponents of the legislation—they wouldn't vote for it in any form—were Delegates Nutter and Charles Poindexter, a right-wing politician who tried to derail the reappointment of Judge William Alexander, the judge who presided over the Pryde and Peterson lawsuit against Virginia Tech President Steger.

If you read the official reports of both the shootings at Columbine and Virginia Tech, as I have, there is repeated emphasis on schools' security plans and the role of those plans in preventing campus shootings. Now, according to the Virginia lower house, the presidents of the state's colleges and universities do not have to comprehend and understand those plans.

Clearly Nutter's promises to the Virginia Tech victims' families to work for greater school safety didn't go as far as it should have. When the state had a chance to do something, as little as it was, Nutter refused to go along with the bill in any form.

Nutter is not alone.

Let's take a closer look at the efforts in Virginia General Assembly by Delegates Bill Janis (R-Goochland County) and Charles Poindexter (R-Franklin County) to delay or kill the reappointment of Franklin County Circuit Judge William Alexander. Alexander was the presiding judge appointed by the Virginia Supreme Court to oversee the trial because all the local judges recused themselves. Judge Alexander initially ruled there was enough evidence of gross negligence that the suit against several current and former Virginia Tech officials, including school president, Charles Steger, could go forward. That ruling may not have gone over well with the right wing glitterati of Virginia's body politic, some of whom argue no one can be held responsible for someone else's actions. Therefore, Seung Hui Cho, and only Seung Hui Cho, is responsible for the mass killings at Virginia Tech. The fact that school and police officials turned a blind eye to Cho's mental illness and threatening behavior is, to them, immaterial. (It should be noted that the gross negligence claim was removed by Alexander just before the trial began in 2012.)

The problem with those who argue that no one can be held responsible for what someone else does, is the failure to take into account the concept of "foreseeability," a legal principle that says if the warning signs are readily apparent, and individuals who are aware of those signs do nothing, then those individuals can be held responsible for their inaction. If you look at the number of warning signs at Virginia Tech they are overwhelming—I have spelled them out in detail in previous chapters.

What more of a warning do you want than a professor threatening to resign unless a student (Cho) is removed from her class because she fears for her safety and the safety of her students? Subsequently, Judge Alexander's ruling may have been viewed as a serious blow to the state and the school.

The *Roanoke Times* reported on the grilling Judge Alexander received during the re-appointment hearings and his opponents may have seized another issue to delay or stop the judge's reappointment in order to mask their real motive. It appears the issue they chose was Alexander's decision to release a grand jury report after the indictment of Franklin County Sheriff Ewell Hunt. The sheriff was indicted on charges of keeping improper records about the employment of his daughter.

Delegate Janis has publicly acknowledged that the judge had the authority to release the report, which the judge did in response to a motion filed by the special prosecutor in the case, Pittsylvania County Commonwealth's Attorney, David Grimes. If Judge Alexander had the right to grant the motion, then what is Delegate Janis doing other than playing politics?

Ultimately, Judge Alexander was reappointed and the lawsuit filed by the Pryde and Peterson families went forward.

The Mental Health Shell Game

Following the mass murders at Virginia Tech the one issue that nearly everyone agreed upon was the need to do more in the field of mental health—to identify and get treatment for those who are a threat to themselves and others. There seemed to be a moment when something might be done. And indeed, Virginia did allocate more money for mental health, but that was 2008; it is now more than five years later and Virginia has backtracked. The state now spends less on mental health than it did on the eve of April 16, 2007.

According to the National Alliance on Mental Illness (NAMI), between FY 2009 and FY 2011, Virginia's expenditures on mental health dropped 9.1% from $424.3 million to $385.8 million.* NAMI also points out that "the risks of violence among a small subset of individuals may increase when appropriate treatment and support are not available. The use of alcohol or drugs as a form of self-medication can also increase these risks." Virginia made these cuts at a time when it was one of the few states running a budget surplus.

---

* *State Mental Health Cuts: A National Crisis*, A report by the National Alliance on Mental Illness, March, 2011.

In his first three years after taking office, Governor McDonnell delivered budget surpluses each year. Virginia's fiscal policy gained national attention. On July 31, 2012, Fox News lauded Virginia's three years of budget surpluses under McDonnell, citing surplus of $220 million in 2010—the first year of McDonnell's four-year term. Fox also said that the Virginia General Assembly had a surplus of $311 million in 2011 and that in 2012 the state had $129 million more in its General Fund than had been predicted. No one mentioned that part of this surplus came on the backs of one of the most vulnerable segments of society, the mentally ill. Fox News did not mention that cuts to mental health services have a potential impact on public safety: the risk of violence among a small number of mentally ill individuals increases when appropriate treatment and support are not available.

Virginia then, has not been starved for cash and its politicians at the highest levels in order to score points with right-wing pundits appear to have intentionally broken promises to the electorate to spend more for mental health.

*　　*　　*

Increased spending on mental health is critical to preventing these shootings. The shooters at the law school, Tech, Tucson, Aurora, and Sandy Hook were all mentally ill. Yet we see what has happened in Virginia—the state cut funds for mental health programs and now Governor McDonnell wants to potentially make the situation worse by privatizing mental health care. Privatization will, over the long run, cost more than if it is in the hands of the state. The quality of care will go down, not up. Privatization will however, probably make some people in Virginia wealthy.

Governor McDonnell's intention to privatize Virginia's mental health system is a betrayal of the electorate and an insult to the victims of the Virginia school shootings. The governor apparently bases his proposal on the system implemented by the former Republican governor of New Jersey, Christie Todd Whitman. The New Jersey system apparently has not saved money, it has led to more vagrancy (and probably crime), and has drastically undercut the quality of mental health.

I personally witnessed an example of the New Jersey program, after spending an evening with a professor and her students from a New Jersey state university. We made over 100 peanut butter and jelly sandwiches and put them in bags along with fruit and water. We then went to the train station in Newark, which was packed with homeless, the vast majority of whom appeared to suffer from some form of mental illness. There were police everywhere (an added taxpayer expense) in an effort to prevent crime and assure commuters they were safe. Based on this experience, New Jersey's mental health care system apparently has not improved and appears to be costing more money than it has saved.

If accurate, then New Jersey's privatization of mental health care is not a program to emulate—it is a program to be avoided.

Virginians should reject any move to cut funds for mental health or to privatize the program. Mass shooters such as those at the Appalachian School of Law, Virginia Tech, and elsewhere were unstable and in need of mental health care. Following the Virginia Tech massacre, President George W. Bush called for greater government spending on mental health.

McDonnell's argument for privatization of mental health care is specious; it is an insult to the Virginia Tech families and victims. McDonnell has tried to conceal from the electorate that he is doing little that is meaningful about mental health care and school safety. For example, in 2011 he launched the "College Campus Safety and Violence Prevention Public Service Challenge"—a jingle contest.

Students were asked to create 30-second videos; something like soap commercials. The Office of Substance Abuse Prevention would narrow entries for online voting. (Neither of the two Virginia school shooters were substance abusers.)

Why the contest? First, to draw attention away from, and perhaps to undercut, the litigation against high ranking Virginia Tech officials; second, to appear to be doing something meaningful, when in fact that is not the case; third, to avoid tackling continuing weaknesses in the law regarding campus safety; and fourth, to cover up the governor's abysmal record as Attorney General during the Tech tragedy.

Governor McDonnell's foolish, shortsighted policy on mental health took a tragic turn on November 19, 2013 when Austin (Gus) Deeds, the son of prominent Virginia State Senator Creigh Deed, stabbed his father repeatedly and then took his own life. Press reports indicated that an emergency custody order was issued for Gus Deeds the day before the attack and he was taken to the Rockridge Area Community Service Center, which treats mental illness and substance abuse. Young Deeds was released because a psychiatric bed could not be found for him. Unconfirmed media reports have indicated that beds were available, but that communication between medical facilities dealing in psychiatric care was so poor that the Rockridge facility was unaware of that fact. No matter what the reason for the young man's release, the Deeds family paid a horrific price for McDonnell's budget cuts. Gus Deeds shot and killed himself after stabbing his father.

McDonnell's budget cuts for mental health are particularly galling when you stop to think that Virginia taxpayers have had to shell out over $570,000 in legal expenses as a result of a federal criminal investigation against the governor. That money would have bought quite a few beds in the state's psychiatric wards.

Willful Blindness

The deceit is not just at the state level; it includes those elected to federal office.

Following the Tucson shooting that killed six and seriously wounded 12 others including Rep. Gabriele Giffords, members of the Brady Campaign asked to meet with House Speaker John Boehner to discuss ways to curb gun violence. Boehner declined. According to the *Huffington Post* (April 15, 2012), he said now is not the time. I would ask, "What better time to discuss ways to curb gun violence than in the aftermath of a member of Congress being shot?"

On the fifth anniversary of the Virginia Tech shooting, Brady Campaign officials asked to meet with Louisiana Senator Vitter to discuss a bill he had introduced making it easier for the mentally ill to buy guns.

According to a Brady Campaign worker, Vitter was too busy.

Boehner isn't too busy to visit tanning booths and Vitter found time to frequent prostitutes. (In July 2007, Vitter was identified by the media as a client of a prostitution service during the DC Madam scandal.)

More recently we have 12 dead and some 50 wounded in a movie theatre in suburban Denver, then two killed and one wounded at a shopping mall outside Portland, Oregon, and now the horrific shooting at Sandy Hook Elementary School in Newtown, Connecticut. So when is the right time to discuss keeping guns out of the hands of convicted felons, convicted domestic abusers, and mentally ill people who are a threat to themselves and others?

*   *   *

House Majority Leader Eric Cantor's meeting with representatives of the Brady Campaign on the fifth anniversary of the Virginia Tech shootings exposed his double dealing.

According to one of the meeting's participants, Cantor expressed his "full support" for keeping guns out of the hands of dangerous people. However, the Majority Leader, who had just returned from speaking at an NRA convention, refused to sign a Statement of Principle capturing the ideas he had just agreed to. The statement calls for keeping guns out of the hands of those who are convicted felons, convicted domestic abusers, terrorists, or people who are dangerously mentally ill.

The Statement of Principle is not a pledge, and Cantor cannot say he is opposed to signing such documents when they advance his career. He willingly signed Grover Norquist's pledge not to raise taxes. Apparently when it comes to the lives of students, staff, and faculty the Majority Leader says no dice—there is nothing in it for me. What a shame. Voters are crying out for politicians with backbone and principle, and Cantor took a pass. He apparently prefers to gamble with people's lives rather than act responsibly.

According to one of the attendees at Cantor's volunteered to those gathered that you have to set standards low around here (Congress), and then proved it. He told them he would not allow a vote on a bill strengthening background checks in order to buy a gun because a Democrat sponsors the bill.

Interest groups, such as the National Rifle Association, have conducted a scare campaign that plays to the basest of human emotions—fear and paranoia. The most blatant falsehood is that the Obama administration is coming to get your guns; closely followed by Washington is going to limit your right to own firearms and when that happens we will be one step away from a totalitarian government that subjugates Americans to the worst forms of repression. The net result? Politicians are spooked. Only now, in the wake of Sandy Hook, are politicians discussing measures to keep firearms out of the hands of those who are a danger to themselves or others. But even measures such as mandated universal background checks for gun purchases and measures limiting high capacity ammunition clips failed to pass in Congress. Neither the federal nor state governments appear to have the will to put their money where their mouth is and to keep mental health care in the hands of government. Neither federal nor state politicians appear willing to vote the money needed to improve mental health.

The result is that we live in a society that over analyzes and limits some of our freedoms and completely ignores life-threatening aspects of others. The bottom line, however, should be that no one has the right to take away another's inalienable right to life, liberty and the pursuit of happiness. When you are murdered on the grounds of the Appalachian School of Law, Virginia Tech, or Sandy Hook Elementary School, some one has taken away those rights. If people's actions or inactions played a role in the killings, they should be held accountable.

When politicians are made to address the issue because the crime is so heinous, such as the massacre at Virginia Tech, they do so with willful blindness—they deliberately fail to make a reasonable inquiry into the crime despite the reasonable awareness of wrong-doing; in this case, the wrong-doing of University President Charles Steger and Virginia Tech Police Chief Wendell Flinchum. According to the dictionary, "willful blindness involves conscious avoidance of the truth and gives rise to an inference of knowledge of the crime in question." The Governor's Review Panel Report, to which I earlier devoted a whole chapter, appears to fall into the category of willful blindness. Even after two revisions, the report still contains apparent errors, including the timeline and other important details, such as when and where the murderer killed himself. Remember, "corrections" to the original report had been requested of Governor Kaine following the publication of the original panel report released in August of 2007, based on information that was only discovered by or disclosed to the families after the legal settlement had been agreed to in April 2008. Prior to that, he refused to reconvene the panel, or to do anything about correcting the record. His successor, former Attorney General Bob McDonnell must have been aware of those errors as well, yet remained silent. What more evidence of willful blindness does anyone need? In effect, then, this says that state officials spent nearly $700,000 on a report that was factually a sham, a report that is supposed to do something in analyzing this nation's worst school shooting and in fact does nothing—and doing nothing is not an option.

According to Christopher Strom, a retired sergeant of the New York police intelligence division, if you look at the Virginia Tech tragedy, you see:

- Criminal possession of stolen property (Seung Hui Cho's medical records were found in the home of the former director of the university's Cook Counseling Center);
- Tampering with evidence in a criminal/civil investigation (critical information about the timeline of events on April 16, 2007 was withheld);
- Witness intimidation (Professor Lucinda Roy who tried to get Cho help, was blackballed by the school administration—some were afraid to have any contact with her for fear of losing their job);
- Obstruction of an official investigation (the police, the ATF, and gun dealers refused to cooperate with the Governor's investigative panel); and
- Possible conspiracy (pressure on school faculty and staff to coordinate with the school administration before talking to the Governor's Review Panel).[*]

Governor McDonnell was Attorney General at that time, and didn't pick up on any of those things.

Most school administrators, professors, and instructors are not clear on what their rights and responsibilities are here in Virginia. They don't

---

[*] *Roanoke Times*, editorials and commentaries, December 29, 2012.

understand that many of the actions of the shooters at the law school and Tech fell under laws governing illegal stalking, and they don't understand their responsibilities to notify families and school officials about potentially violent behavior.

This lack of understanding remains precisely because of the willful blindness by the universities' administrators and state officials participating in the follow up investigations. Doing something poorly, as Tech has done so many times in dealing with the families, is nearly as bad, if not worse, as doing nothing at all.

The O'Neil Story

For William O'Neil and his wife, Jeanne Dube, the recovery has been a long process and O'Neil will never move on until Virginia Tech President Charles Steger takes responsibility and is held accountable for his lack of action on April 16, 2007. O'Neil remembers his exceptionally bright young son, Daniel, who excelled in math and the sciences. Daniel was a determined and diligent young man. Once he put his mind to something he would not stop until he had achieved his goal, whether it was skate boarding or teaching himself to play the guitar and the piano, he would not stop until he mastered a skill.

Daniel earned his undergraduate degree at a small liberal arts college in eastern Pennsylvania—Lafayette College. O'Neil remembers how his son blossomed in his new academic environment. His love for music and the sciences became his passion. Indeed, at school his buddies were all into one or the other, just as he was. But despite being away at school, Daniel's ties to his family remained strong and he called home several times a week.

In his sophomore year, Daniel went to Brussels for the spring semester. No sooner did he land than he called and wanted to come home. O'Neil told his son to give it a chance. And give it a chance he did, he threw himself into his new surroundings with the same determination he approached everything and after a week Daniel was just fine in his new environment.

O'Neil chokes back tears when remembers how close Daniel was to his family, so close that when it came down to a choice of graduate schools, he picked Virginia Tech over Colorado State University, saying he could drive home from Tech.

Daniel approached life at Virginia Tech with the same zest he tackled everything. He loved the beautiful campus nestled in the Blue Ridge Mountains and really liked the big-time sports that Tech offered. He got an apartment and a graduate assistantship and majored in environmental engineering focusing on engineering water resources.

On April 16, 2007, William O'Neil, who works in the advancement office of Connecticut College, was in New Jersey meeting with a college alumnus when he first heard of the shooting. O'Neil and the alumnus had gone to lunch and when he got up to go to the men's room he checked his emails. He noticed an unusually high number of messages from his wife. Returning to the lunch table, he excused himself again, saying he needed to step outside and phone home to see why his wife was repeatedly trying to reach him. It was at that time he first learned of the shootings at Virginia Tech.

O'Neil's wife, Jeanne, told him there had been a shooting at Virginia Tech and she could not reach Daniel on the phone. This was highly unusual, especially because when the Morva shooting had occurred Daniel had called home right away to tell his parents that he was ok.

Returning to the luncheon table, O'Neil explained what was happening and the alumnus suggested they go to his house, turn on the news and try to find out what was going on. O'Neil will never forget the television coverage of Suzanne Grimes's son Kevin being carried out of Norris Hall. When he saw that he left for home immediately.

Before leaving New York, a colleague called O'Neil saying her husband was a State Police trooper and would be willing to contact the Virginia police to try and find out Daniel's status. The answer was, of course, "yes." En route home, the colleague called saying Daniel's name was not on the list of casualties, but that O'Neil should get to Blacksburg right away.

Once home, O'Neil was desperate for news of his son. Finally, he remembered the name of one of Daniel's professors. He got the man's home phone and contacted him. The professor however, knew nothing more than what was on the news.

The O'Neils tried to get a flight to Blacksburg or someplace nearby, but it was impossible. Just as they were about to give up hope of getting to Virginia immediately, a friend, with access to a corporate jet, called. The friend told the O'Neils to go to the airport; he would take care of everything including a car rental and hotel reservations—just get to the airport.

At 8:00p. m., the O'Neils flew to Blacksburg, arriving between 10:00 and 10:30p. m.. A rental car was waiting and a room had been reserved for them at the Inn at Virginia Tech.

Arriving at the Inn, the grim story repeated itself. The O'Neils went to the reception desk and asked for information about their son. They were immediately taken to a room with members of the clergy. The same type of room the Whites, the Pohles and all the victims' families were taken to— the same cold, foreboding style of room where a police officer asked for a picture of their son.

The O'Neils waited for what seemed to be an eternity. Jeanne smokes and they finally decided to go outside so she could have a cigarette. But the O'Neils got only a few steps when the police asked them to go back to the room—it was then that they were told their son was dead. They were stunned. The news was unbearable and the news was overpowering; it was as if all the oxygen had been sucked out of the room.

A compassionate grief counselor from the Red Cross was present and gave them some comfort, but when they returned to the emptiness of their hotel room they faced the arduous, painful task of calling family and friends. They called family members to tell them to go to their parents' houses so someone would be there when they called with the news.

The next few days and weeks were a blur of confusion, disbelief, and pain, but as the reality of what had happened began to set in O'Neil realized something was "not right." The O'Neils heard very little from the school and had no contact with President Steger until August—the same President Steger who was too busy meeting with families to meet with Professor Lucinda Roy. Long before that, however, the O'Neil family began asking questions—primarily, why wasn't there a warning after the 7:15 a.m. double homicide at West Ambler Johnston Hall? The school had very little contact with the families and when school officials did, it was with a sheepish indifference. For example, Virginia Tech asked the families to write down their email addresses so they could be in touch with each other, but no one ever heard anything more about that and never got the list of names. We know now, as was pointed out earlier in this book, that Tech did not want the families to be in contact with each other; school officials did not want the families comparing notes.

Furthermore, the O'Neils began to feel as if the school cared more about public relations than the families—a feeling that was shared by many of the victims' families. The vast amounts of money spent by Virginia Tech on Firestorm ($150,000), and Burson-Marsteller (over $650,000) go a long way to prove the O'Neil's feelings were correct—particularly when you examine the billing for both with the repeated references to consultations for handling and dealing with the media. Furthermore, when you add to those figures to the money the state paid to Arlington-based TriData (over $500,000), to produce a badly flawed "official" report that holds no one accountable, does not address questions such as identifying mistakes in judgment, and in general is a poorly researched, poorly analyzed, and poorly written document—a picture of blatant manipulation and cover-up comes into focus.

All the O'Neils, William, his wife Jeanne, and their daughter Erin, went to therapy—at least briefly. Jeanne openly showed her grief—she would spend hours crying. William held his feelings in. Their main concerned was Erin, who was a teacher in New York. They were concerned that she didn't have much family nearby but were comforted somewhat that she had a cousin and a boyfriend in the city and a circle of close friends.

Jeanne had retired from teaching the year before the shooting, and now there was no way she could go back to work. William initially kept busy with administrative details—closed Daniel's apartment, got his car back to Rhode Island (the O'Neils live in Rhode Island, but William works in Connecticut), and made the funeral arrangements. All these things were therapeutic, they kept him busy and moving forward. But staying home with all the memories was unbearable and he soon decided to go back to work because he needed to keep busy.

The O'Neils still wait for answers; they wait for an explanation; they wait for the truth to be told.

EPILOGUE:

WHERE ARE WE NOW?

"...morality ends where the gun begins."
~Ayn Rand, American novelist, playwright, screenwriter

You cannot make people listen who have plugged their ears; you cannot make people see when they will not open their eyes. Following the Virginia Tech tragedy, a parent of a wounded student asked school president Steger at a meeting with the Administration in Owens Field House, "If you knew then what you know now, would you do anything differently?" Steger said, "No." It was not enough that the families had been traumatized by the deaths and wounding of loved ones, Steger had to underscore that he had learned nothing from the tragedy. He would do it again, follow the same inadequate procedures and make the same poor judgment calls, because to do otherwise would mean that he had something to learn. His callous indifference defies description, but his answer still fits our circumstances: we know more now than we did before April 16, 2007, but we are not doing much to keep our schools and streets any safer than they were before that terrible day. Yes, schools have spent millions of dollars on warning and alert systems, but it takes human beings to activate those systems.

A warning system was in place on the morning of April 16, 2007 at Virginia Tech, but those who could have activated it in time to save 30 lives at Norris Hall procrastinated until it was too late. No one was held accountable for his or her failure to alert the Tech campus. Until there is accountability our schools will not be safe. I am not talking about revenge; I am talking about competence in crisis management. If you are not up to the job, and if you do not do your job, you should be removed and held accountable.

Prior to April 16, 2007, the warning signs in Cho's behavior and faculty concerns were there. Those signs were ignored. School, police and mental health officials knew of Cho's potential for violence, but because of ignorance of the law, incompetence, and a general unwillingness to take action, people in positions of trust and authority allowed Cho's illness to fester until it burst in an orgy of bullets, blood, pain, and anguish. Again, until people are held accountable for turning their backs on signs of imminent violence, our schools will not be safe.

The far-right hysteria over gun control and the Second Amendment has all but doomed any chance of a calm discussion of the best way to keep guns out of the hands of those bent on violence. The Second Amendment should never have been part of the debate on school safety. The issue is not the rights of law-abiding mentally healthy citizens to own guns; the issue is keeping guns out of the hands of terrorists (school shootings are a form of domestic terrorism), convicted felons, and those who are a danger to themselves or others. However, there seems to be no limit to what these right-wingers will say. Backed by the National Rifle Association and gun manufacturers, these people will say and do just about anything in order to prevent a public dialogue over how to keep guns out of the hands of people who are bent on killing or wounding others.

As a nation we have the responsibility to mount an offensive against the gun violence that plagues this country. We need to move forward on many fronts: against the glorification of violence in the media, from bumper stickers to television shows and movies; against video games that glamorize gore and murder; against domestic violence. We have to reject violence as the first and best response to interpersonal conflict.

Following September 11, 2001 we came together and demonstrated the resolve and determination to root out the Al Qa'ida threat. We have spent billions of dollars on two wars and thousands of Americans have been killed or wounded on the battlefield to fight those who use terrorist tactics against us. We showed that, as a great nation, we have the will and determination to put political and philosophical differences aside in a common struggle for the good of all. We must do the same now in a struggle that cannot be solved with soldiers and tanks.

Now, in this struggle against school shootings, it's not a foreign enemy responsible for the killing, it's ourselves. We are sacrificing little children, young adults and innocent bystanders everywhere because the multi-billion dollar gun industry is afraid that effective gun licensing will cut into their profits. Gun advocates use the second amendment to make sure that companies such as Smith & Wesson and Glock make profits by selling military-grade weapons to private individuals. But to quote Professor Bill

Jenkins* from Dominican University, River Forest, Illinois: "We don't use the First Amendment to keep newspapers in business." The Second Amendment should not be used to ensure that gun manufacturers have healthy earnings.

Some sociologists have said that when you scratch the veneer of religion and civilization in which humans are wrapped, you expose a primeval creature capable of the most despicable crimes. You need look no further than the holocaust, the genocide in Bosnia, or the violence on the streets of America for proof of this assertion. The massacres at the Appalachian School of Law, Sandy Hook, the movie theater in Aurora, and at Virginia Tech are ample proof of these despicable crimes. Indeed, it is this primal, visceral instinct, as well as the fear it inspires, that gun manufacturers play upon in pressing for totally unrestricted gun ownership—the right to carry any gun, anywhere, at anytime.

The gun industry has a willing mouthpiece, the National Rifle Association (NRA), to engage in fear mongering saying that the government is coming to get our guns. Nothing could be further from the truth. The Supreme Court has confirmed that the Second Amendment guarantees the right of all American citizens to own handguns and rifles for protection. Furthermore, hunting is a way of life in the U.S.; no one is talking about taking guns away from law-abiding hunters. However, all of the rights granted us in the Bill of Rights have limitations. If you defend unlimited access to guns, including high-powered weapons, you are defending the rights of the Sandy Hook butcher, Adam Lanza, to use a Bushmaster Model XN-15-E25 rife on 20 elementary school children and six teachers and staff. No part of the Constitution was ever meant to give any citizen carte blanche to kill people. According to the research done by Professor Jenkins, 80 percent of Americans (this includes a huge number of hunters) favor tighter gun control laws.

Assault weapons and high capacity clips are designed for military and police use; they are designed specifically to kill people; they are not meant for untrained private citizens' hands. Hunters do not use these weapons; private citizens do not need to protect themselves with an assault weapon. The NRA's position that the Second Amendment guarantees that anyone can own any gun is nothing less than a full-scale distortion of the truth.

---

* On August 12, 1997, 16-year-old Will Jenkins was murdered in a robbery at the aptly named Richmond, Virginia fast-food restaurant, "Bullets." It was Will's second day on the job. A 23-year-old assailant killed him at closing time with one shot in the neck. He died instantly. Will's father, Professor Bill Jenkins, who teaches at Dominican University's Performing Arts Center, has become a prominent victims' rights advocate, working for violence prevention.

Nowhere does the Second Amendment guarantee the rights of terrorists, convicted felons, or those who are a danger to themselves or others to own guns. Here is the Second Amendment: *"Right to Keep and Bear Arms: A well regulated Militia, being necessary to the security of a free state, the right of the people to keep and bear Arms, shall not be infringed."* But when it comes to rights guaranteed all Americans in the Second Amendment, gun manufacturers see no limits. Their actions may be legal, but in pushing for unlimited gun sales, those actions are morally repugnant. Unlimited access to high-powered weapons means:

- That it is much easier for felons, terrorists, criminals, and the dangerously mentally ill to get these weapons;
- That criminals have a disposable commodity that is often hard to trace;
- That unsavory elements of society can buy guns through private sellers without a background check; and,
- That gun traffickers can buy in bulk without any check or explanation (frequently aided by complicit gun dealers who report their inventory "lost.")

Money is at the heart of the gun violence epidemic in this country. Gun sales are profitable, and the gun industry wants to keep it that way. There is no money in limiting the sale of military-style assault weapons such as Bushmasters and high-capacity clips. Indeed, according to Professor Jenkins, "These weapons are the weapons of choice by criminals who want to bring warfare to the streets." A lawyer, who was advising the Virginia Tech families, said to me something along the following lines, "It is the sad truth, but we will have no meaningful gun control in this country until someone finds a way to make a profit out of it."

The NRA is methodically and deliberately dishonest in its efforts to make people think, "big brother is going to get your weapons." In fact, there are only four federal gun control laws:

- The 1930s ban on machine guns
- The 1968 Gun Control Act codifying legal purchasers
- The Brady Background Check of 1993
- The Assault Weapons Ban of 1994 (expired in 2004)

Legally bought weapons were used by a troubled young man to kill children and teachers at Sandy Hook Elementary School on December 14, 2012, and then a few days later by a deranged murderer to kill two firemen and wound two others in New York state.

The loopholes in the three remaining gun control laws are so wide that it makes it easy for anyone to buy a high-powered weapon. Here in Virginia, there is no background check if you buy a weapon at a gun show. Criminals taking advantage of the gun show loophole buy a large number of their weapons in Virginia and then use them in crimes in New York City, according to 2011 statistics released by New York City Mayor, Michael Bloomberg and Police Commissioner Raymond Kelly.

So-called patriots, who defend the Second Amendment to the exclusion of all other rights, are in fact defending the rights of a dangerously mentally ill person to have access to guns that could then be used to, for example, snuff out the lives of 20 children and six of their teachers at Sandy Hook Elementary School.

Is the fear of preserving one's own employment, or the fear of not making a profit so powerful as to justify bending the rules or putting a twist on truth? I believe this question needs to be addressed in not just analyzing the Virginia Tech massacre, but in analyzing school shootings everywhere.

Virginia Tech seems to want to pretend their massacre never happened; the school wants to move on. There was no admission of guilt and no determination to do everything possible to try to ensure that there would not be a repetition of Cho's actions. Tech President Steger and his old boy network* were alarmingly uncooperative and non-communicative in the wake of the April 16, 2007 shootings.

Even if you explain the bumbling mistakes of Virginia Tech on that awful day in April 2007, you cannot explain away the school administration's insensitivity toward many of the grieving families in the weeks and months that followed. You cannot explain away school officials' willingness to cover up. Virginia Tech apparently felt the families would just have to live with their loss, time would pass, they would die and the memories would fade.

But, where are we now? The average citizen who is haunted by the faces of the children at Sandy Hook and wants to do something to prevent future violence faces a gun industry consumed by greed. The gun industry that saturated the legitimate gun-owner market, and apparently looks the other way as sales to criminal elements soar, also appears willing to say anything to prevent tighter gun controls that would cut into those profits. The reality is that the gun industry wants to expand sales no matter what

---

* The following members of President Steger's administration were graduates of the school's class of 1969: University President Charles Steger himself; Frank Beamer, head football coach; Thomas C. Tillar, Vice President Alumni Relations; Ray Smoot, Chief Operating Office and Treasurer of the Virginia Tech Foundation; and Joe Meredith, Corporate Research Center President.

the cost in human lives. The gun industry is powerful, rich, shrewd, and formidable, so it is no surprise that it is succeeding.

Where are we now? We live in a country where there are 85 firearms-related deaths a day; where 30,000 people are killed and another 90,000 are wounded by guns every year. We live in country where there are an estimated 300,000,000 guns in private hands. These figures are from The National Center for Injury Prevention Control, U.S. Center for Disease Control and Prevention, Web-based Injury Statistics Query System (WIAQARS) Injury Mortality Reports, 1999-2006.

Where are we now? We live in a country where powerful people perpetuate the myth that more guns on the streets will mean less crime; where statistics are distorted by special interests; and where the gun industry relies on superficial, visceral, and unfounded emotional arguments to promote its sales. When challenged, these lobbyists and promoters will hide behind the shield of the second amendment, thinking that it makes them invulnerable to criticism.

The truth, however, is that there are limits on all the amendments to the Constitution. In fact, there are whole books devoted to exploring how and when and why limits need to be placed on the amendments. There are limits on what a person can say, so you can't spread lies about someone despite the fact that the First Amendment guarantees freedom of speech. There are limits on how one can go about "pursuing happiness," so you can't steal a car even if you think it the key to your bliss. It follows that you should not be able to possess an assault weapon if you aren't on active duty in the military or with the police. You should not be able to purchase any gun if you have a history of mental illness. The fact that limits are not in place is due to individuals who willfully cloud the issues and obscure the facts surrounding mass shootings for their own benefit.

The truth that victims of the Virginia Tech tragedy desperately want is still lacking. Without the truth, they remain prisoners of their agony. Without the truth, we are doomed to more Sandy Hook-style massacres at elementary schools, high schools, and colleges; more shootings in movie theaters and grocery stores; more workplace murders, and more domestic violence. Where is the next target-rich environment where we will shed more tears, then leave flowers and cards to remember those mowed down by a madman?

Shortly before publication of this book I received the following from Virginia State Highway Patrolman Gary Chafin, a first responder to the French class in Norris Hall:

"I was a small part of that day. I feel I do not throw a shadow around most that were there. But I will always hurt. I will never forget what I saw that awful day, I will run to Matt LaPorte and Reema Samaha. When my time here is done I will beg their forgiveness for not being there first—before the very devil we fear got loose and walked among the young of Tech that would've been giants on earth in their time. Gary Chafin, nearly 7 years removed from the lowest ebb of my life."

The shootings persist—a theater in Florida, a school in New Mexico, a store in Indiana, a school in Philadelphia.

Nothing will change until all segments of society—priests, rabbis, ministers, doctors, lawyers, teachers, professors, politicians, blue and white collar workers, fathers, mothers, aunts, uncles, *everyone*—say enough is enough. Individuals _can_ make a difference by demanding that more money be spent on mental health care, holding people in positions of trust accountable when their actions and inactions result in the deaths of innocent people, and finally, by not reelecting those who are in the pockets of the gun lobby.

This book was written out of respect and love for the victims of shootings, their families, friends, and loved ones. I was warned not to write this account of the Virginia Tech tragedy. One lawyer said to me, "Do you think individuals who would lie about the murder of 32 people will hesitate to come after you for exposing them? They will try to punish you." On the eve of the publication of this book one of my editors sent me an email asking me if I knew the price I would pay for writing this book. She added, I assume you do know the price and you believe it is worth it.

Yes, I do know the price. If this book makes people think; if it makes them realize they have been lied to; if it can move people to action to prevent these shootings; if it can prevent a shooting and save just one life and prevent families from going through the loss of a child in a school shooting—I know the price and it is not too great.

Appendix A

VT Emergency Preparedness, Key Committees, and Witnesses not Interviewed by the Review Panel

Virginia Tech Emergency Preparedness Documents

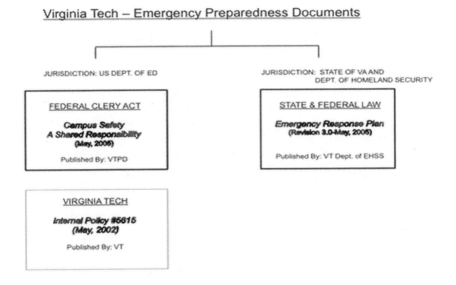

Campus Safety A Shared Responsibility (May, 2005)

This document was created and published by the Virginia Tech Police Force in their Annual Safety Report (ASR) as required by the Federal Clery Act. Jurisdiction for enforcement falls under the US Dept. of Education.

One procedure for issuing "timely warnings" was contained in this document. As shown below, the timely warning procedure did not contain any statement requiring the VT police to receive pre-approvals for preparing and issuing a warning to the campus community from the Policy Group. Additionally, VT police did not have the capability to send an electronic warning to the campus.

"At times it may be necessary for timely warnings to be issued to the university community. If a crime(s) occur and notification is necessary to warn the university of a potential dangerous situation then the Virginia Tech Police Department should be notified. The police department will then prepare a release and the information will be disseminated to all students, faculty, and staff and to the local community."

The panel charged with investigating the massacre at Virginia Tech did not identify this procedure, nor did they provide any detailed discussion of Clery Act requirements in their final investigative report issued following the massacre.

Emergency Response Plan (Revision 3.0—May, 2005)

The following provides a summary of the top two groups in the command chain as defined in Virginia Tech's Emergency Response Plan effective on April 16, 2007. This plan is required per state and federal law, however it is a separate jurisdiction from the US Dept. of Education. The ERRG was the next level below the Policy Group.

This plan also shows that the authority for issuing warnings did not require Policy Group approval.

Policy Group

Members: President, Executive VP, Assoc. VP – University Relations, Provost & VP Academic Affairs, Vice Provost – Academic Affairs, VP – Business Affairs, VP – Information Technology, VP – Student Affairs, General Counsel, Support Staff.

Purpose:
    1.Evaluate institutional effects of emergency

2.Authorize temporary suspension of classes, or campus closure and evacuation

3.Frame emergency-specific policies as needed

4.Assure functions critical for continuity of operations are maintained

5.Address legal issues

6.Collect/analyze data from groups on the impact of the event on university operations

7.Determine and convey business resumption priorities and recovery plans

Emergency Response Resource Group

Members: Vice President in Charge, **VT Police, EHSS, University Relations**, Facilities, Risk Management, General Counsel, Technology and Computer Support, and others

Purpose:

1.Determine scope and impact of the incident

2.Prioritize emergency decisions

3.Deploy and coordinate resources and equipment

4.Provide support to emergency operations at the Incident Command Center

5.**Issue communications and warning through University Relations**

6.Monitor and continually evaluate conditions

7.Other responsibilities

The following illustrates the confusion exhibited by the investigating panel as it related to Virginia Tech's Emergency Response Plan effective on April 16, 2007.

The lack of a thorough understanding of published procedures can be seen via email communications between Phil Schaenman, President of Tri-Data, and Lenwood McCoy, a retired VT Executive who had been appointed by President Steger to serve as liaison between Virginia Tech and the Governor's panel during the investigation. On August 17, 2007, almost four months after the investigation had begun; Mr. Schaenman sent the following to Mr. McCoy;

> *"We have been over this before but I think I still have it wrong. On April 16, who was authorized to send a message as opposed to having the code to send it? Larry Hincker and the police chief for sure, the president too?"*

Mr. McCoy's reply was (in part);

"Phil, the authorization to send a message would have come from the Policy Group provided by the Emergency Response Plan. On April 16, Chief Flinchum would have needed to go through the Policy Group to get a message sent out. As Chief Flinchum reported to you, the university is planning to change the procedure to allow the Chief to send out messages directly."

After viewing the previous slide, you can see that the highlighted comments from Mr. McCoy were untrue. Specifically, it was not the Policy Group, but a group below that which had the authority to issue an alert. That group was called the Emergency Response Resource Group and, per the plan, did not require pre-approval from the President or Policy Group to issue a warning. This was the **second** emergency document that did not specifically direct anyone to receive pre-approval to send out any warning message.

It is shocking, therefore, that when the Governor authorized TriData to issue an addendum to the original panel report two years later that the facts were still incorrect. Specifically, the amended report now stated that approval to issue a campus warning would have to come from the Policy Group **ONLY**!

"However, Virginia Tech's Emergency Management Plan also contained formal emergency alert procedures and these assigned authority for releasing a warning to the Policy Group only." (Panel Report - *The Addendum* – Dec. 2009)

This document was an internal school policy that was never mentioned nor discussed in the Governor's Panel Report issued in August of 2007, or in the two addendums issued by the state.

It was first presented publicly by Virginia Tech in 2010 in their initial response to the US DOE findings that the school had violated the Clery Act. The school, through its attorneys, claimed that this policy was followed on April 16th however, it was not published in Virginia Tech's Annual Safety Report (ASR) as required per the Clery Act.

This internal policy states that in addition to police, the University Relations department will issue warnings to the campus, which was different from the school's published procedure.

"University Relations and the University Police will make the campus community aware of crimes which have occurred and necessitate caution on the

part of students and employees in a timely fashion and in such a way as to aid in the prevention of similar occurrences."

After numerous document appeals, a formal hearing before an Administrative Law Judge and additional appeals, Secretary of Education Arne Duncan upheld that Virginia Tech had committed two Clery Act violations.

First, the school failed to issue a timely warning following the initial shootings at the dormitory, and having two conflicting timely warning procedures. The US DOE also contended that neither procedure was followed as written on April 16, 2007.

The panel charged with investigating the massacre at Virginia Tech also did not identify this procedure, nor did they provide any detailed discussion of Clery Act requirements in their final investigative report issued following the massacre. Why?

Policy Group Meeting Attendees and Other Participants
Morning of April 16, 2007 Following First Shootings in Dormitory
As Recorded by Kim O'Rourke on 04/16/2007

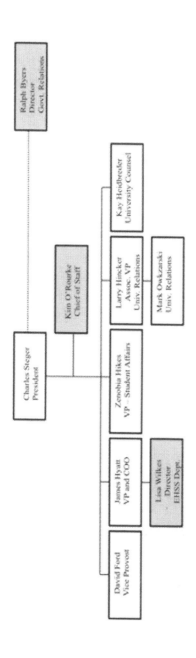

Key Witnesses Not Interviewed by the
Governor's Panel

The diagram to the on the next page summarizes some significant events that occurred the morning of April 16, 2007, and highlights (in bold) the individuals involved.

Reading from the center box and moving out, you will see that these people would have been valuable witnesses for the Governor's Panel to interview, because of their direct involvement in the horrible events of that day.

There is no real explanation as to why these key witnesses were never interviewed, other than what appears to be a desire to minimize potential legal exposure.

0715: West AJ Dorm shooting deaths of Ryan Clark & Emily Hilscher

0810: Police Chief informs Pres. details of shootings and crime scene. 0815: Policy Group meeting participants **Kim O'Rourke** and **Lisa Wilkes** privately communicate with family and babysitter relative to dorm shooting.

0816: Police begin to interview critical witness **Heather Haugh** . 0825: Policy Group meeting begins before witness interview ends.

0840: Haugh Interview ends. **Karl Thornhill** identified as "person of interest". Police told he attends Radford University. **Radford police** notified, along with other law enforcement.

0845: Policy Group meeting participant **Ralph Byers** sends private email to Laura Fornash in Richmond notifying her of shooting details but not to release information. 0940: Cho begins attack in Norris Hall across campus.

April to August: The investigating panel conducted interviews of various members of the Cook Counseling Center, except for **Dr. Robert Miller** who was the Director during the time Cho was temporarily detained. Cho's medical records were missing and not discovered until July of 2009 by **Dr. Miller**, who had been removed from his position.

Appendix B

COMPOSITE VIRGINIA TECH AND GUN VIOLENCE TIMELINE

1984   Seung Hui Cho was born in Seoul, South Korea. He had serious health problems from the time he was 9 months old until he was 3 years old.

1992   The Cho family emigrated from South Korea to Maryland.

1993   The Cho family moved to Fairfax County, Virginia.

1997   Seung Hui Cho was in the 6th grade and teachers met with his parents about his **very withdrawn behavior.**

1999 **(April 20)**   Columbine shootings—12 students, one teacher killed and 21 students wounded.

1999   One of Seung Hui Cho's papers depicted suicidal and homicidal ideations. The paper referenced and celebrated the Columbine shootings. The school requested that his parents ask a counselor to intervene, which led to a psychiatric evaluation at the Multicultural Center for Human Services. **Cho was prescribed anti-depressant mediation.** He responded well and was taken off the medication approximately one year later.

2000	Seung Hui Cho began his sophomore year at Westfield High School. After a review by a local screening committee, **he was diagnosed as having an emotional disability and was enrolled in an Individual Education Plan (IEP) to deal with shyness and lack of responsiveness in a classroom setting.**
2002 **(January 16)**	Appalachian School of Law shootings—one student, one professor, and the dean were killed. Three students were wounded.
2003 **(Spring)**	Seung Hui Cho graduated from Westfield High School with a 3.5 GPA in the Honors Program. **He decided to attend Virginia Tech against the advice of his parents and counselors who thought the school was too big and he would not get adequate individualized attention.**
2003 **(Fall)**	Seung Hui Cho entered Virginia Tech as a business information systems major. He had a difficult time with his roommate over neatness issues and changed rooms.
2004 **(Fall)**	**Seung Hui Cho began his sophomore year and moved off campus.** He complained of mites in his apartment, but doctors told him it was acne and prescribed minocycline. He became interested in writing. His sister noted his growing passion for writing, though he was secretive about content. He submitted a book idea to a publishing house.
2005 **(Spring)**	Seung Hui Cho requested to change his major to English. He submitted an idea for a book to a publishing house; it was rejected.
2005 **(Fall)**	**Seung Hui Cho started his junior year and moved back into a dormitory on campus.** Cho was taken to some parties by his suitemates. **On one occasion he stabbed at the carpet in Margaret Bowman's room with a knife in the presence of others.**

2005 **(October 15)** **Professor Nikki Giovanni wrote a letter to Cho expressing concern about his behavior in her class and about the violence in his writing. Professor Giovanni asked the head of English Department, Professor Lucinda Roy, to remove Cho from her class.**

2005 **(October 18)** **Professor Roy informed Mary Ann Lewis, Associate Dean of Liberal Arts and Human Sciences, and others that Cho read a violent and upsetting poem in class that day, and that her students told her Cho had been surreptitiously taking photos of them. Dr. Roy also said she had contacted Tom Brown, the Dean of Student Affairs; Zenobia Hikes, Vice President of Student Affairs; Detective George Jackson at the Virginia Tech Police Department; and Dr. Robert Miller at the Cook Counseling Center to report the incident and seek advice. Roy said she could remove Cho as long as there is a viable alternative. The Cook Counseling Center advised that though the poem was disturbing, there was no specific threat.** They suggested that Cho be referred to the counseling center. Frances Keene, Director of Judicial Affairs, and Tom Brown both wrote to Professor Roy to advise Cho that any future similar behavior would be referred to Judicial Affairs.

2005 **(October 19)** **Professor Cho and Cheryl Ruggiero met with Cho regarding his situation in Professor Giovanni's class. They discussed the impact of his writing on the class, and warned him that unauthorized picture-taking was inappropriate and was taken seriously by the school.** Cho said his writing was intended as satire and agreed not to take any more photos of classmates or professors. Cho was advised of the study alternative. He also was advised to seek counseling. This was reiterated in an email to Cho following the meeting. Cho was removed from Dr. Giovanni's class and Professor Roy tutored him one-on-one with the assistance of Professor Frederick D'Aguiar. Cho refused to go to counseling. Professor Roy informed the Division of Student Affairs, the

Cook Counseling Center, the Schiffert Health center, the Virginia Tech Police, and the College of Liberal Arts and Human Sciences of the arrangements made for Cho. **Cho's problems and his removal from Professor Giovanni's class were discussed at a meeting of Virginia Tech's Care Team. The Care Team considered the problem solved.**

2005 **(November 2) Cho's roommates and dorm residents think Cho set fires in the dorm lounge and said in e-mails that they reported it to the police. No written police report exists.**

2005 **(November 27) Jennifer Nelson, a resident of West Ambler Johnston (WAJ) resident hall, filed a report with the Virginia Tech police indicating that Cho had made "annoying" contacts with her via the Internet, by phone, and in person. The police interviewed Cho, but Nelson declined to press charges. She did say however that she would testify at a disciplinary hearing.** The investigating officer referred the incident to the school's disciplinary system, the Office of Judicial Affairs. The Office of Judicial Affairs later contacted Nelson, telling her they can only proceed if she files a written complaint. She declined and no hearing was held.

2005 **(November 30) Cho called the Cook Counseling Center following his interaction with the police and was triaged on the phone.**

2005 **(December 6) E-mails among Resident Advisors (RAs) reflected complaints by another female student, Christina Lillizu, who lived on the 3rd floor of Cochrane resident hall, regarding derogatory Instant Messages with foul language sent by Cho under various strange aliases. The RAs also reported the incidents of IMs Cho sent to Jennifer Nelson, and his visit in disguise to her dorm room. Lisa Virga, a resident advisor, sent an e-mail to Rohsaan Settle, a member of the Residence Life staff, detailing a list of complaints about Cho, including reports that he had knives in his room.** Virga was concerned that no one in the dormitory had confronted Cho directly and she thought someone should talk to him. Settle responded with an e-mail to Virga saying they should chat about the knives.

2005 **(December 9) Cho sent unwanted Instant Messages to a third female student, Margaret Bowman. Later he left messages on her marker board outside her room.**

2005 **(December 11) Cho left a new message, a quote from Shakespeare, on Bowman's marker board.**

2005 **(December 12) Bowman returned from an exam and found more text added to the message from the day before. She then filed a report with the Virginia Tech police complaining of multiple "disturbing" contacts from Cho. She requested that Cho have no further contacts with her. When questioned by students about the notes to Bowman, Cho said "Shakespeare did it." Cho called and cancelled a 2:00 p.m. appointment at the Cook Counseling Center, but then called back and was triaged on the telephone a second time.**

2005 **(December 13)** Virginia Tech police notified Cho that he was to have no further contact with Bowman. Cho's suitemate received a message from **Cho saying, "I might as well kill myself now."** The suitemate notified the campus police. The police took Cho to the Virginia Tech Police Department where a pre-screener from the New River Valley Community Services Board **evaluated him "an imminent to self and others."** A magistrate issued a temporary detaining order, and Cho was taken to Carilion St. Albans Psychiatric Hospital for overnight stay and mental evaluation. **No one contacted Cho's parents.**

2005 **(December 14)** (7:00 a.m.) The person assigned as an independent evaluator, psychologist Roy Crouse, evaluated Cho and concluded that **he did not present an imminent danger to himself.**

2005 **(December 14)** (prior to 11:00 a.m.) A staff psychiatrist at St. Alban's evaluated Cho and concluded he was not a danger to himself or others and recommended outpatient counseling. **He gathered no collateral information.**

2005 **(December 14)** (11:00-11:30 a.m.) **Special Justice Paul M. Barnett conducted Cho's commitment hearing and ruled in accordance with the independent evaluator, but ordered follow-up treatment as an outpatient. Cho made an appointment with the Cook Counseling Center and was released.**

2005 **(December 14)** (Noon) The St. Alban's staff psychiatrist dictated in his evaluation summary that "there is no indication of psychosis, delusions, suicidal or homicidal ideation." The psychiatrist found that "his insight and judgment are normal ... Follow-up and aftercare to be arranged at Virginia Tech; medications, none."

2005 **(December 14)** (2:35 p.m.) **Cook Counseling Center received a fax from Carilion Health System with copies of St. Alban's discharge summary and the Pre-admission Screening Form completed by the Community Services Board evaluator the previous day at police Headquarters.**

2005 **(December 14)** (3:00 p.m.) Cho appeared for his appointment at the Cook Counseling Center (for the third time in 15 days). Dr. Miller, the Cook Counseling Center director, received an e-mail notifying him that Cho had been taken to St. Alban's the previous night. Dr. Miller e-mails the Cook Counseling Center staff to alert them "in case this student is seen" at the Center. A Cook Counseling Center staff member e-mailed back that Cho already had been seen in the afternoon.

2006 **January** The Cook Counseling Center received a psychiatric summary from St. Albans. **Neither the Cook Counseling Center or the Care Team take any action to follow up on Cho.**

2006 **February** Dr. Miller was removed from his position following a management study of the Cook Counseling Center. **In**

his hurry to vacate the office, Miller packed Cho's
file and the files of several other students in a box
and took them home. (This was only discovered in
July, 2009 after 30 families had reached a
settlement with state.)

2006 **April**   Cho's technical writing professor, Carl Bean,
suggested that Cho drop his class after repeated
efforts to address shortcomings in class and
inappropriate choice of writing assignments. Cho
followed the professor to his office, raised his voice
angrily, and was asked to leave. Professor Bean
did not report the incident to Virginia Tech
officials.

2006 **Spring**   Cho took Professor Bob Hicok's creative writing class.
Professor Hicok later characterized Cho's writing as not
particularly unique as far as subject matter is concerned,
but remarkable for violence.

2006 **Fall**   Cho enrolled in a playwriting workshop taught by
Professor Ed Falco. **Cho wrote a play about a young
man who hated the students at his school and
plans to kill them and himself. The writing
contained parallels to the subsequent events of
April 16, 2007, as well as the recorded message to
NBC that same day.** Professor Falco conferred with
Professors Roy and Norris, who told him that in the
fall of 2005 and in 2006, Professor Roy and Professor
Norris respectively, had alerted Associate Dean Mary
Ann Lewis about Cho and his behavior.

2006 **(September 6-12)** Professor Lisa Norris, another of Cho's writing
professors, alerted Associate Dean Mary Ann Lewis but
the dean "finds no mention of mental health issues or
police reports" on Cho. **Professor Norris encouraged
Cho to go to counseling with her but he declined.**

2006 **(September 26- November 4)** Cho wrote three more violent stories
for an English class.

2007 **(February 2) Cho ordered a .22 caliber Walther P22 handgun
online from TGSCOM, Inc.**

2007 **(February 9)** **Cho picked up a handgun from J-N-D Pawnbrokers in Blacksburg, across the street from Virginia Tech.**

2007 **(March12)** Cho rented a van from Enterprise Rent-A-Car at the Roanoke Regional Airport, which he kept for almost a month. (Cho videotaped some of his subsequently released diatribe in the van.)

2007 **(March 13)** **Cho bought a 9mm Glock 19 handgun and a box of 50 9mm full metal jacket practice rounds at Roanoke Firearms.** Cho waited the 30 days between gun purchases as required by Virginia law. The store conducted the required background check by police, who found no record of Cho's mental health issues.

2007 **(March 22)** Cho went to PSS Range and Training, an indoor pistol range, and spent an hour practicing.

2007 **(March 22)** **Cho bought two 10-round magazines for the Walther P22 on eBay.**

2007 **(March 23)** **Cho bought three additional 10-round magazines from another eBay seller.**

2007 **(March 31)** **Cho bought additional ammunition magazines, ammunition and a hunting knife from Wal-Mart and Dick's Sporting Goods. He bought chains from Home Depot.**

2007 **(April 7)** **Cho bought more ammunition.**

2007 **(April 8)** Cho spent the night at the Hampton Inn in Christiansburg, Virginia (a town adjacent to Blacksburg) videotaping segments of his manifesto-like diatribe. **Cho bought more ammunition.**

2007 **(April 13)** Anonymous bomb threats were made to Torgersen, Durham, and Whittemore halls. The threats were assessed by the Virginia Tech police and the buildings were evacuated. There was no lockdown or cancellation of classes elsewhere on campus. (Later, during the investigation of the April 16, massacre, no evidence was found linking these threats to Cho's bomb threat note in Norris Hall—based, in part, on handwriting samples.)

2007 **(April 14)**   An Asian male wearing a hooded garment was seen by a faculty member in Norris Hall. The faculty member later told police that one of her students had told her the **doors were chained. This may have been Cho practicing. Cho bought more ammunition.**

2007 **(April 15)**   Cho placed his weekly Sunday night call to his family in Fairfax County. They report the conversation was normal and Cho said nothing that caused them concern.

* * *

2007 **(April 16)**   (5:00 a.m.) One of Cho's suitemates noticed he is awake and on his computer.

2007 **(April 16)**   (around 5:30 a.m.) One of Cho's suitemates noticed Cho is clad in boxer shorts and a shirt brushing his teeth and putting on acne medicine. Cho returned from the bathroom, got dressed and left.

2007 **(April 16)**   (around 6:45 a.m.) Cho was spotted by a student loitering in the foyer area of West Ambler Johnston Hall, between the exterior door and the locked door. He had access to the mailbox foyer, but not to the interior of the building.

2007 **(April 16)**   (around 7:02 a.m.) Emily Hilscher enters West Ambler Johnston Hall, after being dropped off by her boyfriend, Karl Thornhill. (The time is based on her swipe card record.)

2007 **(April 16)**   (around 7:15 a.m.) **Cho shot Ryan Christopher Clark (an RA whose room is next to Emily's). Clark apparently came to investigate noises in Emily's room. Cho then shot Emily Hilscher who had sought refuge under her bed.** Both of the victims' wounds proved fatal. (Ryan died almost instantly, Emily died after being evacuated to a Roanoke trauma care hospital.) Cho exited the crime scene leaving bloody footprints and shell casings.

2007 **(April 16)**   (7:17 a.m.) **Cho's access card was swiped at Harper Hall, which was near West Ambler Johnston and was Cho's dormitory. He went to his room to change out of his bloody clothing,** canceled his computer account, and made preparations for his rampage.

2007 **(April 16)**   (7:20 a.m.) **The Virginia Tech Police Department received a call on their administrative line reporting that a woman in room 4040 of West Ambler Johnston Hall may have fallen from her bed.** The caller was given the information from another student whose room is near room 4040.

2007 **(April 16)**   (7:21 a.m.) **A Virginia Tech Police dispatcher notified the Virginia Tech Rescue Squad that a female student may have fallen from her bed in room 4040 of West Ambler Johnston Hall.**

2007 **(April 16)**   (7:22 a.m.) **A Virginia Tech Police officer was dispatched to room 4040 West Ambler Johnston Hall to accompany the Virginia Tech Rescue Squad**—this is standard operating procedure.

2007 **(April 16)**   (7:24 a.m.) **A Virginia Tech police officer arrived at West Ambler Johnston Hall and found two people shot in the room,** and immediately requested additional police resources.

2007 **(April 16)**   (7:25 a.m.) Cho accessed his university e-mail accounts and erased all his files.

2007 **(April 16)**   (7:26 a.m.) The police dispatcher was advised that there were two gun shot victims.

2007 **(April 16)**   (7:29 a.m.) Virginia Tech Rescue Squad 3 arrived at room 4040 West Ambler Johnston Hall.

2007 **(April 16)**	Additional Virginia Tech Police officers began arriving at the crime scene in West Ambler Johnston Hall. **They secured the crime scene in an effort to lock down the dormitory,** with police inside and outside. The police started their preliminary investigation. Interviews with residents failed to produce a description of the suspect. No one on Hilscher's floor in the dormitory saw anyone leave room 4040 after the initial noise was heard. **A housekeeper in Burruss Hall told Dr. Ed Spencer, Associate Vice President for Student Affairs and member of the Policy Group, that an RA in West Ambler Johnston Hall has been murdered. (The housekeeper received a call from a housekeeper in the dormitory.)**
2007 **(April 16)**	(7:35 am) Police on the scene say they need a detective.
2007 **(April 16)**	(7:40 a.m.) **Virginia Tech Police Chief Flinchum was notified by phone of the shootings in the dormitory.** Chief Flinchum tried repeatedly to reach the Office of the Executive Vice President.
2007 **(April 16)**	(7:51 a.m.) Chief Flinchum contacted the Blacksburg Police Department and requested one of their evidence technicians as well as a detective to assist with the investigation.
2007 **(April 16)**	(7:55 a.m.) **Dr. Ed Spencer arrived at West Ambler Johnston H**all after walking from Burruss Hall. He called Zenobia Hikes.
2007 **(April 16)**	(7:57 a.m.) Chief Flinchum got through to the Virginia Tech Office of the Executive Vice President and notified them of the shootings.
2007 **(April 16)**	(8:00 a.m.) **Classes began. Chief Flinchum arrived at West Ambler Johnston Hall** and found Virginia Tech Police Department and Blacksburg Police Department detectives on the scene. A local special agent of the Virginia State Police had been contacted and was responding to the scene. The Tech and Blacksburg police began to "process" the crime scene. They canvass the dorm for possible witnesses, search

interior and exterior waste containers and surrounding areas near the dormitory for evidence. They also canvass the rescue squad for additional evidence or information.

2007 **(April 16)** (around 8:00 a.m.) **The Virginia Tech Center for Professional and Continuing Education locked down on its own.**

2007 **(April 16)** (8:10 a.m.) **President Charles Steger was notified by a secretary that there had been a shooting. He told her to get Chief Flinchum on the phone.**

2007 **(April 16)** (8:11 a.m.) **Chief Flinchum talked to President Steger on the phone and reported one student was critical, one was fatally wounded, and <u>the incident seemed to be domestic in nature</u>. He reported no weapon found and there were bloody footprints (leading away from the crime scene—<u>this point was not made in the timeline of the Governor's Review Panel Report</u>). President Steger told Chief Flinchum to keep him informed. A staff member discussed the shootings; President Steger decided to convene the Policy Group no later than 8:30 a.m.**

2007 **(April 16)** (8:11 a.m.) Blacksburg Police Chief Kim Crannis arrived at the crime scene.

2007 **(April 16)** (8:13 a.m.) Chief Flinchum requested additional Virginia Tech Police Department and Blacksburg Police Department officered to assist in securing West Ambler Johnston Hall entrances and with the investigation. He also ordered the recall of all off-shift personnel.

2007 **(April 16)** (8:14 a.m.) **Emily Hilscher's roommate, Heather Haugh, arrived at West Ambler Johnston Hall.**

2007 **(April 16)** (8:15 a.m.) Chief Flinchum requested the Virginia Tech Police Department Emergency Team respond to the scene and then to stage in Blacksburg in the event an arrest or search warrant is to be executed.

2007 **(April 16)**   (about 8:15 a.m.) **Two senior officials of Virginia Tech had conversations with family members in which the shootings was discussed.** In one conversation, the official advised her son, a student at Tech, to go to class. In the other, the official arranged for extended babysitting.

2007 **(April 16)**   (8:16 am-8:40 a.m.) **Hilscher's roommate, Heather Haugh, was interviewed by detectives.** She told them that on Monday mornings Emily's boyfriend, Karl Thornhill, usually drops Emily off and then goes on to Radford University. She told the detectives that Thornhill owns a gun and practices shooting. Police then sought Thornhill as a person of interest. **(Note: University President Charles Steger would tell a press conference a press conference at 7:40 p.m.— some 12 hours after the double homicide—that he was told at there was a "person of interest" at 7:30 a.m. and that was part of the excuse for not warning the campus. In fact,** *no "person of interest" was identified until sometime between 8:30 a.m. and 8:40 a.m.***)** Thornhill's vehicle was not found on the campus and officers assumed he had left the school. Virginia Tech and Blacksburg police were sent to Thornhill's home; he was not there. The Thornhill home was put under surveillance.

2007 **(April 16)**   (8:16 am-9:24 a.m.) The police continued canvassing West Ambler Johnston for possible witnesses. The Virginia Tech Police, the Blacksburg Police Department, and the Virginia State Police continued processing Hilscher's room gathering evidence. Investigators identified the two victims. Police allowed students to leave to 9:00 a.m. classes in Norris Hall. **(This last sentence is misleading. The lock down was apparently in place at West Ambler Johnston Hall** *after* **9:00 a.m. Two students pleaded with the police** *after 9:00 a.m.* **to be allowed to leave the dormitory. Those two, Henry Lee and Rachael Hill, were killed in the French class in Norris Hall. The police agreed to break the lock down and allowed them to go to class. Lee and Hill arrived just moments before Cho entered the Madame**

Couture-Nowak's classroom.) The Policy Group convened to plan how to notify students of the double homicide. **Police canceled bank deposit pickups.** Chief Flinchum told President Steger in a phone update that Hilscher's boyfriend was a "person of interest" and probably off campus. **(Note: Remember, President Steger would tell a press conference some 12 hours later that he was told there _was_ a "person of interest" at 7:30 a.m. The false 7:30 a.m. time would become part of the excuse for not warning the campus.) A Policy Group member notified the Governor's office of the double homicide.** Phone calls were made from the Blacksburg Police Department to its units and to the Montgomery County Sheriff's Office and Radford University police to be on the lookout for Thornhill's vehicle. A Policy Group member e-mailed a Richmond colleague saying one student was dead and another critically wounded. "Gunman on the loose," he said, adding, "This is not releasable yet." **The same Policy Group member reminded his Richmond** colleague, **"just try to make sure it doesn't get out."** First period classes ended. The Policy Group began composing a notice to university about the West Ambler Johnston shootings. The Associate Vice President for University Relations, Larry Hincker, was unable to send the message at first Due to difficulties with the alert system.

2007 **(April 16)**   (8:19 a.m.) Chief Crannis requested the Blacksburg Emergency Response Team respond.

2007 **(April 16)**   (8:20 a.m.) A person fitting Cho's description was seen near Duck Pond on campus.

2007 **(April 16)**   (8:25 a.m.) The Policy Group convened to plan how to notify students of the double homicide. Police canceled bank deposits and pickups.

2007 **(April 16)**   (8:40 a.m.) Chief Flinchum told President Steger in a phone update that Hilscher's boyfriend was a person of interest and probably off campus. **(Note: President Steger will tell a press conference some 10 hours later that he was told of the "person of interest"** over an hour earlier and that is part of the excuse for not warning the campus. Steger has never explained the press conference lie.) A Policy Group member notified the Governor's office of the double homicide.

2007 **(April 16)**   (8:40 am-8:45 a.m.) Phone calls were made from the Blacksburg Police Department to its units and to the Montgomery County Sheriff's Office and Radford University police to be on the lookout for Thornhill's vehicle.

2007 **(April 16)**   (8:45 a.m.) A Policy Group member e-mailed a Richmond colleague saying one student is dead and another critically wounded. "Gunman is on the loose," he says, adding, "This is not releasable yet."

2007 **(April 16)**   (8:49 a.m.) The same Policy Group member reminded his Richmond colleague **"just try to make sure it doesn't get out."**

2007 **(April 16)**   (8:50 a.m.) **First period classes ended.** The Policy Group member began composing a notice to the university about the shootings in West Ambler Johnston Hall. The Associate Vice President for University Relations, Larry Hincker, was unable to send the message at first due to technical difficulties with the alert system.

2007 **(April 16)**   (8:52 a.m.) **Blacksburg Public Schools locked down until further information is available about the incident at Virginia Tech. The school superintendent notified the school board of this action by e-mail. The Executive Director of Government Relations, Ralph Byers, directed that the doors to his office be locked.** His office is adjacent to the school President's suite, but the four doors to the President's suite remain open.

2007 **(April 16)**   (9:00 am-9:15 a.m.) **Virginia Tech veterinary college locked down.**

2007 **(April 16)**   (9:01 a.m.) Cho mailed a package from Blacksburg post office to NBC news in New York that contained pictures of Cho holding weapons, an 1,800-word rambling diatribe, and video clips in which he expressed rage, resentment, and a desire to get even with oppressors. He alluded to a coming massacre. Cho prepared this material during the previous weeks. The videos were a performance of the enclosed writings. Cho also mailed a letter to the English Department attacking Professor Carl Bean, with whom he had previously argued.

2007 **(April 16)**   (9:05 a.m.) **Second period classes begin in Norris Hall. Virginia Tech trash pick-up is cancelled.**

2007 **(April 16)**   (9:15 a.m.) Both police Emergency Response Teams were staged at the Blacksburg Police Department in anticipation of executing search warrants or making arrests.

2007 **(April 16)**   (9:15 am-9:30 a.m.) Cho was seen outside and then inside Norris Hall (an engineering building) by several students. He was familiar with the building because one of his classes was there. **Cho chained the doors shut on three public entrances from the inside. No one reported seeing him. A faculty member found a bomb threat note attached to an inner door near one of the chained exterior doors. She gave the note to a janitor who hand carried it to the Engineering School dean's office on the third floor.** A Virginia Tech police captain joined the Policy Group as a police liaison and provided updates as information becomes available. He reported one gunman at large, possibly on foot.

2007 **(April 16)**   (9:26 a.m.) **Virginia Tech administration sent an e-mail to campus staff, faculty, and students informing them of a dormitory shooting "incident." The message contained no specifics, no one was made aware that one student had been killed and another seriously wounded, and there was no hint that a killer might have been roaming** the campus. *The gravity of the situation and seriousness of the threat was played down.*

2007 **(April 16)**   (about 9:30 a.m.) Radford University Police had received a request from the Blacksburg Police Department to look up Thornhill's class schedule and find him in class. Before they could do this, they get a second call that he has been stopped on the road.

2007 **(April 16)**   (9:30 am) The Police passed information to the Policy Group that it was unlikely that Hilscher's boyfriend, Karl Thornhill, was the shooter (though he remained a person of interest).

2007 **(April 16)**   (9:31 am-9:48 a.m.) A Virginia State Police trooper arrived at the traffic stop of Thornhill and helped question him. A gunpowder residue test was performed and packaged for lab analysis. (There was no immediate result from this type of test in the field.)

2007 **(April 16)**   (9:40 am-9:51 a.m.) **Cho began shooting in room 206 in Norris Hall, where a graduate engineering class in Advanced Hydrology was underway. Cho killed Professor G.V. Loganathan. He killed 9 students and wounded 3 others. There were a total of 13 students in the class. Cho went across the hall to room 207 and entered an elementary German class. He shot and killed the instructor, Christopher James Bishop and then turned his gun on the students in the front row. He then went down the aisle and methodically shot others. Cho left the classroom and went back into the hall. Michael Pohle, Jr. and Nicole White were sitting in the front row next to each other. They were among the first students to be killed. Students in room 205, attending Haiyan Cheng's class on Issues In Scientific Computing, heard Cho's gunshots. (Cheng was a graduate assistant substituting for the professor that day.) The students barricaded the door and prevented Cho from entering despite the fact that he fired through the door. In room 211, Madame Jocelyne Couture-Nowak's French class, the students and instructor heard the gunfire. Colin**

Goddard calls 911. A student told the teacher to put a desk in front of the door—which was done. Cho managed to push the door open. He again began his methodical slaughter walked up and down the rows of students. Emily Haas picked up a cell phone and called the police, telling them to come quickly. Cho hears Haas and shot her twice in the head (she will survive). Heroically, Haas played dead and kept the cell phone hidden with the line open. Cho said nothing upon entering the room or during the shooting. (Three students who pretended to be dead survived). *Two students, Rachael Hill and Henry Lee, whom the police allowed to leave West Ambler Johnston Hall despite a lock-down, were killed. The Governor's Review Panel Report glosses over this critical point.*

2007 **(April 16)**   (9:41 a.m.) **The Blacksburg Police dispatcher received a call regarding the shooting at Norris Hall.** The dispatcher initially had difficulty understanding the location of the shooting. Once identified as being on campus, the call was transferred to the Virginia Tech Police Department.

2007 **(April 16)**   (9:42 a.m.) **The 911 all reporting shots fired at Norris Hall reached the Virginia Tech Police Department.** A message was sent to all county EMS units to staff and respond.

2007 **(April 16)**   (9:45 a.m.) **The first police officers arrived at Norris Hall, a three-minute response time from their receipt of the call.** Hearing shots, they paused briefly to check whether they were being fired upon, then rushed to one entrance, and then another but found the doors were chained shut. An attempt to shoot open the chain or lock on one door failed.

2007 **(April 16)**   (about 9:45 a.m.) The police informed the school administration that there had been another shooing. Virginia Tech President Steger heard sounds like gunshots, and saw police running toward Norris Hall. **In the German class in room 207, two injured students and two uninjured students go the door** and hold it shut with their feet and hands, keeping their bodies away. Within two minutes Cho returned. He beat on the door and opened it an inch and fired shots around the door handle, then gave up trying to get into the room. Cho returned to room 211, the French class, and went up one aisle and down another shooting people again. Cho shot Colin Goddard two more times. A janitor saw Cho in the hall on the second floor loading his gun; the janitor fled downstairs. Cho tried to enter room 204 where engineering professor Liviu Librescu was teaching mechanics. Professor Librescu braced his body against the door yelling for students to head to the window. He was shot through the door and killed, but his heroic action saved lives. Students pushed screens and jump or dropped to the grass and bushes below. Ten students escaped this way. The next two students were Shot. Cho again returned to room 206 (the Advanced Hydrology class) and shot more students.

2007 **(April 16)**   (9:50 a.m.) **Using a shotgun, police opened the ordinary key lock of a Norris Hall entrance that went to the machine shop and that could not be chained. These officers heard gunshots as they entered the building. The police immediately followed the sounds to the second floor. Triage and rescue of victims began. A second e-mail was sent by administration to all Virginia Tech e-mail addresses that "A gunman is Loose on campus. Stay in buildings until further notice. Stay away from all windows." Four outside loudspeakers broadcast a similar massage. Virginia Tech and Blacksburg police ERTs arrived at Norris Hall, including one paramedic with each team.**

2007 **(April 16)**   (9:51 a.m.) **Cho had returned to the French class in room 211 for the third time. He killed himself with a shot to the head just as police reached the second floor. Investigators believed that the shotgun blast, when the police entered the building, alerted Cho to their presence Cho's shooting spree in Norris**

Hall lasted 11 minutes. He fired 174 rounds, and killed 30 people in Norris Hall plus himself and would 17 others. The first team of officers began securing the second floor and aiding survivors from multiple classrooms. They also get a preliminary description of the suspected gunman, and tried to determine if there are additional gunman.

2007 (April 16)   (9:52 a.m.) The police cleared the second floor of Norris Hall. Two tactical medics attached to the Emergency Response Teams, one medic from the Virginia Tech Rescue and one from Blacksburg Rescue, were allowed to enter to start their triage.

2007 (April 16)   (9:53 a.m.) The 9:42 a.m. request for all EMS units was repeated.

2007 (April 16)   (10:08 a.m.) A deceased male student was discovered by the police. The police suspected he was the gunman:

- No identification was found on the body.
- He appeared to have a self-inflicted gunshot wound to the head.
- He was found among his victims in classroom 211, the French class.
- Two weapons were found near his body.

2007 (April 16)   (10:17 a.m.) A third e-mail from the school administration canceled all classes and advised people to stay where they were.

2007 (April 16)   (10:51 a.m.) All patients from Norris Hall had been transported to a hospital or moved to a minor treatment unit.

2007 (April 16)   (10:52 a.m.) A fourth e-mail from the Virginia Tech administration warned of "a multiple shooting with multiple victims in Norris Hall," saying "the shooter is in custody" and that as a routine procedure police were searching for a second shooter.

2007 **(April 16)** (10:57 a.m.) **A report of shots fired at the tennis courts near Cassell Coliseum proved false.**

2007 **(April 16)** (12:42 a.m.) **Virginia Tech President Charles Steger announced that the police were releasing people from buildings and that counseling centers were being established.**

2007 **(April 16)** (1:35 p.m.) **A report of another gunshot near Duck Pond proved to be another false alarm.**

2007 **(April 16)** (4:01 p.m.) **President George W. Bush spoke to the Nation from the White House regarding the shooting.**

2007 **(April 16)** (5:00 p.m.) **The first deceased victim was transported to the medical examiners office.**

2007 **(April 16)** (8:45 p.m.) **The last deceased victim was transported to the medical examiner's office.**

2007 **(April 16)** (Evening) **Police continued to investigate whether Karl Thornhill, Emily Hilscher's boyfriend, was linked to her murder and that of Ryan Clark because the ballistics analysis that later tied together the West Ambler Johnston and Norris Hall killings (confirming that Cho's guns were used in both) was not yet completed.** *The Governor's Review Panel Report incorrectly said that the Emergency Response Team, including Virginia Tech and Montgomery County Police, entered Thornhill's home and searched it. In fact, the search took place sometime mid-afternoon around 3:00 p.m. Furthermore, the Governor's report fails to mention that the searchers probably violated the law by not showing the Thornhill's their search warrant before entering the Thornhill home.* **The Governor's Review Panel Report then said, "The ERT searches his residence. Using standard** procedures the ERT members handcuff Thornhill and his family who have come to console him. They were put on the floor while the search was made, because Thornhill was known to own firearms. The search was highly upsetting to Thornhill and his family." *(The Review Panel Report appears to be making excuses for sloppy police work because by this time Thornhill was no longer "a person of interest." Handcuffing the whole family and making them lie face down on the floor some six hours after the murderer ha been apprehended appears excessive.)*

2007 **(April 17)**   (9:15 a.m.) **The Virginia Tech Police Department released the name of the shooter as Seung Hui Cho and confirmed 33 fatalities between the two shootings.**

2007 **(April 17)**   (9:30 a.m.) **Virginia Tech announced that classes will be cancelled "for the remainder of the week to allow students time they need to grieve and seek assistance as needed."**

2007 **(April 17)**   (11:00 a.m.) **A family assistance center was established at The Inn at Virginia Tech.**

2007 **(April 17)**   (2:00 p.m.) **A convocation ceremony was held for the university community at the Cassell Coliseum. Speakers included President George W. Bush, Virginia Governor Tim Kaine (who had returned from Japan), Virginia Tech President Charles W. Steger, Virginia Tech Vice President for Student Affairs Zenobia L. Hikes, local religious leaders (representing the Muslin, Buddhist, Jewish, and Christian communities), Provost Dr. Mark G. McNamee, Dean of Students Tom Brown, Counselor Dr. Christopher Glynn, and poet Nikki Giovanni.**

2007 **(April 17)**   (8:00 p.m.) **A candlelight vigil was held on the Virginia Tech drill field.**

2007 **(April 17)**   (11:30 p.m.) **The first autopsy was completed.**

2007 **(April 18)**   (8:25 a.m.) **A SWAT team entered Burruss Hall, a campus building next to Norris Hall, responding to a "suspicious event," which proved to be false alarm. Tech President Steger's office was in Burruss Hall.**

2007 **(April 18)**   (4:37 p.m.) **Local police announced that NBC News in New York just received by mail a package containing images of Cho holding weapons, his writings, and his video recordings. NBC immediately submitted this information to the FBI. A fragment of the video and pictures was widely broadcast.**

2007 **(April 19)**   Virginia Tech announced that all students who were killed would be granted posthumous degrees in the fields in which they were studying. The degrees were subsequently awarded to the families at the regular commencement exercises, or privately, or in one case, at a Corps of Cadets event in the Fall of 2007. Governor Kaine appointed an independent Virginia Tech Review Panel to review the shootings. Autopsies on all the victims were completed by the medical examiner. The autopsy of Cho found no brain function abnormalities and no toxic substances, drugs, or alcohol that could explain the rampage.

2007 **(April 20)**   **Governor Kaine declared a statewide day of mourning.**

2008 **(February 14)** Northern Illinois shootings—four were killed and 21 others were wounded.

FY 2009-FY 2011 Virginia spent $424.3 million on mental health in 2009, but despite the pledges made after Virginia Tech, to increase spending on mental health, that figure dropped to $385.5 million in FY 2011. Virginia ran a $311.00 surplus in its general fund in FY 2011.

2010 **(January 14)** Virginia State Senator John Edwards introduced a bill to amend and tighten school security. The Virginia

House of Delegates watered the bill down so that the state's college and university presidents do not have to understand the contents of their school's security plans. Virginia Tech employee and then-member of the House of Delegates, David Nutter, refused to vote for the bill in any form.

2011 **(January 8)** Tucson shootings—six were killed and 18 others were wounded including U.S. Representative Gabrielle Giffords. Speaker of the House John Boehner told the media now is not the time to discuss ways to curb gun violence.

2012 **(April 16)** Members of the Brady Campaign met with House Majority Leader (R-Va.) Eric Cantor on the fifth anniversary of the Virginia Tech shooting. Cantor told those gathered he would not allow a vote on a bill calling for stronger background checks in order to buy a gun because it was sponsored by a Democrat. Senator David Vitter (R-La.) declined to meet with the Brady Campaign members, claiming he was too busy.

2012 **(July 20)** Aurora movie theater shootings—12 were killed and 58 others were wounded.

2012 **(August 5)** Sheikh Temple shootings in Oak Creek, Wisconsin— six were killed and four were wounded.

2012 **(December 12)** Clackaman Town Center Mall, Portland, Oregon shootings--two dead.

2012 **(December 14)** Sandy Hook Elementary School, Newtown, Connecticut, 20 first graders and six teachers and school staff were murdered.

2013 **(December 13)** A male student carried a shotgun into Arapahoe High school in Centennial, Colorado and opened fire, killing a 15 year old girl and then himself.

2014 **(January 13)** A retired Tampa police captain shot and killed a 43 year old father in a Wesley Chapel, Florida movie theater in a dispute over texting.

2014 **(January 14)** A 12 year old boy wounded two students at a Roswell, New Mexico middle school.

2014 **(January 16)** A gunman killed two women inside an Indiana grocery store.

2014 **(January 17)** A young male opened fire inside a Philadelphia, Pennsylvania high school gymnasium wounding two 15 year old students.

INDEX

A

Active Shooter Course   279

Addendum, The   28, 53, 55, 57, 60, 63, 67, 79, 98, 112, 113, 115-116, 120, 121, 123, 132, 135-136, 139, 153, 176, 179, 316

Al Jazeera 12

Al Qa'ida   306

Amada, Dr. Gerald   157-158

Alameddine, Lynnette   iii, 269-273

Alameddine, Ross   iii, 82, 269-273

Alexander, Judge William   230-231, 294-295

American Civil Liberties Union (ACLU)   43

Anacostia Senior High School   8

Anderson, Kristina   80, 85-86

Appalachian School of Law   iv, 1, 8, 13 16, 19, 47, 68, 79, 92-93, 111, 161-162, 170-172, 174, 190, 208, 209-216, 257, 275, 284, 288, 290-291, 297, 299, 307, 322

Armstrong High School   7

Ashley, Ross Truett   192

Aurora, Colorado   266, 292, 296, 307, 344

Austin Preparatory School   271-272

Aylor, Moody   260

B

Bagai, Sumeet, President, Student Government Association, Virginia Tech 197

Bailey, Colorado   8

Barnett, Paul M., Special Justice 50, 326

Bertin, Joan, National Coalition Against Censorship   204

Beach High School   7

Beamer, Frank, Virginia Tech head football coach   185, 309

Bean, Carl, Professor 32, 51, 65, 327, 336
Bethel, Alaska 6
Betzel, Cathye, licensed clinical psychologist 60-61, 68, 179
Bickel, Robert 14, 244, 282
Bishop, Christopher James 75, 82, 106, 107, 337
The Black Swan 163
Blacksburg Police Department (BPD) 27, 30-33, 35, 42, 73, 74, 82, 247, 331-337
Blacksburg Public Schools 31, 73, 79, 152, 335
Blackwell, Thomas, Professor 16, 213
Blair, Wendy 262-263
Blank Rome, LLP 187
Bloomberg, Michael 309
Board of Directors, Educational Media Company at Virginia Tech, Inc. 204
Boehner, John, Speaker of the House 292, 298, 343
Boston Herald 270
Bove, Vincent 192
Bowman, Margaret 47, 49, 322, 325
Brady Campaign ii, 5, 88, 258, 259, 274, 275, 292, 298, 344
Branch Davidians 145
Brown, Judy 211
Brown, Randy 211
Brown, Tom, Dean of Student Affairs 48, 58, 59, 323, 342
Buell Elementary School 7
Burruss Hall 26, 27, 80-81, 85, 232, 330, 331, 343
Burson-Marsteller 138, 153, 162-164, 188, 189, 256, 303
Bush, George W., President. 13, 297, 340, 342

Bushmaster Model XN-15-E25 307, 308
Byers, Ralph, Executive Director of Government Relations 31, 73, 79, 125, 234, 236, 237, 238, 249-250, 335

C
California Supreme Court 6
Callison, Myrna, Co-Vice President, Graduate Student Assembly, Virginia Tech 197
Campbell County High School 8
Canellos, Ernest C., Department of Education Administrative Judge 114, 141, 150, 159, 160
Cantor, Virginia Congressman Eric 292, 298, 299, 344
Carilion St. Albans Psychiatric Hospital 50, 62, 125, 163, 261, 325, 326
Cassell Coliseum 78, 341, 342
Cazenovia, Wisconsin 8
Center for Multicultural Human Services (CMHS) 54
Central Intelligence Agency (CIA) 43, 207, 252, 257
Chafin, Gary, Virginia State Trooper iii, 89-91, 310-311
Cho, Hyang Im 53
Cho, Seung Hui ii, iii, 2, 3, 9, 13, 17, 19, 23-26, 32-33, 40, 46-71, 73-89, 93, 105, 107, 114-115, 117-118, 120, 121, 125-135, 138, 144-145, 149-153, 156-159, 161-169, 174-180, 184-187, 190-193, 205, 207-210, 213, 215, 217, 239, 249-250, 263-272, 280, 284,

285, 294, 295, 300, 306, 309,
321-330, 333-340, 343
Cho, Sung-Tae 53
Chumley, Captain 109
Clark, Ryan Christopher 22, 25,
36-39, 72, 73, 150, 151, 166,
231, 238, 329, 341
Clery Act 99, 137, 138, 141-143,
149-155, 159, 160, 163, 165-
166, 246, 290, 314-317
Clery, Jeanne 137
Cold Spring, Minnesota 8
Collegiate Times 193-204
Columbine 7, 10, 13, 14 16, 46, 54,
84, 89,91, 116, 119, 120,
126, 145,192 209-216, 284,
288, 289, 291, 294, 321
Columbine Report 116, 119,
120, 126
Columbine High School 7, 116,
119, 120, 145, 214
Commission on Student Affairs
(CSA) 193-195, 197-198
Cook Counseling Center 48-51,
58-60, 61, 68, 70, 71, 125,
167, 178-179, 213, 264, 300,
323-326
Couture-Nowak, Jocelyne
Professor iii, 30, 75, 82, 83,
89, 144, 332, 336
Crabill, Catherine 10, 11
Crannis, Kim, Blacksburg Police
Chief 28, 30, 42, 247, 332,
334
Crocker, Sue Ellen, President,
Staff Senate, Virginia Tech
197
Crouse, Deriek, Virginia Tech
Police Officer 192
Crouse, Roy, licensed clinical
psychologist 50, 62-64, 66,
68, 325
Cullen, David 211-212, 214

Cultivating Peace: A Student
Resarch Symposium on
Violence Prevention 205
Cusack, Jon 275

D
Dales, Angela iv, 16, 92, 110,
170-172, 209-210, 213-214
Davenport, Ben J. Jr., Rector,
Board of Visitors 197
de Haven, Professor Helen 16,
17, 129, 288
Deming Middle School 7
Deming, New Mexico 7
Denton, Bob, Department of
Communications, Virginia
Tech 203
Denver Post 13
Department of Education
(DOE) 114, 119, 140, 141,
150, 152-155, 157, 159, 163,
168, 316, 317
Dickinson, Laura 142, 143
Diner, Dr. Ralph 138, 148, 187
Division of Student Affairs 48,
71, 198, 213, 323
Dominican Universiy 307
Douglas, Ellen, Assistant
Director of Risk
Management, Virginia Tech
186
Dow-Corning 189
Dube, Jeanne ii, 301
Duncan, Arne, Secretary of
Education 114, 141, 159,
290, 317
Dunlap, James, Associate
Director of Purchasing,
Virginia Tech 186

E

Easterling, W. Samuel, President, Faculty Senate, Virginia Tech 197

Eastern Michigan University 142, 156

Edinboro, Pennsylvania 6

Education Media Company at Virginia Tech, Inc. (EMCVT) 197

Edwards, John, Virginia State Senator 291, 293, 343

Ellsworth, Lucius, President Appalachian School of Law 19, 212, 290

Emergency Response Plan 190-192, 290, 314-316

Einstein, Albert 5, 112

The Elephant in the Ivory Tower: Rampages in Higher Education and The Case for Institutional Liability 16, 129

Essex, Vermont 8

Evans, Garrett 86

F

Falco, Ed, Professor 51, 65, 78-79, 326

Fallon, John A. 142

Family Rights and Privacy Act of 1974 (FERPA) 56, 59, 60, 69, 70, 178

Fayetteville, Tennessee 6

FBI 35, 149, 252, 264, 343

Field, Kathleen 109

Feinberg, Kenneth 138, 149, 220, 221

Fife, Gene 222-223

Fire in the United States 119

Firestorm Solutions, LLC 185

Flanagan, Elizabeth, Vice President of Alumni Affairs, Virginia Tech 222

Flinchum, Wendell, Virginia Tech Police Chief 22, 27-31, 35-39, 41-44, 96, 98-100, 113, 125, 139, 153, 189, 229, 231-233, 237-240, 242, 246-247, 252, 262-263, 274, 290, 299, 316, 331-334

Flint, Michigan 7

Ford, David, Vice Provost for Academic Affairs, Virginia Tech 130

Ford, Gary 260-261

Fort Gibson Middle School 7

Fort Gibson, Oklahoma 7

Forehand, Ron 174-175

Fornash, Laura 125, 236

Foss High School 8

Freedom of Information Act (FOIA) 132, 173, 177

Freivik, Anders Behring 5

G

Gallagher, Mark 96, 109

Gallagher, Tom 96, 109

Gary, Indiana 7

George Washington University 165

Giffords, Gabrielle 11, 298, 344

Giovanni, Nikki, Professor 47-48, 57-60, 130, 164, 167, 213, 323, 324, 342

Glock 19 23, 52, 66, 327

Goddard, Andy ii, 84, 103-106, 108,111, 228 231, 231-238

Goddard, Colin ii, 75, 76, 80, 81, 82, 84, 88, 93-97, 103-106, 111, 115, 228, 231-234, 258-259, 338, 339

Goddard, Emma 84, 103-106, 108, 111

Governor's Review Panel Report 3, 19, 23, 28, 37, 43, 51-53, 58, 75, 79-81, 84-85, 98,

111, 112-136, 174, 176, 178, 233, 246, 247, 267, 299, 332, 338, 341

Grafton, Sue 257

Grant, David, 2008-2009 *Collegiate Times* Editor-in-Chief 204

Graves, Justin, Public Editor, *Collegiate Times* 194

Grimes, David, Pittsylvania County Commonwealth's Attorney 295

Grimes, Kevin 146-149, 265-269, 302

Grimes, Suzanne 146-149, 265-269, 302

Grundy, Virginia iv, 8, 161-162, 170-171, 208, 214, 256-257,

Guerra, Mike 211, 212

Gun Control Act 132, 308

Gust, Mary E., Administrative Actions and Appeals Service Group 152

Guys and Guns: Domestic Terrorism and School Shootings from Oklahoma City Bombing to the Virginia Tech Massacre 2, 12

H

Hall, Bob 236, 240

Hall, Cindy 142

Harper Hall 25, 73, 79, 65, 330

Haas, Emily 75, 82-83, 85, 89, 338

Hagy, Ashley 92

Harris, Eric 145, 211

Hartwick College 280-281

Haugh, Heather 29, 36, 39, 41, 42, 100, 113, 125, 139, 237, 260, 332, 333

Healy, Steven J. 232

Health Insurance and Portability and Accountability Act of 1996 (HIPPA) 69-70

Heidbreder, Kay, university counsel, Virginia Tech 186, 187, 201, 203, 234, 239

Hicks, John 211, 212

Hicok, Professor Bill 51, 65, 327

Hikes, Zenobia, Vice President of Student Affairs 232, 285, 286, 323, 331, 342

Hill, Rachael 30, 40, 75, 81, 115, 144, 333, 338

Hilscher, Beth iii, 259-265

Hilscher, Emily 22, 24-7, 29-30, 33, 36-39, 72-74, 100, 125, 130, 150, 151, 166, 231, 237, 238, 258-265, 329-337, 341

Hilscher, Eric 259-265

Hilscher, Erica 259-265

Hincker, Larry, Associate Vice President for University Relations 31, 41, 73, 79, 152, 186, 190, 197, 203, 232-235, 238, 240, 315, 334, 335

Hokie Spirit Memorial Fund (HSMF) 138, 149, 216-227

Hopkins, Wat, Department of Communications, Virginia Tech 203

Houchins, Debra, Opinions Editor, *Collegiate Times* 194

Huckabee, Michael 11

Huffington Post 298

Hunt, Ewell, Franklin County Sheriff 295

Hunter, Monica, Interim Director of Student Affairs 195, 203

Hyatt, James A. 231

I

Incident Command System (ICS) 119

Individual Education Plan (IEP) 47, 55, 322

International Concepts in Fire Protection 119

International Summit in Transdisciplinary Approaches to Violence Prevention 205

J

Jacksboro, Tennessee 8

Jackson, George, Detective 48, 322

James W. Parker Middle School 6

Janis, Bill 294

Jeanne Clery Dislosure of Campus Security Policy and Campus Crime Statistics Act 159, 165

Jenkins, Bill iii, 307, 308

J-N-D Pawnbrokers 23, 51, 66, 327

John Marshall Law School 16, 288

Jonesboro, Arkansas 6

The Journal of College and University Law 16, 129

K

Kaine, Governor Tim 42, 98, 101, 342

Kapsidelis, Karin, *Richmond Times-Dispatch* 204

Kay, Dr. Jerald 123-125

Keene, Frances, Director Judicial Affairs 48

Kelley, Jesse 11

Kelly, Raymond, New York City Police Commissioner 309

Kellner, Douglas, Professor 2, 12, 13

Kennedy, John F., President 5

Kennedy, Robert, Senator 5

Kennedy, Ted, Senator 270

Kent, Sherman 112

Kilgore, Jerry, Virginia Attorney General 170-172, 210

Kimball, "Jay" Reynolds, President, Virginia Tech Alumni Association 197

King Jr., Dr. Martin Luther 5, 46

Klebold, Dylan 14, 120

Krauthammer, Charles 12

Kretschmer, Tim 13

L

Lafayette College 301

Lake Clifton Eastern High School 7

Lake, Peter 14, 282

Lake Worth, Florida 7

Lake Worth Middle School 7

Lambert, Virginia State Highway Patrolman 171

Lanza, Adam 307

La Porte, Barbara ii, iii, 89-91

La Porte, Matthew Joseph ii, 89-91

La Porte, Priscilla ii, iii, 89-91

Larimer, Patricia, deputy Executive Director of the Virginia Board of Psychology 67, 68

Laughner, Jared 11

Law Enforcement Oath of Honor 21, 44

Lee, Henry 30, 40, 75, 81, 82, 85, 115, 144, 333, 338

Lewis, Mary Ann, Associate Dean, Liberal Arts and Human Sciences 47, 51, 59, 79, 270, 323, 327

Librescu, Liviu, Professor 76, 83, 84, 88, 115, 339
Lillizu, Christina 49, 323
Lincoln High School 6
Listen To Their Cries 192
Littleton, Colorado 7
Littwin, Mike 13
loco parentis 243
Long, Gary, Faculty Senate, Virginia Tech 203
Loganathan, G.V., Professor 75, 82, 336
LoMonte, Frank 203
Lukianoff, Greg, Foundation for Individual Rights in Education 204
Lund, Paul, Associate Dean, Appalachian School of Law 212
Luse, Donald, Association of College Unions International 204

M
Margolis, Healy and Associates 232
Markov, Theodore J., Judge 113
Massengill, Gerald 42, 101, 102, 113, 123, 234, 239
McDonald, Teresa 269
McDonnell, Robert, Attorney General 119, 121, 122, 125, 135, 136, 300
McDonnell, Robert, Virginia Governor 300, 301, 304
McFarland, Derrick 44
McLeese, Michelle, chair of Virginia Tech's Commission on Student Affairs 193-195, 197, 198
McNamee, Mark, Virginia Tech Provost 109, 205, 206, 342
McVey, Timothy 145

Meacham, John 72
Messitt, Peter, Assistant Attorney General for the State of Virginia 99, 113, 140, 231
Meredith, Joe 309
Miglani, Dr. Jasdeep, MD 63
Miller, Dr. Robert, Cook Counseling Center Director 48-51, 70, 125, 167, 176, 177, 323, 326-327
Mitchell, Sara, Editor-in-Chief of the *Collegiate Times* 194, 195, 205
Montgomery County Circuit Court 244
Montgomery County School District 145
Montgomery Regional Hospital 44, 144, 147, 261
Moore, Dr. Warren Moore 18
Moses Lake, Washington 6
Mount Morris Township, Michigan 7
Moxley, Tonia, *Roanoke Times* 203
Myer, Jan, FOIA Administrator, Attorney General's Office, Commonwealth of Virginia177, 179

N
National Alliance on Mental Illness (NAMI) 295
National Association for University and College Center Directors 157
National Rifle Association (NRA) 3, 10, 259, 284, 285, 289, 298, 299, 307-308
Nelson, Cary, American Association of University Professors 204
Nelson, Jennifer 48, 49, 69, 324

New Jersey 91, 97, 101-103, 181, 219, 296, 297, 301
New Orleans, Louisiana 7
New River Valley Community Services Board 50
Newtown, Connecticut 288, 292, 298, 344
Nickel Mines, Pennsylvania 8
No Right to Remain Silent 130,155, 163, 174-176, 213, 282
Norris, Bobbie Jean, Special Assistant Vice President, Virginia Tech 165
Norris Hall iii, 9, 19, 24, 30, 32-34, 36, 39, 52, 66, 72-91, 101, 107-109, 115, 117, 119, 134, 143-147, 150, 152, 165, 205, 207, 222, 239, 248, 251, 268, 269, 272, 285, 302, 305, 310, 327, 329, 333, 336-341, 343
Norris, Lisa, Professor 66, 79
Northern Illinois University 266, 288
Nowak, Jerzy iii, 205
Nutter, David 9, 229, 293-294, 342
NY Alert 279, 281
Nystrom, Lynn, College of Engineering, Virginia Tech 204

O
Odighizuwa, Peter 16, 19, 68, 162, 209, 210, 212, 214
Office of Recovery and Support 87, 189
Oklahoma City 2, 12, 145
O'Neil, Daniel 301-304
O'Neil, Erin 301-304
O'Neil, William ii, 301-304
Oneonta Police Department 278, 279, 280

O'Rourke, Kim 36, 125, 144, 232, 234, 248, 286, 318
Owens, Bill, Colorado Governor 119, 214

P
Palin, Sarah 11
Parker, Walt, Officer 92, 93
Parker, Carol, Professor 17, 18
Penn State 189, 190, 218
Pearl Mississippi 6
Peterson, Celeste 240
Peterson, Erin Nicole 228, 231, 240, 244
Perry, Rob, President, Broad of Directors, Educational Media Company of Virginia 204
Philip Morris 189
Platte Canyon High School 8
Plaza, Ray, Chair, Commission on Equal Opportunity and Diversity 197
Podder, Prosenjit 6
Pohle, Michael 92, 93, 95-103, 180-183
Pohle, Michael Jr. 82, 92, 95-103, 180-183
Pohle, Nikki 95-103, 180-183
Pohle, Sean 98-103, 180-183
Pohle, Teresa 96, 98-103, 180
Poindexter, Charles 294
Policinski, Gene, First Amendment Center 204
Policy Group 26, 28, 30-33, 36, 38, 41, 72, 79, 80, 81, 85, 124, 125, 127, 130, 145, 150-153, 160, 164, 176, 231, 234-236, 286, 290, 314-316, 318, 331-337
Powell, Judge Cleo E. 245-252
Preaction architect 187

Principles of Community 193, 194, 196, 202, 203

Pryde, Julia Kathleen 228, 231, 241-244

Pryde, Karen ii, 241-243

Q

Queensberry, Russell 44

Quintela, Yvette, Co-Vice President, Graduate Student Assembly, Virginia Tech 197

R

Radford University 29, 39, 232, 237, 260

Radford University Police 31, 33, 39, 74, 334-336

Rand, Ayn 305

The Rappahannock Record 209

Red Lake, Minnesota 8

Red Lion Junior High School 8

Red Lion, Pennsylvania 8

Rich, Adrienne 92

Richmond Times-Dispatch 70, 167, 189

Richmond, Virginia 7, 13, 70, 79, 87, 101, 106, 112, 122, 125, 143, 152, 160, 161, 171, 212, 229, 236, 265, 286, 293, 334, 335

The Rights and Responsibilities of the Modern University 14, 15, 243

River Forest, Illinois 307

Roanoke Times 42, 190, 197, 203, 223, 286

Roberts, Larry, Chief Counsel to Governor Kaine 99

Rocori High School 8

Rose Hill Bed and Breakfast 266

Roy, Lucinda, Professor 47, 48, 51, 57-61, 68, 71, 79, 130, 153, 155, 163, 167, 174, 175, 176, 213, 282, 300, 303, 323, 325, 327

Rubin, Mark E., Counselor for the Governor 122

Ruggiero, Cheryl 48, 59, 213, 323

S

Samaha, Joe 106

Sandy Hook Elementary School 9, 16, 17, 266, 296, 292, 298, 292, 296, 298, 299, 307-310, 344

Santee, California 7

Santolla, John, Offier 92

Savannah, Georgia 7

Schaenman, Philip 119, 315

Second Amendment 3, 10, 258, 285, 290, 306-310

Selective mutism 55, 284

Sims, Guy, Assistant Vice President of Student Affairs 195, 200, 203

Skelton Conference Center 108, 207

Special Education Program for Emotional Disabilities and Speech and Language 55

Spencer, Dr. Ed, Associate Vice President for Student Affairs 26, 27, 36, 37, 39, 144, 195, 201, 203, 232, 330

Settle, Rohsaan, Assistant Director Judical Affairs 49, 60, 323

Smith, Marisha 60, 66, 68

Smithfield Police 108

Smoot, Ray 309

Springfield, Oregon 6

Squires Student Center 191, 194, 203
Stafford, D. Stafford & Associates 165
Stafford, Delores A., President & CEO of D. Stafford & Associates 154, 165, 166
Stanley, Ginger, Virginia Press Association 204
State Board of Psychiatry 68
Steger, Charles, Virginia Tech President 15, 28-31, 35, 36, 39-44, 76, 78, 80, 101, 104-106, 110, 113, 125, 139-140, 143, 145, 146, 149-158, 162-166, 175, 184-189, 191, 193, 197, 204-206, 223, 231-243, 246, 264, 273, 274, 282, 285, 286, 290, 294, 299, 301, 303, 305, 309, 315, 332-335, 338, 341-343
Strollo, Dr. Diane ii, 143-146
Strollo, Patrick 143-146
Strollo, Hilary 143-147
Strom, Christopher 303
SUNY-Oneonta 192, 278-281
Sutin, Anthony, Dean, Appalachian School of Law 16, 212
Sutpin, Eric 44
Syracuse University 218

T
Tacoma, Washington 8
Tarasoff, Tanya 18
Tarleton State University 159
Taylor III, Orange 142, 143
TGSCOM, Inc. 23, 326
The Care Team 59, 157, 163, 324, 326
Thornhill, Karl 25, 29-33, 37-41, 72, 74, 81, 125, 156, 233,

237-238, 248, 249, 260, 262, 329, 333-335, 337, 341-342
Thurston High School 6
Tillar, Thomas C. 309
Tolliver, Sheila, Commonwealth's Attorney 92, 93
Thomas, Dave, District Attorney 211
Torgersen Hall 52, 328
Towey, James O., Assistant Attorney General, Commonwealth of Virginia 173
TriData 19, 84, 112-128, 131, 136, 239, 256, 303, 316
Tucker, Tom, Staff Senate, Virginia Tech 203
Tucson, Arizona 7, 296, 298, 344
Turpin v. Granieri 249

U
University of Arizona 8
University of California, Berkeley 6
USA Today 285
U.S. Department of Justice and Human Services 168

V
Valery, Paul 3
Velz, Peter, Managing Editor, *Collegiate Times* 194
Veterinary College 32, 73, 80, 152, 335
Violence on Campus Practical Recommendations for Legal Education 17-18
Virga, Lisa 49, 324-325
Virginia Tech Center for Peace Studies and Violence Prevention iii, 205, 207, 208

The Virginia Tech Center for Professional and Continuing Education 28, 78, 332
Virginia Health Records Privacy Act (VHRPA) 69
Virginia Military Institute 297
Virginia State Police iii, 42, 89, 101, 109, 121, 126, 157, 215, 331, 333, 335, 336
Virginia Supreme Court 141, 244, 247-252, 277, 294
Virginia Tech—Emergency Preparedness Compliance 142, 154, 159, 165, 166, 175, 290
Virginia Tech—Emergency Preparedness Documents 314
Virginia Tech Police Department (VTPD) 25-29, 32, 34, 38, 39, 43, 49, 60, 61, 71, 76, 82, 99, 101, 130, 146, 166, 192, 214, 236, 239, 247, 263, 314, 323, 325, 329-331, 337, 341
Virginia Tech Rescue Squad 25, 26, 330
Virginia Tech Review Panel 42, 113, 153, 343
Vitter, David, Louisiana Senator 292, 298, 344

W

Walther P22 23, 66, 85, 86, 327, 328
Warner, Mark, Virginia Governor 212
Washington, DC 8, 15, 283, 284, 298
Washington Post 12
Washington State University 159
Webb, Kenny 264, 265
West Ambler Johnston Hall 22, 24-31, 34, 36-38, 40, 43, 60,

72, 79, 84, 99, 100, 103, 115, 117, 119, 125, 135, 141, 144, 150, 154-157, 165, 166, 185, 190-193, 205, 238, 239, 246-248, 262, 266, 303, 324, 329-335, 338, 341
West Paducah, Kentucky 6
Westfield High School 47, 117, 322
White, Evan 106-111
White, Michael ii, 106-111
White, Nicole 82, 106-111, 337
White, Tricia ii, 94, 96, 108
Whittemore Hall 52, 328
Wilkes, Lisa 36, 125, 232, 248
Willful Blindness 298-301
Willis, Kent, ACLU of Virginia 204
Wise County, Virginia 212
Woodson Middle School 7
Wolff, Kelly, General Manager, Education Media Company at Virginia Tech, Inc. 194, 203

ABOUT THE AUTHOR

David Cariens is a retired CIA officer who currently teaches intelligence analysis and writing in the U.S. and abroad. He is the author of *A Question of Accountability: The Murder of Angela Dales* — an examination of the shooting at the Appalachian School of Law in Grundy, Virginia and a textbook, *Critical Thinking Through Writing: Intelligence and Crime Analysis*. He contributed to the International Association of Law Enforcement Intelligence Agency's *Criminal Intelligence for the 21st Century*. His new textbook, *A Handbook For Intelligence and Crime Analysts* is slated for publication in late 2014. The author takes no money from the sale of copies of this book. After taxes and expenses, all profits go to the families whose stories are told in the book.

Made in United States
Orlando, FL
26 April 2023